DANGER

WITHIN

Mark W. Danielson

Copyright © 2002, Mark W. Danielson

All rights reserved. No part of this book may be used or reproduced, in any manner whatsoever, without the written permission of the Publisher.

Printed in Canada

For information address:
Durban House Publishing Company, Inc.
7502 Greenville Avenue, Suite 500, Dallas, Texas 75231
214.890.4050

Library of Congress Cataloging-in-Publication Data
Mark W. Danielson, 1952

Danger Within / by Mark W. Danielson

Library of Congress Catalog Card Number: 00-2002109549

p. cm.

ISBN 1-930754-27-2

First Edition

10 9 8 7 6 5 4 3 2 1

Visit our Web site at
http://www.durbanhouse.com

Book design by:
Strasbourg-MOOF, GmBH

This book is dedicated to
my two beautiful daughters
BROOKE & KATIE

Acknowledgements

I especially want to thank my parents, Bill and Mary Danielson, and my surrogate parents, Dick and June Rihn, for their unflagging support. They have molded me into the person I am, providing love, confidence, support, and encouragement.

Also, I would like to thank John Lewis for his vision, and Bob Middlemiss for his mentoring. Their professionalism and friendship made *DANGER WITHIN* a reality.

A special thanks to my flying partners, truckers, hub workers, couriers, and customer service representatives who keep the overnight freight moving, and the members of the US armed forces and law enforcement agencies who protect our freedom so I may write such fiction.

DANGER

WITHIN

The DC-10 thundered through the night hauling fifty tons of cargo. At thirty-five thousand feet, the air was minus forty-five Celsius. Inside it was a living room. Under the spell of darkness jeweled cities passed beneath. No one cared. Three hours to go. But something was bothering Second Officer Kevin Hamilton. A sixth sense from years of flying kept telling him something was wrong. He glanced at Captain Joe Salvetti. He was giving his tired eyes a shot of Visene hoping to renew them. Joe was a small man, but he filled the left seat with authority and experience. Physical size didn't matter in the left seat. There he was king. But Kevin knew that Joe had to stand on his tiptoes to get a peek inside an engine nacelle. He glanced at First Officer Wendy McManus. She too was a seasoned pilot, caught in the seniority system, biding her time. Whatever was bothering Kevin was his problem.

The winter jet stream slashed their groundspeed three miles per minute. Barring a miracle, their million-dollar revenue load would be delivered late, and at the company's expense.

Kevin saw nothing unusual as he glanced over the aircraft systems panel. He must have looked twenty times; each time was the same. The DC-10 required a crew of three, the second officer being the flight engineer, but automation left little for him to do. *Three more pumps for landing.* It didn't take a genius to remember that.

After spending a lifetime strapped to an ejection seat, the DC-10 would take some getting used to. His flattened wool-covered cushion consumed his posterior and cut off his circulation while his long legs cramped under his workstation. Swiveling his chair forty-five degrees made things reasonably comfortable until one of the pilots had to get up.

Although the DC-10 was quiet compared to many airliners, there was still constant high-frequency noise from radios, gyros, and circulating air. The arid climate sucked the moisture from him. It was easier to recline his seatback and prop his feet up than strain his voice in idle conversation. With the autopilot engaged, he watched the miles click by, the pilots' faces aglow in the instrument lighting. A perceptive crew would have noticed the tension in his face.

He managed to push aside his gut instinct that something was wrong and record the engine readings in the maintenance log. This was his first flight as a Global Cargo Express crewmember. He was lucky to be an in-flight secretary. Thousands would trade places in a heartbeat. He recorded the data and set the logbook aside. Watching the minutes tick by, he felt the tension wedge itself back into his brain. "Joe, I'm gonna stretch my legs. Anyone need anything from the back?"

"No thanks."

Wendy shook her head, no.

Kevin passed through the narrow cockpit door into the dark five by fifteen foot cell known as the courier section. It contained a lavatory, meal locker, convection oven, crew luggage net, and two aft- facing chairs for jump seaters. Tonight those courier seats were vacant. He paused, feeling every vibration coming up through his shoes. As he fumbled for the light switch, the air-conditioning pack blasted into high gear, startling him. He stared at the ceiling outlet, wondering what kind of hazardous waste was circulating through those thirty-year-old ducts. Radioactive dust? Anthrax? He shook it off, taking everything else in. The label on the smoke screen, the leaking ice chest, a missing door panel, the draft by the door. There was nothing pretty about the plane's interior. But then, there was no one to impress.

Behind the smoke screen was the cargo net, certified to restrain everything up to nine times the force of gravity. Any impact exceeding that made the net a moot point. Fortunately in the company's twenty-two year history, neither the smoke screen nor cargo net had been tested. Global wanted to keep it that way.

Kevin slid his hand over the vinyl, cool except where the vent spewed. *Things are fine. Get over it.* Lost in thought, he grabbed a water bottle from the cooler, turned out the lights, and returned to his seat. As he fastened his seat belt, his foot kicked the green thermos. "Coffee anyone?"

"Sure," Joe said. "Black's fine."

First Officer Wendy McManus declined, busy programming a waypoint into the navigation computers. An exceptional pilot, her life's story in *Cosmo* buried among breast implant advertisements and orgasm techniques led to five minutes on *The View*. Meeting Barbara Walters was one of her greatest moments. She had no time for coffee.

Kevin was reaching for the coffee jug when a flash on his panel spiked his eye, then disappeared. Uneasy, he checked his instruments, but saw no abnormal indications. *Must've been a reflection.* As he unscrewed the thermos cap, an amber Cabin Cargo Smoke detector illuminated, followed by the Master Caution light. Something bad was happening in the upper cargo area. Something was burning. Within seconds, two more detectors were lit.

It was impossible for Joe to miss the amber Master Caution and Summary lights staring him in the face. They were bright and threatening. The only good news was the red warning lights were still out. He looked at Kevin's panel. Numbers seven, eight, and nine detectors were on; five and six were flickering. "Get your masks and goggles on. Wendy—you've got the plane—I'm working with Kevin."

"I've got the plane," she said, donning her oxygen mask and goggles. Her well-groomed blonde hair was flattened as she rotated the pressure regulator to the emergency position. Neither was a perfect fit; the high-pressure oxygen bleeding into her goggles dried her blue eyes. "Mayday, Mayday, Mayday," she said, broadcasting to everyone on frequency. The international distress signal silenced the airwaves. "Kansas City Center, GlobeEx 3217 Heavy has an inflight fire." While awaiting a response, she set the emergency code in the transponder.

In a darkened radar surveillance room hundreds of miles away, Sam Goodall watched a radar bleep double in intensity. The sight nearly caused him to spill his coffee. It also got his supervisor's attention. "GlobeEx 3217 Heavy, Kansas City Center, I see your emergency ident. Squawk 0170 and state intentions."

"Standby."

The indefinite response could only mean they were in serious trouble. GlobeEx 3217's bleep tracked across the green circular screen, highlighted every few seconds by the radar scan. Sam set his coffee mug aside, anxiously watching, waiting for another call. He marked the tape, should there be an investigation. Kevin closed the vent on the cockpit door and pulled the Cabin Air Shutoff T-handle to shut off the air aft of the cockpit. Assuming everything worked, the smoke would exit through the outflow valve and keep the cockpit clear. He opened the emergency procedures handbook to Cabin Cargo Smoke and set it on the center console so Joe could follow along. Wearing goggles, it wasn't easy to read.

"Every detector's on now," Joe said, his voice scratchy over the intercom.

Kevin stared at the panel. He recalled his fire-fighting training aboard aircraft carriers. His instinct was to fight the fire, but he didn't have a crew to work with. Even if he got to the source, his hand-held fire extinguisher would barely spit on it. Their situation worsened by the minute.

"We'll have to starve it. Wendy, take her down to twenty-five thousand."

Joe's command brought Kevin back. He grabbed the manual pressurization lever and rotated the wheel to equalize the cabin pressure. "Cabin's coming up," he said. Wendy was diving the plane to twenty-five thousand feet. The pressure in his ears confirmed the cabin altitude was rising rapidly.

"Wendy—I've got the radios—you keep the plane," Joe said, struggling to clear his ears. "Center, GlobeEx 3217 Heavy, we need a vector to the nearest airfield—now."

"Joe—we've got fifty-five thousand pounds. You want to dump?" Kevin asked, interrupting him. Joe raised his hand to silence him.

"GlobeEx 3217 Heavy, St Louis Center, Whiteman's at your three o'clock for seventy miles. The weather's clear, winds light and variable."

Whiteman Air Force Base had twelve thousand feet of runway, emergency equipment, an on-site medical facility, and more security personnel than the city of St. Louis. It was an easy decision. "We'll take it."

"Roger, GlobeEx 3217 Heavy, vector three-three-zero for Whiteman, descend at pilot's discretion to four thousand. When able, contact St. Louis Approach on 127.45."

"GlobeEx 3217 Heavy, will contact Approach on twenty-seven-forty-five, PD to four." Joe removed his hand from the radio key, scanning Kevin's panel. Too much fuel. An old saying came to mind. *You can only have too much fuel when you're on fire.* Somehow it wasn't as funny now. He'd land overweight if he had to, but they still had time to lighten the load. "Okay, Kevin—dump to the limits."

Kevin flipped on every fuel pump switch, opened the crossfeed valves, raised the fuel dump switch, and hacked the clock. Fuel gushed from the wing dump masts at seven hundred gallons per minute. From the ground it would look like the space shuttle reentry. Would anyone notice?

Joe considered his options. The cold air was fogging his goggles. He felt Wendy's gaze, waiting for him to make the wrong move. He knew how badly she wanted to be in command. Avoiding her eyes, he checked the aircraft's weight. Landing took priority over starving the fire and Whiteman was getting close. "Wendy—keep her coming down."

"You got it," she said, her voice cold. In a single elegant move she extended the speed brakes, slats, and dropped the landing gear. The nose dropped further.

Joe saw Kevin grab the checklist as it floated off the console. *Jesus!* Staring into the gloom, he realized no simulator ride prepared him for this; the book no longer mattered. His heart banged inside him. *Get the goddam plane on the ground!* "Kevin, how's the dump coming?"

"Forty-three thousand now."

Three thousand 'til the limit: dump's looking good. The pain in Joe's ear was unbearable. The human body wasn't designed to handle such pressure changes. A loud pop relieved the pain, but he felt wetness in his ear. *Ignore it.* He switched frequencies to 127.45. "St. Louis Approach, GlobeEx 3217 Heavy's descending to four thousand." More pain, pressure. He stretched his neck, yawned, and blew his nose at the same time. Finally his ears popped again. *Liquid now. Must've broken an eardrum.* While pondering whether he'd ever fly again, Approach Control called.

"GlobeEx 3217 Heavy, St. Louis Approach, winds are calm, runway your discretion. When able, state souls on board and fuel remaining in minutes."

Stay focused. Joe looked at the fuel totalizer. "GlobeEx 3217 has three souls, two plus hours, and dumping." Passing eighteen thousand feet, he dialed in the local altimeter setting and turned on the exterior floodlights. More vibration as the lights extended into the slipstream. *Ten minutes to go.*

Having little to do, Kevin jammed some damp napkins under the door to block the smoke. For now the cockpit was clear, but it wouldn't last. He beat the laminated checklist against his leg in frustration. His gut feeling had been right, but how'd this happen? *What was the hell was he doing here? He was a goddam fill-in.* Tightening his oxygen mask brought back memories of survival training. An image flashed, but was gone in an instant. Joe's seat made the image clear. It was the Boeing 707 captain—the one who let him sit in his seat; and the seven-year-old kid found his destiny. Thousands of flying hours later, smoke billowing out the fuselage, he was diving at beaded lights against a blackened earth, the plane shuddering from the drag.

While the others worked, he thought back to his meeting Joe and Wendy tonight. Joe with his Italian good looks, calm brown eyes, and olive complexion. At thirty-five or thereabouts, his skin was smooth except around the eyes, the pilot's squint from countless horizons. Probably knew a good Italian restaurant for every logbook entry. Maybe known by his first name. Maybe he got carded, something that would please him. Good pilot. No frills, all business. And Wendy. Kevin watched her, all goggles and mask, her misty blue eyes now gray in the cockpit light. They were tight behind the goggles, constantly moving, confidently scanning the instruments, beyond the cockpit and into the night, ready for Joe's next command. Night flying, he guessed, was taking its toll on her. But he couldn't fault her for being here. Panel lights reflected off her goggles...

Retired from the Marine Corps, Kevin was the old man of the group. Not sure he fit in yet. On probation for another ten months. He watched Joe... everything by the book. Their preflight checks were quick and methodical, cargo doors secured, waiting for him to complete the takeoff data. No pressure—just make it fast. Joe never said it, but he could see it in Wendy's eyes. Kevin avoided her look as he passed the data forward. He went to the back to reviewing the hazardous materials document.

Global relied on its customers to declare anything hazardous, so there was no way to know what they were really carrying. The cargo deck was a sea of containers, a foot along the fuselage walls for a crawl space. The Newark mechanic's last words were have a safe flight. He must know they're not going to Oklahoma City anymore. A question about checklists brought Kevin back into the loop. "In-Range Checklist complete," he said. "Standing by for the Approach Check."

Joe nodded; flipping through his binder for an approach plate he knew wasn't there. Whiteman wasn't a normal alternate. He would have to rely on Approach Control for frequency and guidance information. Whiteman's bright lights in the distance were reassuring.

Wendy shallowed her descent preparing to level at four thousand feet. "Gear up," she said.

"Let's leave it down," Joe said. Her stare prompted an explanation, unnecessary as it was. "No point in taking chances.

It won't hurt our airspeed and we'll burn more fuel." Ready to brief the approach, something caught his eye. *Is that condensation or is smoke coming out the air vents? Did the fire burn through an air conditioning duct?* He checked Kevin's panel. No manifold failure light—must be condensation. But his instruments were disappearing. "Kevin—turn off the packs and pull the ram air."

Kevin recalled the Ram Air T-handle was under a floor panel behind Joe's seat. When he unstrapped and reached for the cover, the oxygen hose jerked his mask over his chin. In the time it took to swap masks with the observer's seat, his eyes and throat were burning. Without the air-conditioning packs on, smoke and fumes were seeping into the cockpit. They hadn't noticed with their masks and goggles on, but the toxic vapors reinforced their predicament. He found the T-handle and pulled, but nothing happened. *Jesus—doesn't maintenance ever check this stuff?* He braced himself and yanked with all his might. Dusty air filled the cockpit, but it cleared quickly. *Why did Joe want the packs off, anyway?* Caught in the moment, Kevin realized he'd forgotten about his fuel dump. Thankfully the automatic shutoff valves worked. "The dump's secured," he said.

Confident that all was under control, Joe assumed aircraft control. Wendy raised her hands confirming he was now flying the jet. "Wendy—call the company. Make sure they're sending trucks."

Kevin was dumbfounded. With everything going on, how could Joe be concerned with delivering freight? Kevin was beginning to wonder about him. Why have Wendy call Ops when his only job was running checklists? Kevin slid his volume lever up to monitor Wendy's call.

"…GlobeEx Operations, 3217's diverting with an inflight emergency." She repeated the transmission several times with no answer. "Must be out of range."

"I'll try while you fly," Kevin said.

"Go ahead," Joe said, reengaging the autopilot and autothrottles.

For the first time since the Master Caution light came on, the plane was under computer control, level at four thousand feet, two hundred thirty knots. Kevin tapped Joe on the shoulder. "I got in touch with Flight Ops. They have a plan for the freight— safety reps are on the way."

Joe raised a thumb, smiling under his mask. He could make out individual buildings now. Unless something else happened in the next four minutes, they had it made. "Call the field in sight." Wendy relayed the information. Approach Control advised there was no other traffic, and passed them to Tower on 132.4. "Flaps 15."

Wendy lowered the flaps to fifteen degrees while keying the mike. "Tower, 3217's with you." Her voice was steady. Hopefully no one noticed her hands shaking. She had been fine flying the plane, her hands on the controls. She expected Joe would take over, but being a spectator was difficult. The airfield was alive; every piece of emergency response equipment awaited them.

Joe glanced over his shoulder. The manual pressurization outflow valve was full open. The plane was depressurized; they shouldn't have any problems evacuating. He called for the Approach Checklist.

Kevin caught the tension in Joe's voice. Now or never, do or die, hours of boredom interrupted by moments of sheer terror, all the clichés—which in flying were all the time. He'd been remarkable controlling his emotions, but now he was having doubts. He knew all hell would break lose once they stopped. The only thing keeping the smoke out was the flowing outside ram air. Without that, all bets were off. They weren't safe until they were out of the aircraft and on the tarmac.

Joe briefed a visual approach to Runway 19. "We'll stop on the runway and evacuate out the windows," he said. "We don't know what's going on back there and I don't care to find out. Kevin— if there's time, read the Emergency Evacuation Checklist. If you guys see something you don't like, tell me early 'cause we're not going around."

Kevin tightened his lap belt and called the Approach Check complete.

Joe disconnected the autopilot and dipped the wing to turn base leg. "Flaps twenty-two, gear down," he said.

"Gear's still down, flaps twenty-two," Wendy said, rechecking the three green lights on the panel, sliding the flap lever into the next detent.

Tower cleared them for landing. "Flaps thirty-five." As the flaps lowered to thirty-five degrees, all eyes were on the runway. The vibration increased. "Flaps fifty." Final flap setting. The plane shuddered as the air pounded the barn-door flaps. When the flaps stabilized, Kevin silently reviewed the Before Landing Checklist. Everything looked good. At a thousand feet above the ground, the computer-generated voice echoed, *One thousand.* "Visual approach," Joe said. A required call; one he knew was being recorded.

Kevin tugged at his seat belt for the fifth time. It hadn't been that tight since his last flight in a jet fighter. His seat between the pilots gave a clear view, but he was also directly behind the console. He moved his seat as far aft as possible for maximum clearance, but made sure he could still reach the ground spoiler lever in case the automatic function failed. *Five hundred.* "Stabilized," Wendy said, confirming the aircraft was properly configured and on-speed. "*Thirty—twenty—ten.*" Joe eased the throttles to idle. Raising the nose slightly resulted in a smooth touchdown. When the ground spoilers deployed, he dumped the nose and stood on the brakes praying the anti-skid would keep the tires from blowing. The rapid deceleration locked their shoulder harnesses, limiting their movement. As the aircraft slowed to a crawl, Joe set the parking brake and secured the fuel shutoff levers, making no attempt to clear the runway. Wendy's hand bumped Joe's as she reached for the Fire T-handles. Once Wendy's hand was clear, Joe turned on the Emergency Power and Thunderstorm Lights, glanced at the others, and tossed his harness aside. "We're outta here."

When Joe cracked his window open, dense smoke forced its way into the cockpit, catching him by surprise. Realizing any delay would put the others in danger, he tossed the escape rope outside, took a final breath, and threw his mask on the seat. Wendy was leaving through the opposite window; Kevin was unstrapped, waiting. *Time to go.* Joe swung out the window, working his way to the ground hand-over-hand. He'd just reached the ground when he heard a scream and a thud. He ran to the other side and found Wendy struggling to her feet. "Are you okay?" She nodded. He guided her to a safe position in front of the aircraft as dense smoke poured out from everywhere.

Kevin's vision was blurred. He located the battery and Emergency Power switches by their distinct features and turned them off. After the cockpit went dark, he noticed red lights dancing in the windows. He remembered his survival training and felt for reference points. Banging his shins, he found the escape rope, its stiff fibers course against his skin. Desperate for fresh air, he tossed the Hazardous Material pouch out the window, balanced on the window frame, and began his descent. As his feet neared the ground, he felt hands on his back and recognized Joe's voice. He relaxed. Nearly blind, eyes swollen, he retrieved the yellow pouch and followed Joe to safety.

Once they joined Wendy in front of the aircraft, Joe swirled his finger in his ear then looked at it. Moist, but no blood. Elated, he drew circles in the ground with his laser pointer. The red beam sliced through the smoke like a knife. Joe smiled. He never expected his mother's birthday present would come in so handy.

Soon the Fire Chief approached, yelling something indiscernible. Kevin handed him the salvaged document pouch and described his cabin cargo smoke indications. The Fire Chief nodded and reached for his microphone. "All units, this is Fire One. Check the right aft section on the upper deck for possible ignition source. We need to get that cargo door open, but— Holy shit!" Flames exploded though the top of the fuselage lighting the sky with fire, a tongue of flame licking the night.

2

Foam and water cascaded over the flaming hulk with little effect. Fire wafted and sucked at the night like an evil magician's wand. While Kevin, Joe, and Wendy watched in disbelief, the Fire Chief shook his head. Other options were needed. It was Joe who first spotted the car. "More company," he said.

Now everyone was watching the approaching dark colored sedan bearing a white eagle on the front. Kevin was about to say "Bird Colonel," when he noticed Wendy's grimace. "You okay?"

"Rope burns," she said, holding her hands, humiliated. She was damned good at what she did—proved herself every day. Now this. Her pride hurt more than her hands. "I was half way down when—"

"There they are." Two attendants burst from the ambulance and raced towards them. Joe swabbed his ear again. Still no blood, pain's gone. He and Kevin kept quiet, concerned about their careers. Wendy wasn't as perceptive. After showing them her hands, she was headed for the clinic, a prisoner of the medical corps, her anger evident in the rear window.

The staff car halted, killed its lights, two doors opened. Two men stood for a moment, shadows in the smoke and gloom, and approached in perfect cadence. The taller man spoke first. "Welcome to Whiteman," he said. He wore a flight suit, the other something more formal. He extended his hand to Joe, but did so with grace of habit, a tall man looking down, but with respect. "I'm Colonel Moran, Base Commander. This is Colonel Reynolds, the base Safety Officer." Moran's gaze fixated on the inferno, its flames reflecting in his eyes. "What a bitch. I see the Fire Chief's trying new options."

"She was a good plane," Joe said, his black eyes marbles in the golden light. Moran was a gentle giant. He wasn't so sure about Reynolds. Anyone staying in the background was either a yes-man or untrustworthy. "I'm Joe Salvetti. This is Kevin Hamilton."

Handshakes were exchanged. "Sorry you lost her, Joe. Hard to believe you even got her down. Pretty damned lucky, I'd say. What happened?"

Joe wiped a hand across his mouth. It left a smear of ash across his jaw. "We were eighty miles east when we got indications of a fire. Whiteman was our best option."

"Well, I'm glad you got her down safely." A smile tugged at Moran. Nothing like this had ever happened under his watch. Other than the normal alerts, the base operation was monotonously predictable. "Believe it or not, you actually helped us out."

Joe's head cocked like the RCA dog's. "Say again?"

"Joe—our response crews need to be tested now and then. As far as I'm concerned, this is no different than a no-notice inspection." He gazed into the darkness. "It would've been a mess if you'd crashed out there, but this is no sweat." He looked around. "Say—aren't there three of you on a DC-10? Where's your other crewman?"

"The ambulance just took my FO to the clinic. Wendy McManus—she had some nasty rope burns—slid down the rope."

"Ouch. I'm sure the doc will take good care of her, though." He glanced at his Safety Officer. "Colonel Reynolds—any questions, or can they wait?"

"We're glad to cooperate," Joe said quietly, "but we do have union guidelines—"

"Understood," Reynolds said, stepping forward, his face finally visible in the light. He kept wondering if Moran was going to give him a chance to speak. The gutted hull of the DC-10 seemed ready to collapse, its metallic sculpture melting, spewing aluminum lava. "We should get out of here. Like Colonel Moran said, you did a great job tonight. We'll let the investigators figure it out."

Joe's eyes hardened in the dancing light. The National Transportation Safety Board, not to mention the media with their shoving fists, microphones, and obnoxious questions, would soon be down on them. Having twenty–twenty hindsight, they'd sift and question, push and probe, rehash and conjecture, and still not get it right. No pilot wanted that sort of thing in his record. He needed time with his crew. "Colonel, can someone drop us off at the clinic? I'd like to check on my FO."

"Sure." Moran made a quick survey of the ramp; the fire wasn't going out anytime soon. "By the way, if you want to stay on base, I'll get you some rooms at the Visiting Officers Quarters. It's no five-star hotel, but it's quiet."

"Thanks, we'd appreciate it. Just need a place to crash, if you'll excuse the pun."

Moran laughed for the first time. "Good one. Listen Joe, I can keep the press off you for a few hours, but that's it. If they get wind of you being here, they'll be all over—"

"I know," Joe said. He was drained, eager to make some calls. His mind was going eight miles a minute. He couldn't fall asleep if he had to.

As they piled into the staff car, Colonel Moran added, "Global's always done a great job supporting the Air Force. Whatever you need, just say the word."

"Thanks again, Colonel." Joe studied the back of their heads, catching Moran's eyes in the mirror. Could Moran and Reynolds be trusted? He'd forced them from bed, yet they seemed eager to help. If they were sincere, it must have been because of those military charters Global flew to the Middle East. Nice they finally had some redeeming value.

The DC-10 continued to burn, its flames throwing themselves against the night. The car turned and it was gone. Nobody looked back, but Fate toyed with them. Reynolds' words rode out over the hand-mike to Tower. "Nice job tonight."

The Tower's static voice lifted over its tension. "Thank you, sir."

Moran caught Kevin in the mirror. "Something wrong with your eyes?"

"Irritated from the smoke," he said, downplaying the discomfort.

"Better have the doc look at 'em while we're there."

Kevin nodded, rubbing them again. He felt like he'd taken two elbows to the eyes, swollen, watering. His career depended on his vision. Perhaps Moran was right.

Moran scanned his mirror, finding Joe deep in thought. "Joe, I've been around long enough to know that you and your crew need some time alone. Take advantage of the VOQ. Everything else can wait."

Joe nodded. *Who to call first? The union or Flight Ops?*

They surprised the sergeant at the clinic. Colonel Moran, himself. He should have been ready, but the colonel rarely stopped by. Then again, it wasn't every day a DC-10 demolished itself on their field. He stood rigid, struggling with his composure. "Sir!"

Moran stopped two feet in front of him, eyes flowing from the sergeant's trembling feet to his sweaty forehead. "Evening, Sergeant." He elected not to say anything about his dozing; the adrenaline rush would keep him alert the rest of his shift. "We're looking for the woman crewmember."

"Yes, sir—she's in exam room one. Would you like me to page her, sir?"

"That's all right. We'll find our way." As they started down the hall, Moran spun around. The sergeant snapped to attention like a robot, except his face was red. Moran looked through him down the hall. "I think one of the other crewmembers ducked into the restroom. Would you point him in the right direction when he comes out?"

"Right behind you, Colonel," Kevin said, dabbing his eyes.

Moran pushed on the door, peeking inside the exam room. Aside from the cutaway model of the human body on the cabinet, eye chart on the wall, a few medical tools, and an exam table, the off-white room could have been a brig. The worn tiles and stained vents suggested no budget for upgrades. The Air Force doctor pushing retirement sat with his back to them, his eyes tired, finishing his bandage. Wendy cued him someone was there. He glanced their way, then went back to what he was doing. Hopefully they weren't more patients.

"Hi, Doc. Looks like you're just about done," Moran said. "I've got another one for you—eye irritation."

The doc swung his stool around, expressionless. "Lemme see." He pulled at Kevin's eyelids, canted his face into the light, then reached for some eye drops. The fluid ran down Kevin's cheeks. "You're fine," he said, handing him a tissue. "Use these drops every four hours. Nothing to worry about, but don't expect a good night's sleep."

Kevin was about to say, "Like there's any chance of that happening," but restrained himself. He squinted, the old man's wrinkled hospital garb a reminder of their intrusion. The doc spent less than thirty seconds before making his analysis. He'd have his regular doc check him out once he got home. Kevin tucked the eye drops into his pocket. "Thanks, Doc."

Moran sensed Joe's anxiety. "Hey, Doc—how about joining us for a cup of coffee? I'm buying."

"Sounds good. Lord knows I can use it," he said, tossing his latex gloves in the biohazard bin. He left with the colonels.

Joe smiled. "Alone at last," he said, noting the iodine-stained gauze and tweezers on the tool tray. No bloodstains anywhere. "So Wendy—how ya doin'?"

"Not great," she said, staring at her gauze-covered hands. Every throbbing heartbeat reminded her of the rope slide. "Thanks to that damned rope I've got imbedded fibers. The doc did his best to clean everything up, but he says it'll take a lot of soaking and ointment before the fibers work themselves out."

Joe nodded, thankful it wasn't more serious. "Hope you're ready for a sim check when we get home. I'm sure they'll want to know what we screwed up."

Wendy's eyes narrowed. "Say again? If I go, I'll be watching from the jump seat," she said, waggling her bandaged hands.

Joe laughed. He knew she couldn't fly, but it was fun teasing her. She had a short fuse, but once you got her out of the plane she was a different person—most of the time. Her smile was irresistible, her figure stunning. If he were a foot taller, he might be tempted to ask her out. Then again…"That was the Base

Commander," he said, his thoughts returning to business. "He got us rooms at the VOQ—thought it would make things easy."

"So what are we waiting for?" She leaped to the floor and led the way.

They found Moran in the break room, his feet propped on the table, conversing with Reynolds and the doc. Moran lifted his cup, smiling. "Care for some coffee?"

Reynolds rose from his chair. "If you'll excuse me, I have work to do."

"Me, too," the doc said, following him out the door.

"We'll pass on the coffee, but we could use a ride to the VOQ," Joe said.

Moran tossed his Styrofoam cup in the trash and held the door. "Sure."

It took five minutes to get to the VOQ, barely enough time to yawn. The Colonel's handing Joe a bulky envelope soured the mood. "Sorry, Joe. Government red tape. Fill 'em out when you can. Colonel Reynolds needs them to document our emergency response. It helps with our operating budget."

Joe opened the envelope, staring at the forms. He didn't have time for this crap. He forced a smile and tucked the package under his arm. "We'll get 'em done."

The VOQ was a nondescript cinderblock building the same color as everything else on base. The government must get a great price for that paint, he mused. Once inside, the lobby took on surprising grace. Overstuffed chairs, potted plants, a chandelier. Moran did well. After photocopying their airline IDs, the clerk handed them their keys. "I think we should go to my room and compare notes to get our story straight," Joe said, squeezing Moran's package.

Wendy shook her head. "I need a break."

"And my pupils are dilated," Kevin said, backhanding the tears from his eyes. "I agree with Wendy. I can barely see. God, these eye drops burn."

Joe sighed. He had little choice but to grant a reprieve. He'd start on the paperwork while they rested. Make some calls. Time well spent. He checked his watch, barely meeting their eyes. "You've got three hours. Sleep fast."

Kevin switched on the light, tossed the key on the desk, and read the instructions for the eye drops. Everything seemed legit, so why didn't it relieve the pain? Wearily he reached for the phone. Take some time, he reminded himself. Don't get Nancy and the kids upset. They're stressed enough from the house-hunting trip. He collected his thoughts while the hotel desk transferred him to their room. "Hi, Babe."

He caught her off guard. Four-thirty in the morning was too early to be home. She sat up, suddenly wide-awake. To a squadron commander's wife, a phone call in the middle of the night could only mean trouble. "What happened?"

Her voice was cold, business like. He found confronting her more difficult than the emergency. "We had some aircraft problems. We're staying over at Whiteman Air Force Base. We have VOQ rooms. I think you should plan on flying home without me."

There was nothing reassuring about his voice. He was trying to protect her again. Didn't he know he couldn't put anything past her? She rested her hand against her forehead; glancing at the boys, now sound asleep. "Why are you at an Air Force base? And where's Whiteman?"

He blew it. He could see her face; that look of disgust. Still, what could he say without making the situation worse? Surely she could read between the lines. "In Missouri. It was our closest divert. The plane broke, we landed."

"So you're off duty then? You want me to book a later flight?"

"Not yet. We've been extended in the field." His stomach wrenched. "How's the hotel?"

"It's okay. Maybe we should've stayed at Cherry Point."

Kevin sank into his pillow, staring at the family portrait in his wallet. "I've been thinking the same thing. I really miss you and the boys. I bet they're driving you crazy."

"Actually, they've been great. Of course right now they're a couple of snoozing lumps. You want me to wake them so you can say hi?"

"No, that's okay. They'd never get back to sleep and we both know they need it."

His words were strained. She didn't dare ask for details, but she couldn't stop worrying. "Kevin, are you sure you are all right? Your voice sounds hoarse. Do you have a cold?"

Her voice was on edge. God, he hated this. He should be with her, not in some VOQ room. He'd spent enough time on military bases—couldn't wait to leave. "I'm fine, Nance." He held the phone to the side and coughed. "Just a combination of no sleep and dry air. I'd give anything for a lozenge." He took a sip of water, then another. The moisture wet his throat, but did nothing to soothe it. Tears flowed, but from what? Too much time away. Too many deployments, too many missed birthdays. And they'd moved twice before the kids were in elementary school. Was moving to Oklahoma City a good decision? It would eliminate his commute, simplify everything. His thoughts returned to the fire. It bothered him he couldn't say more. The DC-10 would be on the news when they woke up. Nancy would be livid.

"Kev?" Nancy was still on the line, not wanting to let go.

"Yeah?"

"When will you be back?"

"I'm not sure. No airplane right now. Nance—I'm sorry I woke you. I just needed to hear your voice. I really need to get some sleep. Big day ahead. I love you."

"You, too." The line went dead. She stared at the phone. God how she hated being protected. Whatever it was she could handle it. Wasn't she the one who handled Mac Gerard's funeral? Didn't she hold Karen's hand while they lowered her husband's flag-draped coffin into the ground while his FA-18 squadron was at sea? Didn't Kevin trust her? She brushed her cheek, thankful it wasn't a war zone this time.

Kevin blinked at the mini-fridge, humming just enough to be irritating. She knew he loved her. For now that's the best he could do. He smelled of soot and fire and sweat and fear. It impregnated his skin. His eyes kept tearing up. He tossed his clothes in the bathroom and buried himself under the covers, but the stench was too much. No choice but to shower. *Dammit!* He was nearly scalded when someone flushed a toilet. Seems every VOQ was the same. He soaped up one last time, the water sluicing down his lean body. Then the flight came skulking back, tightening him up. Something had been wrong. He'd gotten up and looked around. Instinct. A pilot's instinct. Still half wet, he dragged his aching body into his bed and fell asleep.

Whiteman's concrete reflected in the Citation's landing lights. Bill Kessler fixated on the DC-10 as his corporate jet taxied in, its charred skeleton more dinosaur than tri-jet. The blue Follow-Me truck led them to a spot near the control tower that flaunted an Air Combat Command shield. A camouflaged Security Policeman blocked their exit. Bill noted his M-16. "Good morning, gentlemen," the sergeant said, his voice older than his appearance. "Welcome to Whiteman. I'm here to brief you on our ramp security procedures." Bill nodded. "We take our flightline security seriously, so display your company ID at all times. Consider the red line an electrified twenty-foot fence. Failure to use the checkpoints will land you face-down on the tarmac with a rifle pointed at your head. Any questions?" Satisfied he had their attention, he backed out of the aircraft.

Bill made his way forward, massaging his throbbing headache. He'd been up all night, and taking orders from a gun-toting kid didn't help matters. He stepped from the Citation and retrieved his luggage.

"Oh—Colonel Moran's expecting you," the sergeant said. "Base Operations is right in front of you. Ask for him when you go inside."

"Thanks." Bill recognized the name from the welcome sign. Dragging his bag, he felt he was in a time warp. He hadn't served in thirty years, yet the base infrastructure looked the same. Only the planes changed. Maybe that was a good thing.

"Hey Bill," one of the Citation pilots yelled. "Any idea how long we'll be here? This was our fifth leg today—we need some rest."

"No idea. I'll know more after I meet with the colonel."

Kevin awoke with the coordination of a drunk, knocking the phone to the floor. It couldn't be Joe—he still had fifteen minutes. The line went dead when he picked up. He resisted the temptation to slam the phone down. He didn't dare lie down again or he'd be late for sure. He slung his feet over the side, pausing to let the blood flow to his brain. No choice but to wear his grimy uniform.

As he stepped into the lobby, a balding man in a loud sport coat rushed to his side. No one from the FAA dressed like that. *Must be a reporter.* The man reached for his hand, but abruptly backed away from the fire stink. "I take it you're one of the GlobeEx crewmembers," he said.

Kevin managed a smile. "Recognized my charred uniform, huh? I'm Kevin Hamilton—and you are?"

"Oh—sorry." The man transferred his Global ID to his coat pocket. "Let's start over. I'm Bill Kessler—Flight Safety Manager for Global Cargo Express." Kevin's eyes roamed the lobby among a sea of uniforms. "Les Cresanko's around here somewhere. He's with Flight Operations."

Kevin was looking for Joe when the desk clerk interrupted. "Sir, you have a call."

He expected Joe, but it was a woman asking if he was Captain Salvetti. He spotted Joe and waved him over. He pointed out Bill Kessler as he passed him the phone.

Joe crowded the counter, angered by Marsha Woods' voice. How did the *International Press* get his name? More importantly, how did she know where to find him? Whatever happened to Moran's promise? He knew Moran was too good to be true. "Marsha, I'm sorry, but I can't talk right now. I suggest you contact the Global Cargo Express public relations department. I'm sure they'll be happy to give you a statement." He hung up before she could respond. He smiled at the clerk, keeping his hand on the phone. "Colonel Moran assured us complete privacy, so if anyone outside the government or Global Cargo Express asks for a DC-10 crewmember, we're not here." The clerk made a mental note of it. *Where the hell is Wendy?* He dialed another number.

Sergeant Keri Wilkins's voice reflected confidence and calm, a seasoned blend of protocol and the female sex. As Colonel Moran's secretary, she was used to hearing "captain" and presumed Joe was another low ranking Air Force officer. She made no attempt to contact the colonel, instead telling Joe he was out. Joe didn't buy it, but asked for the Public Affairs Officer. Second Lieutenant Gavel came on the line.

"Lieutenant, this is Captain Salvetti, Global Cargo Express. Are you aware of our aircraft mishap?"

Gavel had spent all morning preparing incident reports for Colonel Moran and the Pentagon. He would've laughed had he not been so tired. But why was Salvetti so angry? His pen found a note pad, doodling as he spoke. "I'm well aware of your situation, Captain Salvetti. What can I do for you?"

"A reporter from the *International Press* just called—asked for me by name. Any idea where she got my number?"

"It didn't come from me. I've been talking to your company PAO though. Maybe you should ask him."

Bullshit. Why would anyone at Global invite the press? "Look—Colonel Moran promised to keep the press off our backs. Please make sure that happens. We're at the VOQ. Call me if there's an emergency—otherwise we're not here."

"I'll do what I can." Gavel's pen added the finishing touches to a well-endowed woman's breast.

Joe handed the clerk the phone, wondering how much she'd overheard. He noticed Wendy, Kevin, and Bill talking—hopefully nothing about the mishap. He joined them, gripping Bill's waiting hand. "Good to see you again, Bill. Hi guys. How are the hands, Wendy?"

"Throbbing." Her white bandages were stained with serum. She needed to soak them again, apply more ointment. When would the pain medicine kick in?

"Bill, I don't mean to sound rude, but we still need to go over some things."

"You mean I'm gonna have to eat all these doughnuts myself?" He smiled, dangling a grease-stained bag. "Come on, Joe. Let's find a room and sort this out. I assure you everything's off the record."

Joe frowned. "I don't think so—not without a union rep. You know the rules." Donuts or not, the pilot union was the only group who'd look out for their careers.

"You and I both know the union won't have anyone here for hours. Be reasonable, Joe. Global's screaming for some facts."

His first thought was to say, "screw you," but he thought better of it. He couldn't win that battle, and he couldn't stall either. At least not without severe repercussions. His ploy might hurt the union as much as him. God he was tired. He should've taken a nap instead of work on those goddam papers. "All right, Bill, but remember—this is strictly off the record."

"Promise."

The veneer conference table seated twelve, but there were only ten chairs. The paneled walls made the room smaller; its dim lighting shrank it more. In the far corner sat a plant identical to the ones in the lobby, the only sign of life. Two pictures of B-2 bombers hung on opposite ends of the room. Bill tossed the donut bag on the table. "Have at it," he said, grabbing for a glazed.

Joe explored the contents of the bag. He preferred chocolate covered, but there were none. He settled for an old fashioned. "So when'd you get in, Bill?"

"Two hours ago, but I didn't want to disturb you. I've already spoken to the air traffic controllers and flight safety personnel. Have you seen your plane?"

Joe shook his head, grabbing another donut before passing the bag to Wendy.

"There's not much left, I'm afraid."

Joe said nothing. A tap at the door caught their attention.

The man wore blue jeans and a tweed sport coat with black Tee. His hair was tousled. Must have shaved on the way. "Global Cargo Express?"

"That's right. I'm Bill Kessler, Global Safety."

"George Lenholder—NTSB," he said, flashing his ID. "Mind if I join you?"

Joe couldn't believe Bill invited him in. As Bill introduced everyone, Les Cresanko walked in. *Christ. Global Flight Operations is here, too? What the hell's going on?*

Cresanko looked at the players, noting there wasn't anyone from the union. The pilot union's mishap reaction team was made up of line-holding pilots who volunteered their time. He assumed they were assembling a team now. The union team could observe the NTSB and conduct their own investigation, but they had no official capacity. However, in some cases they had uncovered facts that not only changed the NTSB's conclusion, it saved the pilots' careers. "Joe, why don't you and your crew call the union?"

Joe nodded. As they left, Lenholder grabbed a donut and checked his watch.

They retreated to Joe's VOQ room, where he handed Kevin the forms. "Look these over while I call the union," he said and turned away. Al Dansen, the pilot union president, answered on the first ring. "Al, forgive me if I sound irritable, but the NTSB and Global reps are here, yet there's no mishap team. Where are they?"

Al continued searching for names on his computer screen. "We're still working on it, Joe. Sit tight and make sure no one makes any statements."

"Easy to say when you're not the one getting calls from the *International Press*."

Al lifted his hand from the mouse. "Pardon me?"

"You heard me. Marsha Woods called me this morning. The base information officer implied Global tipped her off. I don't know who's lying, but I'm pissed."

"I'm sure, but keep your cool and don't worry about the press. We both know the public doesn't give a damn about cargo planes."

"Gee thanks, Al. That's real comforting."

Dansen scanned his mishap guide. "Joe, I'm sure you know this, but here's a few pointers. First, make sure everyone agrees on what happened. Second, fill out your NASA forms. Third, don't bullshit anyone—state the facts. Finally, since no one from the union's there, try to record your interview sessions and give us a copy. Don't be badgered into giving bad answers. If you're not sure about something, say so. For whatever it's worth, I trust Bill and Les."

Joe noticed the National Aeronautic and Space Administration forms that Kevin set aside. As base commander, Colonel Moran was looking out for them, tossing the NASA forms in with the others. The Aviation Safety Reporting System was a joint venture between NASA and the FAA to improve flight safety through anonymous pilot reporting. Submitting an ASRS meant legal protection should the FAA file a flight violation. It was a win-win program, but pilots only had a few days to file the report if they wanted any protection. "Keep working on that team, Al. We'll do our best on this end."

Wendy was soaking her hands when Joe asked if she'd completed a NASA form. "You're kidding, right?"

Joe closed his eyes, stretching his back. It had been a long night. Where did he lose control? He gently dried her hands, warm to the touch, meeting her eyes as he applied ointment. "I'll tell you what—we'll do them together. Wendy, I'll fill yours out, but you'll have to sign your own name." Lost in thought, he barely noticed her nod.

They spent forty minutes completing the forms and discussing the mishap before returning to the conference room. Joe was convinced they could present the facts without compromising anything. He stopped in the doorway, taking in the changes, the distinct military atmosphere. Colonel Moran sat calmly near the middle of the conference table. His blue uniform was immaculate, award ribbons pushing his wings to his epaulette, his flight cap with its eagle insignia lying face-up on the table. His hands were clasped together, resting on a notepad, a confident smile on his face. There had been many conferences here, times when the Colonel had maneuvered with far more agility than in a B-2's cockpit—and advanced his career. His body language was clear: I'll finesse this one. He had a light colonel with him, probably another safety officer. Joe, Kevin, and Wendy found their seats. The B-2 bombers still hung suspended in place and time. The green plant offered its waxy leaves to the air conditioning. "Sorry it took so long," Joe said. "I thought I'd made enough copies. I had no idea we'd have such a large group."

"It's okay, Joe," Bill said, his eyes apologizing to his host.

"I hope you don't mind us sitting in," Moran said. "This is Lieutenant Colonel Bateman, my Aviation Safety Officer."

Cresanko winked, trying to assure Joe it was all right. But it wasn't. Joe looked at Moran. "Colonel, do you think we could get some microphones and a recorder before we begin? The union suggested we tape the meeting."

Lenholder popped his knuckles. How much longer could they drag this out?

"Sure," Moran said. "It'll take about twenty minutes. Since we're starting so late, why don't I have lunch delivered so we can keep working?"

"That would be great," Bill said. Bateman left with Moran.

Lenholder studied the completed forms. No surprises there. Most of the information was generic and gave little description of the event. A DC-10 diverting with cargo smoke wasn't much. "Joe, what was your first indication of the problem?"

Bill raised his hand. "George, let's hold off until we get the tape recorder," he said.

Lenholder gathered his documents and rose from his chair. "Sure. If you'll excuse me, I have to make some calls. I'll be back."

Joe relaxed. The only ones left were Global employees. The atmosphere changed. He could breathe again.

"What's that guy's problem?" Wendy asked. "He seems put out."

Bill shrugged. "Probably tired like everyone else."

"No—I think he figures we're stalling," Joe said. He squeezed his hands together, concerned over the formality of their informal debriefing. Al told him to tape the session, but how would that help if someone said the wrong thing? Wendy and Kevin were unpredictable. He'd lost control and didn't like being on the defensive. "Bill—we did everything by the book and have nothing to hide, but why the audience? I thought this was between us."

"Relax, Joe—no one's here to hang you."

Joe scoffed.

It didn't start until George Lenholder showed up in his blue jeans and tousled hair. Why did Bill look worried? His job wasn't in jeopardy. Did he think they screwed up, or did he know something more about the fire? Whatever it was, he wasn't saying a word.

Before long, three audio/visual technicians were pushing a large equipment cart into the room with Colonel Moran and Aviation Safety Officer Bateman close behind. They set up six microphones linked to two tape recorders, positioned so as to pick up everyone's voices. Moran looked pleased. Lenholder returned to his seat just as the tests were concluding. "Thanks for your help, gentlemen," Moran said, excusing the airmen. "I'm told lunch will be here within the hour."

"Super." Bill closed the door and moved to the head of the table, checking to make sure everyone was back. "It appears we have a quorum. Before we get started, I'd like to set some ground rules. George—I'll be leading the discussion." Lenholder nodded, hardened eyes fixed on Joe. "This is an information-gathering session. Any knowledge obtained through this interview can only be used for safety-related issues. Anyone can ask for clarification or offer a follow-up question, but no faults will be assigned or implied. Anyone attempting to do so will be asked to leave. Finally, this has been an emotionally draining experience so I ask that you treat the crew with respect." There were no objections. "Colonel Moran, will you please start the recorders?"

Moran punched the buttons, raising his thumbs after the red lights came on.

Bill was reviewing his notes when he noticed the anger in Joe's eyes. Joe felt betrayed. Hopefully he'd forgive him. This wasn't what either expected, but it was too late to turn back. He stared at the mike as he began.

"The purpose of this interview is to disclose facts relevant to the inflight fire and subsequent destruction of DC-10-30, tail number N103GE, operating as Global Cargo Express Flight 3217 on January 7, 2003. The flight originated in Newark, New Jersey, and was enroute to Oklahoma City, Oklahoma, when the plane diverted to Whiteman Air Force Base, Missouri, at 0233 local. I'm Bill Kessler, Safety Manager for Global Cargo Express. Also in attendance are Flight 3217's crew, Captain Joe Salvetti, First Officer Wendy McManus, and Second Officer Kevin Hamilton. Mr. George Lenholder is here from the NTSB, Colonel Scott Moran and Lieutenant Colonel Bob Bateman representing Whiteman Air Force Base, and Mr. Les Cresanko from Global Cargo Express. It's now 1123 local, January 7, 2003. Captain Salvetti, would you describe the circumstances that led to your diverting into Whiteman?"

Joe leaned forward in his seat, still perturbed by the formalities. He described their indications, actions, and decisions in such intimate detail there was little room for interpretation. His calm voice left no doubt he was as much in command of the debriefing as he was his aircraft. He occasionally called upon crewmembers Wendy and Kevin to add detail, and when finished, sat back in his chair and waited.

Moran shifted in his seat, looking at Lenholder, waiting for a challenge from the NTSB rep.

Bill smiled, Moran looked away. "Thanks, Joe. Are there any questions?" The only movement came from Lenholder's pen. The door opened and a young man in a white apron said their lunch was ready. "Come on in."

Everyone welcomed the turkey sandwiches, French fries, and sliced fruit. Even Lenholder seemed impressed. Bill took a bite of sandwich, thinking about the mishap. Past experience showed it could take months to find the ignition source, but everything he'd heard made sense. It *had* to be something in the cargo. Hopefully the crew could resume their flying duties quickly. He needed to compare notes with the Global Ops rep, Les Cresanko.

Kevin set his food aside. The recorders were off. If he was to say his piece, and possibly end his career, now was the time to do it. His stomach churned. "Colonel Moran—thanks for your support and making us feel welcome." He took a sip from his water glass, his eyes on Bill. "Joe, Wendy—forgive me, but I can't sit here without saying something about our Dangerous Goods situation. I may be new, but I also know that fire didn't start in the Haz can. It couldn't have since the Haz can's in the forward section. I don't know about you, but I find that very disturbing. I mean, who the hell's checking this stuff? Where's the security?" He sat down.

Bill's jaw dropped. Bringing up DG handling was insane. Hazardous materials were their cash cow. How dare Kevin imply someone didn't follow procedures. True, this was an informal proceeding, but did he *want* to be fired? "Ah, Kevin—at this point we have no idea what caused the fire. We won't know whether it was cargo or aircraft related for some time. I understand your frustration, but give the investigators a chance to sort it out, okay?"

Kevin confirmed the tape recorder was still off. "Bill—how could it be aircraft related without any abnormal indications? And yes—I'm pissed about nearly becoming a crispy critter. All I'm asking is for better cargo screening. Passenger airlines can't carry hazardous materials anymore, but we'll haul anything. Give us your nukes, your anthrax, your incendiaries, your infectious substances. And we're not alone. You remember when FedEx had that radiation leak? Everyone on the plane got exposed, all because something wasn't packaged right." He paused to look around the room. No one was smiling.

Joe looked away. Didn't he make it clear that Kevin should only speak if spoken to? While he shared his concerns, this wasn't the place to vent. Thanks to him, the FAA might investigate Global's shipping operation, and that could seriously impact their jobs. *Way to go, Dumbshit.*

Moran read the tension in Joe's face. He stared at the photo of the B-2.

George Lenholder ran a hand through his tousled hair then set his pencil down. "Kevin—how long have you been with Global?"

Kevin looked at Joe and Wendy. They froze him out. The green table used to evaluate pilots came to mind, only now these guys were the judges. No longer was this an inquiry about the DC-10. Now it was about him. "A couple of months," he said. A face came to mind. A squadron mate he'd voted out of the Naval Aviation fraternity. A damned fine pilot, but he set his own rules. His career ended with the stroke of a pen. His eyes met Lenholder's. "This was my second flight out of training— actually my first if you don't count the deadhead."

"No kidding? That's a heck of a way to break into a new job."

Kevin loosened his collar, smoke smell wafted up. "Look, George—I know what you're implying, but I've been working with hazardous materials for twenty-two years—most of it in the Marine Corps—most of it a lot more hazardous than what we carry around. I'm not placing blame, but I do believe some undeclared Haz caused the fire. It's the only thing that makes sense. The customer's the weak link because Global has to take their word for what they're shipping. Since it costs more to ship hazardous material, a lot of nasty stuff slips by. Unfortunately, I doubt we can prevent a reoccurrence without jeopardizing the business."

Bill stood. "Well, Kevin, thanks for your candor. Joe—since he brought it up, would you care to comment?"

Joe shrugged. "Kevin has a point. It'll be interesting to see what the investigators come up with." Kevin waited. Would he keep his job or be blackballed from the industry?

Lenholder finished reviewing the DG declaration. "According to the loading document, no hazardous material was anywhere near the rear of the aircraft. I'm sure the FBI will get involved in this one."

"You think it was sabotage?" asked Bill.

"Who knows? No one's ever determined why TWA Flight 800 went down. Of course, your DC-10 didn't explode like TWA's

747, but it still raises questions about cargo handling." Lenholder looked around the table, stopping at Joe. "Frankly, I'm surprised you're not more concerned about the possibility of arson."

Bill shook his head. "Now hold on, George. A lot of things could've started that fire—even a hydraulic leak if the conditions were right. Let's not jump to any conclusions."

"I'm not, but we have to consider all the possibilities, and the FBI's best suited to investigate those aspects."

The room was tense. Sabotage added a new dimension. Worse than a hijacking. There was limited cargo access. Nothing a crew could do to protect against it. The conversation ceased while the tables were bussed.

Bill Kessler resumed the interview after a ten-minute break. By 1430, everyone was ready to leave. "Thank you for your time," he said. "I'm going to let the crew gather their belongings and send them back to Oklahoma City. George, would you mind coming along to verify they are only removing their personal effects?"

"Sure, but I want to take some photos before they disturb anything."

Colonel Moran was removing the tapes from the recorders. "I can provide a photographer if you'd like. I'll also have these tapes transcribed and send copies to everyone."

"That would be great, Colonel," Bill said.

"I'm sure you'll need hangar space."

"Can you arrange that?"

Moran smiled. "I'll assign a liaison to make sure your needs are met." He stood, winking at Kevin. "No point in having authority if you don't use it."

Before they left, Moran and Bateman shook hands with Joe and Kevin, and patted Wendy on the shoulder, staring awkwardly at her bandages. Lenholder left with them. With everyone gone, the room fell silent around its B-2 bomber photos and potted plant.

Wendy glanced at Joe on the way to their rooms. "I can't wait to get out of these clothes." Joe was still mulling over Kevin's betrayal. Wendy was angered by his distance. "You're lucky, Joe. No one notices *your* appearance. Imagine being a woman. I'm ashamed to be seen in public."

Joe nodded. "Don't be so hard on yourself," he said. "You look great with or without makeup. See you in the lobby."

Bill yelled at them as they were about to go in their rooms. "The Citation pilots will be ready in forty-five minutes. Meet you at the van." Joe, Wendy, and Kevin went to clean up.

The SP at the flightline security checkpoint matched their ID pictures to their faces. Bill hadn't seen that level of security since his last trip to Moscow, but was glad the guard took his job seriously. He stared at the red line, wondering if the others knew about the restricted entry points. "Stick with me," he said. Lenholder's NTSB car was right behind them.

The DC-10 came into view as they entered the ramp, its fuselage hinged at the wing root, tail resting on the ground, tail-mounted engine pointed skyward. Their once-proud bird had been reduced to rubble. Oddly, the American flag below the engine nacelle still gleamed. "It just kept burning," Bill said. "They never got to the source. The Fire Chief thinks the tail broke from all the water. Believe it or not, we might be able to deliver some of the cargo. The lower cargo deck's pretty much intact."

Joe barely heard Bill's words, stunned by what he saw. Everything behind the upper cargo door was gone. The damned thing looked like a pickup truck with wings. But why? He flew it in for Christ's sake. He noticed the Aviation Safety Officer, Lt Colonel Bateman, climbing down the cargo loader ladder, camera over his shoulder. "What the hell's going on?"

"I don't know," Bill said, observing Bateman. "Wait here."

Bateman met Bill half way. "Hi Bill. I took a few shots, but nothing's been disturbed. You and George will get copies. By the way, their personal effects look fine."

"That's good to know."

The Air Force photographer arrived as Lt Colonel Bateman was leaving. The base's seldom-used portable stairs had a flat tire so a cargo loader had to do. Once the loader stopped at the cockpit level, Wendy pushed her way inside. The courier deck was soaked, but the cockpit was just as they'd left it, charts out, emergency checklists open, Kevin's "3217 Heavy" sticky note on the instrument panel. She backed out of the way so the photographer could get some shots.

"The Citation's waiting so don't waste any time," Bill said.

Kevin turned around. "What's the rush, Bill? This beast is a helluva lot more than a burned out hulk. It saved our lives."

"You're right—poor choice of words. They'll leave whenever you're ready."

Kevin removed their suitcases and set them on the loader while Joe gathered their flight deck belongings. Wendy moved out of their way, inspecting her bag. "God dammit!"

Her words caught Kevin's attention. He looked at her, noticing her moist eyes, vulnerable for the first time. "Hey—a soaked suitcase isn't so bad," he said.

"I can't wait to get the hell out of here." A breeze flipped her singed hair into her face, its smell reminding her she'd escaped a fiery death. The escape rope dangled out the cockpit window. Her eyes smiled.

Kevin made a final sweep through the cockpit, removing his flight folder from under the desktop. Joe had yet to say a word. Not much of a crew anymore. Like Wendy, he wanted to change clothes, but it wasn't an option.

"You're going home by yourselves," Bill said. "You'll each get a copy of the transcripts. The union gets one, too. I'm sure we'll have more questions, but until then, make the most of your time off."

Time off? Would it be permanent? Kevin boarded the Citation and fastened his seat belt, the smell of burned cloth now a constant companion. Was it cold or just him? He didn't look forward to another interrogation. This time he'd keep his mouth shut. Ideally he'd get a reprieve. Maybe another trip. But not for a while. If word got out about his comments at the hearing....And then there was Nancy.

Kevin awoke when the Citation's main gear met the runway. Joe looked at Wendy. She was lost in thought, her arms hugging her, struggling to find another minute's sleep. The sounds of muted cockpit conversation and jet engines made Kevin shiver.

Other than the mechanic directing them into their parking spot, the ramp was deserted. Smoke from the diesel auxiliary power cart rose in the calm air, trash from the evening's package sort littered the tarmac. Kevin frowned. Quite the contrast from when he returned from the Gulf War where thousands of people lined up waving American flags. He picked Nancy out of the crowd, her lips saying, "I love you," the boys yet to come. But this was a different time and place, a lesson in civilian life. This time he was a survivor, not a hero. Dad always said, "Never expect anything and you won't be disappointed." Kevin could still see his face, thoughtful, reflective, yet carrying a little pain.

Ten minutes later, their crew bus arrived. Why it wasn't waiting for them was bothersome, but since Joe said nothing, he wasn't about to. When they arrived at Flight Operations, Kevin thanked the bus driver and unloaded their bags, taking a moment to strap Wendy's Jepps bag onto her roller suitcase. "You need help getting these to your car?"

"No thanks. Hope you get some sleep." She wasted no time disappearing into the nearby parking lot, her wrist pulling her suitcase.

Kevin caught Joe's eye as he hooked his bag. "So, what are your plans?"

Joe raised his suitcase handle, avoiding Kevin's eyes, heading inside. "I'm gonna stop by the union office."

Kevin's stomach stirred, his throat burned from bile. Would it be like this the rest of his career? Kevin the whistleblower? He shadowed Joe. "Mind if I tag along?" Joe's silence grated. "Look, Joe—I'm sorry about what happened back there, but I couldn't just sit back and watch. I'm a team player, but I'll never be someone's yes-man."

Joe stopped, firing a look. "Neither will I, but you should've warned me. You made me look like an idiot, Kevin. It's not what you said, but how you said it. I thought we had an understanding." He paused to grind a hand into tired red eyes. "Look—we're both stretched thin. Come if you want, but *I'll* do the talking."

"Agreed."

Kevin relaxed, following Joe through the maze into a part of the building he never knew existed. To imply solidarity, Global provided the pilot union with an office in the far corner of a hangar. The musty scent of old wood suggested a sixty-year old building, its framework now hidden behind paneled walls, false ceilings, and dim fluorescent lighting. Al Dansen had spent the last five hours getting a mishap team together and was now soliciting volunteers to fly their trips. He saw them in their soot-stained uniforms and cradled the phone. "Hey, Joe—good to see you."

"Hi, Al. This is my SO, Kevin Hamilton." While they shook hands, Joe stretched. He felt like an old man. Maybe twelve hours of sleep would help. "Al, if I had any brains I'd be outta here, but I wanted to make sure everything was in order."

Dansen sat back in his chair. "Everything's on track—in fact, you probably passed our response team beak-to-beak," he said. "They should be landing right about now. I wished they could've been there for the debrief."

Joe shrugged. "No sweat, we taped everything. Bill Kessler's supposed to be sending transcripts. By the way—looks like the FBI's gonna get involved."

"Seems logical."

"Yeah, but it won't be good if they find the company negligent. Al, doesn't Global have an obligation to give us a safe work environment?"

Dansen checked the hallway to make sure no one was within earshot and closed the door. "This doesn't leave the room, but the scuttlebutt is some kind of improperly packaged electronic gear started the fire. Of course no one's admitting anything, but the fact the rumor spread so quickly makes me wonder."

"Ah, yeah. Rumors. They run amuck at Global." Al's revelation was no different than talk of mergers, planes, and new pilot domiciles. Why'd he bother passing it on? It wasn't like Al. "Any idea what'll happen to us?"

Dansen sighed. "Unless you hear different, plan on flying your line."

Joe stared. "Say what? Who's ever heard of a captain flying right after a mishap? Besides—I'm not ready to fly. And what about that time off Bill promised?"

"Bill doesn't have any authority in that area and we're short on pilots. I'm not saying it's right, but since there's no FAA violation, the company can fly you once you've had a legal rest period. Talk to your flight manager, Joe—see what he says."

Joe's face flushed. He'd been Al's first officer, respected him. Where was the support? The fire in his eyes? "You sure you're not in management?"

Dansen looked at his computer screen, pretending to read something important. "Joe, you're tired, scratchy. Go home and get some rest. By the way, I'm sure the crew force would love to hear your story. Would you and your crew mind talking about it at the Wednesday night pilot meeting?"

Kevin bit his lip. How could Dansen be so bold? Even if Joe agreed, what could he contribute? He'd pulled a few levers and dumped some fuel, but for the most part was along for the ride. He didn't need any more scrutiny.

Joe twisted the doorknob. "I'll let you know about the meeting." He turned. "Just for the record, Al—Kevin did a great job tonight. My second officer got sick so they flew Kevin out to replace him. Kevin's first trip out of training and he ends up in the corporate jet—can you believe it?" He grabbed his bag and slipped into the hall.

Kevin reflected on Al's words: beak-to-beak, scuttlebutt—fighter pilot terms for meeting a plane head-on and hearsay. Dansen must have been Navy—but even old fighter pilots don't back down. Al knew Joe shouldn't be flying, so why didn't he call the schedulers and tell them to pack sand? Kevin nodded at Dansen and left to catch up with Joe.

Joe said nothing as they came to the duty office. Too late for the night duty officer, too early for the day shift, he scribbled a note while dialing Crew Scheduling. "Hi, Betty—Joe Salvetti. Say, I wanted to confirm I'm replaced for tonight's flight."

She hesitated. "Just a minute, Joe."

Joe's doodling intensified. There was typing in the background, but no one was talking. What's going on? "Betty? You still there?"

"Yeah—sorry for the delay, Joe. I wanted to make sure there wasn't a mistake. Wendy McManus is on sick leave and Kevin Hamilton's out of reserve days, but you're still listed for tonight's flight."

"What? That's insane!" Joe's head throbbed, his cheeks numbed. The pressure behind his eyes was unbearable. He couldn't focus. He rarely lost control and hated this. He stood there with the stink of violence and fire on him. "Betty—I'm sorry, but I'm in no shape to fly. Show me on sick leave." He slammed the phone and left. Pilot shortage or not, he wasn't flying tonight.

Kevin squinted into the light, his eyes still irritated from the smoke. Not wanting to startle the kids, he changed into a polo shirt and pants, still damp from the fire hoses. He drove the rental car to the hotel where Nancy and the boys were staying, wishing he could turn back time. There was no escaping the ordeal. Every yellow streetlight became a smoke detector; red, a Master Warning.

His heart tripped with the engine. When he arrived, he couldn't open the door. He was emotionally and physically spent. He took a moment to wipe his mouth and smooth his hair. He looked like hell.

Nancy ran to him, shaken, angry. "Why didn't you tell me about the fire?"

The boys were in the tub laughing; they didn't know he was home. He took her in his arms and squeezed. He saw the fear in her eyes. "I figured if you heard my voice, you'd know I was okay."

His soiled clothes reeked. She couldn't stop scanning his red eyes. She freed herself from his embrace. "My God, Kevin—I kept seeing the fire, the wreck, it won't leave me. I never got back to sleep. I'm stuck here in this hotel room—"

"I'm sorry, Nance. I—"

"You know, Kevin, I figured life would be a cakewalk after the Marine Corps. But this? For Christ's sake, you're gone for two months of training, then your plane's destroyed?"

"Nancy—"

She pulled free, her face flushed. Images flashed. Things from the past; a look into the future. "So what happens now?"

"Unless I hear something different, my schedule goes as planned."

"So this is what I can expect? Three days together, then you're gone for ten days of reserve? And this is your dream job? What about *my* life? What about us? We both wanted kids, but I never expected I'd be raising them on my own."

"Hey—wait a minute, Babe."

"And stop calling me *Babe*. I hate it when you do that!" She turned her back. "I don't think I can handle your being gone every other week."

He moved closer, wrapping his arms around her. "I love you, Nance."

She felt a chill. His breath warmed her neck. Her heart thumped. She turned to face him. "Damn you, Kevin—it's not fair. Why do I love you so?" She buried her head in his shoulder, catching the smell of his clothing, hearing his own pounding heart. She kissed his parched lips. "You sure you're okay?"

He nodded. "Nancy—I love you so much. I should've told you. When I was up there, I feared I'd never hold you again."

She unbuttoned his shirt, pulling it off, tossing it aside. He tasted her lips, her curves melting into him. As his hands explored her, the boys called out. She sighed. "You'd better get them."

Kevin threw the bathroom door open, spreading his arms wide. "Hi Guys."

"Daddy," they shouted. Soap, toys, sponges, splashing water.

He toweled them dry and emerged with a clean kid in each arm. "Hey, Mom—look what I found."

Jake's nose curled, pointing to his dad. "Mommy, Daddy stinks." He looked at Nancy and back at his father. "Daddy—why's mommy crying?"

Kevin rubbed Jake's wet head. "She's just glad to see me," he said. He tickled Jake's belly. Not to be ignored, Randy wrapped his arms around Kevin's neck. "Hey—take it easy, you little Munchkin," he said, throwing Randy over his shoulder. He pinned Randy's arms against the bed and planted a sloppy kiss on his belly, blowing until the repulsive sound brought a fit of giggles.

"Can't catch me," Jake said, waving his hands behind his ears, curling his nose.

"Oh really?" Striking fast, Kevin flipped Jake on his back and blew on his belly. Nancy joined the romp, tickling Randy until he begged for mercy. In five minutes it was over. Reality closed on him like a vise.

"Kevin, if you toss me those hideous clothes you're wearing, we'll take them to the cleaners. Maybe they can do something with your suitcase, too."

He stepped into the bathroom, chucking his dirty clothes, clinging to his towel. "Thanks." After hearing the front door close, he immersed himself in steamy silence. The warm water soothed, but he was still haunted by the debrief. Why did he speak up? Why didn't he just sit back and watch it play out? Didn't he trust Joe? No wonder Joe was upset. He let the shower cascade over him, increasing its heat and pressure until it turned him pink. After toweling himself, he made his way to the bed, out before his head hit the pillow.

The phone was ringing in his dream, his flight manager saying he was released. The smell of smoke alerted him. One eye opened, then the other. It was no dream; his pillow reeked of smoke, he was holding the phone. He listened intently. "Kevin, we want you back in the air as soon as possible. There's no sim check so plan on flying when you return."

"Thanks." Still half asleep, he cradled the phone, unconcerned. The safety standards were the same for all airlines. This was a fluke. Accidents happen. Global was probably reviewing their cargo acceptance procedures. Just then, the door flew open.

"Daddy!"

He barely had time to cover himself before the boys reached the bed. He grabbed one in each arm, pulling them close. "Gotcha."

Nancy watched, her eyes studying him. He needed more sleep and wouldn't get it. He was so good with them. It's what kept her love alive while he was away. Once the boys moved from the bed she nestled close. Her fingers stroked the hairs on his chest. "So—did you get any rest?"

He slid his arm under her neck, nuzzling her nose, her perfume inviting. "I dunno—what time is it?"

The covers outlined his form. She moved closer, blowing in his ear. "Mmmm—you smell so good. I could eat you alive. Do you want some…clean clothes?"

He rolled onto his side to keep the sheet from rising. "Oh—you're bad, blowing in my ear like that."

She smiled, her eyes inviting, devilish. "Sometimes I like to be bad."

Her lips were her best feature. Full, soft. The boys were far away, yet obstinately right there.

Nancy told them to go play. She moved closer to Kevin, spreading her scent. She kissed his ear. Then the tease was over. "So tell me, Kevin—what *really* happened."

Kevin stared at the boys. Their hotel room offered no privacy. The boys would be listening, trying to hear. He felt sick, but he had to say something.

"Well?"

"I was scared, Nance. You and I both saw a lot in the Corps, but it's different when it happens to you. For the first time, I understood why my dad never wanted to talk about World War II—not that this approached that. About all I can say is the crew and I handled the emergency. That's the way it is—something goes wrong—you handle it. That's why we do so many EP sims. It's just that—"

"What?"

"It's hard to explain. I know it sounds like I'm covering it up, but I'm not. Nothing like this has ever happened at Global. It was bad luck, that's all."

Nancy pulled back. "Bad luck? So you're saying you can handle anything?"

"For Christ's sake, Nancy—you think I don't fear burning planes?"

"Shhhh. The boys."

As Kevin looked up, the boys' heads snapped around. He whispered, moving as close as he dared. "Look, Nance, the important thing is that no one got hurt. I can't imagine anything like this happening again. Don't you remember what it took to get this job? Give it a chance, will ya?"

Nancy lay on the bed staring at the ceiling, her face turned to stone. "This isn't working, Kevin. I'm thinking we should hold off on our move. You're gone all the time. The boys and I have friends in North Carolina. Why do you want to uproot everyone to move to this company town? You can't escape Global out here. Everyone we meet will know you were in that mishap. You'll be the topic of every grocery conversation, delivered over the bananas. "Oh look, there's Kevin Hamilton. Do you think he's accident-prone? Say, cashews are on sale. I love cashews.""

He glanced her way. "Aren't you being a little overdramatic?"

"No."

He shifted in the bed, distancing himself. "You're right. Who says we have to rush into this? Of course, we've moved lots of times and everything's always worked out—but we'll give it some time. I admit reserve duty sucks, but that's the way it is when you're new. Consider this, though. By moving here, we'd have a lot more time together and a lot less stress." He wasn't reaching her. His words faded into her fragrance. He was better off watching television with the boys while she packed their suitcases. They could still catch the later flight. Wordlessly he dressed and joined the boys on the floor, an arm around each one.

By seven p.m. they were flying to Raleigh, North Carolina. The whole family was tired; the boys were asleep before the plane leveled off. Nancy seemed apprehensive about flying, but it was their only way home. With the cabin lights dimmed, passengers asleep, flight attendants seated, it seemed a good time to try again, make his case. He squeezed her hand. "This is the best flying job I'll ever get, Nance. Good pay—eventually I'll have lots of time off. If you knew about the close calls I had flying those canceled checks, you'd be glad I have this job."

She stared at the candy wrapper in the seat pocket. "But I do know, Kevin."

"Say again?"

She looked at him. "You have no idea how many sleepless nights I spent worrying about you. Flying light planes in ice storms in the middle of the night is insane. In fact, I need a logbook—a logbook so I can record my hours of worrying while you're away. Multiply the hours in your logbook times three, Kevin—because that's how long I've worried about you."

Kevin didn't know what to say. He sensed others were listening, though no eyes were on him. He squirmed in his seat.

Her hand closed over his. "You have to fly. I know you had to take those crappy jobs to keep your proficiency. Don't you think I sympathize? I'm the one who watched you drag yourself through the door every morning. I knew how tired you were."

"So you realize I'm now working half the hours for twice the pay, right?"

She smiled at that. "I remember the day Global called. You were so excited, your smile could've lit up a football stadium."

Kevin smiled, remembering. "Yeah—I couldn't believe it. I'd about given up. Felt like no one in the big league wanted me. Strange, but I still don't know what it takes to get hired by a major airline."

She rested her head on his shoulder. Maybe it wasn't so bad. She'd accepted her role, how could she expect him to change now? She tried to accept it was a fluke that Kevin was on board that flight, but it didn't quiet her fears. But fears or not, she couldn't imagine a life without him. "Kevin, I'll always worry about you, but I guess working for Global is no worse than your being in the Marine Corps. Just be careful, okay?"

Jake opened an eye. "Yeah, Dad—be careful," he said, bearing a gap-toothed grin.

Kevin buried his pillow in Jake's face. The little toad must have heard everything. Thankfully they'd limited their conversation to flying.

At best, the Boeing 727's jump seat was cramped, but the ride was free. Watching the second officer balance fuel and make radio calls made him appreciate the DC-10's larger, quieter cockpit. He'd escaped duty in the "lawn dart" by virtue of his social security number, which gave him a higher seniority number. He closed his eyes and shuffled his feet to keep the circulation flowing. Still another two hours to Oklahoma City.

It was an odd lifestyle; something he was still getting used to. Sharing a crash pad with five other new-hires was like living in a frat house, but without the parties. First-year pay didn't yield many options; a crash pad was the only way to make ends meet. He had just gotten to sleep when his roommate handed him the phone. It had to be Crew Schedules. "Hang on," he said, fumbling for the light switch and notepad. He read everything back and slid into his uniform, reviewing his note while he brushed his teeth. *Pairing X115. Flight 3209 to Los Angeles, twenty-hour layover, 1854 back.* Not bad. Five minutes later he bolted out the door.

When he entered the flight planning room, anxiety crowded in. As he checked the flight release, he realized nobody knew him or cared. The room was so jammed, his best friend wouldn't have recognized him if he were standing five feet away. He didn't know his captain or first officer. Did they know anything about him? He grabbed a coffee jug and boarded the crew bus.

Flight 3209 pushed back two minutes early, each crewmember engrossed in their duties, no time for pleasantries. Passing eighteen thousand feet, Captain Jack Henshaw engaged the autopilot and relaxed. "So, Kevin—what's it like being engulfed in smoke?"

Oh, Christ. Suddenly aware of the air conditioning, lights, and vibration, he saw Joe and Wendy's faces. They were staring at him, mouthing, "Go snuff the fire, Kevin!" He checked his panel; no lights. All was calm, just a dream. Wendy and Joe disappeared. "It wasn't much fun," he said.

"I bet. We sure lost a lot of lift capability because of it. Global had to wet-lease a DC-10 from World."

"Sorry—what's wet leasing? Is it bad?"

"Bad? Kevin—everything in this industry revolves around scope. When Global wet leases, they not only lease a plane, they're leasing pilots, too—and that means someone else is flying our freight. If that trend continues, we could be out of a job."

Kevin nodded, turning his chair to report his off times. He reflected on Henshaw's words as Flight Operations read back the information. Was he being blamed for the mishap or was the captain just frustrated? He centered his chair again. "It never should've burned," he said, angered by the insinuation. "The fire trucks were dousing it within seconds, but they never got to the source. I'm sure it was something in the cargo."

The captain took a moment to answer a radio call. He looked back at Kevin. "Nothing surprises me," he said, mulling over the notion. "I heard the FO got burned."

"Where'd that come from?"

The captain shrugged. "That's what I heard."

"She lost her grip and got rope burns on her hands. No big deal."

"Oh—glad that's all it was. I'll pass it on. Of course you've heard about the drug money, right?"

Kevin shook his head, hiding his smile. If this story was anything like Wendy's burns, he couldn't wait to hear it. Nothing moved faster than airline gossip. A good rumor or joke could travel the world in less than twenty-four hours.

The captain's face grew serious. "When they sorted through the lower cargo bay, they found boxes full of hundred-dollar bills wrapped in plastic and no one's claimed 'em. Rumor has it that if it's not delivered in a certain period of time, the company gets to keep it. Hell, between that and the insurance money, Global's gonna make out like a bandit."

The FO laughed. "You've been watching too many movies, Jack."

Kevin scanned his panel. "Has anyone actually seen this money?"

"Beats me—just repeating what I've heard," Henshaw said.

If it were true, it was undeclared cargo, just like whatever started their fire. The news was troubling. "It'll be interesting to hear what the company says about it."

Henshaw burst out laughing. "Christ, Kevin—what've you been smoking? This isn't the military—they don't share secrets. We'll be lucky if we know something about your mishap in two years. Hey—how about a refill?" he asked, passing his coffee cup.

"Any plans for LA, Jack?" the FO asked.

Kevin stirred the coffee, awaiting Henshaw's response. It was strange being on the road with time to spare, no meetings, no deadlines. He had to think how he'd spend his layover. What a contrast from flying canceled checks. Barely enough time for a nap before climbing back in the cockpit. Images of sunshine and tanned hardbodies scalded his brain. He could almost hear the waves, shorebirds. This was definitely a change for the better. "I'm gonna run on the beach," he said, handing Jack his coffee.

"Cause it clears your head, right?" the FO asked, nudging Jack.

Kevin smiled, half-listening to their talk about beach babes while thinking about the recovered money. Was it tied to the fire? Were they carrying illegal drugs? Could it have been an inside job? He went to the lav and splashed water on his face. In the mirror, his face was gaunt, his hands shaking.

Seven months passed and to everyone except Kevin, his mishap was old news. Nancy had adapted to the lifestyle and their move to Oklahoma City made his reserve duty effortless. When he wasn't called out for a flight, he was playing with the boys or working on Nancy's endless to-do list. For now they were content living in a rental house. Life was good. His bedroom eyes met Nancy's, knowing the boys were asleep. He wrapped his arms around her, sliding her nightgown over her shoulder, her fragrance lingering. "I don't have to leave for another four hours."

Her hand reached for his thigh. "Hmm. What could we do with that time?"

"I was thinking maybe we should check out the bedroom," he said with a grin. "I was wondering—what do you think about putting some crown molding in the bedroom?"

"I'm not sure," she said. "Maybe you should show me."

Kevin was still wearing a smile when he walked into Flight Ops. He hadn't flown in a week and getting airborne was the icing on a perfect day. He spotted Wendy McManus typing at a computer terminal and caught her eye.

"Hey Kevin," she said, holding her hands high. "Look—no scars."

What a smile. He'd never seen her smile before. His memories were of her blue eyes faded to gray in the cockpit illumination.

Appropriate or not, he hugged her. She was beautiful and knew it. Every pilot at Global must've hit on her at one time or another. Nice to see her let her guard down. "That's great. How long were you out?"

"About four weeks, but I only used eight days of sick leave thanks to my bid line and vacation. Believe me, I've learned to appreciate my health. What are you up to?"

"Same as always—still on reserve. Where are you headed tonight?"

"Back to Newark, I'm afraid. Haven't been there since the accident. Can't say I won't be thinking about Whiteman AFB."

Her comment about Newark brought him back to the mishap. His smile disappeared. Why did the investigation take so long? Cover-up came to mind.

"Penny for them."

Kevin looked up. "Oh, nothing special. Well, you're busy and I've got to find a computer terminal. Good seeing you again. Fly safe." She waved without looking up.

Seeing Wendy reminded him to send another query to Flight Safety about their mishap; his tenth e- mail on the subject. Like the others, it would go unnoticed, but he'd keep bugging them until they responded. He banged on the keyboard, lost in thought. *Inside job, cover-up.* It ended when a key flew off.

5

As civil and freight aircraft weaved contrails across the Oklahoma sky, Cougar Industries designed their first internal combustion engine. In that same year, Global Cargo Express launched its fledgling fleet skyward, competing in its own arena of commerce. While Cougar Industries struggled against impossible deadlines on engine development, Global struggled with pilot schedules, light revenue loads, and staggering fuel costs. Since the bottom fell out of the oil industry, it was no coincidence that both companies were established in Oklahoma City, where premium warehouse space now rented for pennies on the dollar. Reacting to insider information, Derek Goldstein sold his trucking company before the bust with visions of developing a fuel-efficient diesel engine. If he succeeded, he'd sell thousands to the trucking industry and ride the wave of success.

He'd gone to the Massachusetts Institute of Technology with an engineer named Arvid Kizka, a man of remarkable insight. Goldstein e-mailed the Boston engineering firm where Kizka worked, hoping for a response, yet unsure he'd remember him.

Kizka was enticed by Goldstein's offer. As a mid-level engineer working mediocre tasks, he was eager to head his own project. He could handpick five engineers and was given two years to develop an engine. Failure to meet Goldstein's timeline meant they would all be out of a job. He accepted the challenge, sight unseen.

While Goldstein's original intent was to transform the trucking industry, the federal government was so impressed, they issued Cougar Industries a grant to develop an efficient automobile engine. On the verge of a breakthrough, the oil crisis ended, gas lines disappeared, and Goldstein's market was lost. Financially strapped, he had no choice but to sell his designs to the automobile and gasoline conglomerate that wanted his engines off the market. Ironically, even though Cougar Industries' engines never saw production, communal fear still made them profitable.

Goldstein continued pursuing his dream on a shoestring budget, confident that once gas prices doubled, consumers would be demanding fuel-efficient vehicles. But he was equally convinced the real money was in replacement engines for semi-tractors, and Kizka's latest design was promising. In his wildest dreams, he never envisioned an engine that could power a twenty-ton tractor-trailer rig while delivering over thirty miles per gallon, but they were nearly there. If successful, this engine would make him a legend. Dad had to be smiling from above.

Although Kizka's ¾ scale Ultima E850 prototype supported his computer models, it failed to gain enthusiasm from U.S. manufacturers. They wanted to see the real article before making any commitments. Intentional news leaks of a full-size prototype sent Cougar's stock soaring, but also put Goldstein under pressure to demonstrate the engine before his market lost interest. Without consulting Kizka, he issued a press release announcing the Ultima E850 would be unveiled on July 3, 2004, proclaiming it would free America from its dependence on foreign oil. He anticipated a full house.

With the unveiling less than three weeks away, Kizka's team labored to the brink of exhaustion. On June 25th, the full-scale prototype was wheeled out of the lab for the first time in weeks. Following several modifications, the engine was hooked up to its test bed. All eyes were on Kizka as he prepared to turn the key. Kizka held his breath and flicked his wrist. Cylinders pounded, exhaust tubes swelled, cheers and applause erupted as the engine came to life. "Gentlemen—we own the future."

With the engine monitors showing everything performing to specifications, Kizka left the engine running and locked the facility. When he returned twenty-four hours later, nothing had changed. He turned the key over to his technicians and made his way to Goldstein's office. The secretary sent him in. "Good news, Boss. She's still purring like a kitten."

Goldstein walked over to the bar and opened the mahogany cabinet. He filled two highballs with ice and poured a shot of Chivas Regal, handing one to Kizka. "To the future, Arvid," he said, raising his glass. He took a sip and escorted him to the easy chairs located near his window. Goldstein set his glass on a copy of *Fortune* magazine. "So—are we ready to hit the market?"

Arvid found a coaster and set his glass down. "Not quite. We need more testing in the semi. Still working on the overheating, but we should have that licked in the next few days."

Goldstein looked over his reading glasses, his eyebrows raised. "Exactly what do you mean by that? We've only got a few days."

"I know, Boss. We'll be ready."

Everything did come together on the morning of July 3rd. Red, white, and blue banners adorned the otherwise drab building, the early sun reflected off its mirrored windows. Every seat was filled with representatives from the trucking industry. Goldstein wasn't surprised. He delayed his entry to increase tension among the potential investors, vigorously rubbing his hands together. When he gave the nod, blaring trumpets startled everyone but their host. As they turned in their seats, Goldstein paraded down the center aisle like an evangelist, eyes wide, teeth gleaming. "Good afternoon, and thank you all for coming," he said, taking center stage. "As you know, for over two decades Cougar Industries has been leading the way in energy-efficient engines. Today you will witness the future—our latest design, certain to revolutionize the transportation industry and launch interstate commerce into the next century. It's with great pleasure that I present the Ultima E850." Trumpets sounded, strobe lights flashed. He tugged on a golden rope and the sapphire velvet drape rose. Spotlights focused on the pristine 4-stroke, 32 valve, turbocharged V-10 engine. The presentation was spectacular.

Goldstein lowered his hands to silence the thunderous applause. "Don't be fooled by this prototype's sparkle. It's powered a fully loaded eighteen-wheeler for thousands of miles under a variety of road conditions. In fact, I'm pleased to say it's surpassed even my own expectations." As he finished his sentence, the lights dimmed and curtains parted, exposing a wall-sized movie screen. Without missing a beat, the video presentation showed a semi racing up a steep incline. "As you can see, the Ultima E850's eight hundred fifty horsepower easily traverses even the most challenging routes, yet with half the fuel consumption of its nearest competitor. While fuel cells are a novel concept for pleasure vehicles, they lack the raw power required for hauling cargo." More clips of the semi driving in snow, the desert, and rain. The curtains closed and the spotlight focused on Goldstein. "I predict the Ultima E850 will replace today's diesel engines within the decade. Trucking companies that want to stay in business will either retrofit their rigs or buy one of the new aerodynamic tractors we're designing to complement our engine.

"While our prior fuel efficient engine designs were shelved before production could take place, there is no stopping the Ultima E850. I promise you this engine will see production within a year, even if I have to build it myself." Silence filled the room. Following a dramatic pause, Goldstein smiled. "Of course, you all came here to see the engine, not listen to me boast. Please allow me to introduce my chief engineer, Mr. Arvid Kizka. Arvid will lead us through today's demonstration. Arvid?"

A lean man wearing a clean white smock and thin mustache shook Goldstein's hand as he stepped onto the stage. Streaks of gray accented his wavy brown hair, and his eyes sparkled with enthusiasm. As he took center stage, another curtain rose, revealing a panel of switches and dials. Kizka clasped his hands and looked around the room, squinting into the lights. "Good morning. It's my privilege to show off our baby, but first we'll go over the E850's performance specifications. You should all have a copy in front of you so, if you would, please follow along." Papers shuffled, heads turned. "As you can see, the E850 boasts a forty-seven percent increase in horsepower and a one-hundred fifty percent increase in fuel economy over the leading diesel." He ignored the mutterings from the audience. "I understand your skepticism. After all, if this were possible, why'd it take so long to develop, right?" Heads nodded. "The truth is the necessary advances in metallurgy only recently came about, and I'm sure others are racing to catch up. Regardless, I'm certain that today's demonstration will convince you the E850 is real."

The cynics quieted as Kizka rolled a shiny object between his fingertips. "Gentlemen, this microchip is the heart of the Ultima E850 system. It regulates everything, including the integrated Heads-Up Display. The HUD is a key element that directs the driver to a specific gear for optimum performance. While later versions will incorporate an automatic transmission, we decided to retain the manual transmission for now because most truckers prefer shifting."

Kizka's laser pointer identified the instruments, the audience's attention focused, the room still. He spoke in layman's terms, yet technical enough to show expertise. Their eyes shifted between their papers and him. "You'll each receive a printout of today's test results, so please return your attention to me." He waited until he had their interest. "Thank you." He caught Goldstein's nod from the sideline. "As you can see, the instruments read zero, and the time and date are correct. This is a loud demonstration so I'll be speaking through an intercom. Please put your headsets on so we may proceed." He paused. "Okay, now raise your hand if you can hear me." Satisfied, Kizka removed the key from his smock and inserted it into the ignition switch. "Here we go. Three, two—" With the flick of a wrist, the engine burst into life. The audience seemed impressed. "Please direct your attention to the computer display," he said, using his laser. "Note the engine is idling at five hundred RPM, yet its fuel flow is barely off the peg. Now watch as I increase it to two thousand RPM to simulate sixty miles per hour on a level highway." Kizka shouted into the mike, "Note the fuel consumption. Thirty-five miles per gallon is no mistake." Their nodding heads reminded him of those mechanical dogs in car rear windows. "Now I'll simulate driving east on Interstate 80 from Salt Lake City, one of the steepest grades a trucker can encounter." The engine roared as it simulated downshifting two gears, its reverberation vibrating the floor. "Note the E850 is still delivering an unbelievable twenty-one miles per gallon." The skeptics began shaking their heads. "Finally, as we descend into Denver over I-70's Loveland Pass, the E-850 is delivering over forty miles per gallon even with engine braking."

Goldstein surveyed the audience, wondering who would make the first bid. Suddenly, it seemed as though the engine quit. Kizka smiled. "Don't be alarmed, folks. We're back at idle RPM. I'll let the engine cool while I print out the data sheets." He pressed a button and paper flowed. One of his assistants quickly gathered the sheets and disappeared. Kizka turned off the ignition and removed his headset. "You can stow your headsets now. The data sheets will be available shortly. This concludes the formal demonstration. Are there any questions?"

An executive in a gray suit raised his hand. "How soon can we expect production?"

Kizka smiled. "That depends on the investor, but we hope to see a production line within a year."

Another suit raised his hand. "Where's the semi?"

"Out back. We pulled the engine for today's demonstration and will resume testing once we have an investor."

With the questions turning non-technical, Goldstein took the stage and shook Kizka's hand. "Thank you, Arvid. I think he deserves a round of applause, don't you?" The applause died and Kizka resumed his position off stage. "Again, thank you all for coming," Goldstein said. "If anyone wants to talk business, my secretary will gladly set up an appointment. Otherwise, I wish everyone a happy and safe Independence Day."

"Excuse me, Mr. Goldstein?" a suit asked before Goldstein made his exit. "Let me get this straight. I admit your engine delivered some amazing specs today, but is this the only prototype?

I mean—that doesn't seem like a smart way of doing business. What's your backup?"

Goldstein's smile was assured. "Additional prototypes require huge capital investments and the E850 isn't our only project. As CEO, my first priority is to be fiscally responsible to our shareholders, and such frugality has kept Cougar Industries profitable during the lean years. Of course, any investor will share in our success. The E850 prototype is a major breakthrough, but we will continue to push the technological limits as it progresses into the production stage."

"Exactly how much investment capital are you looking for?"

"Sir, that's a business question and one which I must defer. Again, I'll be happy to discuss such matters in private."

Another man stood. "About that computer-controlled shifter—how do you know a driver will manually shift to the correct gear?"

Goldstein looked at Kizka. "Arvid, would you care to explain that feature?"

Kizka returned to the stage, hands clasped in front of him. "Good question. You all know that overcoming boredom is one of the most difficult challenges for long-haul drivers." Heads nodded. "In that regard, our HUD helps counter white-line fever by projecting an electronic image into the driver's line of sight. Assuming the HUD is properly adjusted for the driver's sitting height, basic information like speed, fuel, and RPM is impossible to avoid, but it also tells the driver what gear to be in. Whenever the computer detects the engine isn't in optimum gear, it flashes an advisory for sixty seconds. If no action is taken, a non-canceling alarm sounds until the condition is corrected. In this sense, our HUD may actually keep drivers awake while improving engine efficiency. We hope this side benefit will reduce accidents attributed to sleep deprivation."

The man nodded. "Sounds good," he said. "So, when can we expect to see this automatic transmission you spoke of?"

"That's impossible to predict since it's still under development. However, we are actively seeking a partner to fabricate it based on our computer model. Please let us know if you or anyone else is interested in that venture."

Goldstein saw Kizka's assistant come in with a stack of papers. To the assistant's surprise, Goldstein grabbed them and began distributing them down the rows. "These are the data sheets Arvid promised. Please note the time and date in the upper right-hand corner agree with today's presentation. The original's on file if anyone cares to compare it." He paused for everyone to look over the information. "Any more questions?"

"Just one," gray suit said. "How much time does your prototype have on it?"

"The Hobbs meter reading is three columns down. Today's demonstration brings the E850 to one hundred thirty-three point three hours. Approximately seventy of those hours were spent in the lab, the rest in the test vehicle." Gray suit nodded and went back to the stats. "Gentlemen, I seriously doubt there is another prototype that has undergone such rigorous testing. We have repeatedly pulled the E850 to improve performance. By our estimates, each logged hour is comparable to several hundred hours of actual long haul driving. We're ready to proceed to the production phase whenever you are." He rubbed his moist hands. "Arvid—thanks again for that superb demonstration," he said, smiling. "Gentlemen, it's been a pleasure hosting you. Help yourselves to some refreshments in the foyer, and again, have a pleasant holiday."

The audience moved about, some lingering for a closer look at the E850 while others exchanged small talk. Arvid noticed Goldstein escorting a Japanese gentleman out the side door. He smiled. Once the room emptied, he patted his warm engine and turned out the lights.

Months passed, yet still no word on the DC-10 fire. Kevin tried, but he couldn't let go. Before the mishap he never worried about seeing his family again; now the thought lurked in his brain. His marriage had become an emotional roller coaster. All was fine until he got called out. Then Nancy was on edge, increasingly bitter over his absences.

He went to the FAA Flight Standards District Office hoping they could tell him something. It seemed unlikely, but he was desperate. He took a seat, thumbing through an old copy of *AOPA Pilot* when a woman's voice startled him. The well-dressed woman in her thirties smiled from behind the counter. "I'm Kevin Hamilton. Is there a safety inspector around?"

"Sure. I'll be right back." She went into the back room and came back with a man in a tie and wrinkled white shirt.

"I'm Art Sorrel," he said, shaking hands. "What can I do for you, Mr. Hamilton?"

"Please—call me Kevin." Sorrel nodded. "I was the Second Officer on the Global DC-10 that burned." He said it as though it should mean something, but the woman and Sorrel only stared, waiting. Kevin smiled. "I'm sorry. About fifteen months ago Global had an inflight fire. The plane burned after we landed. I was on that plane." Sorrel nodded, eyebrows raised. "Well, I've never seen or heard anything as to what caused the fire, and wondered if you'd seen anything in the way of an accident report. You can understand how frustrating it is not hearing anything."

The woman went back to shuffling paperwork, but kept listening. "Kevin, I'm not sure you understand the FAA bureaucracy," Sorrel said. "The FAA is regulatory, not investigative. My job entails change recommendations and regulation enforcement—that's it. Unless I stumble onto it in a magazine article, I wouldn't know anything about your mishap. It's not that I don't care—I'm just not in that loop. Have you talked to the NTSB?"

Kevin glared at Sorrel. He resented being patronized, especially in front of the woman. "Art, I wouldn't be circumventing the NTSB if they were liberal with their information. I'm sorry to have bothered you. I assumed you got messages on all the airline mishaps." He prepared to leave, but stopped short of the door. "By the way, don't you issue ADs if you determine a mishap was the result of a mechanical problem?"

Sorrel nodded. "FAA Airworthiness Directives are based on NTSB recommendations, but I don't know of anything that concerns your mishap. Correct me if I'm wrong, but wasn't that a cargo fire?"

"That's right."

"Well, that explains it. There weren't any ADs because it wasn't aircraft related."

Sorrel was heading back to his office when Kevin called to him. "Wait a minute. Isn't the FAA's job to enhance flight safety?" Sorrel nodded. "Then what's being done to enhance cargo screening? From what I've seen, all that changed after the ValuJet crash was passenger carriers were prohibited from carrying hazardous cargo. We're the ones who are hauling all that crap—what's being done to protect us? How many cargo planes do we lose before something's done about our safety?"

Sorrel stared at the counter. How could he tell this persistent pilot that change is effected by the political climate? The woman retreated into the back room. Sorrel lowered his voice. "Look, Kevin, I can see why you're frustrated, but the FAA doesn't make changes unless it's sure it will achieve the desired results. In your case, nothing's gonna happen until the NTSB releases their final report and right now they're at an impasse. I'm sorry I can't help you. You'll probably have more success talking to your company's safety office."

Kevin smiled. "I guess my problem is when I was in the Marine Corps, the Aviation Safety Officer was required to send weekly updates until the final mishap report was released. Why's the civilian world so secretive?"

Sorrel shivered, the air conditioning chilling his perspiration. "There isn't any cover-up if that's what you're implying." He leaned over the counter. "Kevin, there's more to this than just an investigation. The NTSB seals their reports until they're made public. That way there aren't any negative implications to affect a company's future."

"You're talking liability."

"Yes—and that's something the military's generally excluded from. Unlike the military, it may take years before the final mishap report is released. My advice? Let it go. It's not a perfect system, but that's how it is."

Kevin left. He closed his car door and slumped in his seat, staring at the Global DC-10 that roared overhead. He recalled the ValuJet DC-9 that crashed into the Florida swamp minutes after takeoff because of improperly packaged cargo. The fire spread quickly; the crew was dead before it hit. No survivors. The same was true with Swissair Flight 111, although that one was an electrical fire. Either way, inflight fires were unforgiving. He could have just as easily become a statistic. The thought was staggering. But the more he searched for the truth, the more it alienated his family. Nancy didn't care that seeking professional counseling could lead to him losing his medical certificate, his job, his life. Another knife twist in his gut. The pain was getting worse.

Back home he walked into the living room, plopping onto the couch without saying a word. Nancy kept her distance, thankful the boys were out back. "Well? How'd it go?"

He just sat there, staring at the floor. "The FAA doesn't know a damned thing. The safety inspector referred me to Global, if you can believe that. Tell me, Nance—am I going nuts?"

She nuzzled close, stroking his hair, worried. Same talk, different day.

He met her sad eyes. "I'm sorry." He kissed her forehead, started to place an arm around her, but backed off. "Seems I'm always taking this out on you. You're my best friend, yet I keep hurting you."

"We're both hurting, Kevin—just for different reasons."

"I know. But I can't believe we rely on strangers to declare what is and isn't hazardous material. They have no clue that those DG documents determine our safety."

"And why should they? It's not their problem."

"That's my point. Get it there by sun-up—nothing else matters." He didn't notice the look in her eyes as he paced the floor. "That FAA inspector implied corporate profits dictate their regulations. It makes sense if you think about it. If they didn't, they would've introduced new cargo screening procedures a long time ago. If the FAA had done more after the ValuJet crash, maybe I wouldn't have had a mishap." Only when he finished did he realize Nancy had retreated to the kitchen. "Did you hear anything I said?"

Nancy stirred her coffee. "Yes—I heard it all. In fact, I've heard it so many times I can recite it in my sleep. How do you know what the FAA did? For God sake's, Kevin, this isn't the Marine Corps and you're not the safety officer. Why can't you let it go? Did it ever occur to you that Global might not want the public to know their security procedures? Next you'll be telling me you're trying to get 60 Minutes to do a story on it. Get over it."

Kevin's eyes roamed the room. He noticed a split in the hardwood floor. Where'd it come from? And there—a crack in the drywall. Did the house have foundation problems? He'd just vacuumed the cobwebs. How did they return so fast?

Nancy moved in front of him, hands on her hips. "Kevin, you can't deny you've changed. I love you, but we can't go on this way. You're always in a bad mood and all you talk about is that damned accident. It's been over a year, Kevin. Do you even care about the kids? Me? I've tried to understand. I keep praying things will change. But they don't. Haven't you noticed how the boys avoid you now? They're afraid you'll yell at them. Either you figure out a way to change or the boys and I are leaving."

He stared at the ceiling, dust on the ceiling fan, a nail head pushing through the drywall. But he couldn't deflect her words. He'd lost her. Why'd it take so long to realize how selfish he'd been? Why hadn't he noticed the boys keeping to themselves? How could he be so blind? When he moved next to her, she didn't pull away. "I'm sorry, Nance. God knows I never meant to hurt you or the boys. And you're right—there's no excuse for my short fuse. I allowed myself to get caught up in this. I only hope you can forgive me. I love you—I'll do everything in my power to move on." He held her hands. She said nothing. She'd heard it before. *Forgive Me*, Dialogue One all over again. "Say—why don't we take the boat to the lake? I'll throw some sandwich stuff together and we can be outta here in minutes. What do you say?"

She nodded, moving to the back door. "I'll tell the boys." But her words were listless. She sounded old.

7

Following several months of intense negotiations, Cougar CEO Derek Goldstein finalized his contract with Tigress CEO Hisao Yoshimura. Yoshimura was as large as he was astute. His narrow eyes were difficult to read, but on paper everything looked good. The Tigress Automotive Company of Tokyo agreed to a multi-million dollar contract with Cougar Industries to manufacture the Ultima E850 engine. Should the prototype fail to meet specifications, Tigress would return the engine at their expense and forfeit one million dollars. Pretty straight forward. That money would keep Cougar Industries solvent for years.

Yoshimura insisted the prototype E850 arrive in Japan for evaluation within the next five days or the contract was null and void. It was a condition of trust that Goldstein hadn't anticipated. Reluctantly he agreed. They sealed their affiliation with a handshake. Yoshimura's hand consumed Goldstein's. He would've made a good sumo wrestler.

Upon learning of the agreement, Chief Engineer Arvid Kizka asked if he could personally handle the shipping arrangements. Goldstein agreed, knowing no one cared more about the E850 than Arvid. Kizka chose Global Cargo Express because of their reputation for delivering oversized, time-critical, international freight. The E850 was drained of its oil and fuel. Dehydrator plugs were installed to absorb internal moisture. Working under the threat of termination, Kizka hovered over the workers, making sure its pallet was built to Global's specifications. Satisfied, the engine was then bolted to the pallet and sealed. Kizka stenciled, "PRECIOUS CARGO—HANDLE WITH CARE" in bold letters on the side, hoping it would make a difference.

The crate was loaded on the flatbed and Kizka double-checked it for security. He delivered it to Global's package sorting facility two hours before their cutoff time. The security cameras took everything in as he went into the office. He'd completed all of the shipping declarations ahead of time. No reason for anyone to tamper with the crate.

A cheerful female customer service representative assisted him with the arrangements. "That should do it, Mr. Kizka. Your engine will be transferred in Los Angeles before flying on to Anchorage, Narita, and then trucked to Tokyo. It will take three days because of the international date line."

"That's fine," Arvid said. "Oh, do you have a fax machine I can use? I need to fax copies of everything to both parties."

The woman hesitated, then looked at the invoice. The least she could do was throw in a couple of phone calls. "If you write the information on a couple of cover sheets, I'll take care of it."

"That's great. Thanks." He noticed the pallet being loaded while he worked on the cover sheets. He paused, watching the pallet until it disappeared inside the aircraft.

"Is everything okay, Mr. Kizka?"

He smiled. "Just fine. Here you go," he said, sliding the papers to her. Everything he'd worked for was about to pay off.

Kevin Hamilton climbed out of the oversized bed, well rested after his stay at the Manhattan Beach Barnabey's Hotel. It was only his second stay here, but he loved its narrow hallways, replica oil paintings, and red wallpaper that hinted at brothel décor. He took in the surroundings. His four-poster bed, heated towel rack, and fireplace were pure elegance. Hard to believe he was there.

He found his inner child while running on the beach. Nothing like sand between his toes and pounding waves to rid him of old fears. He couldn't wait to see Anchorage. He'd have to be quick exploring the town since they'd be deadheading home fourteen hours later. Life was good. If only Nancy were here. She deserved a second honeymoon.

The day passed too quickly. Soon Kevin was back in the aircraft performing his preflight duties. He placed a sticky note reading "GlobeEx 002" above the captain's INS computer. There were no outstanding maintenance discrepancies. It looked like they'd make their 1130 takeoff.

He saw himself fishing Ship's Creek; the silver salmon were running. Imagine Nancy's surprise if he brought back fresh fish. She'd have him slap it on the grill while she whipped up some veggies. The boys loved salmon. The moment faded when the mechanic brought the fuel slip.

During his walk-around inspection, he spotted a small pool of liquid on the tarmac. As he bent over to touch it, a drop splattered him from above. He dipped his finger in it, rubbing it. Red, slimy, oily smell; definitely hydraulic fluid. He shined his flashlight into the wheel well, but couldn't pinpoint the source. He stopped his preflight and contacted maintenance. Any hydraulic leak was unacceptable.

Kevin was discussing the leak with maintenance when Captain John Armishaw approached. One of Global's first black pilots, Armishaw's large frame and muscular forearms suggested he'd played football in his younger days. He had a reputation for being soft spoken and a fine pilot. Kevin was at ease the moment they met. "So, what's going on, Kevin?"

Kevin watched First Officer Lonnie Stevens climb the stairs. Tall, lean, his receding hairline robbed him of his youthful physique. The mechanic hurried off. "We've got a hydraulic leak," he said to Armishaw. "The mech went to get a ladder, but said to press on. They'll keep us advised."

John nodded. "Everything else okay?"

"Sure is. I can't wait to get going."

John smiled. "You may as well come upstairs. I'd prefer you do your preflight after they complete their maintenance."

Kevin nodded, following him up the stairs. Once they finished their cockpit duties, John reclined his chair and propped his feet against the footrest ledge on the instrument panel; one of the few comforts afforded to pilots. "I heard a funny joke the other day," he said. "A woman looks in—" A violent jolt interrupted his thought. People were yelling outside. "What the hell?" His first intuition was it was an earthquake, but the ornamental columns across the ramp weren't moving. More yelling, two maintenance trucks converged on the scene. "This can't be good. Better check it out, Kevin."

Kevin saw several mechanics pointing fingers, cursing. When he reached the ground, he noticed the cherry picker. *Holy shit.* His dream trip was disappearing. He flew upstairs to spread the news. "Looks like we'll be here a while. They ran a cherry picker into the inboard flap."

Kevin expected to see rage, but John's expression didn't change. He left everything as it was and rose from his seat. "Relax, Kevin. We'll be flying this trip no matter how long the delay. No point getting excited. Let's have a look."

Though futile, Lonnie continued programming the ship's navigation computers.

John checked his watch as he headed out the cockpit door. It wasn't the first time a plane had been damaged by ground equipment, but he couldn't remember it ever happening on a dry ramp. "Aren't you coming, Lonnie?"

Lonnie leaped from his seat. "You bet."

The senior mechanic was saying something when they reached the ground. The flight crew maintained their distance until he waved them over. "Sorry, Captain, but you might as well take your stuff inside. I have no idea whether we'll fix it or find you another plane, but if we have to fix her, it'll take several hours."

John nodded. "Do what you can—keep us posted." He turned and headed for the stairs. Lonnie and Kevin followed.

In the pilot lounge, Kevin reviewed his e-mail while John called Flight Operations. Kevin joined Lonnie in the TV room, surprised to find him asleep.

John came in an hour later, flipping on the lights. "Bad news, guys. No spares. They have to replace the inboard flap and leaking actuator. They have the parts, but it'll take 'em at least three hours. Ops isn't as optimistic so they're sending us back to the hotel. Barnabey's van's on their way to pick us up. Looks like it'll be a long day."

Kevin checked his watch, converting local time to Zulu. LA was eight hours behind Greenwich, England. They wouldn't take off until at least 1800 local—six pm. He was tired, but not sleepy. Nothing harder than trying to sleep on command.

John rubbed the sleep from his eyes as he called the maintenance supervisor for an update. "Yes, captain—everything's going together nicely," the supervisor said. "We've got a full crew working on it. We want you out of here, too. We need the gate for the evening sort. We told Ops to plan for a 0115 launch. Guess they didn't tell you."

"I'm sure they'll be calling shortly. Thanks for the update." John cradled the phone, jotting 0115Z on the notepad next to his bed.

At 2335Z, Ops called, asking they get airborne as soon as possible. Armishaw smiled. That's the way it is—make sure they're legal, then ask for the impossible. He called Lonnie and Kevin. "Looks like we're a go," he said. "Meet me in the lobby ASAP."

John couldn't believe Lonnie beat him downstairs. "Get any sleep?"

"A little," Lonnie said. The thrill was gone. The job had become a means to an end. No point in worrying about when they left, so long as he got paid. The only day of a trip that mattered was the last day. Regardless of where they stayed, he never got enough rest. "I may nod off along the way."

"Yeah, I know what you mean. Just let me know so one of us stays awake."

Kevin came in from loading his bag in the van. "Hi guys. Obviously the fishing trip's out, but at least we can have a nice dinner."

"We'll see," Armishaw said. "Right now, sleep sounds better."

Kevin went straight to the aircraft while John and Lonnie went inside Flight Operations to finish their flight planning. The absence of maintenance trucks and cargo loaders was assuring. The new flap's paint didn't match, but everything seemed in place, the hydraulic leak gone. He hoped to block out within the next thirty minutes.

The maintenance paperwork was in order, everything looked good. Having time to spare, Kevin rechecked every switch and circuit breaker. When he finished, he reclined his seat, awaiting the others. When he heard John's booming voice in the courier section, Kevin was upright, ready to pass him the maintenance log. "She's not pretty, but it looks like she'll fly."

"That's reassuring. Everything loaded?"

"Yes, sir. Here's the paperwork." He laid the weight and balance, takeoff data card, and Dangerous Goods declaration on the center console. "The coffee and catering are on board. I'm ready when you are."

John paused, wondering if they'd delivered fresh catering. The last thing he needed was food poisoning. Surely they'd replaced it. In any case, there was no time for more. Out the corner of his eye, he saw Kevin reclining his seat. "Don't tell me you're tired, too?"

Kevin looked at John, unsure how to take the remark. "Oh, no—just getting comfortable."

John smiled. "Hey, relax. I was just giving you a hard time." He handed back the paperwork and maintenance log. "All right—let's get outta here."

Kevin went to the back, handing copies of the paperwork to the ramp agent, then closed and armed the entry doors. When he returned, John and Lonnie were verifying their flight routing in the INS computers. They finished the Before Start checklist just as the mechanic was checking in over the intercom. "Ground to cockpit—your doors are closed and locked. Standing by for the push."

"Roger, stand by," John said, checking to see Kevin's door warning lights were out. Lonnie called for their pushback clearance. Ramp Tower and Ground Control gave clearance. "Cockpit to ground—let's shove it." John's remark failed to raise a response from the mech who'd heard it too many times. The plane lunged as the giant tug pushed them back from the gate with the ease of a body builder pushing a hot dog cart. "Start three."

"Turning three," Lonnie said, punching the right outboard engine's start button. The floor vibrated as the engine rotated. Four minutes later their checks were complete and they received taxi clearance to Runway 25L.

John pointed out an old stucco across from the FedEx ramp. "See that building over there? That's the original terminal building."

Kevin studied the twin-towered art-deco building and its attached hangar, its ornate Spanish tiles a striking contrast to its surroundings. It exuded dignity, but now sheltered cargo bins instead of DC-3s. "It looks familiar for some reason."

"That's because they used it in a Bogart movie way back when. Can't remember the name for some reason. Anyway, they moved it here instead of tearing it down—too valuable to destroy."

"Casablanca," Lonnie said.

"Say again?"

"Casablanca. That's the name of the movie."

"Oh yeah," Kevin said, picturing Bogart bidding his woman farewell, smoke billowing as the plane's engines start up, propwash blowing their clothes. Aviation's romantic period. The time to be an airline pilot.

Lonnie switched to Tower as they approached the runway. Tower knew their sequence, no need to call. They'd issue their clearance when they could. John anticipated having to cross 25L to take off on 25R, but Tower surprised them with an immediate takeoff on the left, winds light and variable. "Below the line," he said.

As Kevin raced through the final checklist items, John slid the throttles forward.

"Power's set," Lonnie said. "Eighty knots."

John checked the gauges and engaged the autothrottles. All systems were go. The heavy aircraft barreled down the runway, its nosewheel thumping as it skipped over the centerline lighting and patched concrete. The main gear followed the nose and they were off—four hours late.

Kevin glanced at the waves pounding the deserted beach, the coastline disappeared, lights from anchored tanker ships dotted the sea. A quick scan of his instruments, then back outside. Malibu was in the distance, an endless string of white and red defined its roads. He watched the airspeed build, anticipating John's call.

"Slats retract, After Takeoff Check."

Kevin waited for Lonnie to retract the slats and disarm the spoilers, then reached up to rotate the dial-a-flap wheel to the zero-flap position. As the aircraft accelerated to 250 knots, he turned on the cargo vents. "After Takeoff's down to the line."

At ten thousand feet, John eased the nose over to accelerate to 320 knots and retracted the landing lights. Still heading out to sea, Kevin noticed the moon's reflection. He looked up to see a full moon, the stars dim through the haze. Good to be airborne.

Climbing at three thousand feet per minute, they reached their initial cruising altitude of thirty-one thousand feet sixteen minutes after takeoff, one hundred-twenty miles from LAX. John set the airspeed bug at max speed to make up whatever time he could. Once they burned some fuel, they would climb to Flight Level 350, but that was two hours away.

Their last meal was seven hours ago and everyone was starving. As Kevin prepared to get up to put their catering in the oven, his seat bucked like a rodeo bull. With the force of a tornado, the cockpit door flew open, invisible hands tugging at him. His lungs blew out air like someone punched him in the stomach. All hell broke loose, the cabin altitude alarm blaring, cabin altimeter climbing like a second hand. He clung to his seat and grabbed his oxygen mask.

John lunged for the controls, using his left to find his mask. He could handle the rapid decompression, but why was the plane rolling and pitching down? Did the new flap break off? He countered with aileron and rudder. It wasn't working.

After donning his mask, Lonnie squawked the emergency code, awaiting John's instructions, the blackness of the sea and sky merging as one, the attitude indicator his only clue as to what was going on.

Only one red light shined; the cabin altitude warning light showed the cabin had exceeded ten thousand feet and was climbing fast. "Something must've blown," Kevin said, forcing his words against the flow of pressurized oxygen. "We still have three good engines and all hydraulics. Flaps, slats are up and in—nothing's wrong."

"Well *something's* fucked up!" John said, cursing to himself over having to take his right hand off the yoke to push the intercom button. "Lonnie—give me a hand."

Lonnie matched John's movements, jamming his left foot against the rudder pedal while holding full left aileron, but the aircraft continued its roll. Passing forty-five degrees bank, there were no signs of the plane righting itself.

When Candy Barrington assumed her Los Angeles Center workstation five minutes ago, everything had been running smoothly. Now she stared in disbelief at the highlighted radar blip, its only direction down. Her finger squeezed the mike. "All aircraft stand by—GlobeEx 002 Heavy, Los Angeles Center, the airspace below you is clear. When able state the nature of your emergency."

Kevin thought about answering. Their situation was critical, but John wasn't saying anything. He recalled Joe's reaction to his speaking up at their debrief. Follow orders. He had to wait. For the second time in his life, he was coping with an emergency for which there were few written procedures. *Nancy—the boys...God help us.*

While the aircraft performed its own version of an emergency descent, Kevin ran through the procedures for rapid decompression. There had to be a reason why the spiral was tightening. Their airspeed was good; she wasn't in a spin. She acted as though the right engine's thrust reverser had deployed, but there were no matching indications. He continued to scan the gauges. Nothing made sense. Even if the reverser deployed, it didn't explain their loss of cabin pressure. Did the flap break off and punch a hole in the fuselage? A definite possibility, but the flaps showed full up. Cold air frosted the insides of the windows, but he was sweating. Could it have been a bomb? The pitching and yawing tormented his inner ears. He had to look outside to keep from puking. How long could their aircraft survive such violent maneuvering? By all rights, they were already dead.

John extended the slats, deployed the spoilers, and retarded all three power levers to idle. He pulled back on the yoke, expecting the nose to rise. Instead, the bank angle increased and the nose dropped further. The plane flew as if the flight controls were reversed. He scanned Kevin's panel, eyes wide open.

"Hydraulics are good," Kevin said, reading his mind.

Of course they were. Wouldn't have slats and spoilers if they weren't. John's left leg was cramping. "Lonnie, I'm dying here—keep that rudder in!" he said over LA Center's frequency. "Let's try leveling her at fifteen." It was impossible to reach the console to use the intercom button, so he used the paddle switch on the yoke to transmit. Center would get the idea. The thought occurred to him they might be his final words.

Candy Barrington heard the desperation in the pilot's voice through her headset. She could only imagine what was going on up there. GlobeEx 002's crew wasn't talking to her. A call from her might be distracting. She'd already alerted her supervisor and switched her other aircraft to another frequency and controller. Now all she could do was watch, listen, and wait.

"If we can't hold her at fifteen, we'll try for ten," John said. His left knee was locked in the rudder pedal, still holding full left aileron, but the pitching and rolling wouldn't stop. It was an aerodynamic phenomenon. What was keeping them from rolling inverted?

Kevin began dumping fuel as soon as they went out of control, their erratic white trails highlighting their graveyard spiral. He needed to dump eighty thousand pounds, a safe landing a remote possibility. He helplessly watched the coastline lights reappear every twenty seconds. Shooting through fifteen thousand feet, the altitude alarm only added to their chaos.

John ripped off his oxygen mask and tossed it aside, no longer needed at this altitude. The others followed suit. "Goddam it, Lonnie, keep your foot in there! Kevin, tell Center we had a structural failure. If we don't make it, at least they'll have a clue."

Finally, something to do. Kevin didn't hesitate keying the mike. "Mayday! Mayday! Mayday! LA Center, GlobeEx 002 Heavy has had structural damage and is out of control. Advise Search and Rescue we may be ditching." Trying to stay ahead of the game, he found the ditching checklist.

"Lonnie—you gotta help me out."

"Dammit John, the pedal's against the stops. For all we know, we don't have a rudder!"

John grew desperate. Less than a minute to impact. He jockeyed the throttles, sliding them fore and aft in every imaginable combination. The windscreen was blotted out by water, no horizon. Miraculously, the corkscrew was breaking. He pulled back on the yoke with all the energy he could muster. He didn't care if he bent the plane. The nose began to rise, the rotation slowed. When the spiral stopped, they were heading out to sea. He was fighting physical endurance as much as the plane. Even if they turned her around, he probably couldn't land. No one was talking. Everyone knew his recovery only prolonged the inevitable.

Barrington stared at her radar screen. Suddenly her eyes lit up. "Look. They broke their descent." Every controller in the crowded room switched screens. Cheers and applause broke out. 002 was going to make it. She watched the blip track across the screen. "GlobeEx 002 Heavy, you're out of my airspace. When able, contact SoCal Approach on 128.75. They're aware of your situation. Good luck." She released the mike button, pressed her folded hands to her lips, and prayed.

At nine thousand feet, the ocean wafted like an endless black flag. John analyzed his plane's aerodynamics. The nose didn't rise until he increased power on the right engine. The plane always rolled right. The drag was on the right side of the aircraft. They were getting lighter as the dump continued. The aircraft was under control, but barely. He'd have to slow the aircraft if they were going to land. His stomach tightened. "I've got to see how this thing handles," he said. "Speak up if you're uncomfortable." The plane vibrated from unbalanced power settings, but the cockpit remained silent.

John scanned the horizon, a thin line separating black from black. He'd remain over water in case something went wrong. No need to jeopardize anyone on the ground. He adjusted the power, slowing to two hundred knots. He anticipated the buffeting, but suddenly the right wing dropped, the horizon climbed in the windshield. *Shit!* The bank reached 35 degrees before he could firewall the right engine. He kept number two at 75%, idle on one. Once again, the wings were leveling, but the altitude warning sounded. "Set eight thousand," he said, his eyes burning from his sweat. The altitude warning sounded again. "Christ—I can't hold her. Prepare to ditch."

John's words went straight to Kevin's heart. He pictured the hijacked Boeing 767 ditching in the shallow waters off Africa, its wings ripped apart, fuselage breaking, tumbling. Most likely they'd meet a similar fate, their wing-mounted engines acting like giant scoops. Three hundred fifty thousand pounds of metal carried a lot of inertia; would the 9G net hold? Point Mugu Naval Air Station was nearby, but could they get there in time to save them? He saw the lights of Oxnard and the darkness between them. They were going down, and all he could do was read a goddam checklist.

Lonnie picked up the hand-held mike, his hand trembling as he switched frequencies. "SoCal Approach, GlobeEx 002 Heavy is ditching. Advise the SAR we're pointed at Oxnard."

Kelly Sandusky had been monitoring their progress on radar for the last fifteen minutes. She'd alerted the Coast Guard. No other planes were on her frequency. Everyone was ready. She was hoping the outcome would have been different. She keyed the mike. "GlobeEx 002, SoCal Approach, roger. The SAR's been notified."

John remained steadfast, a leader to the end. It was an honor flying with him. Kevin's head was spinning with thoughts of Nancy and the boys, rotten luck, the buddies he'd lost and was about to see again. John's voice brought him back. *Twelve minutes to impact.* Assuming nothing changed for the worse, that is. As much as Kevin tried to make peace with himself and God, he wasn't ready to die. He couldn't. Nancy would never forgive him. He ripped the life vests from their seat backs and handed them to John and Lonnie. "Put these on," he said. "Just don't inflate 'em 'til we're out of the plane. Maybe we'll make it to one of the islands."

John's leg was numb and shaking uncontrollably. Lonnie's didn't look any better. "Kevin—tell Approach we'll stay on this heading until two thousand feet, then commence our final approach."

While Kevin spoke, Lonnie pressed his body into the seat, locking his leg for maximum rudder input. Images of the American Airlines Airbus losing its tail crossed his mind. Thankfully their tail was metal and Lonnie was wrong. It would take a miracle to survive. He prayed Lady Luck was in the jump seat.

Frank Bottoms was in his office when he first learned of GlobeEx Flight 002's emergency. As watch supervisor for Southern California Approach Control, he was responsible for all radar-controlled traffic in the low altitude sector. He rushed to Sandusky's station. Leaning over her chair, he stared at her scope in disbelief. His last two cups of coffee were bursting his bladder. 002 was going down. "Do we have a clear freq?"

Sandusky sighed. Bottoms must have gotten the job through nepotism. He was the last thing she needed. She felt his warm breath, but dared not look his way. "Affirmative," she said. If he interfered in any way...

Bottoms' eyes shifted from her scope to the room. Tension crackled. No one spoke. In fact, no one seemed to be doing anything. But what *could* they do? They'd seen it before, a PSA jet nose-diving into the water when a despondent hijacker took over the controls, an Alaska Airlines MD-80 meeting the same fate when its elevator jammed. You never get over it.

"They're eleven west of San Miguel Island descending through ten," Sandusky announced.

Bottoms picked up the landline to LA Center, relaying 002's position. Due to 002's unpredictable needs, Center slowed all inbound traffic inbound to LAX, placing twenty airplanes in holding patterns, some as far away as Phoenix. SoCal Approach hurried to get as many on the ground as possible before 002 attempted an emergency landing in the opposite direction. Three aircraft opted to divert into Ontario while others were preparing to go to San Diego and Orange County. He nearly knocked over Sandusky's mug as he moved closer. "Things are stacking up. We've got to get them on the ground."

Sandusky glanced at him over her shoulder. "Look Frank, we're doing all we can. Point Mugu and the Coast Guard have been alerted. Everyone knows 002's ditching."

"Did anyone call Camp Pendleton to see if the Marines have any flare-equipped aircraft to light up the area? That water's cold—they'll need all the help they can get."

"I'll call once I'm sure what 002's gonna do."

He patted her shoulder. "You're busy—I'll make the call." He picked up the phone. After passing his request, he dialed Global Cargo Express' Control Center, surprised by the woman's calm. "Ah, yes—this is Frank Bottoms with SoCal Approach. Are you aware of Flight 002's situation?"

"I'm sorry," she said, her voice old but sweet. "Mr. Bottoms was it? What about Flight 002?"

"Something happened—they're out of control. They're gonna ditch."

Martha Gloflin's face tingled. Her son was a pilot for Global. "What happened? Where are they now?"

Bottoms studied the scope. "Near the Channel Islands. We're doing all we can—the SAR's been alerted. Everyone's hoping for the best."

Gloflin's hand shook as she looked over the emergency checklist on her desktop. "Mr. Bottoms, can I get a phone number for verification?" she asked.

"Certainly." After giving her the information, he asked her name. She told him she wasn't leaving until this was over. "Neither will I," he said. "I'll keep you informed, Martha." Bottoms cradled the phone, returning his attention to the scope. As 002 descended through two thousand feet, he grabbed a mike. "GlobeEx 002, turn south immediately—terrain!"

The aircraft was bucking like a hooked marlin. *Terrain! Terrain! Whoop Whoop, Pull Up! Whoop Whoop, Pull Up!* "Kevin—pull the GPWS breaker," John said. It was taking all his concentration to keep the aircraft under control; he didn't need Bitchin' Betty telling him he was close to dying. The frantic call from SoCal merely confirmed what he was seeing in front of him. "Okay, Lonnie—let's ease off the rudder and bring her around." As the airplane banked to the right, the nose dropped. *Jesus!* It would've been easier balancing a beach ball on his nose. Pain shot through his leg. *Too late to put Kevin in Lonnie's seat.*

Shadowed peaks rose in their side windows as they banked, the moon's reflection sliding up the wing. Thankfully the sea appeared calm. He was maneuvering for lineup when SoCal Approach called. "Answer them, Kevin."

Kevin reached for the microphone. He spoke calmly, knowing this was their last radio transmission. "Approach, GlobeEx 002 Heavy estimates three minutes to impact. Aircraft behaves like it has severe damage to right side. Do not expect the aircraft to float. Send the SAR. 002 out." He tossed the mike under his desktop, tightened his life vest and harness, and resumed making peace with God.

As Kevin scanned the cockpit, its dim lights reminded him of what his flight instructor said about forced landings at night. "Always turn the landing light on, Kevin. If you don't like what you see, turn it off." He said it tongue in cheek, but it had merit. *Forget the bullshit. Concentrate on your exit. Do it for the boys.* Kevin felt for reference points like they taught him in blindfolded underwater escapes. They would help maintain orientation.

"One thousand," Lonnie announced, watching the radar altimeter. The waves danced. Ditching may have worked for World War II bombers, but not jumbo jets. With the radio receivers off and the Ground Proximity Warning System disabled, Kevin became aware of their breathing, the swirling air, the ocean in the windscreen. Time stood still. In seconds it would be over.

Frank Bottoms understood the finality of Flight 002's transmission and removed his headset. Soon the blip would vanish from the screen. Twenty-four years as a controller and he'd never felt so helpless. He stood on the chair rubbing his hands together. "All right, people—listen up. It's a SAR scenario now—we'll run it on this freq. Tell Center LAX is open. Let's get the others down before they run out of fuel."

Kevin admired their ghostly spirals from the side window. Did anyone else see the beauty in its reflection? *Five hundred.* Lonnie's voice had the same monotone as the computer-generated GPWS. John made a final adjustment to parallel the swells. Kevin felt like he was watching the scene play out from above. Overcome with thoughts of his family, he looked at the Cockpit Voice Recorder microphone. "Always remember I love you," he said. *Two hundred.* His heart grew cold, strangling his chest.

One hundred. Looking good. *Fifty.* John eased back on the yoke, sandwiching air between the wings and the water, slowing their descent to three hundred feet per minute. Even with max power on number three, their airspeed had slowed to one hundred thirty-five knots. *Forty.*

"Lonnie, slide your seat back—now," John said, his leg shuddering.

Thirty. Twenty. With his remaining strength, John reduced their descent to one hundred feet per minute in a near wings-level attitude. *Ten.*

"Brace!"

The right wing sliced the water, snapping their bodies sideways, shoulder straps biting into their necks. Almost immediately, they were thrown in the opposite direction. Briefcases, maps, trash tossed about, hitting them in the head, filling their eyes with debris. The aircraft bellowed as its metal frame twisted and sheared. Lonnie covered his arms over his head while John fought the controls mouthing indiscernible words. The shearing wings propelled the cockpit forward, sending it tumbling end over end. Squeezing his eyes shut, Kevin clung to his seat.

When their capsule came to rest, Kevin heard the unnerving sound of rushing water, then it was cold against his skin, swirling, numbing. He was dazed but alive. He looked for the others, but it was pitch black. Someone was moaning. "Put your oxygen masks on," he yelled. He released his seat belt and abruptly fell out of his seat, hitting his head on his desk. It hurt like hell, but he now knew which way was up. They had to get out before they were pulled under.

Lonnie felt Kevin's hand on his shoulder, forcing a mask to his face. He pushed himself off the side window, taking the mask from him. "I'm okay," he said, pleased his arms absorbed the brunt of the impact. His head throbbed. "How's John?"

Kevin raised his mask. "Don't know," he said, leaning over the console. He began shaking him, but John failed to respond. Fortunately the air bubble that was keeping them afloat was on John's side. As Kevin reached over to slip a mask over John's face, the capsule moved. He froze, shivering from the cold. They wouldn't last without a raft, but they had to get out—now.

After fitting John's mask to him, Kevin went to look for his flashlight. Somehow it was still in his cup holder, even though everything else in the cockpit had been tossed about. He shined it through the cockpit door, relieved to find the smoke screen intact. The cockpit had severed aft of the side entry doors; the slide/rafts should still be there.

The nose began rising like a sinking ship's last gasp. Kevin put on a courier mask and dove for the entry door, pulling its emergency release lever. The nitrogen charge blew the door into the ceiling and sent the slide/raft to the surface. Hopefully it wouldn't drift away before they got out. He swam back into the cockpit.

Their metal tomb was becoming increasingly unstable, rolling and rising capriciously, as it had in the air. Kevin lifted his mask as he broke the air bubble. Lonnie was tugging on John's leg when Kevin tapped him on the shoulder. "The raft's deployed, but we're sinking fast. We've got to get out of here—we're gonna lose the raft."

Lonnie lifted his mask. "I'm not leaving John."

The full moon shone through the windshield like a train's headlight. Kevin could see. He positioned himself behind John's unconscious body, sliding his arms under John's armpits and locking his hands together. He couldn't leave either. They'd succeed, or die trying to get John out.

Light reflected off the blood spurting from John's head. Of more concern was his left leg, jammed under the mass of crushed metal, broken glass, and twisted wire that was once the instrument panel. John's leg emitted sickening sounds as Lonnie twisted and pulled, but nothing happened. He pulled harder. *Crack.* John's leg dangled like a socket wrench, but was still caught. As Lonnie slid his hand down John's leg to get a better grip, he felt the sharp bone sticking through the skin. Overcome with fear, he popped his head up and ripped off his mask. "He'll lose his foot if I keep pulling."

"So be it. Keep pulling—I'll tug on his armpits."

Lonnie slipped his mask on and dove under the dash. He forced his way forward, trying not to cut himself. His progress was halted when his mask caught, breaking its seal. Cold water rushed in, bubbles churning a mixture of air and seawater. Had he not been SCUBA diving, he might've taken a breath. Instead, he backed out, refit the seal, and blew hard to purge the mask. He knew the seal broke because the oxygen line wasn't long enough. There wasn't much time. He inhaled deeply and tossed his mask aside so he could move about more freely. He could feel Kevin tugging on John's body, but he wasn't going anywhere unless he could free that foot. He slid his arm under the instrument panel, scraping something along the way. Sharp pain ran the length of his forearm as salt water penetrated his muscles. He wanted to scream. The pressure was building in his lungs, but there was no turning back. He'd either free John, or yank his foot off. His arm was on fire as he reached around the flight control assembly, his blood clouding the water. He wrapped both hands around John's foot, twisting and tugging with all his strength. Finally it broke free and John's body was ejected from its seat.

Kevin had John halfway to the door when Lonnie came up for air, but John's oxygen hose stopped him. Kevin took a deep breath and tossed their masks aside, pulling John's body through the cockpit door, grateful for the water's buoyancy. Clinging to John with one arm, he found a courier seat oxygen mask. He took a quick breath and slipped it over John's face, then found the second courier mask. The indigo sea made it impossible to find Lonnie. Hopefully he was right behind him. His ears told him they were sinking. The raft would float away once the tension line broke. His body was succumbing to the cold. If he stopped, they were all dead. He stripped their masks and forced his way through the cabin door, pulling their life vest cords once they were clear. Their inflated vests shot them to the surface like corks.

Kevin's first taste of air was bittersweet, but the raft was drifting away. He had no choice but to let go of John and swim for it. He scanned the surface, but the only two strobe lights were his and John's. "Lonnie!" He called several times to no avail. Dragging the raft with the tether between his teeth, he kicked and pulled, but when it ended up on the backside of the wave, it pulled him backwards again. John was getting further away. It would've been easier pulling a car up an icy hill.

His head pounded, muscles ached. He kept going because he had no choice. He found John unconscious, lying on his back, breathing on his own. His elation disappeared seeing that Lonnie was still missing. As he tethered the raft to John's vest, an unworldly groan came from the aircraft. In horror he watched the cockpit slip below the surface, its nose vertical in its final salute. "Lonnie!" He looked around, desperate for help. "Lonnie!"

He thought he heard a faint groan. It wasn't coming from John. He snapped his head side to side, his heart racing. "Lonnie—where are you? Talk to me. I'll find you." Spotting a third strobe light, he swam with Olympic determination, aware John and the raft were drifting away.

Lonnie held his hand up, the strobe light highlighting the blood draining from his arm, his muscle sliced clear to the bone. Exhausted and panicked, he nearly passed out. He felt Kevin's hand rubbing his head, saying something about being glad to see him. Everything merged together. His mind was in a fog. He felt himself being pulled and tried to fight it.

"Relax, Lonnie—I've got you. Lie on your back—kick your feet if you can. We've got to get to the raft."

Lonnie started kicking, aware of what he needed to do, the taste of seawater lingering.

It took fifteen minutes to reach John. They clung to the side of the raft catching their breath, shivering, alone, frightened, but determined to survive. "Lonnie, I'll need your help to get John in."

"What do you want me to do?"

"Get in the raft. I'll give you a boost."

Lonnie winced as the salt dried. He pulled with his good arm while Kevin pushed from below, flopping aboard. He leaned over the side, extending his good arm. "I'm okay. Bring him over."

Kevin maneuvered John's body to where Lonnie could reach him. Without the buoyancy, John's massive body became a struggle. Lonnie pulled while Kevin pushed. Lonnie puked when he saw John's legs break the water. His left leg was twisted like a wet towel, foot dangling, bones sticking out. Kevin strained. "Come on, Lonnie—pull."

Lonnie wrapped both arms around John's torso and fell backwards pulling John on top of him. By the time he rolled John on his side, Kevin was aboard. The strobe lights showed red blood oozing out of John's blue skin. He'd stopped breathing. He had a weak pulse, but they'd lose him if they didn't do something fast.

Kevin laid John on his stomach, forcing the seawater from him, then turned him over to begin CPR. As water lapped the side of their raft, he squeezed John's nose to breathe into him, listening for air leaks in his lungs. Thankfully John's chest rose and fell with Kevin's cadence. Two minutes later, John's head moved, then his chest heaved, gasping for air. Kevin turned John's head to the side as he began spitting up. When the pain hit, he bellowed. Kevin hugged him. "Thank God you're alive."

John was in massive, unending pain. He didn't know where he was. The strobe lights blinded him, but he made out Kevin's eyes. "Jesus, Kevin, back off."

Kevin gave him some space. He tried to smile, but his face was a numbed mask. "What's the matter? Never been hugged by a white man?"

"Holy shit!" Lonnie shouted.

Lonnie pointed at the two dorsal fins splitting the water. Thanks to his blood, every shark in the Pacific Ocean was headed their way. By inflating the ends of the slide/raft, they had transformed it into a seaworthy craft, but it was still a precarious perch in a big ocean.

"Forget about them," Kevin said. "Wrap up your arm and find the emergency supplies while I work on John. I've got to stop his bleeding."

Lonnie stripped his shirt and wrapped it around his arm, securing it with a knot. He shivered as the air chilled his naked torso. There had been no time to don his jacket.

While Kevin worked, John's eyes softened. "Hey, thanks for saving my life."

"You've got it all wrong," Kevin said. "You saved ours."

John nodded, his face frozen. "Help on the way?"

Kevin looked into the frigid dark. Nothing but the moon's reflection on sullen water and dim stars. "It'll come."

Their strobe lights were disorienting, but they would aid in their rescue and sporadic lighting was better than none. Kevin worked to stabilize John, using whatever he could find to dress the wounds. Hitting a nerve sent John into convulsions, hideously tossing his foot in the air. "Lonnie—pin his leg down." Lonnie threw his body over John's legs while Kevin struggled to think.

"Will this help?" Lonnie asked, pulling his penlight from its sheath. He'd forgotten it was attached to his belt.

"Yeah."

John's condition was getting worse, his eyeballs were rolling up. While Kevin worked on a splint, something leaped out of the water, splashing Lonnie. Lonnie backed up to the center of the raft. "Sharks!" he said.

Kevin looked at the graceful silhouette. It circled twice before spouting water. "It's a porpoise," he said. "If anything it should keep the sharks away." John's ghastly features made his stomach heave. "Keep him still, Lonnie. If I don't do something about this foot, he'll lose it for sure."

John was moaning, rolling his head from side to side, drifting in and out of consciousness. Kevin leaned over him, trying to understand his words. "Oh, God. My head." John grabbed his head, trying to quell the skull-splitting pain. "What's left of the jet?"

Kevin held John's hands to keep him from ripping his bandages. "Easy, John. You have a nasty gash and I don't have any extra supplies. If you're gonna hold your head, then press on the bandage so it'll stop the bleeding."

For a moment, John's eyes were quiet. He was in shock and pain, but he understood what Kevin was saying. He rested his hand over the bandage, putting a small piece of cloth between his teeth to bite on.

Kevin splinted his leg using his shirt and a small raft paddle. His lips were numb from the cold. "Any pain besides your head?"

"Hell yes—my body's freezing and burning at the same time. What happened after Lonnie called ten feet?"

"Easy, John—it's not important. We'll have lots of time to discuss it later." Kevin went back to tightening the tourniquet. When John screamed he loosened it slightly, then secured the knot. He placed his hand over John's head. His pulse was stronger, but the skin clammy. "Can you feel your left leg?"

"Of course. The whole thing's on fire."

Kevin's mouth was frozen. At least John had feeling in his leg. He rested his hand on John's shoulder. "You've got a bad fracture in your left leg. It's splinted. Try to relax. Help's on the way." *Where in the hell's the SAR?* He could see the glow from Point Mugu Naval Air Station. Someone should've been here by now.

Frank Bottoms hit the elapsed time; the SAR clock was now running. Kelly Sandusky looked away as he approached, busy talking on the landline. "Where's the SAR?"

"Hold on," Sandusky said to the Coast Guard dispatcher. She looked at Bottoms. "The Coast Guard's enroute from LA, Point Mugu's helo broke, and the Marines don't have anything with flares. The Coast Guard should be there within the hour." She resumed her conversation with the Coast Guard dispatcher.

Bottoms nodded, listening to his controllers sequence aircraft into LA's four parallel runways. All departures were halted until they'd landed all the fuel-critical aircraft. Everything was under control; they'd done it without him. When he returned to his office, he saw the note bearing Martha's name. She answered in her sweet voice, probably a grandma, and a great one at that. "Martha, this is Frank Bottoms. 002 has ditched off Santa Cruz Island. The Coast Guard's enroute." Her weeping made it real amongst the blips and static, the squeal of mikes.

Nancy dropped the phone, collapsing on the bed. She stared at CNN, waiting for word from Global. A news bulletin tracked across the bottom of her screen. "A cargo DC-10 belonging to Global Cargo Express ditched off the coast of California. The Coast Guard is enroute to retrieve any survivors…A new round of energy problems for California as environmentalists…" Global's sympathy was an obligatory call. "We're there for you." A pillow muted her screams.

The crew huddled together to retain body heat. Waves tossed their bodies as they slipped under the raft. Nothing could stop their shaking. The sky was alive with blinking lights, but nothing was heading their way. They drifted. Didn't anyone see their strobe lights? Were they being mistaken for fishermen? Another wave rolled them.

Kevin shuddered. Closing his eyes didn't stop the nightmare. He heard Nancy's father recounting his albatross; a story from World War II he was compelled to tell over and again. Nancy would leave the room. Her father's destroyer was sent to rescue a B-17 bomber crew that had ditched. He could almost smell her father's pipe smoke. The image was frightening. When the ship pulled alongside, the bomber crew was bobbing like corks, but no one spoke. Pulling them aboard showed the sharks had a field day, the only thing left being their upper torsos. He sat up, searching. The waves tossed their raft like a toy.

✈

Frank Bottoms noticed the CNN reporter's live broadcast as he entered the break room. He moved closer.

"…Moments ago, two Dolphin helicopters departed the Los Angeles Coast Guard Station, hoping to recover the crew of Global Cargo Express Flight 002," the reporter said. "A press release issued by Southern California Approach Control, noted the cargo DC-10 disappeared from radar approximately five miles southeast of Santa Cruz Island near Oxnard. Destined for Anchorage, the tri-jet struck the ocean less than forty minutes after taking off from Los Angeles International Airport. Reportedly, the crew's final transmission said they had suffered structural damage, although officials have refused to comment. The NTSB and FBI are enroute to the scene.

"We asked Global Cargo Express if hazardous cargo may have been responsible, as was the case in the DC-10 they lost a year ago, but they declined to comment. At this time we don't know if Flight 002 carried any hazardous cargo. We will continue to monitor this story and provide updates as information becomes available. This is Brent Whitlock, CNN News, Los Angeles." Bottoms filled his coffee cup and returned to his office, closing the door behind him.

✈

Kevin felt the vibration before hearing a sound. "Help's on the way," he shouted, loading a pencil flare into its casing. "Close your eyes." He aimed the flare high and to his side. His frozen thumb liberated the trigger and there was a brilliant flash. The flare climbed a few hundred feet before igniting into a brilliant red glow that drifted towards the sea. He fired a second, then grabbed the signal mirror. He placed the mirror behind his strobe light and aimed it in the direction of the noise, moving it up and down, and side to side. No way a pilot could miss that. Two bright lights broke the darkness, flashed twice, then came on steady. The survivors waited, the cold immobilizing them into a numbed silence.

Minutes later their raft was bathed in light. The helicopter went into a hover a few hundred feet to the side, lowering its rescue basket to the sea. As it moved closer, Kevin swam to retrieve it. The cold took his breath away. His arms and legs barely moved. Only his life vest kept him afloat. He was being pelted by the helicopter's downdraft and could barely see. Lonnie never heard his calls for help. The chopper dragged Kevin and the basket alongside the raft. Kevin stayed in the water to hold it steady. "Gggget Jjjjohn in thhhe bbbbasket."

John's agony was audible as they eased him into the basket. Kevin flung a numb arm and the basket was lifted into the air. The Dolphin's landing light went out as it made a sharp turn for the coast. The second Dolphin's light came on as it maneuvered into position.

"Llllonnnnnie—gggget inn." Lonnie dragged himself into the basket, waving with his good arm. When the basket returned for him, Kevin let go of the raft and pulled himself in, barely able to grip the sides. He shuddered under the downdraft. Then he felt himself being pulled out of the wind. He wanted to hug the aircrewman, but his arms wouldn't move. The aircrewman wrapped him in a blanket.

It took fifteen minutes before his shivering began to subside. Kevin had to thank the rest of the crew. He made his way forward, leaning over the console to pat the pilots on the back. "Ttthhhhank yyyyou," he shouted, his ears ringing from the noise.

With the Dolphin flying on autopilot, the woman pilot in the right seat turned around to shake his hand. "Glad to have you aboard," she said. "Are you hurt?" Kevin shook his hand, his teeth chattering. "That's amazing. What about the others?"

"Lllllonnnie's gggot aaaa ggggash—mmmy cccaptain's hhhurt bbbad."

"Oh yeah. He must've been the first one aboard. They didn't want to wait. Say—is there anyone you want to call? I can connect you via a phone patch."

Kevin's eyes widened. "Yyyyes!" He dragged the pencil across the pad and passed it forward.

Moments later, the pilot handed him a headset. "It's ringing," she said. "Make sure you tell her to say 'over' after each sentence. This is an open radio band."

He couldn't believe it when Nancy answered. "Nnnnnnance—" He tried again. "Nance—it's mmme. I'm okkkay, over."

She nearly fainted. "Thank God—oh, thank God."

"We're hhhheading for a hhhhospital, bbbbut I'm ffffine, ovvver."

"I love you, Kevin. I love you."

"Yyyyou tttttoo," he said. "Mmmmmmmst go. I lllllooooove yyyou, Nnnance. Ovver and ooout."

Frank Bottoms cracked his door open so he could monitor CNN while working on his reports. Brent Whitlock's latest report caught his attention.

"I'm at the Coast Guard Station in Los Angeles where I've just learned all three crewmembers of Global Cargo Express Flight 002 miraculously survived the crash and are enroute to an undisclosed hospital. Two Dolphin Coast Guard helicopters spotted distress flares while homing in on their emergency beacon and plucked them from the ocean within ninety minutes of their crash. The names of the crewmembers are being withheld, but we understand the captain and first officer sustained serious injuries while the second officer is uninjured. There's no word as to what might have brought the massive plane down, but one witness claims to have seen a missile strike the aircraft. Nearby Point

Mugu Naval Air Station and Vandenberg Air Force Base both test-fire missiles, but neither have commented on the incident. To recap, all three crewmembers from Global Cargo Express Flight 002 have been rescued. Brent Whitlock, CNN, Los Angeles."

Oxnard was closer, but Los Angeles Methodist Hospital had a trauma center and the difference in travel time was an acceptable risk. Used to police patrols, none of the residents noticed the Dolphin hurling over their houses at five hundred feet.

John's helicopter occupied the landing pad when they arrived, its blades scribing a white arc. While his helicopter hovered to the side, Kevin watched a horde in hospital garb whisk him away. Even from two hundred feet, it was clear John was in distress. He said a prayer for him and watched the helicopter depart.

The pilot maneuvered her Dolphin for a smooth touchdown as she'd done hundreds of times before. A doctor and nurse wearing goggles for protection climbed aboard and turned their attention to Lonnie. "Get him to ER," the doctor said. The nurse tugged at Kevin's arm, wanting him to follow. They had wheelchairs and warm blankets waiting.

Kevin's body tingled as warmth returned to his body. They pushed him through the spotless hallway at a hurried pace through several double doors, exit signs reflecting off the tiled floor. The smell brought back memories of getting his appendix out. Was it pine or ammonia? The nurse's station whipped by. He heard moans, but they weren't coming from John. Kevin imagined John's eyes rolled back in their sockets, the doctors asking him questions while a nurse held an oxygen mask to his face, John's ligaments a tangled web like the wires in their cockpit. It was more than he could bear.

He felt a hand on his shoulder, reassuring eyes looking at him, a white curtain draped around him, a small bed next to him. "Whhhere's Lllonie?"

"They're taking care of him," she said. "Right now, I need you to slip out of your clothes and put this gown on." She handed him a gown and slipped outside the curtain.

Kevin looked at the gown on the bed, ties in the back. He was wet, but didn't want to remove his blanket. The nurse asking if he was changed yet prompted action. He slipped his Tee shirt, soaked shoes, and pants off, shivering as he put the gown on. Immediately, he wrapped himself in the blanket. "Okkkay."

"I'm going to take your temperature," she said, slipping the horn-shaped device into his ear. It beeped almost immediately. "Ninety five point three," she said. "Let's get you in the hot tub—you need to warm up."

She wheeled him into a room that had a stainless steel tub. He suspected the whirlpool bath was used for physical therapy, but didn't ask. As she drew the water, he wondered about Nancy, his sons, John, and Lonnie. He wanted to speak, but his mouth wasn't cooperating. The bone-penetrating cold wouldn't let him go.

"Okay—it's all yours. I'll check back with you in a bit. Add water if you need to, but don't fall asleep, okay?"

Kevin nodded and waited until she left. He slid the gown off and stepped into the water. The water wasn't hot, but it burned his skin. Slowly, he settled into the bath and found the timer that turned the jets on. Immediately, the water churned. Thoughts of the helicopter downdraft brought a cold sweat to his forehead. He turned it off, white knuckles gripping the tub. He didn't notice the nurse return fifteen minutes later.

"How are you feeling?"

Kevin crossed his legs, hiding himself with his arms. "Better," he said.

"You sound better. Let me take your temperature again." She repeated the procedure. "Ninety seven—not bad."

"That's almost normal for me. How are John and Lonnie?"

"I believe John's still in surgery. Not sure about Lonnie."

"Can I see them?"

"I'll see what I can do. Are you ready to get out?"

"As long as you get me another warm blanket," he said. "I'm still pretty chilly."

"No problem. Here's a towel. I'll be back in a minute."

Kevin toweled himself and was tying the last bow when the nurse returned with a preheated blanket. He wrapped himself in it, bathing in its warmth. He remembered Nancy telling how wonderful it felt in the delivery room, but he never appreciated it until now. "So can I see Lonnie?"

"Sure," she said, pulling a wheel chair over. "Hop in."

The doctor paused as Kevin was wheeled in, nodding mid-stitch. Kevin flinched as he watched.

"Nurse—find him a bed," the doctor said. "He's going into shock."

Kevin didn't remember getting into bed. He looked around the room. He was fine—so why was he here? Home was fourteen hundred miles away. Why was Lonnie in the room with him? He caught a whiff of perfume.

"Good evening, Gentlemen. My name is Lanai."

Kevin's eyes met hers. They were soft, inviting, with the same sparkle he saw in his kids. "When can I go home?"

"They want you to spend the night," she said. "Mr. Stevens—how's your arm?" Lonnie was high on painkillers, grinning like a fool, gawking in a fantasy world. When she took his wrist to check his pulse, he stroked her arm. Lanai smiled, tucking his arm under the covers. "I see you're in La-la land, Mr. Stevens. I'm afraid Mr. Hamilton's the only company you can expect and I don't think he's your type. Ring if you need me," she said on her way out.

Kevin stared at the phone, afraid to pick it up. It took three tries before he dialed Nancy correctly. On the third ring, she spoke into his needs and fears.

"I've been waiting for your call," she said. "Are you all right?"

"I am now," he said.

She lay on the bed staring at his picture, hand over her heart, feeling its pulse through her nightgown. "God, it's good to hear your voice."

"Sorry my teeth were chattering. There was so much I wanted to say. I was so cold, Nance. I thought about you when they wrapped me in a delivery room blanket."

She immersed herself in her own blanket, pressing the soft material to her face. "When can you come home?"

He watched Lonnie trace something magical in the air with his fingers. "I think tomorrow. I'm not sure about Lonnie, but I know John's gonna be here a while. John's my captain." He sensed her fear. "How are the boys?"

"They're fine," she said. "Of course, they're asleep. Call them tomorrow."

"I will." She was alluding to his last mishap. She forgave him, but it never went away. When he closed his eyes, he was in the cockpit being dragged down, his chest ready to burst under the pressure. *Lonnie!* He was hyperventilating. He opened his eyes, surprised to see Lonnie in the bed next to him, sound asleep.

"Kevin? Are you there?"

"Ah, yeah—I'm really tired. I'll call you tomorrow, okay? I love you."

"You, too." The phone fell to the floor as she missed its cradle. His rapid breathing, the hesitation—it was the same when he awoke from nightmares about the fire. God help them both. She couldn't do that again.

When the nurse came in, Kevin was clinging to the phone, sound asleep.

10

Derek Goldstein's alarm went off at five am as it did every day. He hated being ignorant about worldly matters and made a point of watching CNN Headline News before climbing out of bed. He was drawn to the Global DC-10 crash, dialing Global's toll-free number while he watched. Following numerous computer prompts, he reached a live customer service representative. "Ah, yes—I'm watching a CNN story about your DC-10 crash," he said, running his fingers through his gray hair. "I just shipped some precious cargo to Tokyo. Can you see if it was on that plane?"

"Certainly, sir," the woman said. "May I have your tracking number?"

"Hang on," he said, tossing the covers aside. He ran into his office and dug out his paperwork, then picked up the extension. After providing the tracking information he was put on hold. He tapped his fingers on the desk, half-listening while his mind wandered.

"Mr. Goldstein?"

"Yes?" Her tone had changed. She didn't need to say more.

"I'm sorry, but your shipment was on that flight. At this point we have no idea about its cargo's status, but you may want to contact your insurance company."

Goldstein began yelling. "You expect me to contact my insurance company? Young lady, your company just destroyed a revolutionary one-of-a-kind engine. I assure you your company will pay for it. I assume you'll call when you know more?"

The woman had been in this job too long to be intimidated. "Mr. Goldstein, I'm sure someone will be contacting you concerning your loss, but it will take time to clear this matter up. Again, I'm sorry for your loss."

"Yeah? Well not as sorry as you're gonna be!" He slammed the phone down and swiped his hand across the desk, sending papers flying. The goddam bitch had no clue how this would affect his business. Hopefully Tigress would grant an extension. If Tigress refused to wait for a replacement engine, Global would pay.

———

Nurse Midge Hellerman was eager to finish her rounds so she could burn a cigarette. It had been a long day. She had guests coming for dinner; she needed to clean the house. If she hadn't forgotten to thaw the roast, things would have been fine.

Kevin smelled smoke. He was sound asleep, but it was as real as the pillow he was lying on. He was surrounded by fire and smoke. Something was tugging at his arm. He couldn't move. He was trapped.

"Take it easy, Mr. Hamilton," Midge said. Why did she always get the difficult patients? She pinned his arm under hers, applying pressure to his wrist. She used her weight to her advantage. "Open your eyes, Kevin. I'm only taking your pulse."

Kevin heard her voice, but couldn't wake up. His free arm thrashed about. He squeezed his eyes shut, panicked. The smoke intensified. "Nancy. Help!"

Midge gave up. She set his arm down and stroked his forehead like she would a child. "Wake up, Kevin. You're having a nightmare."

It wasn't Nancy, but her voice was sincere. He opened his eyes, surprised to see a frowning woman hovering over him. He looked around, disoriented, groggy.

"You were in a plane crash," Midge said, ready to call the doctor. "You're in the hospital. How many fingers am I holding up?"

Slowly they came into focus. "Two," he said, incensed. "Why does Lonnie have bandages on his arm? Why doesn't he wake up?" He felt a hand on his arm. It was the woman again. He read her nametag. Her touch was coarse.

"Lonnie had a large gash—it was sewn up. He was pretty sedated—may sleep another six hours." He looked at Lonnie and back at Midge. "I'm told you were asking about Mr. Armishaw," she said.

Armishaw? Kevin's mind struggled to sort things out. Of course. John Armishaw—his captain. "Captain Armishaw," he said to her. "Tell me all you know."

"They were able to save his foot," she said, patting his arm. "You guys were lucky to get out. Now do us both a favor—sit back and relax so I can take your pulse."

Kevin sat back. When she finished with him, she waddled over to Lonnie's bed, tucking his limp arm under hers. "It's still dark outside," Kevin said. "Why'd you wake us up so early? How can anyone get any rest around here?"

"Shhh." Midge studied her watch's second hand.

Lonnie awoke, surprised to find a plastic tube imbedded in his wrist. "What's this thing?" he asked, his voice slurred.

Midge didn't look up. "You were dehydrated," she said. She set his arm down and recorded his vital signs. "The doctor should be making his rounds within the hour."

"Great," Kevin said. "The sooner the better. I want to get out of here."

"Lonnie, Kevin will probably be released today, but you should plan on being here a couple more days," Midge said. Lonnie stared at his tube. "It's temporary. You were exposed to a lot of bacteria and we don't want to risk infection." She met Kevin's eyes. "I'll see you again before you leave. Lonnie—let me know if anything's oozing. By the way, the evening nurse felt sorry for you both. Kevin, she retrieved your shirt from ER before they tossed it—had it bleached and your uniforms washed. Everything's hanging in the closet."

Kevin's eyes lit up. "Was it Lanai?"

Midge nodded, leaving in need of a smoke.

Kevin tossed the covers aside and swung his feet onto the cold tiled floor. Why hadn't the NTSB stopped by? Someone from Global's LA facility should've checked on them by now. Then again, maybe they did, but he was too doped up to remember. Either way, he was leaving as soon as the doctor released him. If the doc was running late, he'd go see John. If anyone wanted to talk, they'd find him.

He emerged from the bathroom with a towel around his waist, unaware that Lonnie was watching his every move. His uniform was tattered, but clean. He didn't notice John's faded bloodstains until he buttoned the shirt. While slipping the last button through its hole, he noticed a spectacular sight. Outside, a bright orange horizon welcomed a new day. Last night he wasn't sure he'd see another.

"Whatcha doin', Kev?" Lonnie said.

Kevin turned, surprised to see Lonnie awake. "Just checking out the sunrise. It's beautiful. How you feeling?"

"Buzzed. Whatcha doin' all dressed up?"

"I'm gonna see John," he said, searching under the bed for his shoes. He checked the closet. He sat on the bed, looking around, dumbfounded. They were nowhere in sight, but he didn't dare ask. If Midge found him dressed, she'd shackle him to the bed. Maybe no one would notice if he went in his black socks. "Don't tell anyone where I went. I should be back before anyone knows I'm gone." Lonnie nodded, scratching at his IV tube.

Kevin moved down the hallway, managing to avoid the nurse's station, but he startled an elderly volunteer in pink stripes pushing a flower cart. "Excuse me," he said, hoping his smile would keep her from checking his uniform. "I'm looking for a patient named John Armishaw. He's recovering from surgery and I don't have any idea where he is. I don't have much time."

"Wait here—I'll see what I can find out."

Kevin nodded. He ducked into a corner and waited.

"There you are," she said.

"So what did you find?"

"According to the nurse, he's not to be disturbed." She couldn't help noticing Kevin's battered Global ID badge, torn uniform, and no shoes. "You know—I think I have a flower delivery for Mr. Armishaw. Those vases can get pretty heavy. I could use a hand."

"You're my kind of lady, Agnes," he said, reading her nametag. "Lead the way."

The freight elevator swallowed them. He watched Midge pass by as the doors were closing. Thankfully, she didn't look his way. Once the elevator began to move, Agnes said, "He's in 517."

John heard the door open and turned to look. "Whoozaire?"

Kevin bit his lip. John's leg was elevated by a series of wire supports; steel rods pierced his blood-soaked bandages. "It's Kevin," he managed. "How ya doin', John?"

John squinted, unable to focus. "Hey, Kev—whassup?"

"Keep it down. I'm not supposed to be here." Kevin took a seat next to his bed, the *Cosmo* on the floor piquing his curiosity. No coffee cups and sundry items anywhere. Whose was it? "I wanted to see you before I left. I'm getting discharged today."

John drew his tongue over the roof of his mouth several times to moisten it. "What day's it?"

"Tuesday. We came in this morning. They must've given you the same sleeping pill they gave me. I was really out of it when I woke up."

John smiled, his eyes empty. He meant to ask about Lonnie, but drew a blank. "So how you doin', Kev? How's—Lenny?"

"I'm fine—and except for a few hundred stitches in his arm, Lonnie's fine, too." He studied John's face. Veins popped out his forehead. His knuckles were white. Kevin held a water glass to John's mouth. John swirled his tongue inside, then wet his lips. Kevin set the glass aside. "John—do you remember the crash?" John nodded. "You know, you did a helluva job getting us down safely. I'm sorry you took the brunt of it."

John smiled. "Thanks, man."

"John—has anyone contacted you? The NTSB? FBI?"

"Kev—I don' know which way's up, man. I feel like pukin', but I won't 'cause it hurts too much. For all I know, a hundred people could've talked to me already. How long you been with Global, Kev?"

"About a year and a half."

John's laugh was quiet, riding over the pain. "Oh, man—don' make me laugh. This is your second mishap? No offense, but I ain't flying with you again."

"Hey—who told you?"

"Kev—everyone knows 'bout chu, man. Do me a favor—pumme on your negative airman list, okay?"

"Sure, John," he said, forcing a smile. "But seriously—I've feared something like this might happen ever since that inflight fire. Not that it would happen to me, mind you—just that it would happen." Kevin watched the renewed intensity in John's eyes. "Did you hear about the drug money?"

"Not that again."

"It's true, John. One of the guys in accounting confirmed it. Global made a lot of money on that fire. They kept a million bucks in crisp hundred dollar bills because no one claimed it. You know it was an FBI DNA synthesizer that caused the fire, right? The chemicals weren't packaged right. It wasn't intentional, but why'd the FBI refuse to accept responsibility even after the investigators confirmed it was the cause?"

John's fingers began to respond. Pain flowed through him like a river. He closed his eyes. "You're ex-Marine, right?" Kevin nodded. "Any combat?"

"Three campaigns—why?"

John scraped his tongue over the roof of his mouth. Kevin moved the water glass closer. John took a sip and nodded. His pain brought a clarity he hadn't possessed since the accident. "I think you're overreacting." Kevin frowned, but listened. "Look, Kev—I've hauled tons of bombs to the MidEast and never had a problem. Our security folks screen the cargo with drug-sniffing dogs and x-ray machines before it's ever loaded. They've been doing that for years, but it got even tighter after the attack on the

World Trade Center and Pentagon on 9-11. I can see how money might slip through, but explosives? No way. If that new flap came loose, it could account for our roll and yaw. If it bent back and hit the fuselage, that would explain the depressurization." He reached for the water again.

"You really believe that? Think about it, John—we never lost hydraulics."

"Look, Kev—I'd be hard pressed doing my job if I thought someone was tryin' to blow me out of the sky. Call it what you want, but this was an accident, just like your fire. Nothin' more, nothin' less."

Kevin's foot kicked the *Cosmo* as he rose from the chair. He picked it up and set it aside the bed. "Has anyone from your family been here?"

"Beats me."

John's abruptness was unexpected. It crossed Kevin's mind he'd overstayed his welcome. "Well, I'd better get going before the warden misses me. Can I get you anything? Clothes, magazine?"

John nodded. "Magazines would be great. Sports magazines. A swimsuit issue."

Kevin smiled. "I'll see what I can find." He backed into Midge, her arms folded.

"Busted," John said.

"What do you think you're doing?" Midge said. "I figured if I kept your shoes locked up you'd stay put. The doctor made his rounds and I had no idea where you were. You made me look like an idiot." She was still nagging as they slipped out the door.

Two men in Navy-blue windbreakers bearing yellow NTSB lettering on their backs turned around as Midge held Kevin's door open. "You must be the elusive Mr. Hamilton?" one said. Kevin nodded. "I'm Chris Friarson, NTSB. This is Kirby Ward. Glad you're okay. The Navy's handling the salvage operation," he said. "Fortunately you ditched in some relatively shallow water so we'll be able to recover the wreckage. We just finished with Lonnie—can you describe what happened?"

Kevin looked around the room. No legal advisors or union reps here—again. He hesitated, but Lonnie gave him the nod. Since Friarson was asking what he saw and not what he thought, he felt obligated to answer. He described the loss of cabin pressure and John's struggle to keep the plane flying. "Much of the time I couldn't tell which way was up. Captain Armishaw tried a bunch of power settings before regaining any control. He and Lonnie were amazing."

Friarson jotted notes as though he'd heard it before. "Was there more drag on one side or the other?"

"I couldn't say—I wasn't flying. Lonnie could probably answer that one."

Friarson sighed. "Okay—how long did it take for the cabin pressure to equalize? Minutes? Seconds? Anything would be helpful."

"I really don't know," Kevin said. He recalled his anger and frustration from the first mishap. It took months to rid himself of it. Would this be any different?

"Kevin? You okay?"

"Yeah—I'm fine, just preoccupied. Look, I know first-hand how time expansion affects the brain in crisis situations. I'm afraid any estimate on my part would be worthless." He heard a noise and turned around. Friarson was putting his notebook back in his pocket. "The cabin VSI was pegged when we lost pressurization. I'm sure the Flight Data Recorder will tell you more."

Friarson looked at Ward. "Hopefully the captain will be more enlightening."

As part of her shakedown cruise, the Salvage and Rescue ship *USS Atlantis* was docked at San Diego Naval Station. The two hundred fifty-five foot, multi-task vessel was preparing to return to her homeport in Hawaii when Third Fleet Headquarters ordered her to front the DC-10 recovery. With twenty salvage divers assigned to his crew, Commanding Officer Lieutenant Commander Ed Battock was mystified why Third Fleet ordered him to wait for two additional divers. The duty officer informed him the FBI handpicked those divers from the Explosive Ordnance Disposal team at the Coronado Amphibian Base. They were to assist in the investigation, but offered no other explanation. Battock was miffed.

Prior to becoming skipper of *Atlantis*, Battock served as Executive Officer aboard the *USS Grapple*. He was highly experienced in underwater salvage operations, and felt confident his crew would perform well. He knew the area. If the Coast Guard's chart coordinates were accurate, it was close to where the Alaska Airlines MD-80 crash took place, the water no deeper than one hundred fifty feet, shallow enough for SCUBA. The weather forecast was good; the salvage operation should go smoothly.

The two EOD divers were to report no later than 1300 hours, but neither had shown. Battock paced the bridge, his face tense. *Atlantis* had to be underway by 1400 to meet her on-station time; failure to do so would reflect poorly on him and his crew.

He considered telling Third Fleet they couldn't wait, but feared it might curtail his CO tour. With less than six years to retirement, muddying the waters wasn't an option.

Standing six foot one, two hundred fifty pounds, Battock commanded respect. His eyes sunk into a weathered face, aged it beyond his thirty-six years. His Naval Academy rugby experience honed his no-nonsense ethic that it took teamwork to get things done.

He postponed Quarters fifteen minutes in anticipation of EOD's arrival. His anger mounted. His crew was waiting. He frowned at Executive Officer Lieutenant Brent McClintock as he flicked his cigarette overboard. "Let's go, XO."

A senior petty officer noticed the door open and a khaki pant leg step forward. "Attention on Deck!" he said, his chin tucked against his chest, arms pinned at his side. The officers walked past columns of rigid bodies.

Battock carried his stern expression to the podium. "Eyes on me, ladies and gentlemen!" He read them. They knew something was wrong. Why else would he call an assembly? "All liberty is canceled until further notice. We've been ordered to recover a civilian airliner and will ship out within the hour. You may have heard a DC-10 ditched off the Channel Islands last night. It'll take ten hours to get there—we'll commence dive operations upon arrival. Our delay is with the two EOD divers I've been ordered to take on. They have yet to arrive, but I'm confident they'll be here soon. EOD will be in charge of the site until it's rendered safe. *Atlantis'* divers will be restricted to being safety observers until I say otherwise. I don't know these other divers, so I'm asking you report anything unusual. Any questions?"

A unanimous, "No, sir!" broke the silence.

"Very well—At Ease." Bodies slackened. "Make no mistake about it—this is a dangerous assignment. We're assisting the NTSB and FBI so it's critical you document everything. A single piece of wreckage may hold the key as to what brought the plane down. Be safe; don't assume anything. Nobody talks to anyone about our mission unless cleared by me, especially the…"

A loud *thump* interrupted Battock. Two muscular men stood in the entry. "Sorry, Skipper," the taller man said. "We're your EOD divers. Where should we stow our stuff?"

Seeing Battock's nod, Ensign Truman called the formation to Attention. "Carry out the Plan of the Day," Battock said. He returned Truman's salute and headed towards the entry, the XO following close behind. He stopped in front of the EOD divers. "XO, you're excused," he said, his eyes locked on the taller man. When they were alone, he asked EOD to meet him on deck.

The two divers fell in behind Battock. He didn't stop until he reached the bow. The salty air revived him. He lit a cigarette, taking in the men in camouflage fatigues. Smoke streamed out his nostrils. "I'm Lieutenant Commander Battock," he said. They were unflinching; wore no rank. "I have no idea why I've been ordered to take you, but while you're here, you're under my command and I hold you to the same customs and courtesies expected of Navy personnel." He took another drag from his cigarette, crushing it in the butt can. He'd been trying to quit for weeks. "I expect you to address me as sir and render proper salutes when reporting for duty. You've embarrassed yourselves in front of my crew with your lack of military bearing. I trust that won't happen again."

"No, sir," the taller man said, stepping forward. "I'm Lieutenant Commander Duncan and this is Petty Officer Ray. Frankly, I don't give a damn about your petty operation. We just got back from a real assignment. Shitty as it was, at least it meant something. Airliner salvage. Christ—we didn't volunteer for this any more than you did, but I guess we're stuck working together for a while. By the way—I resent your addressing me this way in front of Ray."

Battock's fists tightened. "Petty Officer Ray, find the Senior Chief—he'll show you to your quarters." He watched Ray leave. "Mister Duncan—you're out of line. You're a commissioned officer in the United States Navy. Conduct yourself accordingly. If you can't do that, then I suggest you and Petty Officer Ray get off my ship and I'll submit a report to your commanding officer."

Duncan looked at the moored warships. He extended his hand. "Perhaps we didn't get off to the best start," he said. "I'm Dan. Sorry we interrupted Quarters. Until we determine the site is safe, Petty Officer Ray and I will be the only divers allowed inside the wreckage. Once we're done, it's all yours and we'll get off your ship. If you can live with that, then I guess we have a partnership."

Battock nodded. He and Duncan held the same rank, and that demanded he be treated with the same privileges as any other O-4. "I'll put an extra bunk in my quarters."

"Thanks, but if you don't mind, Ray and I will bunk in the wardroom."

"Suit yourself, but I'm not placing it off limits."

"No sweat. You ready to shove it?"

Battock frowned. "We'll be casting off soon."

"Good."

When Battock arrived on the bridge, the crew was standing by. He leaned over the railing, watching his crew cast off. In short order, *Atlantis* was making its way through the crowded waterway, surrounded by pleasure boats. They steamed past row upon row of them, a tribute to the area's affluence. San Diego Bay was as gridlocked as the interstate, but it was a perfect day for sailing. As they passed abeam Point Loma's narrow peninsula, an S-3 submarine hunter from North Island Naval Air Station swooped overhead. They rounded the point and the seas tossed them from side to side, foaming the deck. Battock came alive. He was in his element. He ordered a secure-equipment check.

The coastline was a sight to behold, clear air, blue sky, swooping seagulls. He tapped his cigarette pack, then put it back. "XO, I'll be in my quarters."

Atlantis arrived on scene at 2200 hours. They deployed the side-scan sonar to conduct a grid search. As the ship passed over the crash site, the crew scanned the water for debris. Rainbow oil slicks appeared minutes after the sonar picked up some elongated returns. Battock was confident they'd found the DC-10. "Boatswain—ten degrees port and drop anchor."

The young sailor spun the wheel.

Ten minutes later, *Atlantis* was anchored, pointed into the wind. The Boatswain secured all engines. *Atlantis* was ready to commence dive operations. Battock sensed Duncan's presence, but ignored him.

"Congratulations, Skipper," Duncan said, looking over the sonar returns. "Looks like you found her all right. We'll get ready. Do you have any underwater lights?"

"Of course, but I'm sending the remote down before anyone gets wet. This thing's pretty broken up and I want a better picture of what we're dealing with. I'm thinking we might wait until morning."

"Say again? With all due respect, we have a job to do and the sooner we get on with it, the sooner we'll be off this tub. Besides, underwater currents might be destroying evidence as we speak. We'll make do with spotlights. We'll be ready in fifteen minutes."

Battock nodded. Duncan was right. He couldn't justify delaying the dive. "We'll launch the inflatable."

From a distance, Battock watched Duncan and Ray check their gear while the outboard-powered raft awaited them. Duncan stopped what he was doing when he noticed the two *Atlantis* divers. "What the hell are you doing in my boat?"

Battock moved closer. "Skully and Smitty are your safety divers."

"I don't think so. EOD works alone."

"Sorry, Commander, but you're not diving without 'em."

Duncan's face flushed. *Another power play.* He dropped his gear and pulled Battock aside. "We know what we're doing and we intend to do it alone."

"Dan—if this were a combat mission, I'd say no problem, but it's not. You're my responsibility, so I insist my divers be in the water anytime you're diving." He smiled. "Think of them as your Guardian Angels."

Duncan went to the inflatable to survey their equipment. One diver held an MK 21 deep water diving helmet in his lap, its intercom wire and oxygen hose draped over the side. The other wore SCUBA. "Fine—they can go. But remember, they're *not* going inside the wreckage. I don't have time to rescue any wannabees." Battock said nothing. "It's probably a hundred foot dive, so give us thirty minutes to locate and survey the fuselage. If it's safe, your crew can start plotting the wreckage on the next dive."

Battock nodded, watching Senior Chief assist Skully with the MK 21 helmet. Skully confirmed he was ready and gave an intercom check. Duncan looked over his divers as he sat on the side of the raft. The raft wasn't going anywhere. They were using it as a dive platform. Duncan bit his mouthpiece, covered his mask with his hand, and fell over backwards, followed by Ray, Smitty, and Skully. Battock hacked his watch, watching a trail of bubbles rise from their fading lights. He went to the communications room to monitor the dive.

The room was alive with background noise as sailors manned their positions in the dimly lit room. Skully's scratchy breathing over the loud speaker confirmed his intercom was working. Ten minutes later he made his first report. "EOD's located the main fuselage. Nothing unusual. Now they're securing a buoy line."

"Skully, this is the Skipper. Where are you now?" No response. "Skully—how do you read?" No response. "We're still hearing his breathing. His headset must've failed. Let him continue." McClintock nodded.

Skully hovered thirty feet above the EOD divers, unaware of his intercom problem. He strained to move closer, but his trailing life support hose slowed his pace. If he tugged on the line, Senior Chief would misinterpret it as a signal to abort, but EOD out-distanced him. He barely arrived in time to see them check out the fuselage. "Skipper—there's a hole about eight feet in diameter on the right side of the aircraft," he said. "The skin's peeled like a grape. The cockpit's on its side about fifteen yards away, but the fuselage is upright and pretty much intact. I don't see the tail or wings."

The technician trouble-shooting Skully's intercom problem shook his head. "Sorry, Skipper. The problem must be on his end. He can transmit—just can't receive."

Battock nodded. "Senior Chief—you think we can raise the fuselage intact?"

Senior Chief studied the sonar image. "The largest piece must be at least fifty feet, Skipper. Even if we raised her, nothing short of a flattop could carry her."

Battock settled into his chair. "XO, draft a message to Third Fleet. See how they want to handle this—and be creative so they don't think we're stalling."

"Yes, sir."

A need for a cigarette sent Battock outside. Tapping the pack into his palm, he scanned the horizon, wondering why they were still alone. It didn't make sense; nothing about this operation did. The damp air chilled him. It was nothing like Hawaii.

"Skipper," Senior Chief said. "Skully reported EOD went inside the fuselage."

"How'd they get in?"

"Through the hole."

Battock nodded, checking his watch. The SCUBA divers were running low on air. There'd be little time to save them if anyone got trapped. "Senior—have the rescue divers standing by."

While Senior Chief relayed the order, Skully made another transmission. "I see bubbles coming out the hole," he said. "Now light. They're coming out, Skipper. By the way, Senior—next dive I want SCUBA. How can I watch them if I can't move around?" There was no answer. "Okay, Skipper—everyone's out. We're coming up."

Senior Chief picked up the PA mike. "Now hear this. Prepare to recover divers. That is all." He replaced the mike. "Skipper, I'm gonna monitor the recovery."

Battock nodded. "I'll join you."

Smitty was the first to surface, soon followed by Skully, Duncan, and Ray. They'd shed their gear by the time Battock and Senior Chief arrived. "How'd it go?" Battock asked.

"There's a big hole on the right side with razor sharp metal protruding from it," Duncan said, busy toweling his face. "The pattern suggests something exploded inside the aircraft. You'll need to hold off on the survey and keep everyone clear until we've had a better look inside. Petty Officer Ray's one of the best underwater demolition experts in the Navy. If anything needs to be disarmed, he can do it, but we'll need some additional equipment and bigger tanks for our next dive."

"Take whatever you need," Battock said.

"Thanks." Duncan held his grease board up for Battock to see, his finger for a pointer. "Here's a rough sketch of what we found. This is the cockpit—the main fuselage is here. I didn't see them, but I assume the wings broke off in this direction—probably a ways behind. It doesn't appear the currents have disturbed anything, but that could change any time. The cargo area's a mess—it's gonna be hell searching for explosives. We only had time to check out a couple containers."

Battock studied the diagram. "Should we pull the cans so you can maneuver better?"

Duncan shook his head. "Too risky. If there's anything in there, moving the cans might set 'em off. We'll know more after our next dive."

Battock was curious how moving the cargo could set anything off after a crash like that. From what had been described, everything on board had either moved, twisted, compressed, or otherwise been destroyed. "I'm waiting to hear from Third Fleet. Better get some rest. We'll resume operations in the morning."

Duncan's head snapped up. "Say again? We're not here to sit on our asses and play pinochle." Seeing the sailors looking their way, he lowered his voice. "Look, Ed—Ray and I don't need baby-sitting. We're diving as soon as our rest period's up."

Battock grabbed the PA mike. "Now hear this. This is the Skipper. Dive operations are suspended until 0600 hours. Repeat—dive operations suspended until 0600. That is all." He looked at Duncan. "Your dive—my ship. If you've got a problem with that, take it up with Third Fleet."

Duncan slapped Ray's shoulder. "Let's get outta here, Tim."

Skully moved closer, helmet in hand. "I couldn't help overhearing, Skipper. What's Mister Duncan's problem?"

Battock watched Duncan and Ray. "He's tired. By the way—you need to get your helmet fixed—you never heard a word I said." Skully turned the helmet over, playing with the connection. "Have a tech look at it," Battock said. "Anyway—how was it down there?"

"It was too damned dark. I was shark bait on a tether, and once they went inside, I couldn't see jack. I'm not sure I served any purpose, especially if we didn't have com."

"You did fine, Skully. I heard everything. Any way a water impact could've caused that hole?"

"No, sir. It looks just like the *Cole*, only it's bent outwards."

Battock recalled the terrorist attack on the *USS Cole* in Yemen. If that were the case, a mechanical failure didn't cause the crash. "Thanks, Skully. Better get some rest—you've got a busy day tomorrow."

"Yes, sir."

Once the deck cleared, the only lights came from the bridge and position lights. Battock's cigarette glowed red. This job was getting to him. He couldn't escape Duncan, his smug look, disrespect, and angry eyes. Ray was a follower, Duncan a different story. Unable to sleep, he went to the wardroom to confront him.

The wardroom was dark, the moon casting strange shadows through a porthole. There were no sounds, no breathing. He flipped on the light. Nothing but tables, chairs, and the picture of *Atlantis* underway. Duncan and Ray were gone. Checking the deck, Battock found two sailors enjoying a smoke. "How you guys doin'?"

"Fine, sir."

"I don't suppose you've seen the EOD divers, have you?"

"No, sir, but we only got here a couple minutes ago."

"No sweat. Tomorrow's a busy day. Get some rest." The sailors nodded. Making his way to the bow, Battock listened to the chorus of singing wires, a bustling flag, slapping waves. He watched the bow rise and fall over the swells. Still no sign of Duncan or Ray. When he returned to the quarterdeck, McClintock was finalizing the message to Third Fleet. "How's it coming, XO?"

"All done, awaiting your signature."

"Thanks, Brent. By the way, have you seen Lieutenant Commander Duncan?"

"No, sir—but I've been here for the last hour."

"Come on—let's take a walk." Outside, Battock raised his collar and stared at the water. "Something's not right, Brent. I can't find Duncan or Ray. In a few minutes I'm gonna make an announcement asking they report to the bridge. I've got a hunch they dove against my orders. Find Senior Chief and tell him I want Bends and Darby ready to dive as soon as I give word. Make sure they know they're only diving if I give the order—and if they go, their only role is to see what Duncan and Ray are up to, not disturb them. Oh, yeah—make sure someone takes an infrared camera. I'll need proof they violated my orders to get them off my ship."

"Yes, sir—on my way."

Battock gave him ten minutes and picked up the microphone. He regretted disturbing his crew, but it was the only way to prove his hunch. "Now hear this," he said, his voice echoing off steel walls. "This is the Skipper. Lieutenant Commander Duncan and Petty Officer Ray report to the bridge. Repeat—Lieutenant Commander Duncan and Petty Officer Ray report to the bridge. That is all." He checked his watch. As expected, neither showed.

On Senior Chief's order, Bends and Darby flipped over the sidewall and descended into the abyss. Unlike the last dive, the ship's floodlights remained off. Once they found the buoy line, they turned their flashlights off. Bends pulled himself down hand-over-hand with Darby at his heels. Bends saw a faint light coming from inside the fuselage. As he prepared to take a photograph, he felt a tap on his shoulder. Darby was signaling he had a problem and needed to surface. Bends tapped him on the shoulder indicating he understood, but he was drawn to the light in the fuselage. It had to be coming from the EOD divers, and his orders were to prove they were down there. Duncan was an ass and he wasn't about to let his CO down. He'd abort the dive once he took the pictures.

Bends snapped a photo, but couldn't shake the feeling he wasn't alone. There was no horizon, no up or down, nothing but indigo. He took a few more. His breathing intensified as he prepared to stow his camera. When it came, he couldn't breathe. *Thud!* The camera fell from his hands as he doubled over in pain; his flashlight spiraled towards the fuselage. He'd lost the buoy line and was disoriented. He exhaled, holding his hand above his regulator for the bubbles. Their rising provided direction and he began a slow ascent.

He was fifty feet from the surface when he saw light. Suddenly he was hit from behind, his mouthpiece knocked from his teeth. He had no feeling in his arms or legs. His mouthpiece was spewing bubbles but he couldn't reach it. The pressure was building in his lungs. His eyes bulged. Something grabbed him. He was being dragged down in a trail of bubbles. When the pressure became unbearable, he screamed and seawater rushed in. There was a sudden calm. Then he was floating. At peace.

Duncan found the anchor chain. He tapped Ray on the shoulder and made a slow ascent. There'd be hell to pay, but he did what he had to. He surfaced cautiously, removing his facemask to avoid a reflection. A lone speck in a large sea, no one noticed. Ray clung to the anchor chain as the waves pushed Duncan into the gray hull. Duncan moved side to side until he found the knotted rope. He slipped off his tank and climbed the rope, his bulging muscles stretching against his wet suit. Hanging by his fingers, he peered over the deck at eye level. He could see several people looking over the stern, but the bow was clear. After climbing aboard, he pulled on the rope while Ray climbed. Once Ray was aboard, Duncan coiled the rope and stashed it with the rest of their gear. They quickly changed into the sweats they'd hidden and walked into the wardroom. Duncan flipped on a light and broke out a deck of cards. "Five card stud, Joker's wild," he said.

Ray smiled. "You're on."

12

Darby shook his head as he pulled himself aboard. The pain was unbearable, like someone held a welding torch to his brain. Senior Chief's lips were moving, but all he could hear was a high-pitch ringing. Cupping his hand over his ear did nothing to relieve the pain or the noise.

"What's wrong? Where's Bends?" Senior was shouting so loud, Battock feared he'd wake the crew three decks below.

"I can't hear you. I've got an ear block," he said, scanning the deck. "Where's Bends? He was right behind me."

"Better get him to the pressure chamber," Battock said. McClintock, the XO, took him away.

Senior Chief kept tugging on Bends' safety line, giving the signal to abort, but there was no response. He tugged again, but now the line was taut and wouldn't budge. "Something's wrong, Skipper."

Battock grabbed hold and yanked, but it may as well have been the anchor. His heart accelerated. "Turn the floods on," he said.

As Senior Chief flipped the lever, a circle of light surrounded the ship. Curious fish began surfacing, sailors gathered, neither knowing what they were looking for. "Bubbles on the port side," Senior said.

Battock ran to the left side of the ship where a continuous flow of bubbles broke the surface. He picked up the PA, forcing himself to remain calm. "Now hear this. This is the Skipper. We have a diver down. Repeat—diver down. All divers report for rescue operation. Repeat—all divers report for rescue operation. That is all."

Sailors scrambled on deck, emerging from every door and ladder. EOD Lt Commander Duncan was among them, stopping next to Battock. "What's going on, Skipper?"

Battock met Duncan's eyes. It was all he could do not to knock him overboard. "Where the hell've you been?' he asked. "I paged you and Ray over forty minutes ago."

Duncan shrugged. "We took a shower, had a smoke on the bow, then went to the wardroom. Ever notice how the wind blows the noise? Anyway, we never heard your page—sorry. So, what's all the commotion about?"

Battock glared. "I figured you and Ray took an unauthorized dive so I sent two divers to look for you—and one of them's still down there. Give it to me straight, Dan—did you make a second dive?"

"No. Look, Ed—I admit I was upset about you calling it quits, but that's in the past. You need help with the rescue party?"

"No—I've got plenty of divers. Wait in your quarters. I'm not through with you." Duncan shrugged and walked away. Battock looked at his divers, their eyes wide with concern. "Listen. Bends is in trouble—his safety line won't budge. We spotted continuous bubbles off the port side, but now they've disappeared. Senior will assign the divers. Whoever goes, do not—repeat, do not enter the wreckage. Any questions?" The frogmen looked at each other. "No? Then find him."

The divers rushed Senior Chief to get assigned to the detail. Losing a shipmate was hard, but Bends was one of the best. Three divers soon went over the side, one wearing an MK 21, two in SCUBA. Five more stood by.

"Senior—get on the horn and order a medivac," Battock said. He couldn't imagine losing someone on a shakedown cruise. He felt drained. His problems with Duncan would have to wait. He returned to the bridge to make a logbook entry. He opened the green canvas notebook and set his ballpoint pen in motion.

2107 hrs. EM1 Van "Bends" Dyer is missing, presumed drowned, while searching for EOD divers. Senior Chief and I spotted continuous bubbles near the marker buoy. Three divers dispatched for Dyer's rescue. SAR helo requested.

He tossed his pen aside and found himself tapping his cigarette pack again. Disgusted, he crumbled the pack and tossed it in the trash. "Skipper—they found him," Senior Chief said over the intercom. Battock ran. He met Senior Chief in the com room, monitoring the dive. "How is he?"

Senior's head bowed. "There's metal sticking clear through his body," he said. "Bends is gone, Skipper. Even worse, the crew's surrounded by sharks."

Jesus! "Dammit, Senior—he's not gone 'til I say he's gone. Get our—"

The MK-21's intercom interrupted him. "We're attaching a line to him now, Senior. Okay—he's free now. Pull him up."

McClintock burst into the room. "Skipper—the Coast Guard should be here within thirty minutes."

Battock nodded. "Get our best corpsman up here, XO. Make sure he knows CPR."

The XO's eyebrows rose. "Mind if I try, Skipper? I used to teach CPR."

"Hell no. Give Bends your best shot."

A mixture of blood and water oozed from Bends' torso as they laid him on deck. There was so much blood it was impossible to tell if sharks attacked him on the way up. Sailors formed a half-circle around him in uneasy silence. Senior Chief stripped Bends' diving equipment and cut away his wet suit while the corpsman grabbed whatever he could to stop the bleeding. There was just enough pulse to keep his arteries spurting.

The XO rolled Bends onto his stomach. A repulsive sound emerged as he slid his palms over Bends' lower torso, shooting fluid from his mouth and wounds. Bends was turning blue. He needed oxygen. Too many air leaks. The corpsman plugged the wounds with gauze, then McClintock rolled him on his back.

Sailors watched in horror as the life drained from their shipmate. No matter how many bandages the Corpsman wrapped, more blood escaped. Bubbles rose from the red pool as the XO breathed air into Bends' chest.

As word spread about Bends, several began crying while others backed away, the sight too much to bear. Battock watched his crew. Casualties were a reality in war and this was a warship. If they couldn't take this, how could they perform in combat? He'd address that later. He dropped to his knees, taking Bends' hand. "If anyone knows a good prayer, now's a good time."

The Dolphin helicopter was nearly overhead before they noticed. "Kill the floodlights," Battock said. The chopper's spotlight would be sufficient.

The Dolphin crew discharged the cable's static on the water, then delivered the basket with surgical precision. Battock shielded Bends' face from the downdraft while McClintock and Senior strapped him in the basket. The swirling winds dried his eyes as the basket raised, blood dripping onto the deck. The white and orange helicopter disappeared, speeding towards the same hospitalto which it took the DC-10 crew.

Battock looked around, surprised to see LCDR Duncan in the background. He wiped his bloodied hands on his pants. His crew backed out of the way as he approached Duncan. "I thought I told you to stay in the wardroom."

"The entire crew was on deck, so I stayed. Sorry about your diver."

Battock turned his back on Duncan to address his crew. "All right everyone—listen up. You all did a great job tonight.

Unfortunately, Bends' fate is out of our hands. May God be with him. We still have a mission to do. Try to get some rest." He nudged McClintock as he walked away. "I'll be in my quarters, XO."

McClintock nodded. Battock came upon a young female sailor in shock, unable to leave. This was her first cruise. He remembered reading her file. She was from Muleshoe, Texas. Eighteen years old. Did she really know what she signed up for? "You have to let it go," he said. "With any luck Bends will pull through. Get some rest."

Her blonde hair blew in her face, sticking to her cheek. She hugged her thin frame, shivering in the breeze. "We just started going out."

"Like I said, get some rest."

Once the group dispersed, the XO found a bucket and scrub brush. He heard a noise; another pail appeared. Senior Chief dipped his brush into the bucket without saying a word. McClintock threw some water on the deck to rinse it clean. Either man could have assigned a work detail. The job took an hour, but when they were done, all traces of Bends were gone.

Captain Battock lay on his bunk, hounded by demons. His insomnia worse than ever, he struggled to collect his thoughts. He returned to the bridge and picked up the logbook.

> *<u>DC-10 mishap (continued.)</u> Following the first dive and under night conditions, two divers were dispatched to confirm the security of the buoys. Petty Officer Darby is recovering from a broken eardrum; Petty Officer Dyer was found impaled on the fuselage. He is unconscious, enroute to LA hospital. Dive operations to resume at 0600.*

He stared at his entry, repulsed by his lies. They would've expelled him from the Academy for it. He tossed his black government pen in the book and pushed it aside. He wished he could include his suspicions about Duncan and Ray, but lacking hard evidence, it could only lead to complications. Where was Duncan tonight? Did he dive or not? He had to send Bends and Darby down. A CO had to be willing to risk his crew to accomplish the mission—that's Navy doctrine. But he was accountable. Should it come to a Summary Court Martial, he'd make sure no one else shared the blame. He took a sip of stale coffee and placed a call to Third Fleet. Why'd he toss those goddam cigarettes?

Ignoring the choppy turbulence and noise, the Coast Guard aircrewman furiously pumped Bends' chest, but got no pulse. Hopefully the trauma team could breathe life into his body. His knees sent the helicopter's vibration directly to his brain. His helmet wasn't enough to ease the throbbing.

It took thirty minutes for the helicopter to arrive at Methodist Hospital. The doctor removed the cap from a long needle and shot adrenaline directly into Bends' heart. At the same time, a nurse inserted an IV into Bends' wrist. They whisked him into the emergency room, feverishly working for forty-five minutes. In the end, Petty Officer First Class Van Dyer was pronounced dead on arrival. His demise was passed in a fax to the Department of the Navy.

Global Captain John Armishaw marveled at the pilots flying the rescue and air ambulance helicopters. They arrived day and night, sometimes four in an hour. No sooner did they land, they were airborne again. He feared it may be the closest he'd come to flying again.

His ears tuned in an approaching helicopter. There was no mistaking the sound of the HH-65A Dolphin. He sat up in bed, curious whom the Coast Guard was bringing in this time of night. He waited until it took off before pushing his call button.

The nurse arrived within minutes, relieved he wasn't in distress. She inspected his dressings as she approached the bed. "What's the problem?" she asked.

John stared out the window. "I'm having a lot of pain. Is there anything you can give me?"

The nurse studied his face, his expression inconsistent with pain. "I'll check." She returned a few minutes later, arms folded across her chest. "I'm afraid you're at your limit, but I'll talk to the doctor. Would you like something to drink?"

"No thanks." His eyes went back to the window. "I don't suppose you know anything about that Coast Guard helicopter that just took off?"

She smiled. "Hon—helicopters come and go around the clock," she said. His eyes were troubled, glazed, his pain more emotional than physical. "Tell you what—if you promise to relax, I'll see what I can find out."

John nodded, trying to ignore the throbbing in his wired-up leg. How any blood made it to his toes was beyond him.

The nurse wasn't smiling when she returned. She'd lost some color. "They brought in a Navy diver investigating your plane crash." John strained to push himself up. She rushed to his side to settle him. "I'm not going to finish unless you lie down and relax." John fell back. "They said he was impaled on the aircraft. It was pretty bad."

John stared at his leg. "Impaled? Was there a hole—what?"

She pulled the covers to his chin as though he were a child. "Now don't get all worked up. You didn't cause it. I told you everything—don't make me wish I hadn't."

John closed his eyes and waited. She turned out the light and left. Before the door shut, he'd turned on his reading light and was dialing the Global safety manager's number. Bill Kessler was out, so he left a voice mail for him to call back.

The phone rang an hour later. "Thanks for returning my call, Bill," John said, wide-awake. "I know you're busy, but I just learned a Navy diver was killed investigating our mishap—impaled on the fuselage. You know anything about it?"

"No, this is the first I've heard about it. Who told you this?"

"I watched the Coast Guard bring him in so I asked the nurse. No one should've died out there."

"I'm sorry, John. I know it must be hard, but remember you didn't cause his death. I'll check with the FBI and NTSB to see what they know. If they haven't heard about it, I'm sure they'll want to know more. By the way, thanks for your mishap statement. Sounds like you guys had a helluva ride. Sorry you got hurt. I'm recommending you and your crew for the Outstanding Airmanship Award."

"Have they retrieved the data recorders yet?"

Kessler sighed. "Not as far as I know, but I'm sure that's a priority. Listen, John, I'll stop by when I get to LA. Rest assured Global's as concerned about your recovery as they are the mishap. We'll get to the bottom of this. Leave the investigating to us."

John cradled the phone and leaned against his pillow. His head throbbed against the pressure bandage. Sure, Global was concerned about him—but only 'cause he was costing them money. He considered calling Kevin, but it was past midnight in Oklahoma City. He'd call him first thing in the morning.

A young boy's voice answered politely. "Good morning," John said, fighting pain. "This is Captain Armishaw. I work with your dad. Is he home?"

"He's with Mommy."

An image came to mind, a reunion, Kevin wrapped in his wife's arms. Then another image. A young diver, impaled in their wreckage. Kevin needed to know. "If he's not asleep, I'd like to speak to him." He heard the phone bounce off the floor, footsteps, the boy calling, "Dad. Telephone." He smiled. The pleasures of fatherhood. Too bad he missed out.

"It's probably the NTSB," Kevin said to Nancy. "Hello?"

"Hey, Kev—John Armishaw."

"John!" He covered the phone, turning to Nancy. "It's my captain from LA." She nodded, listening intently.

"Listen, Kev—sorry to wake you, but I have some disturbing news."

Kevin closed his eyes. "What's up?"

"I watched a Coast Guard helicopter come in last night. They brought in a Navy diver who'd been investigating our wreck. They say he was impaled on the wreckage, but they couldn't give any details. Bill Kessler didn't know anything about it either. It's not right, Kev. No one should've gotten hurt. I don't know what's going on, but I figured you'd want to know." He heard Kevin's breathing. "Kevin?"

"I'm here," he said, rubbing his face.

"I'll be in the shower," Nancy said, slipping out of the bed.

He watched her go, getting his response ready for John. "Sorry to hear about the diver, but I'll be honest—I can't let it get to me this time. My family's suffered enough."

John wished he could let it go so easily. He'd never lost anyone before. "Sorry, Kev—I shouldn't have called. Don't know what I was thinking. Well, actually, I do. I thought maybe you'd know someone in the Navy who could find out what's going on. I'd sure like some answers."

Kevin listened to the shower running. He could speak freely now. Kessler's ignorance didn't surprise him, but he could tell John was troubled by the diver's death. How far was he willing to commit himself, though? "John, I don't know if you were ever in the service, but I was in the Marine Corps—not the Navy. There's a huge difference, but I'll see what I can do. I'll go through my old phone lists, who knows? You say Kessler's still in Oklahoma?"

"As far as I know."

Kevin chewed at a nail. "So what did he say when you told him about the diver?"

"Nothing—just that I wasn't responsible, that's all. I'm sure he made some inquiries after speaking to me, though."

"Well, I'm obviously out of the loop. No one's contacted me since I gave my statement. Doesn't seem anyone's too interested, does it?"

"Nope." John winced as more pain shot through his leg. "Hang on, okay?" He took the pill he'd been saving and set the glass aside. "I'm back. Anyway, it didn't sound like Bill. He could've been overwhelmed. Just my feeling."

"Has there been anything on the news about this?"

John pressed his water glass to his forehead, its chill a welcome relief. "Don't know—I haven't turned on the TV. Hang on—maybe there's something on the local news." He punched the remote, flipped through the channels. "Nope—I don't see anything. Listen, Kev, I know you're busy so I'll let you go. I'm obviously not going anywhere so call me if you hear anything, okay?"

"I will—and you do the same. Get well, John."

Kevin cradled the phone just as Nancy stepped out of the bathroom. She dropped her towel as she'd done many times before, but this time her smile was tentative, shaped by worry. "The phone call?"

"Yes." He patted the bed.

She slid under the sheets, but kept her distance. She waited.

"Anything you want to talk about?" she asked.

"Not really. It was John—my captain. He wants me to check around some Navy records."

"And you'll do it, of course."

"I'll give it a try anyway. I reminded him I was Marines—not Navy."

When the tap came at the door, Nancy slipped on her robe and tossed Kevin his pajama bottoms. Once he was dressed she opened the door and let the boys in, standing aside so the dog and boys could make their charge.

Kevin smiled around his worry, his arms open wide. He held his dog Brutus at arm's length while pulling the boys close. "Hi guys. Man, it's good to see you." He pulled them into a group to defend himself against Brutus' slobber.

When he looked across the open door, Nancy was gone.

The smell of pancakes filled the kitchen. He met Nancy's eyes. They needed to talk. Nancy set a plate in front of him. "The boys set the table," she said.

"That's great," he said, spreading some butter. "Thanks, guys."

After breakfast, he and Nancy sat on the sofa while the boys played. Jake was flipping through the TV channels when an update on their crash seared Kevin. "Wait, Jake." He grabbed the remote.

> "…when a Navy diver investigating the DC-10 crash perished. The USS Atlantis frogman apparently became entangled in the wreckage and suffocated after his oxygen ran out. He was flown to Methodist Hospital, but attempts to revive him failed. The diver's name is being—"

Kevin switched back to the cartoon station and handed the remote to Jake. "Sorry son—I thought it was something else." He placed his arm around Nancy, forcing a smile.

"Kevin?"

"Let's go upstairs," he said.

Nancy followed him into the bedroom, locking the door behind her. Her stare was cold. "How could you do that to the boys?"

"That report's pure bullshit, Nance. John told me that diver was impaled on the fuselage."

"Oh, God—like that helps." It was the inflight fire all over again. "Kevin—I supported you through twenty years in the Marine Corps, but this life is even more insane. I worry every time you leave on a trip. When you were talking to John, it was like you were still in that plane crash. I was listening at the door—heard everything you said. I'm sorry about the Navy diver, but why does that concern you? For God's sake, Kevin—don't be consumed by this. I won't go through it again."

He held her, needing her touch and embrace. He caught the scent of her perfume. He didn't cause that diver's death anymore than he did the crash. They moved to the bed. "You have every right to be angry with me, but please hear me out," he said. "John, Lonnie, and I need to know what brought our plane down. I admit I was obsessed the last time, but it truly appears there's been a cover-up on this incident. Think about it, Nance—why all the lies? What terrorist group would waste their time blowing up a cargo plane? Hell, our story barely made the news. This has to be about money. The question is—" Nancy squeezed his arm, pointing out the shadows under the bedroom door. He nodded, escorted her into the bathroom, and turned on the shower. "Thanks. I didn't see them. Anyway—it had to be a bomb, and whoever planted it didn't want any survivors. The FBI and NTSB's lack of interest makes me wonder if they're in on it. John implied Bill Kessler was acting strange, too." Nancy rolled her eyes. "Look—John called me at great cost, he's in massive pain. He saved my life, Nance—I owe him."

Nancy stared at him. "Personally, I think you've both lost it. If the government were trying to cover something up, wouldn't they send investigators just to avoid suspicion? What's next, Kevin? Accuse Global of planting a bomb to get rid of an old airplane and reduce the crew force?"

"No, but I can't believe so little's being done—especially when someone died." She turned away. "I promised John I'd call some folks. I'll be in the office."

"Fine, but remember what I said. I mean it, Kevin—I won't go through this again." She started to walk off, but stopped. "Do you enjoy being gone for days at a time, dragging a suitcase in the middle of the night, or is there something else you'd rather be doing?"

He stared at the portraits on the dresser, her beautiful smile shone in every photo. College. Nancy in her cheerleader outfit, him in his football uniform. Their wedding day, flowers in her hair under an arch of baby's breath and roses. The military ball, him in his tux, she in a black formal. Pictures of the boys. The perfect couple. How could their lives be taking such a turn? "Nance—you know I've got to fly. I can't imagine doing anything else."

She opened the bedroom door. "Come on, boys—your dad needs some time alone."

Kevin lay on the bed, drawn to the ceiling light. The frosted bulbs consumed him, reminding him of the smoke-filled cockpit at Whiteman AFB. Before long, everything else in the room disappeared. He didn't ask for this. Why should he quit his job? Had Nancy forgotten about the two pilots in his A-4 squadron who each ejected twice? They didn't quit. Two days later, they were begging to fly. It was no coincidence that both went on to become airline pilots just like him. He couldn't stop living because something might happen. More accountants died each year in car crashes than pilots in airliners.

He went downstairs to get a cup of coffee. He couldn't believe it when Nancy met him in the kitchen and wrapped her arms around his neck. Her eyes probed his. "Do what you have to—just get our lives back."

"I'll make those calls." He paused. "I know that cost you."

"Just get our lives back."

Kevin sifted through boxes of old paperwork, curious why he'd saved them. The only ones that mattered were his discharge orders. Who cares about old bombing and strafing scores or pilot qualifications? He tossed aside fifty pounds worth before finding the listing for the Inspector General at Camp Pendleton. The base was close to the mishap site; it seemed likely they'd know something.

Gunnery Sergeant Betty Pearson answered the phone. Gunny for short, her voice was hard, determined. She had a stack of paperwork that needed to be filed. Answering the phone was a distraction.

"Hello, Sergeant. This is Lieutenant Colonel Hamilton—retired Marine Corps. I'd like to speak to a legal officer, please."

"Sorry, Colonel, but I'm the only one in the office right now. If you'd like, I'll have one of the staff officers return your call. What does this concern?"

"The death of an active-duty serviceman." She took down his phone number and hung up. He went into the family room to join the others. "I sure don't miss the Corps," he said. "This woman—God, she was unflinching. I mean she—"

Nancy smiled. "Treated you like a retiree?"

"Yeah—I guess she did." He looked at the boys. "Who wants to play 'Go Fish'?"

Forty minutes later the phone rang. He ran to his office, eager for some news.

"Colonel Hamilton, this is Major Isabelle Garcia returning your call. I understand you were inquiring about a deceased service member. Was he or she a relative?"

"Ah, no. Actually, it concerns the Navy diver who died last night. He was investigating the DC-10 crash that I was—"

"This is about a sailor?" Her tone changed. "Colonel, we only handle Marines. I suggest you contact the Navy IG at the Coronado Amphib Base or the San Diego Navy Yard. Maybe they can help."

"Do you have their numbers handy?" He wrote them down and hung up.

Next, he called the Navy staff officer at the Coronado Amphibious Base and gave the same spiel. Without being a relative, it was unlikely he'd get any further with them, but he had nothing to lose.

LCDR Woolsey was about to leave for a staff meeting when Petty Officer Karen Ritowski asked if he'd take the call. He listened to Kevin's introduction, checking his watch several times. "Certainly I'm aware of the incident, Colonel, but if you're not a family member, I fail to see your connection."

"He died investigating our accident," he said. "I want to know if there's a connection between our accident and his death.

The Navy wouldn't send an unqualified diver down to investigate. Something's not right."

"Colonel, while I agree the diver's death was unfortunate, it's a bit presumptuous to imply his death was something other than an accident. Do you have any proof?"

"Not yet."

"I see. Well, I'm afraid there's nothing I can do for you. As for your mishap, I hope the investigative agencies have some answers before long. Good—"

"Wait. Did you hear anything I said? Something's not right—"

Woolsey sighed. "Colonel, I happened to be the officer who took your call, that's all. Other than that, I have no involvement in the case. Even if I had, I couldn't release any details until the JAG investigation's complete. Your best source is probably with your own company. Good day."

14

Skipper Battock lay in his bunk, thinking about Bends. He stared at the picture of his father in his Navy uniform, wondering how he had handled crew losses as skipper of a destroyer. He'd just drifted off to sleep when his alarm went off. He sat up, surprised he was still dressed. His mouth was stale, his eyes stung. He clambered out of bed, splashed water on his face, and slipped on a fresh uniform. It would be a long day.

The crew stood at Attention awaiting his orders. Battock studied their faces as he walked through the ranks. The personnel inspection took up valuable time, but he needed to know they were ready to resume their duties. They couldn't hide the uncertainty in their eyes.

"At Ease," he said. "Ladies and gentlemen, we've all had a long night. I regret to inform you that Petty Officer Dyer never regained consciousness. Bends was pronounced dead on arrival. I'd like to say a few words on his behalf before we resume dive operations." He paused to clear his throat. "Circumstances required that I order a second dive last night. I'm not going to discuss that decision. During that dive, Bends got tangled in some shrapnel and sustained mortal injuries. This tragedy reminds us that our mission entails great risks. Our first dive will be at 0630. I'm counting on you to perform your duties with the utmost professionalism. Two safety divers will accompany Lieutenant Commander Duncan and Petty Officer Ray at all times. Any questions?"

XO McClintock moved closer. "Bends' memorial service?" he asked.

Battock nodded. "Thanks, XO. There'll be a memorial service for Petty Officer Dyer at 1900 hours. I expect all available personnel to attend in the uniform of the day. I'll pass along information concerning a family memorial service as it becomes available. Ensign, take change and carry out the Plan of the Day."

The XO and Senior Chief followed him out the door, leaving Ensign Truman to dismiss the crew. Battock returned to the bridge and slumped in his chair, rubbing his fingers over his temples. His head pounded. He reached for his cigarettes, but remembered he'd thrown them away. He didn't believe Bends got stuck in the wreckage, but his crew didn't need to know that. Bends was a top-notch diver. He wasn't supposed to go near that wreckage—so what happened? And why didn't he abort with Darby? Something tapped his shoulder.

"Sorry to wake you, Skipper."

Battock blinked, embarrassed he'd fallen asleep on the bridge. "Glad you did, Senior. Guess I'm worse off than I thought."

Senior nodded. "Sir, you didn't say who you wanted diving this morning."

"Up to you, Senior. I sure hope they got more sleep than I did."

"Yes, sir."

Battock downed three aspirin with his coffee and stood over his XO. McClintock was reviewing the ship's log, too engrossed to notice. Battock kept his voice to a whisper. "I'm thinking you should assume command."

McClintock's head spun, surprised to see him. "Say again? Are you sick?"

"No, but my judgment's clouded. I had nothing to justify that dive. Nothing but a gut feeling. Make sure you tell that to the JAG—and don't hold back for my benefit. I accept full responsibility for what happened."

McClintock noticed Boatswain Angelina Martinez staring. "Care to step outside?"

Battock nodded and headed for the door. "We'll be outside if anyone needs us."

The overcast skies and damp air chilled them. They huddled in a corner. "Skipper, with all due respect, have you lost your mind? No—don't answer that." McClintock paused. "Sir, in my twenty-one years of enlisted and officer service, you're one of the best CO's I've worked for. Don't blame yourself for what happened. It was an accident—and it wouldn't have happened if Bends had followed the rules. He knew it's against Navy policy to dive alone, but he ignored it. Although he must've had a reason."

Battock sighed. "I meant what I said about the JAG."

Duncan was making final adjustments to his gear when he noticed Battock. He stopped what he was doing to extend his hand. "Ed—again, I'm sorry about your diver. I know how it feels to lose a member of your team." Battock said nothing. "Seriously. It's been a long time and I don't care to talk about it. Just know that I feel."

"Thanks," Battock said, watching his divers huddle in the inflatable.

Duncan grabbed the rest of his gear. "You guys ready?"

"Ready when you are, sir," Ray said.

"Then let's get wet." Duncan readied his mask and mouthpiece and flipped over the side, leaving a trail of bubbles.

Skully was the last one out. He'd insisted on being among the divers and willingly wore the MK-21 helmet he so despised. Bends was his roommate in dive school. He wanted to see the fuselage for himself. His descent was slower than the divers in SCUBA. "Skipper, this is Skully—do you read?"

Battock listened in the communications room. "Loud and clear, Skully."

"Roger—you're loud and clear, too. The visibility's much better today. The EOD divers have reached the hole—they're poking at something."

Battock leaned forward, studying Duncan's whiteboard map. "Skully—where are you relative to the hole?"

"Level with it—maybe twenty feet away," he said. He still felt like shark bait, but at least there was security in numbers. "Duncan and Ray just went inside—I can't see them anymore."

Battock jotted notes as he listened. Mostly it was doodling, but Duncan's map and the sonar scan gave him enough information to follow along. He wished he were diving with them, but too many years had gone by. "Keep me informed, Skully." He set his mike aside and looked at McClintock. "What do you think, XO?"

McClintock shrugged. "Does he have a camera with him? It might come in useful."

"Don't know," Battock said. His face flushed. Something about last night. Suddenly he rose to his feet, his eyes wide. "Didn't Bends have an infra-red camera?"

McClintock smiled. "I'm with you. Skipper. I'll check with Senior Chief."

Christ, if they found Bends' camera...

"Skipper. We're coming up," Skully said, struggling to reach the surface. "We're aborting the dive! Repeat—we're aborting!"

"We'll be ready, Skully." He switched over to the ship's intercom. "Boatswain—start the engines. Be ready to move on my command." Battock switched over to the ship's PA, thoughts of disaster on his mind. "Now hear this—this is the Skipper. Divers aborting. Repeat, divers aborting. Stand by to recover divers and secure equipment. Anchors aweigh. Prepare to evacuate once divers are aboard. Repeat—prepare to evacuate. That is all." He tossed the mike aside, fighting his way against a stream of sailors to get to the bridge. He didn't care much for Duncan, but Duncan wouldn't be aborting unless the divers were in imminent danger. Skully's voice echoed that. He took his seat, ready to give the command once he heard from Senior Chief. "Angelina, what's the status?"

Boatswain's Mate Martinez stared at the gauges. "Sir, the engines are running, anchors aweigh, maintaining steerage, standing by to move out."

"Good. Stand by for full speed."

Each second was molasses. Battock chewed his pen, craving a cigarette. The pen was a poor substitute, but it's all he had. No information was coming in. He needed to see what was going on. "Boatswain—stand by for my orders over the intercom. I'll be on deck."

"Aye, aye, Skipper."

Battock slid down the ladder on his hands and raced to the stern. They were just pulling the last diver aboard when he arrived. Every diver was accounted for, but their rapid ascent put their bodies at risk. Duncan waved his arm to get the ship moving, out of breath, unable to speak. Battock ran for the intercom. "Boatswain, this is the Skipper. Firewall it—maintain heading."

It wasn't a proper command, but Angelina knew what he meant. She forced the throttles to the stops and held on. The ship responded, churning the sea into foam.

Once *Atlantis* was underway, Duncan breathed easier. He shed his gear and unzipped his wet suit, ignoring the pounding in his chest. "A bomb," he said to Battock. "I tripped something—couldn't take chances. We'll need the remote to see what we're dealing with before we attempt to disarm it."

Battock pondered his report. "What do you mean you tripped—"

When the explosion came it was a sullen rumbling, then seawater was hurled into the air, showering metal fragments in a stink of explosives and dead fish. It loomed over them, the shock wave rocking them hard. Battock grabbed the railing just before a mountain of water broke over the stern. When the water sucked back, he saw Duncan clinging to the railing, his body over the side. He slid on his belly, grabbing Duncan's wrist.

Duncan scrambled aboard, spitting seawater as he tried to catch his breath. "Jesus Christ!"

It was the first time Battock saw fear in Duncan's eyes. Duncan made the right call. If he hadn't aborted when he did, they could've lost the ship. "You all right?"

"Yeah, I'm fine. Do we still have everyone?"

"Everyone's accounted for, Skipper," Senior Chief said.

Battock gripped Duncan's hand. "Good job, Dan. Senior—I'll be on the bridge."

Battock found his white-knuckled Boatswain holding a steady course for Hawaii. Had the situation not been so dire it might have been amusing. "Boatswain, all stop."

"Aye, aye, all stop." *Atlantis* drifted to a stop, maintaining steerage.

Battock stared at the settling sea, the debris, and gutted fish. If Duncan saw a bomb, why didn't he disarm it? Isn't that why EOD was there? And how could a bomb survive the ditching? For that matter, how could there be a tripwire on a cargo jet? Now they may never know what happened. He picked up the mike. "Now hear this. This is the Skipper. We will maintain present position and suspend dive operations until further notice. All hands on deck to recover debris. Use extreme caution—objects may be razor sharp. That is all." He looked at the radar. No surface contacts within twenty miles. *Where in the hell is everyone?* "Ensign—you have the watch. The XO and I will be in the com room."

McClintock and Battock had grown close during their short time together. He followed Battock into the high-tech room, crammed with electronic gear and dim lighting. Battock ordered the Signalman to take a break. McClintock moved closer, waiting for Battock to break the ice.

Battock's face was red. "Shit! I need a cigarette," he said.

"Sorry, Skipper—can't help you there. What's wrong?"

"Duncan. He said he hit a tripwire, but tripwires don't usually have timers. They're intended to keep intruders out—cause an immediate explosion. So why would there be a delay? To give us time to evacuate? Duncan must be behind this. And what a great cover. He destroys the wreck and comes out a hero." He looked at McClintock, nostrils flaring. "Confine Duncan and Ray to their quarters. Use armed guards if necessary, but keep 'em there 'til I can get them off my ship. They no longer have a mission. When the water clears, we'll use the remote camera to survey the damage. No one dives until I say so."

McClintock was about to comment but thought better of it. "Yes, sir."

"Oh, Brent—low profile it as best you can. No one else needs to know about Duncan." McClintock nodded and left. Battock picked up the secure line to speak to the Third Fleet Duty Captain.

Captain Giles sat in his chair at Third Fleet headquarters, pondering his retirement. Another year will make thirty. The desert might be a nice change from the sea. Golf every day. Visit the grandkids every couple of months. He looked around the office, phones lined up, duty logs in place, sailors and officers standing by for the next disaster. It would come. It always did. But hopefully not on his watch. The phone rang. "Captain Giles, Duty Officer."

"Sir, this is Lieutenant Commander Battock, Skipper of the salvage ship *Atlantis*. We're on station with the DC-10 wreck near the Channel Islands and just witnessed a powerful underwater eruption. One of our divers reported seeing a bomb and aborted the dive. *Atlantis* evacuated the area. Floating debris suggests at least part of the wreck was destroyed."

"How's your ship and crew, Commander?"

"Sir, *Atlantis* is fine—no injuries. We're remaining clear, but will scan the site with sonar and the remote camera within the next few hours."

"Where'd the explosion come from, Skipper?"

"I'm not sure, but I have reason to believe the EOD divers I was forced to bring aboard had something to do with it. Sir, I'm requesting the FBI come aboard *Atlantis*. As a civil aircraft, this would fall under their jurisdiction. It wasn't an accident."

Giles tossed his pen down. He watched the red second hand rotate around the oversized dial. Bad timing. Forty-three minutes and he would've been off duty. "Let me get this straight," he said. "You're saying Navy divers sabotaged your operation? Do you have anything to support that claim, or is this a gut feeling?"

"Sir, as absurd as it may sound, I've had problems with Lieutenant Commander Duncan since he came aboard. I don't trust him or Petty Officer Ray. I assure you I wouldn't be asking for your assistance if I didn't believe they were responsible. They were the only ones to enter the aircraft, and the ones who aborted the dive. Duncan said he saw a bomb—hit a tripwire. I don't know why they'd destroy a wrecked civil aircraft, but that time bomb provided them with a perfect alibi. I have Duncan and Ray confined to quarters and want them off my ship as soon as possible. I'm hoping the FBI can give us some answers. Sir—will you help me?"

Captain Giles hesitated. He had no choice but to honor Battock's request. He owed him that much, CO to CO. "For your sake, Commander, I hope you find something to back up these allegations. I'll see what I can do. In the meantime, keep this to yourself and stay out of harm's way. I'll call when I know something."

"Thank you, sir."

Giles took a moment to make a logbook entry, keeping the details to a minimum. He thumbed through his reference book and found the number for the FBI.

Battock's body trembled from withdrawals. He saw his career going down the shitter; the perfect start to a dreary day. He stared at the black desk phone, anticipating its ring. Probably recycled from a decommissioned carrier. Some things never changed. He downed the last of his coffee. Declaring mistrust for a fellow officer is a serious infraction, but there was no turning back. He stepped outside and leaned over the railing. Some of his crew were sorting through the metallic fragments and objects. No question it was from the aircraft, but why was it destroyed?

15

Hearing the doorbell, Brutus charged the front door while the boys raced him. Brutus won. Kevin set his newspaper aside and got to his feet. "Don't open the door," he said, fearing it was a reporter. Before he got to the hallway, Jake had the door open. Brutus bared his teeth, blocking the entry. A man in a brown suit was eyeing their Doberman, his body stiff. "Brutus, heel." Kevin said. Brutus backed up to him, growling at the suit. "Jake, take Brutus in the other room. I'll see what this gentleman wants." He waited until the boys left. "Sorry about that," he said, glancing at the man's badge. "What can I do for you?"

"Paul Sterling, FBI. Are you Kevin Hamilton?" Kevin nodded. "May I have a word with you, sir?"

Kevin stepped outside, pulling on the door so the others wouldn't hear. Before it shut, something grabbed it. Kevin turned around, surprised to see his wife. "Oh, hi Nance. This is Paul Sterling. He's with the FBI."

She extended her hand. "Hello."

They both looked at Sterling for an explanation. He hesitated. "Mrs. Hamilton, if you don't mind, I'd like to speak to Mr. Hamilton alone. Could you give us a minute?"

Kevin reached for her hand and pulled her next to him. "I'd like her to stay."

"Very well. Mr. Hamilton, I'd like you to come downtown to discuss the DC-10 crash. The wreckage blew up—we need some answers."

Kevin's smile faded. "Give me a minute," he said, escorting Nancy inside.

"I'll be in the car," Sterling said, walking to his Chrysler.

Kevin spoke before Nancy had a chance. "A diver dies and now the wreck blows up? Now do you believe me?" Nancy's mouth opened, but no words came. "Remember what you said. Do whatever it takes. Doesn't look like I have a choice. I'll call when I know something."

Nancy held the door open. The boys crept up, watching their dad leave without saying good-bye. How long this time?

Kevin waved to them as Sterling backed out of the driveway. "Brutus may look intimidating, but he's really a sissy," he said. "Hope he didn't scare you."

"I don't scare easily," Sterling said.

"So, what about this explosion?"

Sterling scanned his mirrors. "Special Agent Pentaglia will fill you in. He flew in from LA to talk to you."

"You're kidding," Kevin said, staring at Sterling. "I'm flattered, but why would anyone come that far to see me? Hasn't he heard of a phone—e-mail?" Sterling didn't answer. "Does Pentaglia think I had something to do with the bomb?

"Like I said, he'll fill you in. I can't speak for him."

Kevin watched a vortex of dust and debris cross their path. Oklahoma was flat and dry. It sure as hell wasn't any place he'd call home. He missed the trees, the ocean.

Sterling's silence made time stand still. Since they were going to the FBI office, Kevin probed Sterling for his opinion on the Oklahoma City bombing. "I'm curious, Paul—how'd you feel when McVeigh gave up his appeals and they finally executed him? Did it give you a sense of justice? Closure?"

Sterling's eyes were too bright. "Lethal injection was too easy," he said. "They should've hung him from the highest tree near the site. But then, my opinion's never mattered much."

Sterling stopped talking, waiting for the security gate to open. He pulled inside and waited for the steel gate to close. A side door led to a confining concrete staircase. Their steps echoed as they ascended. The security guard matched Kevin's picture to his face and wrote down the information from his driver's license. Kevin attached the visitor's pass to his coat pocket and followed Sterling.

"Special Agent Pentaglia will be here shortly," Sterling said, holding open an office door.

Kevin was alone in an empty conference room. He stared into one of the several portholes small enough for surveillance cameras. He waited.

Pentaglia watched the video monitor from an adjoining room. Usually, visitors made smart aleck comments to the cameras. It was apparent it would be best to be up front with Kevin Hamilton. "Keep it rolling," he said to the other agent.

Pentaglia entered through a door on the opposite side of the room. "Good morning, Mr. Hamilton."

"Morning." Kevin studied the agent. Pentaglia probably played sports, stayed in shape. His five o'clock shadow shaded narrow cheeks. Brown eyes probed.

"Thanks for coming." Pentaglia said. "Coffee?"

"No thanks."

Pentaglia rocked back in his chair. "I'm sure you're wondering why you're here." Kevin nodded. "Did Paul tell you about the explosion this morning?"

"He mentioned it. Pretty strange."

"Well, the CO from the salvage ship requested our help with that. I imagine this'll get pretty complicated." Kevin nodded again. "What's your involvement in this mess, Mr. Hamilton?"

Kevin shrugged. "I was a crewmember on the plane, we had a rapid decompression, ditched, and survived. Then I came home. I hope you didn't fly all this way to hear that."

Pentaglia smiled. "How about starting from the beginning?"

Kevin retold his story. "I'm curious—why didn't you visit me in the hospital like the NTSB? Why the sudden interest? Is it because the story made bigger headlines after the Navy lost a diver or what? Why are you here?"

"Easy, Kevin," Pentaglia said. "May I call you Kevin? Call me Mike. Anyway, you didn't see us, but we were involved the moment your plane went down—before *Atlantis'* CO requested our help—before the explosion. Of course, that's not why I'm here. What caught my attention is your personal pursuit in this matter."

Kevin's eyes widened. "Pardon me?"

"You know—all those phone calls you've been making. In particular, the one you made to that Navy JAG officer in Coronado. Commander Woolsey, I believe."

Kevin leaned forward. "Isn't that an invasion of privacy?" Brown eyes probed. "Listen, Mike—I've got every right to conduct my own investigation. I promised a friend I'd find some answers and I'm not one to break promises."

"Hey—relax, Kevin. Don't be so defensive. Woolsey felt a bit threatened, that's all. Said you knew more about the salvage operation than he did. You survived—it's over for you. Why's this thing so important?"

Kevin flashed his family photo. "Here's three reasons," he said. "Mike, my family and I have been through hell. My first flight with Global was an inflight fire thanks to your DNA machine, and I didn't care much for ditching on my last flight. I can't believe a call from Woolsey would bring you here from LA, so do me a favor and cut the crap, okay? I have a lot of stuff to do at home."

Pentaglia smiled. "It's a shame you can't express your feelings, Kevin. Would you feel better if I told you some FBI agents are about to board the salvage ship?" Kevin raised a brow. "That's right. As I said, *Atlantis'* Skipper shares your suspicions. He thinks the underwater demolition experts he took aboard planted that bomb. So now I've leveled with you, how about telling me the rest of your story?"

Kevin studied the man across from him. How would he use the information? Was this entrapment? "I already gave my statement."

"I know. I've read it, but did you have any unexpected events? You know—unusual cargo? Delays? Come on, Kevin, tell me what you know. It's off the record."

"But you're taping, right?"

Mike shrugged.

"Did you know about our maintenance delay in LA?" Mike shook his head. Kevin told him about the damaged wing flap and their stay at the hotel. "It took about four hours to fix it, but the plane flew fine. Forty minutes later we were drowning."

Mike stared. "Let's find a map."

Kevin followed him into a nearby room that had various maps of the world stapled to the walls. Encrypted documents crowded a desk.

"Okay, here's the Pacific Ocean and you were going to Anchorage, so if you'd taken off on time, where would you have been four hours later?"

"Mike, I'm really not qualified to answer that. I'm responsible for the aircraft's systems, not navigation. You'd be better off asking one of the pilots."

Mike sighed. "Kevin, work with me, all right? Trust me—I'm on your side. If I weren't, I'd have you under surveillance instead of talking to you. Now, assuming there was a time bomb on board and you took off as scheduled, where would you have been four hours into the flight?"

Kevin paced off four five-hundred mile intervals and placed his finger off the Canadian coast, south of Alaska. "We were flying an ocean route so we would've been here," he said. "Damn. If we'd been on time, we would've disappeared without a trace."

"Just as I thought. We're hoping the load manifest will give us a motive or link. We're still going to recover the wreck, though. Clues don't vanish easily."

"What about that Navy diver? You think his death was an accident?"

"Off the record? No."

Kevin took a seat, taking in the surroundings. Fax machines, computer terminals, phone lines, portable radios, and maps crowded what looked like a tactical planning room. He speculated on what types of missions were planned here. "How'd the diver die? I mean, I heard he was impaled, but on what? How?"

"There's a hole in the fuselage. Right side. That's how we know it was a bomb."

"I knew it," Kevin said, slapping a fist to his palm. "No one believed me. My captain kept insisting—" He stopped mid-sentence, not wanting to drag John into this. "I still don't get why you need me. Where do I fit in?"

"Like I said, I want to know why you're so interested in the investigation. Kevin, I understand your frustration and anger, but I've never known anyone to go to the extremes you have."

"I already explained my motive. I haven't trusted investigators since my last mishap. Besides, I did aircraft investigations in the Marine Corps. I know what it's like."

"I see. Oh, by the way, Global's doing an excellent job of tracing your plane's cargo. Did you ever see the load manifest?"

"No, but there's no reason to. All we ever see is the Dangerous Goods declaration, and that's only because I have to inspect the Haz can to make sure it's loaded right. Sometimes they stack stuff to the ceiling, but that wasn't the case with this flight."

"I don't envy you," Mike said. "Your DG situation's kind of like us breaking down a door, not knowing what's on the other side." He stared at the map again. "You do realize this wasn't some senseless act of violence? Someone had a motive."

"I agree," he said, keeping his money theory to himself. "You think it's a conspiracy?"

"No." Mike smiled, reaching for Kevin's hand. "Well, Kevin, I've taken enough of your time. Thanks for coming down." He held the door open and looked down the hall. "Hey, Paul? Would you mind taking Mr. Hamilton home?" As Sterling headed their way, he handed Kevin his business card. "If you think of anything else, call me—day or night. My number's on the card."

Kevin slid the card into his pocket without looking at it. He couldn't believe the interview ended so abruptly—and right after he mentioned conspiracy. He followed Sterling down the hall, crunching the new data with one goal: watching out for himself, Nancy, and the kids.

Kevin and Nancy were sitting at the kitchen table having breakfast. It had been two days and Pentaglia hadn't called. Their breakfast was quiet, both being polite, each thinking about the investigation.

Jake jumped up to answer the phone. "Dad. It's a guy from schedules."

Kevin sighed. "This should be interesting. Be right back." He patted Nancy's hand and took the call in his office.

"Second Officer Hamilton?" the man said in a hurried voice. "This is Bill Martin—how you doin'?"

Kevin felt a surge go through his body. Bill Martin wasn't a scheduler—he was his flight manager. "Fine, Bill. What can I do for you?"

"To be honest, we're in a bind. Normally I don't get involved in this sort of thing, but Skeds says you're the only one who can take this flight. They asked me to call and see if you'd take a draft trip—assuming you're up for it."

"I dunno—tell me more."

"It shows in fourteen hours and everyone in the chain's cleared you to fly, but I need to know how you feel about flying so soon. Tell me the truth—no pressure to fly."

"I'm fine," Kevin said, flattered by his sudden importance, mulling over the possibilities of his first draft trip. Time-and-a-half pay would come in handy; make up for a trip he'd dropped. Nancy walked in the office. She listened as he read it back for her benefit. "Just to confirm, it shows in fourteen hours, fly to LA, layover twenty-four hours, fly to Newark, layover for thirteen, then home." He covered the mouthpiece. "I'll be gone less than three days and pick up eleven hundred bucks. What do you say, Nance?" Nancy nodded approval. "Sure, Bill—I'll take it."

"Great. Your pairing's X331. I'll notify Skeds."

Kevin cradled the phone. Nancy saw his unease. She sat in his lap, wrapping her arms around his neck, giving him her warmth. He hugged her. "We still have the whole day ahead of us," he said. "No reason to change our plans."

"I'll tell the boys."

He enjoyed a day of fishing with his sons while Nancy visited friends. The sun took its toll, but a brief nap and shower revived him. He looked forward to getting airborne. It felt like he and Nancy were a team again. Her understanding how important this was even made the drive to work enjoyable. Only the deserted streets reminded him it was the middle of the night.

Kevin wasted no time in the crew lounge. After checking in on the computer, he made a copy of the flight release, grabbed a pot of coffee, and headed for the crew bus. The ramp was alive with tugs pulling trains of containers, loaders reloading, handlers sliding demis through cargo doors, fuel and maintenance trucks cruising by. Same chaos, different day. He felt fine. When he reached the second level, he froze. His bags were slipping, feet wouldn't move, heart pounded, people were staring. He grabbed the railing and forced his way into the plane, sweat beading from his brow.

He set his bag aside, light-headed, terrified. He opened the cockpit door and saw Lonnie leaning over the console, struggling to free John. After rubbing his eyes, they were gone. Dear God. How could he do his job? There were no replacements; Bill Martin said so. If he backed out now, Global would lose the flight and he'd be grounded for a psychiatric evaluation. No choice but to tough it out.

He took his seat and reviewed the maintenance log. It was difficult to concentrate; he couldn't recall what he'd just read. He was going through the motions, but nothing was registering. A tap on the door startled him. He opened the door.

"How ya doin' this morning?" the mechanic asked, unusually cheerful considering the late hour. He smiled, handing Kevin the fueling receipt, the smell of jet fuel consuming his clothes.

Kevin managed a smile. "Just fine. How about yourself?"

"Couldn't be better. It's clear, warm, the plane's been flying good, and I haven't had a late push all evening. From the looks of things, you might even get out early."

"Super," he said, checking over the receipt.

"Well, I'll get outta your way. Have a good flight. Holler if ya need anything."

"Thanks." Kevin pulled the door shut and mopped his brow. Hopefully the mech thought it was from the heat. The mechanic's right—it is a good night to fly. He began to relax. He completed his cockpit setup with renewed confidence and went outside to do the walk-around. The captain and first officer were climbing the stairs as he inspected the left engine.

Kevin returned to the cockpit and introduced himself. The captain leaned over his seat to shake his hand. "Terry Betterman," he said in a heavy southern drawl. "This here's Sam Drago. So this is a draft trip for you, eh?" Kevin nodded, unsure of the connotation. "Looks like the drinks are on you," Betterman said, hacking with a disturbing cough. "How's the jet?"

"No gripes, the coffee and catering are on board, and they're about to close the cargo door. I'm told we can expect an early push."

"Can't git much bedder'n that. C'mon, Sam—let's git our rears in gear so we can git outta here."

Kevin took his seat. As predicted, they pushed early. He set his fuel and hydraulic pumps and called ready for start. All systems were normal.

Betterman recited nonstop jokes while he taxied the plane. It was against company policy, but he was too close to retirement. Following each punch line, he laughed, regardless of his crew's reaction. It wasn't that the jokes were crude or that he'd heard them before, but Kevin couldn't help thinking how the accident investigators would react when they reviewed the Cockpit Voice Recorder. Ironically, once Betterman set the parking brake and it was okay to talk, he clammed up. An endless stream of white lights from arriving aircraft kept them grounded.

Ten minutes later, there was a break in the traffic and GlobeEx 3702 was cleared onto the runway, awaiting final takeoff clearance. When cleared for takeoff, Betterman advanced the throttle levers. Kevin scanned his panel, then focused on the forward engine instruments. The nose pitched up twenty degrees, leaving the white and green airport lights below, the full moon reflecting in the irrigated fields.

The line of thunderstorms was visible before they appeared on radar. Floating like giant mushrooms, they changed color as lightning illuminated them. Few would ever witness such majestic beauty. Kevin wished his kids could see it. Betterman picked a heading that would keep them clear.

When they leveled at their cruising altitude, Kevin got up to retrieve their catering. He noticed a foul odor as he bent over the icebox, and it wasn't the catering. Pilots joked about things going bump in the night, but after all he'd been through, he no longer found it amusing. He set their lunch boxes on the courier seat and turned on the galley lights. Against his better judgment, he unzipped the smoke curtain and sniffed the air, but found nothing out of the ordinary. The pilots were expecting their meals; everything looked fine. He turned out the lights and headed back to the cockpit.

The smell intensified when he neared the lavatory. He set the meals aside and opened the door, gagging from the stench. He slammed the door, angered he'd let an improperly serviced toilet get to him. He passed the catering forward and returned to the lav, knowing that no one could use it in its present condition. He should've caught it on his preflight. Not only did the plane bake in the sun all day, someone had closed the air vent. He held his breath, opened the vent, and poured several bottles of water down the drain, hoping to dilute the residue. He slammed the door and returned to his seat.

"Everythang okay?" Betterman asked, chewing on his sandwich.

"Yeah, but don't use the head unless you have to."

Betterman nodded, staring at his empty coffee cup. "I was about to send Sam back to look for ya."

"I'll make sure it gets serviced in LA," Kevin said.
Betterman nodded.

The first hint of sunshine appeared in the side windows. They'd been flying all night and looked forward to getting to the hotel. At thirty-five thousand feet, the sun rose quickly, its brilliant colors a curse. Like vampires, nightfliers needed to be asleep before the sun came up. The long days of summer made that difficult.

When they landed in LA, Kevin was exhausted. His fishing expedition and anxiety had taken their toll. He needed rest, and waiting for the hotel van only added to his frustration.

The van showed ten minutes later. The driver jumped out, nervously loading their bags. "I'm sorry," he said. "I had to get gas."

Betterman rested his hand on the man's shoulder. "That's all right. I would've been real ticked if we'd run out on the way to the hotel."

16

Kevin awakened to the maid's vacuum cleaner four hours after getting to bed. "Do Not Disturb" signs attracted housekeepers like moths to light. He pulled the pillows over his head and burrowed under the covers.

He awoke an hour later, unable to sleep any longer. He turned on the light and found Methodist Hospital in the White Pages. John was awake when they transferred his call. "Hey, John—it's Kevin. I'm in town and thought I'd stop by. You gonna be around a while?"

"Oh, sorry, Kev—I'm doing the Ironman competition this afternoon. You on a layover?"

"Of course. You don't think I'd pay to see you, do you?" He heard Armishaw laugh. "I'm on draft—their last hope, if you can believe that."

"Man, I can't believe you're flying already. They must've been desperate. So, when can you come over?"

"I'll be there around one—unless that would interrupt your soap opera."

"Real funny—see you at one."

Kevin pushed John's door open, happy to be a visitor instead of a patient. "Hey, Dude—good to see you."

"Hi, Kev. Thanks for coming, man."

John's wounds looked the same. Kevin positioned himself to avoid looking at his protruding rods. He spent the next hour filling him in.

John's eyes narrowed. "What do you mean the wreck blew up?"

"It gets worse. Pentaglia told me the diver was impaled on a hole. So far the Navy's managed to keep both incidents from the media and no one's asking questions. It wasn't the flap, John. It was a time bomb."

John rolled his head on his pillow. "Makes sense, but I still can't believe it."

"I know." Kevin struggled to keep his eyes open. "John, I've got to make some calls and take a nap. I wish I could stay longer."

"No sweat. Oh—thanks for the magazines, Kev. I really appreciated it. Stay in touch." Kevin nodded and got up to leave. "Oh, Kev? I look forward to flying with you again."

Kevin smiled. "See you later." He pulled the door shut.

A chill came over LCDR Woolsey at the mention of Kevin Hamilton's name. Did he know he'd called the FBI? He picked up the phone. "Colonel Hamilton, I'm afraid I can't talk right now. I'm on my way out the door."

"Hold on, Woolsey. Why'd you have the FBI call me in? Thanks to you, instead of spending time with my family I had a meeting with Special Agent Pentaglia. Of course, he already knew I had nothing to do with the mishap."

Woolsey relaxed. "Sorry. I thought I was doing the right thing. Guess I overreacted."

"Maybe. Then again, I might've done the same thing. Anyway, no hard feelings. So, I hear you were assigned the JAG for that Navy diver. How's it going? You know he was impaled on a hole, don't you? What was his name again?"

Woolsey stared at Dyer's file in his "IN" basket. "Surely you don't expect me to provide any details, do you?"

Kevin reeled in his line to add more bait. "Not really, but I figured since his name's been released, you'd at least confirm the spelling. I heard it on this morning's news." The bait dangled.

"Well, I suppose I could do that," he said, opening the file "His name was Van Dyer—DYER. Petty Officer First Class. He was assigned to the salvage ship, *USS Atlantis*. It's a shame. It was their shakedown cruise."

"*Atlantis* was on her shakedown cruise? That's incredible—not that it's anything like ditching a DC-10 or having the wreckage blow up."

"You know about the explosion?"

A smile came over Kevin's face. "That's right. Pentaglia told me."

"Who else knows?"

"Beats me. Any idea why someone would want to destroy the wreckage?"

"Nope, but then it's not my concern either. My only involvement's with Dyer. Anything beyond that is a whole new JAG investigation. I will say the *Atlantis* crew owes their lives to those EOD divers though. If they hadn't noticed the explosives, we might've lost a ship, too."

"Perhaps—unless EOD planted the bomb."

Woolsey sighed. "Colonel, this conversation's gone far enough. I won't tolerate such unfounded accusations."

"I understand, but what if those divers weren't really Navy? What if they were posing as Navy divers so they could destroy the evidence?"

"Colonel, I—"

"Commander Woolsey—my plane blew up from a time bomb and now the wreckage is destroyed. Don't you think there's a possibility that those EOD divers aren't who they claim to be? Even *Atlantis's* skipper has suspicions. Think about it—for all we know they could be FBI or CIA. Who else could get them in like that?"

"That's enough," Woolsey said. "Good day, Colonel—and don't call back." He slammed the phone down, fearful he'd compromised the investigation. He listed Kevin as a witness in Dyer's JAG investigation in case someone traced his phone conversations. He didn't like it, but Kevin's speculation had merit. He went into the reception area and approached his chief yeoman. "Chief, I need background checks on PO Dyer, LCDR Duncan, PO Ray, and retired Marine Lt Col Kevin Hamilton." The Chief took the list, staring at him. "Don't ask," Woolsey said.

77

The CH-46 Sea Knight blended into the haze as it lifted off from North Island Naval Air Station. The three FBI agents looked out of place in the helo's webbed seats in their pleated slacks, loafers, and navy blue windbreakers. Their helmets reduced the thunder from Sea Knight's twin rotors. Conversation was impossible. While their bodies vibrated, they watched the coastline from a thousand feet.

The helo lifted off two and a half hours after Battock's conversation with Captain Giles. Since *Atlantis* lacked a helo pad, they would be lowered via the jungle penetrator, an obscene looking device that bore a strong resemblance to an oversized fishing lure. It was designed for the Vietnam jungle, but proved to be a universal rescue device. The agents stared it, each wondering who'd be first.

An hour into the flight the pilot pointed out *Atlantis* while the co-pilot established communications. "*Atlantis*, November Juliet Two One Three, five south for pickup."

Ensign Truman watched through his binoculars. "Roger Two One Three, we have visual. Winds are light from the west. Request you approach from the stern; two to evacuate."

"Roger, *Atlantis*, we have two requesting to come aboard."

Ensign Truman looked at his skipper. Battock nodded, his arms folded across his chest. "Very well."

The pilot went into a hover two thousand feet aft, two hundred feet above the waves while the aircrewman opened the helo's door and swung the hoist. The crewman unfolded two pegs and waved the agents forward. Two of the agents looked at each other, then approached. They sat down. The crewman double-checked their security strap and connections and swung them overboard. Their pants tightened around the crotch, their legs dangled over a frenzy of concentric circles. The downdraft whipped at their windbreakers as they huddled against the device. One hundred feet above the water, they felt the downdraft change as the pilot maneuvered them over *Atlantis*. Someone was grabbing their legs. Seconds later, a sailor unstrapped them. He took their helmets and passed them to Duncan and Ray.

Duncan and Ray frequently used the penetrator and kept specially equipped torso harnesses for such occasions. They connected their quick-clips to the device and slung their bags over their shoulders. Duncan saluted Battock as the penetrator lifted off.

EOD's mission was over, they were off the ship, life was good. The aircrewman swung them aboard and closed the door. As Duncan slipped off his torso harness, he noticed the man flashing a badge. The agent stood between Duncan and Ray. "Special Agent Kidman, FBI," he said, shouting over the noise. "I'm escorting you to North Island. You have any weapons?" Duncan and Ray shook their heads. "What's in your bags?"

"Diving equipment, clothes," Duncan said.

Every diver carried a knife. Kidman kicked their bags aside, making sure no one moved. "We'll talk later."

Back on *Atlantis*, XO McClintock escorted the agents to the bridge. Skipper Battock was busy making an entry in the ship's log. "Sir?"

Battock turned. "Gentlemen—welcome aboard," he said. "I'm Ed Battock, CO of *Atlantis*." He sized up the trim men with medium builds and short hair. They might have passed for sailors had they not had FBI in twelve inch letters across their backs.

"I'm Special Agent Jim Barnes and this is Special Agent Greg Landis. Greg's the explosives expert. What happened this morning?"

"You don't waste time, do you?"

Barnes shook his head. "Don't want the trail to get cold."

"I see. Well, everything's in the logbook," Battock said, handing it over. "We'll discuss it after you've both read it. You hungry?"

Barnes steadied himself as a swell rolled the ship. "Maybe some coffee," he said.

"Sure. Follow me and watch your knees. Those knee-knockers are hell on shins."

Barnes and Landis looked at each other.

Battock led them through a tunnel of watertight doors to the officer's mess. The small room sat to the side of the mess hall. Barnes noted the vinyl seats and green tiled floors. "You sure you're not hungry?" Battock asked, passing them some coffee. "Chubby's a great cook. He can fix you a slider—I mean burger—in no time."

Barnes grabbed his cup as the ship rolled the other way. His face grew pale, skin clammy. "Ah—maybe later." He delved into the logbook entries with Landis looking over his shoulder.

"Be right back." Battock returned with a hamburger patty, scrambled eggs, fries, and two biscuits smothered in gravy and stuffed a fork full in his mouth. "Don't mind me," he said. "This operation's been a disaster from the start. We left late 'cause I had to wait on those two EOD divers. Then I lose a diver and the wreckage within the first twelve hours. Duncan and Ray were on scene both times. I can't prove it, but I'm sure they planted that bomb. Unfortunately, they got away."

Barnes smiled for the first time. "We left an agent aboard the chopper." Battock stopped his fork mid-stroke. "They're being escorted to North Island; Captain Giles from Third Fleet is waiting.

If anything suggests they had something to do with the explosion or Dyer's death, they'll be placed under arrest and taken downtown."

Battock nodded. "That's great, but the wreck's destroyed. How do you expect to prove anything?"

"There's always evidence," Landis said. "In this case, we may have to dig a little harder, but we'll find something. Do you have a remote camera on board? We can tell a lot from the debris pattern. I'd also like to inspect any recovered material. My equipment's supposed to arrive on a later flight. They wanted us here ASAP."

"Anything you need and we have, you're welcome to it. I cleared out a stateroom for you."

"Thanks. Have you talked to anyone from the NTSB?"

Battock attacked his biscuits and gravy. "As I told Captain Giles, nothing about this mission makes sense. Normally we'd have a fleet of ships swarming over the site with NTSB inspectors, but we're all alone. It's one thing to be first on scene, but there's not even a Cutter to help out. You're the first outsiders to get involved."

"Others are on the way," Landis said. "I know for a fact that at least ten NTSB members are gathering data in LA, talking to air traffic controllers, going over audio and radar tapes, waiting to analyze the Cockpit Voice Recorder and Flight Data Recorder. Retrieving those recorders is a top priority."

Battock pushed his empty plate aside. "You actually think they survived?"

"Maybe. Then again, I haven't seen the wreckage. Skipper, I know things haven't gone the way you wanted, but at least you got EOD off your ship."

"My diver was murdered."

"We don't know that," Barnes said.

Battock shook his head. "Well, I'm glad you're here. Thanks for coming. We were preparing to side-scan the crash site when you arrived. I figure if anything else were going to go off, it would've exploded by now. Any objections?" Landis shook his head. "It shouldn't take more than an hour." Battock got up. "Feel free to sort through the aircraft fragments on the aft deck. I'll be on the bridge. If you don't mind, bring me my logbook when you're done."

Atlantis plunged over the swells during her grid search. The sea was rough, white caps spraying the deck. Agent Landis was struggling to find his sea legs. He made his way aft and found the metal fragments under a tarp. He knew from the green primer paint they were from the DC-10. He sorted the pieces, smelling and inspecting each one. No doubt they were damaged from a secondary explosion.

Landis felt *Atlantis* lose way and mush down, then she was drifting. He stopped what he was doing and moved to the rail. Sailors were lowering something over the side.

The XO noticed him watching. He approached, holding onto the railing as he walked. "It's the remote camera," McClintock said. "You're welcome to join us in the control room if you want to see. The Skipper and Agent Barnes are already there."

"Sure—that would be great." Landis clung to a metal fragment from the DC-10 and followed McClintock.

The remote camera made several passes over the wreckage. Several sections survived intact. The cockpit had moved twenty yards south of its first position. The main fuselage had disintegrated.

Battock and Landis compared the camera's live transmission to the diagrams Skully and Duncan gave him. "Can you sweep this area?" Barnes asked, pointing to an area of small pieces. The robot moved in. "Perfect. These markings are definitely fuselage. Wow—look at all those cardboard boxes."

"Yeah. How did they manage to survive?" Battock asked.

"Well, they're all outside the twenty-foot crater. The explosion must've blown their containers apart and they spilled out."

Landis moved closer to the monitor. "There's no question the underwater explosion was more powerful than the first one," he said. "Do you have a vacuum? I'd like to retrieve the shrapnel. It'll help determine the source and strength of the bomb."

"Sure," Battock said. "But how much do you want to bring up?"

"Let's get these first," he said, circling an area with his finger. "You've already completed a basic survey—the NTSB won't mind. You see how the crater's deeper on this side?" Battock nodded. "That means the blast occurred on the right side of the fuselage. Assuming the first bomb was hidden inside a container, a seventy-pound charge might leave a ten-foot hole in a pressurized fuselage, but in order to overcome the pressure and energy-absorbing tendencies of seawater, it would require at least twice that to disintegrate the wreckage like this. Theoretically some unexploded ordnance could've survived the ditching, but it's more likely a second bomb was planted later."

"Precisely," Battock said. "That's why I say Duncan and Ray did it. They were the only ones to go inside the fuselage."

Landis noticed the tech listening in. He moved closer to Battock. "Skipper, we need facts, not speculation. By your own admission Duncan saved your ship, so let's not jump to conclusions. Even in a military court of law, everyone's innocent until proven guilty. Hopefully, I'll know more after I analyze the pieces."

Battock nodded. "You're right. Sorry. Any reason why we can't resume dive operations?"

"That's your decision, but I don't see how anything else could've survived."

"Then I'll get my divers ready. You'll have your debris within the hour."

"Now hear this. Quarters in five minutes. Repeat, Quarters in five minutes. That is all."

Agents Landis and Barnes watched sailors scrambling to form ranks. They stood to the side as Battock addressed the crew. "Special Agent Barnes and Special Agent Landis are here to determine why the wreckage exploded. We've surveyed the site with sonar and remote camera and I've determined the area is safe. Our new mission is to find the data and cockpit recorders and recover whatever's left of the fuselage. Before we get started, Special Agent Landis has a few words of caution. Agent Landis?"

Landis was blindsided by his introduction. He cleared his throat. "Thank you, Skipper. As Commander Battock said, we believe the area is safe, but there's always a possibility of unexploded ordnance. Someone went to great lengths to disrupt this investigation, and our only hope of finding who's responsible is to recover as much material as possible. Retrieve the larger pieces before vacuuming. Handle every object with care. Please don't contaminate the evidence. The most seemingly worthless piece may be the one that identifies the type and location of the explosives. Any questions?" No one moved. "Great. Well, thanks for your attention and good luck." Battock assumed command. "Remember—safety is paramount. We'll abort anytime someone suspects danger. Treat every scrap with care. Keep track of your diving buddy. Above all, don't do anything stupid. I want all divers ready in twenty minutes. Bring nets, baskets, sacks—anything you can find to recover debris. Bring up everything that isn't natural to the ocean. Senior Chief, please have a diver take a video camera to complement the remote camera." Senior Chief nodded. "If you find something, mark where you found it and send it up. Any questions?"

"No, sir."

Captain Giles watched the tall sailboats in the distance as the Sea Knight approached the sand-colored Base Operations building at North Island Naval Air Station. He was a long way from comfortable thoughts about retirement and golf. He was supposed to be off duty. What would he tell the admiral about this episode? Giles had to defend Battock's position and investigate the allegations, but he was eager to hear Duncan's version.

Giles held onto his hat, shielding himself from the rotor blast. The aircrewman led three people away from the aircraft. He assumed the middle two were Duncan and Ray. Once they were clear, the aircrewman returned to the helicopter and it taxied away.

Giles studied Duncan and Ray, their well-toned bodies, hard faces. He motioned them forward. "This way," he said, holding the door open. The men walked into a secluded room off Base Operations' foyer. The VIP room was normally reserved for visiting high-ranking officers, but Giles needed privacy. "Help yourselves to a drink," he said, gesturing to a six-pack of Coca Cola on ice.

Ray followed Duncan's lead and grabbed a Coke.

"I'm Captain Giles. I hope you had a pleasant flight."

Duncan popped the top, wiping its spray on his pants. "It was fine," he said.

"Sir, I'm Special Agent Kidman."

Giles nodded. "Welcome to North Island." He took a sip of Coke, staring at Duncan and Ray. Duncan stared back. The air conditioner whispered in the background. He now understood why Battock was frustrated with Duncan. "Gentlemen, Agent Kidman and I are trying to understand what happened aboard *Atlantis*. Since the Skipper or XO can't be here, I'm asking for your assistance in their place. Lieutenant Commander Duncan, Skipper Battock said you were the one who discovered the explosives this morning. Can you describe what you saw?"

Duncan shrugged. "Ray and I were poking around inside the fuselage, prying a few containers open. I saw something that looked like plastic explosives. A few seconds later, I felt resistance—like a tripwire. I don't know how I missed it going in, but I figured it was gonna blow. When it didn't, I gave the signal to abort and everyone shot to the surface. *Atlantis* barely got out of there in time. The force lifted the fantail and showered us with water and debris. We were damned lucky no one got hurt."

Giles watched Ray taking in the plush surroundings, a true follower. "Yeah—good thing you spotted that bomb, but why didn't you disarm it?"

"We weren't prepared. I'd intended to take some tools along, but since it was an exploratory dive, I decided they might get in the way. I mean, I honestly didn't believe anything could've survived the crash. Besides, the electrical leads must've been buried in the rubble. In any case, since we're still alive, I figure I made the right call to abort."

Kidman shifted in his seat. "Petty Officer Ray, did you ever see the bomb?"

"No, sir, but I was making sure we didn't cut our oxygen hoses. When Mr. Duncan backed into me and ordered the evacuation, I left." Ray looked at Giles and Kidman, convinced they didn't believe him. "Sirs—I'd stake my life on Commander Duncan anytime, anywhere. His word can't be questioned in our line of work."

"I see," Kidman said. "Lieutenant Commander Duncan—you're the senior officer in your disposal unit and an explosives expert. Have you seen a lot of action?"

"Yes, sir."

"The Gulf?"

"And other places."

Kidman smiled. "I'm sure. I'm no explosives expert, but I also find it odd that a bomb of such destructive power could survive an inflight explosion and ditching. I think a second bomb was planted after the crash. What do you think?"

Duncan took a swig of Coke. "That's certainly a possibility."

Giles was unnerved, glimpsing a trained methodical killer. "You said you didn't see any wires or a timer—so what made you think you had to evacuate? I'm not saying you made the wrong decision, but I'm curious how you figured you hit a tripwire in a wreck with garbage scattered everywhere. Maybe it's just me, but if I felt a tug at my flipper, I would've figured I snagged a piece of metal."

"It felt like a tripwire," Duncan said, staring. Giles was now the hanging judge, Kidman the jury, their minds already made up. "Captain—before you ask, we didn't plant any explosives. I didn't expect there'd be unexploded ordnance on board, but there was. If I had it to do over again, I'd make the same decision. Ray and I wouldn't be here if we hadn't evacuated when we did."

"Lieutenant Commander Duncan," Giles said, "this is an informal inquiry. No one's accusing you or Petty Officer Ray of anything. In fact, based on Skipper Battock's report and your own testimony, I'd say you deserve credit for saving *Atlantis*. All we're trying to do is piece this puzzle together so the NTSB and FBI will know where to concentrate their efforts."

Duncan nodded.

"So you and Ray were the only ones to go inside the aircraft?" Kidman asked.

"As far as I know, but I can't speak for the *Atlantis* crew. You see, Skipper Battock sent a couple of his divers down after he canceled dive operations. I have no idea what they did while they were down there, but Dyer's death proves they were near the fuselage. For all I know, Dyer could've planted the bomb."

"I'm sure the investigators will look into that aspect," Giles said, coldly. "Anything else?"

Duncan shook his head and downed the last of his Coke. He crushed the can and tossed it in the trash basket.

Kidman stood. "Captain, if it's all right with you, I'd like to keep their equipment for analysis. It may contain residual traces that can identify the type of explosives."

"Fine with me," Giles said.

"Hey—wait a minute," Duncan said. "We need that stuff."

"Relax, Commander. I've already spoken to your CO. You're both relieved of diving duties until this investigation's complete. You'll be carrying out administrative duties until further notice."

Duncan kicked his bag over to Kidman. Ray slid his.

Kidman inventoried their equipment, noting their knives. He gave the divers and Captain Giles hand receipts. "I'll have these returned as soon as possible."

"Very well," Giles said. "Commander Duncan, there's a van outside waiting to take you and Petty Officer Ray back to Coronado. I'll be in touch." Duncan and Ray walked out, surprised to be free.

Kidman watched the Navy van drive off. "Skipper Battock has reason for concern," he said to Giles. "Duncan's too cool. He knows we consider them suspects. Hopefully their equipment bags will reveal something. Trust me—the lab will know if they had any explosives in there."

Giles raised an eyebrow. "But that's their mission," he said. "They must've carried explosives before. How can you make a connection to this disaster?"

"Chemical shelf-life," he said. "Like DNA testing, there's little room for interpretation."

Giles nodded. "You know—if you remove the bias and take Duncan's word, Dyer makes a good suspect. After all, they did find him pinned to the fuselage. Jesus—I can't believe I just said that. Fred, I've got to go. Thanks for the help."

"Have a good one, Captain."

Kidman mulled over the possibilities as he closed his trunk. Were they headed down the right path with Duncan and Ray? He'd check into Dyer's past when he got to the office. Maybe he was disgruntled over some punitive action, a bust in rank, passed over for chief. But didn't they find his body some ten hours before the explosion? His ship was directly on top of the wreckage. But if he intended to take out his shipmates, why not plant the bomb aboard *Atlantis*? The more he reasoned, the more absurd it seemed. One thing was for sure; Duncan and Ray's equipment bags should provide some answers. He was eager to get to the lab. As he started his car, he wondered how Agents Barnes and Landis were doing back on the ship.

Skipper Battock spotted a small armada on the horizon as his crew prepared to dive. He'd received word that three commercial ships would be supporting him in lieu of Navy vessels. The largest ship was the four hundred foot *Scavenger*. *Scavenger* was longer and lower to the surface than the multi-role *Atlantis*, with high-lift cranes able to recover large pieces. Battock turned his attention to his crew. They would dive as scheduled.

		Skully toddled the ocean floor in his MK 21 helmet. He'd become accustomed to it and liked maintaining communications with *Atlantis*. He saw the remote camera passing overhead and waved. "Hi, Skipper."
		Battock smiled. Then he noticed something near Skully's foot. He zoomed in on a smooth, cylindrical object. "Skully, look down. What do you see?"
		"Looks like a flashlight," he said. "I'll send it up." He tossed it in a bucket, tugged on the rope, and went back to searching the floor. He shuffled his feet and kicked up a rectangular object. His heart thudded when he realized what it was. "Skipper—I found a camera. It looks like Bends'."
		"Send it up." Battock looked at McClintock. "The sand must've protected it from the blast," he said, reviewing Duncan's

diagram. "Bends must've dropped them, but if he was pinned to the right side of the aircraft, how'd they end up on the left?" McClintock shrugged. Battock took over the remote camera's controls and maneuvered the camera over Skully. "Show me where you found the camera, Skully."

Skully saw the remote camera and pointed at the floor.

"Thanks. Keep looking." Battock returned the controls to the sailor. "This could be our big break, XO. Have someone get Bends' camera to the photo lab as soon as it gets here. Make sure they know it's important. I want those photos."

"I'll handle it," McClintock said.

Battock stared at Special Agent Barnes. "I never believed Dyer's death was an accident," he said. "Bends wouldn't go anywhere without his flashlight or camera. The guy was murdered."

"Careful, Skipper. Those are important pieces of evidence, but I'm not sure they'll point to murder. It'll be tough proving Duncan and Ray were involved."

"But that's your job."

"Actually, we're here to determine the cause of the explosion. Of course we'll look into the possibility of murder as well, but we need more than your gut feelings. Let's put them aside 'til we see what's on that film, okay?"

"Fine, but—"

"Skipper—*Scavenger*'s on the radio," Ensign Truman said over the intercom. "She's fifty yards to port."

"I'll be right there." Battock headed for the door. "Be back in a few."

"*Atlantis*, this is *Scavenger*. We have three NTSB inspectors requesting to come aboard. Request transport instructions."

Battock peered through binoculars from the bridge. *Scavenger* sat so low in the water it merged with the horizon. "*Scavenger*, *Atlantis* has divers in the water," he said over the radio. "Request you maintain present position. We'll send an inflatable over."

Battock watched the inflatable raft speed towards *Atlantis* with four souls on board. He grinned, watching the inspectors get sprayed as the raft skipped over the waves. All three were clinging to the raft; probably none had been in deep water before. Two sailors stood by to receive. Battock left the bridge to greet them. "Welcome aboard," he said.

"Thanks." The tall, confident brunette woman stepped forward to shake hands, her long hair tangled and damp from the trip. She tucked it behind her ears, unconcerned with her appearance. "I'm Kathy Jennings, senior investigator, NTSB," she said, presenting her ID. "Sorry it took so long to get here. We should've been here last night, but *Scavenger* returned to port with some mechanical problems. Her Skipper wanted the other ships to stay with him in case he had more problems. Anyway, we're glad to be here. We brought some lab equipment for an FBI agent—Landis I believe."

"Thanks," he said, grabbing the bags. "He'll be glad to get it. Let's go inside. I'd like to monitor the dive while we talk."

When they got to the control room, Battock introduced Jennings' team to Agents Barnes and Landis and briefed them on the operation. "Oh, Greg—here's your equipment."

"Great," Landis said. "I'll be in my room." The explosives expert took the bag and left.

Kathy Jennings, as senior investigator, was eager to see the pictures from Dyer's camera. Hopefully they showed the wreckage before it was blown up. The video monitor showed nothing but destruction. Everything was so distorted it was impossible to determine the flight path.

"Excuse me," Battock said, noticing his XO vying for his attention. McClintock handed him an envelope containing four dark photographs. "Just those four on the roll, Skipper. Bends may as well have been using regular film."

Battock spread the photos on the table, noticing two of the pictures had light spots in the middle. He barely made out the fuselage. "These are from Petty Officer Dyer's infra-red camera," he said. "Until now, we had to assume his death was an accident. These photos prove he wasn't alone that night."

Agent Barnes scratched his head. "How'd you come up with that?"

Kathy looked at Battock.

Battock pointed to the center of one of the pictures. "This glow's coming from inside the fuselage. It has to be from another diver's flashlight. Remember, Dyer had his camera so he must've had his flashlight. You can tell he was well above the fuselage when he took these pictures. He must've seen the light and knew something was going on. That's probably why he didn't abort with Darby. I figure something must've happened before he could get closer. We were the only vessel in the area and everyone was accounted for—except Duncan and Ray, that is. That's why the light had to come from Duncan or Ray. One or both of them must've overpowered Bends before they skewered him to make it look like an accident. Duncan said they were taking a smoke break on the bow, but they weren't there when I looked, and there aren't any witnesses to back up their claim. Duncan maintains they weren't in the water when Dyer was diving."

Barnes rubbed his forehead, studying the photos. "Isn't there another explanation for the light? Maybe the moon's reflection—lights from your ship?"

"Not at that depth," Battock said. "Besides being dark, the visibility was poor. No way it's surface lighting. Look, Jim—this photo clearly shows the light's coming from inside the fuselage. We didn't turn the floods on until after Dyer was missing. Besides, any reflection would've been outside the aircraft, not inside."

"I agree," Kathy said, holding the picture. "The DC-10's electrical lines were severed and the batteries would've been dead by then. There's no way it could've been the plane's emergency lighting. Someone had to be inside."

"Well, that certainly gives a new perspective, doesn't it?" Barnes said. "The thing is, there are so many red herrings anything's possible. Greg Landis's evidence is pretty straightforward—either there was a bomb or there wasn't. If you'll excuse me, I need to see if he's come up with anything."

DANGER WITHIN

Agent Barnes was hit by a strong breeze as he stepped outside. The salty tang was something he could never get used to. He didn't mind airplanes, but sea duty was another thing altogether. He placed a call to Kidman on his cell phone. "Hey, Fred? Jim Barnes. You still with your EOD companions?"

"No," Kidman said. "I'm half way to LA. Why?"

Barnes watched the deck rise and fall. A chill came over him from the sweat evaporating. He stared at the Channel Islands so he wouldn't puke. They were the only things on the horizon that appeared stationary.

"Fred, we have a situation that requires you meet with them again. I can't say much over the phone, but you need to take them downtown. Call me when you have them in custody."

"Will do."

Barnes returned to the control room. He knelt next to Skipper Battock, keeping his voice down. "I just talked to Kidman—the agent in the helo with EOD's Duncan and Ray. Unfortunately, they were released, but he'll bring them in for further questioning. I need to make a few more calls. I'll be back shortly."

Battock nodded, continuing as though nothing happened.

Kidman pulled off the freeway to call the Coronado Amphibian Base Commanding Officer. He was on hold, waiting for Captain Iverson to answer. "Good afternoon, sir. This is Special Agent Fred Kidman, FBI."

"What can I do for you, Agent Kidman?"

"Sir, I need your assistance to detain two men from EOD Mobile Unit Three. I met with Lieutenant Commander Dan Duncan and Petty Officer Tim Ray earlier today concerning an incident aboard the salvage ship *Atlantis* and need to speak to them again."

"What incident?"

"A Navy diver died and there was an underwater explosion while they were aboard. I need to clear up some details. Would you have the Shore Patrol pick them up for me? It'll take me a couple of hours to get there."

"Talk straight, Kidman. Are they under arrest or not?"

"No, sir. But they are suspects. I'm hoping they'll cooperate so we don't have to arrest them."

Base CO Iverson rested his head against his high-back chair, staring at the pounding waves. This was his base, his men. He resented outside investigators, but it was prudent to cooperate with the FBI. "It could take a while. I'll call you when they're in custody, but you should know I'm doing this under protest."

"Yes, sir. Thank you."

Agent Kidman tucked his phone away and headed back to the LA office. He'd return to San Diego when he had time. Right now, he had background checks to do on Duncan, Ray, and Dyer. The computer network was thorough, but it took time. His eyes grew weary. Why hadn't Iverson called back? Agent Barnes was waiting. He called Barnes to give him an update.

Barnes happened to be on deck, surprised to hear his cell phone ring. "Barnes."

"Hi, Jim—it's Fred. The Amphib Base Commander told me he'd pick up Duncan and Ray, but I haven't heard back from him. So far, the background checks on Duncan, Ray, and Dyer have come up empty."

"Why'd you bother with Dyer?"

"Something Duncan said in the debrief. No big deal."

Barnes didn't press it. "Keep searching," he said. "Like I said, I can't go into details, but Duncan and Ray are dangerous. Use caution."

"Sure, Jim. Later." Kidman hung up. He debated passing Barnes' warning to Captain Iverson at the amphibious base, but the SPs were armed; they knew their jobs. He went back to the computer. What did Jim Barnes know that he didn't?

Two hours later, Kidman received a fax from the Navy Bureau. Dyer graduated at the top of his diving class, had never been in trouble, advanced quickly, and received the Navy Achievement Medal from his last command. Duncan and Ray's records weren't much different, both highly decorated veterans. How could either have committed such a horrific act against Dyer? He dialed the lab. "Find anything in those EOD divers' bags?"

The technician was replacing several items in their duffle bags as he spoke. "Some traces of explosives," he said, "but that was expected. I haven't been able to date anything yet though. Things aren't going as smoothly as I'd like. I need more time—so many variables. It'll be tough getting a warrant based on this."

"Keep digging," Kidman said, studying his computer screen. The tech's report and background checks reinforced Duncan and Ray's innocence. So, why was Barnes convinced they were dangerous? Duncan may have been rude, even disrespectful, but Kidman never feared for his life around him, and Ray just sat there. The phone broke his concentration. He recognized Captain Iverson's voice.

"We haven't been able to locate Duncan or Ray," the base commander said. "They're off duty and could be anywhere, but we'll keep looking. But before I go to General Quarters on this, I'd like to know more. I don't like detaining my personnel without cause."

"Sir, as I said, we're trying to wrap up some loose ends. I don't know what's happening aboard *Atlantis*, but the agent on board wants another meeting. He also made a point of saying Duncan and Ray are dangerous."

"I'll have to reserve judgment on that. I've been reading a lot of message traffic about the explosion and Dyer, but nothing that's addressed Duncan or Ray's involvement. Frankly, I'm not thrilled about all this fuss over a civilian cargo jet. Why the US Navy got involved is beyond me, but that decision's well above my pay grade. As far as I'm concerned, this should've been civilian contract all the way."

"I understand your feelings, Captain, but that's a moot point."

Iverson stared at a picture of D-Day. Amphibious assault landings during its finest hour. That's what he was there for—not frivolous involvement with law enforcement agencies. "Look,

Kidman—if all you need to do is talk to them, why can't I have them call you? It'll save you a trip."

"Sir, with all due respect, I need them in LA."

"Fine—I'll let you know if we find them."

Kidman's phone rang shortly after Iverson hung up. It was Agent Jim Barnes asking for an update. Kidman reported the lab tech's comments and Iverson's situation. Things weren't going well on either end. Explosives expert Agent Greg Landis had yet to make a breakthrough. "I'm telling you, Jim, from what I've seen and heard, they're unlikely suspects."

"Fred, maybe if I were in your shoes, I'd feel the same way. We need to talk. See if you can get a chopper to get me off this tug. Greg can stay behind and keep working with the fragments. The NTSB's also here—it's getting a little crowded."

Kidman laughed. "Yeah, right. The last time you were on a boat you complained for months. The NTSB won't bother your investigation, but I'll see what I can do. Maybe the Sheriff's Department can give us a hand," he said, thinking out loud. "Oh, yeah—Mike Pentaglia's on his way back from Oklahoma City. I'm sure he'll want to be included in our meeting."

"Sure, why not?" he said, eager to hear from Agent Pentaglia. "Of course, there won't be a meeting 'till you get me outta here." Barnes heard Kidman laughing in the background. "Enjoy the laugh, Fred. Next time I'll make sure you'll be the one riding the giant suppository." The ship's motion knocked him off balance. He cursed as his shoulder hit steel. Kidman laughed some more. "God dammit, Fred, I mean it. Get me off this boat! And keep digging. There's got to be something on Duncan and Ray."

Kidman placed another call. Deputy McKessler from The LA County Sheriff's Aero Bureau answered the phone. "Yes, Deputy, this is Special Agent Kidman, FBI. I was hoping you could help us out this afternoon. We're investigating that DC-10 accident off the Channel Islands and one of our agents needs to get off the salvage ship as soon as possible. Any chance one of your choppers can give him a lift?"

Deputy McKessler jotted down Kidman's name, underlining FBI. Mutual aid was an essential part of law enforcement, but helicopter support had become difficult to justify. "If it were up to me, I'd say yes, but our budget limits us to routine patrols, rescues, and emergencies. We don't have funds for non-essential missions."

Kidman's jaw dropped. "You're kidding. You guys have a bigger fleet than most of the world's armies. Don't you guys fly all the time?"

"Not anymore. We've got a lot of choppers, but unless all hell breaks loose, we're not doing much flying. You know how it is—feast or famine."

Kidman massaged his neck. He'd spent all afternoon on the phone and looking at a computer. Advil gave him no relief. "How about if I come up with the funds?"

"I suppose that would be a different story."

"Good. You'll have your money."

McKessler called back minutes later telling him a helicopter was on its way. Kidman called Barnes. "Good news," he said. "A Sheriff's helicopter is on the way—should be there in the next thirty minutes or so. All they have is a horse-collar, though. And don't be surprised if you have to explain yourself when you get back. It nearly took an act of Congress to get that chopper."

"It'll be worth it."

"I'll be waiting."

Agent Barnes pocketed his phone and returned to the meeting, eager to get out of the cold. He'd been in and out of the room so often, no one paid any attention "A helo's coming to pick me up, Skipper," he said to Battock. "I've got an important meeting back at the office. Mind if I take these photos along?"

Battock looked at Kathy. She didn't raise any objections. "Sure, but leave the negatives here."

"No sweat, but make sure nothing happens to them. We won't have a day in court without 'em."

Battock nodded.

Agent Barnes waited on the deck. He heard a noise on the horizon. Soon a large helicopter came in view. A helmeted sailor guided the Sikorsky H-3 over the aft deck while another assisted Barnes with the horse collar harness. Barnes stepped inside, raised the harness around his torso, and signaled he was ready. As the chopper took up the slack, Barnes felt the wind getting sucked out of him. He took short breaths, watching the ship get smaller. He relaxed as the aircrewman pulled him inside. The H-3 dashed towards the federal building.

When he got to his office, Kidman and Pentaglia were talking with a man he didn't recognize. He tapped at the door to get their attention. "Sorry to interrupt."

Agent Mike Pentaglia turned around. "Hi, Jim—come on in. This is Second Officer Kevin Hamilton. He survived that DC-10 crash you've been investigating. Kevin, this is Special Agent Barnes."

Kevin stood to meet his hand. "Pleased to meet you."

"You, too," Barnes said, wondering why a civilian was there. "Must've been quite a ride. So, what brings you out here, Kevin?"

"It's a long story," Mike said. "We first met in Oklahoma City and, by coincidence, he's out here conducting his own investigation." Barnes fired a sharp look.

"Actually, I'm here on a layover," Kevin said, "but I am checking into some things. I kept running into dead ends so I talked to Captain Iverson—the Amphib Base CO. He referred me to your office and Mike happened to answer the phone. Mike offered to pick me up to compare notes, so here I am."

Mike smiled. "You won't believe Kevin's luck, Jim. This is his second major mishap in two years. I mean, we've all had our share of bad luck, but do you know anyone who can top this?"

"Nope."

"Of course, Kevin's not amused," Mike said. "He wants to see this investigation through even if he has to do it himself. That's why he's here."

Kidman moved on. "Well, Jim—what's so important that we had to spend a couple grand to get you off *Atlantis*?"

Barnes didn't want Kevin there, but it was evident he wasn't leaving. He spread the photos on the table, pointing to the first. "It's hard to see, but this was the fuselage before the explosion. We estimate the photo was taken about twenty-five feet above the fuselage. This illumination you see coming from the over-wing inspection windows proves someone was inside the fuselage when Petty Officer Dyer took the photo. That's significant because *Atlantis*' CO had canceled dive operations for the night. When Duncan and Ray failed to report as ordered, he sent Dyer and another diver down to find them. As you know, one aborted, but Dyer remained behind. Dyer's camera and flashlight were found buried in the sand here," he said, pointing to the diagram. "We assume he dropped them while being attacked. These were the only pictures on the roll."

Kidman studied the photos. "So you're saying Duncan and Ray planted a bomb, then attacked Dyer and drug him down and pinned him to the fuselage?"

Barnes nodded. "I admit we don't have much to support it, but these photos speak for themselves."

Kidman passed the photos to Pentaglia. Barnes' theory was ugly, but plausible. "I can see why you'd want to talk to them," Kidman said, "but neither Duncan or Ray have any prior arrests and both have enviable service records. Why risk everything to murder a fellow Navy diver and blow up a civilian plane wreck? It doesn't make sense."

"What makes you so sure those divers are legitimate?" Kevin asked. He felt their eyes on him. "Service records can be manufactured with the right connections—the CIA does it all the time. Has anyone talked to someone who served with Duncan or Ray?"

Mike Pentaglia smiled as Kidman shook his head. Kevin was an outsider, but that made him fearless.

"Doesn't it seem odd," Kevin went on, "that Duncan and Ray were placed on a ship that already had twenty divers on its crew who are trained in underwater salvage? I'm no underwater demolition expert, but I've never heard of a bomb going off a day after a plane crashed. I intend to find out who ordered those EOD divers be on board and why. If Duncan and Ray are responsible for Dyer's death and planted the bomb, chances are they're just pawns in a conspiracy we know nothing about."

"Interesting theory, isn't it," Pentaglia said.

"This stinks, Mike," Kevin said. "There's got to be a reason our plane was brought down. Find it and you'll find whoever's responsible."

Mike thought about it. "When do you have to be back, Kevin? I mean—how much time do you have before your flight actually departs?"

Kevin glanced at his watch. "I've got three and a half hours—why?"

"If I get you off your trip, would you be willing to help with the investigation?" Tension mounted. Agents Barnes and Kidman made sure Mike knew they objected to having a civilian on the case. But Mike was the senior man. "What's the number for your scheduler?"

Kevin wrote the number down and passed it to him.

"Be back in a minute. Help yourself to some coffee, guys."

Mike went into a smaller office and dialed the number. "Hi—this is FBI Special Agent Pentaglia. I'm working with one of your pilots out here in LA—Second Officer Kevin Hamilton. You need to replace him on this afternoon's flight. I need him for a few days to help with a federal investigation. I'll let you know when I'm done."

The Global Cargo Express scheduler laughed when Kevin's activity sheet appeared on the computer screen. "You're kidding, right?"

Mike frowned. "Actually, I'm quite serious. We're trying to resolve some issues from your DC-10 crash. You may recall he was on that flight."

The scheduler adjusted his headset as he studied the computer monitor. "Look—maybe he can come back tomorrow. He's due to launch in a few hours. We're paying him overtime 'cause there's no one else. Surely it can wait until tomorrow."

"No—I can't. Every minute that goes by means the investigation's getting cold. Let me ask you something. What happens if he's in a car wreck or gets sick? Wouldn't you find a replacement then?"

"Of course, but in that case we'd have a justifiable delay. We don't have any pilots based in LA—it'll take time to find a replacement."

"Then I suggest you get busy. Like you said, you've only got three hours to find someone."

"But—"

"Look—I know it sucks, but this is a criminal investigation. If you'd prefer, I could place him under arrest and hold him for forty-eight hours."

The scheduler slumped in his chair. "That's all right. Give me a number where I can reach you and I'll run this past the duty officer."

"I can hold. If you prefer, I'll talk to him. I want to make sure Kevin gets the same pay he's getting now, and is at my disposal until he's no longer required."

"I'm not sure where the duty officer is right now—I'll have to page him."

"Fine. I'll be expecting his call."

"Well, Kevin—looks like you'll be working for me for awhile."

"Pardon me? Don't I have a say in the matter?"

"Hey—you're getting full pay. Time-and-a-half as I recall."

Kevin didn't like it. Besides, Barnes and Kidman didn't want him there. He thought of Nancy, the boys. "You know, Mike, I was looking forward to flying my trip."

Mike's face went stone cold. "I'm surprised. You seemed so dedicated in Oklahoma City. I thought you wanted answers. Guess I'll call 'em back."

Whatever it takes. "Wait," Kevin said. "I do want answers—even have my wife's blessing on it."

Mike looked at Kidman and Barnes. "I'm feeling a lot of tension," he said. "Kevin—why don't you to start from the beginning? I want everyone to hear what happened on your flight and your conspiracy theories. Nothing can be used against you so don't hold back."

Kevin took a seat. He didn't see any tape recorders or cameras, but could he trust Mike? What if he were part of the conspiracy? What about Kidman and Barnes? He knew nothing about them. His mind was spinning. He remembered his debriefing at Whiteman AFB. "You sure you don't want to record this?" he asked Mike, hoping to keep a copy for himself. "I can talk without it, but you might want to refer to it later."

Mike slapped his leg. "You see, Jim? That's what I like about him." He reached into his desk, pulled out a small tape recorder, and hit the record button. "Okay, Kevin—you're on."

Once again, Kevin recounted his experience. It gave Kidman and Barnes a perspective they didn't expect. He was gaining ground. Kevin dismissed his fears and detailed on whom he'd spoken to and why, and briefed them on JAG protocol and how he'd obtained privileged information from LCDR Woolsey at the Coronado amphib base. An hour passed and it felt good getting everything in the open. Mike looked pleased. Hopefully something positive would come from it.

Mike was amazed at how Kevin had learned so much without access to government resources. He turned off the recorder. "I'm curious, Kevin—how'd you develop such an extensive network?"

Kevin smiled. "Marines have to be resourceful," he said. "I didn't have a network when I started, but I've met a lot of people who are equally interested in finding the truth. It wasn't hard to get information."

Kidman dumped two files in front of Kevin. "You're obviously well versed in military procedures. How about reviewing these personnel records? These guys look clean to me, but I'd like your opinion."

"Sure."

Kevin scrutinized the files, surprised at their detail. Unlikely the FBI or CIA would've come up with anything so extensive or convincing. He didn't expect to find respect for Duncan or Ray, but from their records, he would've been proud to have either under his command. He looked at Kidman. "Did you notice that both men received medals for heroism as SEALs three years ago?" Agent Kidman shook his head. "Well, did you notice they've worked together for the last five years?"

"I must've missed that one, too," Kidman said. "Officer/enlisted fraternization is frowned upon, but in their line of work, they probably developed a pretty tight bond. Do you have any details during their time together as SEALs?"

Kidman leaned back in his chair. "What's the big deal about them being SEALs?"

Mike cleared his throat. "Fred's spent his entire career as an FBI agent."

Kevin looked at Kidman. "It's extremely competitive to become a SEAL, but once you're in, you're in for life. You don't rotate in and out of the SEALs like a squadron mechanic. That's why it's odd they both went from the SEALs to EOD. Anyway, being SEALs explains their medals for valor. I imagine whatever went on that day solidified their relationship."

"I'm not following you," Mike said. "What relationship?"

"SEALs, EOD, and grunt Marines come from the same mold. They trust each other to watch their backs—you know, brothers-in-arms. Anyway, it's not uncommon to develop close bonds throughout the rank structure—especially in combat. They've seen their buddies dismembered, disemboweled, and cut down. When they return home, they've changed. Many are embittered by their lack of respect from those who take freedom for granted.

Most of their missions remain classified, so few know what they did. They resent the fact they can't talk about it. I remember returning from overseas, disgusted to see protest rallies for the first time. Of course, after the Gulf War and Afghanistan, we were heroes—at least for a while. Anyway, from what I've seen, I seriously doubt Duncan or Ray had anything to do with Dyer's death or planting a second bomb. If they did, I imagine their combat experience played a role."

Mike stared at the ceiling, deep in thought. Kevin got up and poured himself a cup of stale coffee. He took a sip, grimaced, and forced it down.

"Thanks for your insight, Kevin," Mike said. "It's obvious we don't know Duncan or Ray well enough. Jim, get a search warrant for their apartments. Fred, you've been working with the Navy—call our Washington office to have someone visit the Navy Bureau. I want to know more about their time as SEALs. Have them track down a fellow SEAL and get some feedback. It may take a while, but we'll—" The phone rang. Mike got it.

"This is Andy with Global Cargo Express crew scheduling. Per your request, Second Officer Hamilton is off the trip and will remain at your disposal with full pay until we hear he's no longer required."

"Thanks, Andy. I'll be in touch." Mike propped his feet on the desk and leaned back in his chair. "That was your scheduler. You're officially part of the team."

Kevin nodded. "I'd like to call my wife."

"Have at it." Mike slid the phone over. "C'mon, guys—let's stretch our legs."

Kevin waited until they left. "Hi Nance. How's it going?"

Nancy turned down the TV, glancing at the time. "Kevin? Don't you have a flight? Don't tell me you've had another accident."

Kevin laughed. "No—nothing like that, but you won't believe this..."

19

Kevin cradled the phone, Nancy's anger still with him. She wouldn't go back on her word, but she made it clear she didn't like it. And he shared her fears. It wasn't like flying combat in the Marine Corps. There, he was wrapped in armor plating with sensors telling him if someone was firing at him. Here he was defenseless.

"Everything okay?" Mike asked, walking back in the room.

"Yeah."

"It's late. I'll take you back to the hotel. We'll start in the morning."

Kevin's alarm went off at eight. He shaved and dressed and waited for Mike's call. The phone rang while he watched Headline News.

"Hey, Kevin. Mike. When can you come downtown?"

"Anytime."

"Great—I'm in the lobby."

"Give me a minute." He cradled the phone and sat on the bed, feeling a panic attack coming on. He felt fear—even more than climbing the DC-10 stairs after the accident. His chest tightened. He was suffocating, breaking into a cold sweat. He struggled to breathe. When the attack left him, he prayed he wouldn't have another in front of the others. His flying days could be over. He washed his face and left the room, determined never to let it happen again.

When the elevator doors opened, Mike was flashing a toothy grin. "Hi, Kev."

"Morning, Mike. Either you have great news or you got lucky last night."

"Unfortunately, it's the former. Let's go. We'll talk on the way."

When they got in the car, Mike handed Kevin a manila folder that had "RESTRICTED USE" stenciled in red ink on both sides. "I just got this from the Washington office. We still lack a motive, but Duncan and Ray aren't as clean as we thought. Go ahead—take a look." Kevin skimmed through the highlighted lines while Mike drove. "As you can see, they were both kicked out of the SEALs for doing a little business on the side. Nothing too outrageous, mind you. In fact, using SEAL equipment for pleasure diving's kind of funny, but after their CO counseled them, they went and did it again. Their CO had enough and got 'em transferred to EOD."

Kevin looked up. "I'm confused, Mike. What's the connection between government fraud and murder? I mean, government fraud's a hot item and carries stiff penalties, but I don't see how it leads to conspiracy and murder. Besides, if they were guilty of fraud, they shouldn't have gotten new assignments. A good CO won't pass on his problem children to another command."

"He must've still considered them assets. Besides, that way he avoided having to explain how they managed to borrow his equipment."

"Makes sense," Kevin said, "but why wasn't that in their records?"

"Because their CO wanted to get promoted. Special Agent Freeman called from our DC office. Turns out Freeman served in the same SEAL unit as Duncan and Ray. He knew everything."

"But hearsay isn't evidence, even if it's first-hand. And if it's true, how does borrowing government equipment provide a motive to blow up a DC-10?"

"Beats me. I'm hoping Duncan or Ray will tell us."

"So you found them?"

"Not yet—be we will."

Kevin laughed. "You realize those guys will die before they rat on each other."

"Maybe, but we won't know 'til we talk to them. Captain Iverson over at the amphib base said they're now officially listed as AWOL. Seems they never came back after their shore leave expired. From what I recall, being absent without leave is a pretty serious crime in itself, but running from the law implies guilt. Why would they disappear if they didn't have something to hide?"

"Maybe they'll have a good explanation."

Mike shook his head. The conversation was over. A few minutes later, he pulled into the federal building parking lot. "As far as I'm concerned, Duncan and Ray became federal fugitives when they went AWOL. We're working on their warrants now."

Kevin stuffed the contents back in the folder and handed it to Mike. "Why do you need me if you're so sure about Duncan and Ray?"

"Oh, I forgot to mention what the lab found. Care to see? That is, if you still want to be a part of the investigation."

"Why not? I've already missed my flight."

The elevator doors opened on the third floor of the FBI facility. The walls were dingy, floor tiles cracked, paint chipped, dust stains on the vents. He followed Mike into a small room blocked by a long counter. An older man in a white smock and thick glasses looked up from behind his desk. "Hey, Tony—how ya doin'?"

"Okay, Mike. Who's your friend?"

"Tony Perini, meet Kevin Hamilton. Kevin—Tony. Kevin's the guy I told you about that survived the wreck." Mike nodded at Kevin. "Tony's one of our best lab technicians."

Tony picked up a fractured piece of metal with his gloved hand and showed it to Kevin. "This is what Mike wanted you to see. The agent on board *Atlantis* had it specially delivered. He's convinced it contained the initial explosive charge."

"May I hold it?"

"Sure. Watch the sharp edges."

Kevin examined it, rotating it. It reminded him of the samples he'd studied at Naval Aviation Safety Officer School in Monterey. The biggest lesson he learned during his six-week course of mishap investigation was every fragment bore clues. How many times did he hear that?

It looked like cast steel, but it was too light. He rubbed his finger over a flat surface. It was coarse with small bumps; the texture of a die-cast product. He held it to his nose and sniffed. He passed it back to Perini. "Interesting alloy," he said. "From its thickness, I'd say it's a casing of some kind. It's not from our plane though."

Perini held it to the light. "I agree, but I'm not sure what it's from either. I'm hoping a few more tests will reveal something. I've never seen anything like it. It's so strong it contained a massive explosion. I agree with Greg Landis, our explosives expert. The bomb that brought your plane down was inside this casing."

Kevin was drawn to the fragment. Holding it in his palm, he felt the anger build. "Maybe now John will believe this wasn't an accident."

"Say again?" Perini said.

"I said this proves it wasn't an accident. Mike—any feedback from the load manifest yet? It might help determine what this is and who it belonged to."

Mike nodded. "We're still working on it."

"If you liked that fragment, take a look at this one," Perini said.

Kevin held it to the light, studying it from every angle. "Smells and looks the same to me."

Perini smiled. "That's because you can't see the difference with the naked eye. The chemical analysis found traces of a second explosive material. In other words, there was definitely a second bomb. See how this piece is bent?" Kevin nodded. "That means the secondary explosion was outside this component—just the opposite of the first. I haven't figured out what triggered it yet, but I will." He looked over his glasses. "Underwater blasts tend to contain explosions and things don't burn. I'm hoping we'll get enough fragments to rebuild the casing."

Kevin tried to imagine what the casing might have looked like. Something that large and bulky would have been on a pallet, but he didn't recall seeing one. If the pallet were loaded in the back, the demi containers would have blocked his view. He picked up a fragment with his fingers, holding it to the light. Perini was right—there was something special about that metal. Maybe special enough that someone didn't want anyone else finding it. Perhaps that's why there was a second explosion. He handed it back. "Thanks, Tony—nice meeting you."

"Still one of the best, Tony," Mike said.

"The best." Perini went back to his desk.

Kevin followed Mike into his office. "Well, Kev—now do you think Duncan and Ray should be our prime suspects? We've got more than enough for their warrants. Be right back. Help yourself to some coffee."

Kevin studied the photos on the desk. Why would two respected Navy divers plant explosives in a wreck when there's no way they could've had anything to do with the inflight explosion?

Mike returned an hour later. "Sorry it took so long, but I just got two one-way tickets to jail; one for Mr. Duncan and one for Mr. Ray. By now, every law enforcement agency in the country should have copies of their warrant. They'll be in custody soon."

"Well, Mike—it sounds like you've got this case wrapped up, so if you don't need me for anything, I'll try to get a flight out of here."

Mike stared. "So you don't want to see this through, eh?"

Kevin smiled. "Be honest, Mike. Don't you think it's time I backed out? You've seen how Fred and Jim look at me. They don't want me here. How about taking me back to the hotel?"

Mike headed for the door without saying anything further.

"Hey, Mike? Do me a favor and hold off on calling the company, okay? I have a couple more things I want to check out."

"Want to play hooky, eh? Why not? I'll cover you a while—but stay in touch."

"I will."

Kevin figured the only way he could check on Navy diver Petty Officer Dyer's JAG investigation was to do it alone. He rented a car and drove to the Naval Amphibious Base at Coronado. Once he got outside the LA metropolis, the sprawling city gave way to rolling hills and lush farms with mansions nestled amongst them. It was a simpler place where birds soared and grapes grew. Even the commuters seemed more relaxed.

It took two hours to reach the Silver Strand, a thin minced strip along the beach. The Strand was the only route to the assault training base and provided beautiful vistas, the Pacific Ocean on one side, San Diego on the other. He presented his retired military ID to the sentry and got directions to the base administration building. A young woman petty officer greeted him at a counter. "I'm looking for a JAG officer—Lieutenant Commander Woolsey."

She didn't recognize the name. "One moment, sir." She went into another office and returned to the counter a few minutes later. "Sir, Lieutenant Commander Woolsey's in a different building. You can call him if you like. I'm sure he'll give you directions."

"Thanks." He accepted the phone and placed the call. Thankfully, Woolsey was in. "Commander Woolsey—Colonel Hamilton. Say, I'm in town and was hoping we could get together. Is there a time that might be convenient?"

"Sorry, Colonel, but as I've told you before, I have nothing to say to you."

Kevin turned away from the counter. Woolsey was like rainbow trout—cautious, but would eventually take the bait. "Too bad. I figured I could help you."

"How's that?"

"Well, I just left the LA FBI office and they had some pretty interesting evidence. Thought you'd be interested. It's privileged information, but I figured I owed you one."

"How long will it take you to get to Coronado?"

"Like I said—I'm in town. Actually, I'm on base. Where's your office?"

Woolsey stared at the stacks of files and books scattered throughout his office. Hamilton would think he was a disorganized slob. Still, he wanted to hear what he had to say. He picked things up while he gave directions. "My office faces the flagpole. Room 227. You can't miss it." Minutes later, Kevin tapped at his door.

Kevin was escorted into Woolsey's office. Woolsey was a heavy-set man with dark hair and black-framed bifocal glasses. Not surprisingly, his only ribbons were "gimmees." Sea Service and Sharpshooter Marksmanship were fine for a new ensign, but hardly fitting for an officer of his rank.

Woolsey looked over Kevin. "So, Colonel, what can you do for me?"

Kevin stared out the window. How did this legal officer rate a window view of one of the finest vistas in San Diego? Several assault ships were maneuvering off the beach. "Nice view. Seems the Navy always got the better base locations."

"Why are you here, Colonel?"

"The FBI's convinced that two EOD divers from this base murdered Petty Officer Dyer. They have warrants for their arrest. Know anything about that?"

Woolsey stared. "So, now we're talking murder, eh? Interesting. Everything I've heard says it was an accident."

"That's what I thought, but new evidence suggests otherwise. Personally, I don't know what to believe anymore. I mean, sure—Dyer could've been murdered, but I can't believe Duncan and Ray did it. What do you think?"

Woolsey leaned back in his chair. "I think you're wasting my time. And who are Duncan and Ray?"

"If you recall from your JAG investigation, Duncan and Ray were the EOD divers aboard *Atlantis* when Dyer died."

"I shouldn't even be handling Dyer's case, but since we're the nearest base with Navy divers, it got dumped on me like everything else. I don't have time for this crap. I'm supposed to be a base legal officer doing wills, keeping the CO out of trouble—not murder investigations. You see this in-basket? What do you really want, Colonel?"

"How old was Petty Officer Dyer?"

"I don't know."

"Well, how convinced are you that his death was an accident?"

"Like I said, I've never seen any evidence to the contrary. His CO's explanation was pretty cut and dry; underwater currents forced Dyer into the wreckage. That's good enough for me. After all, he was there, I wasn't. Now, if the FBI proves that's not the case, that's fine, too. I'll just change the document to reflect their findings."

"Commander—how much time have you actually spent on this investigation?"

Woolsey looked away. "I haven't been keeping track."

"Have you seen Dyer's autopsy report? Talked to anyone about the sea conditions that day?" Woolsey shook his head. "So, what were the underwater currents that day? Have you interviewed anyone from *Atlantis*?"

"No. I don't know."

"Commander Woolsey—if I were your reviewing officer, I'd be demanding answers to those questions and more. Anything less is a sham. Then again, maybe the Navy's different."

"Like I said," Woolsey said, slowly, "I shouldn't have been tapped for this investigation. I begged my CO to give it to someone else, but he insisted it was my turn. We're always getting hit for JAG investigations. Do I have the answers to Dyer's case? Of course not. That's why it's still on my desk." He turned to face Kevin. "I have nine months left before the Navy kicks me out. And my last hurrah's another goddam JAG investigation."

"You should call Petty Officer Dyer's parents," Kevin said. "I'm sure they could enlighten you on how their son's life was cut short in the line of duty. You owe it to them and the Navy to do a quality investigation."

Woolsey took off his glasses. "Want to see his file?"

"That's what I came for." He studied each detail in the autopsy report; severe trauma to his right-rear ribcage, lungs punctured—rear entry. The diagram made Dyer look crucified, yet the official cause of death raised a flag. Wouldn't he have water in his lungs if they were punctured? From what he saw, the only area free of puncture wounds was where Dyer's SCUBA tank protected him. Kevin must have read the CO's statement four times. He looked at Woolsey, astounded. "Did you read this?"

"I scanned it."

"Reading between the lines, it appears Commander Battock believes Dyer was murdered. He's also the one who requested the FBI get involved. I can't believe it took me this long to catch on." He closed the folder and handed it to Woolsey. "You really need to find out what the currents were like that day. Anything short of a tsunami wouldn't have enough force to impale him like that. Didn't you find it odd they ruled his death a drowning?"

"Like I said, I just scanned it."

"Oh, right. So, think about this, Commander. Dyer's most severe injuries were to his backside. So I'm supposed to believe he drowned and then the currents threw him against the fuselage. Doesn't sound likely, does it?"

Woolsey picked up the phone and placed a call. After speaking to the oceanographer, he cradled the phone. "The sea currents frequently exceed ten knots in that area, but according to his data, it was probably less than five at the time Dyer was diving." The phone rang. Kevin waited. "That was the Duty Officer," Woolsey said. "Duncan and Ray were picked up in Catalina."

"Did he say where they were taking them?"

"LA."

"Can I get a copy of Dyer's file?"

"Tell you what, Colonel—do the JAG for me and the file's yours. Of course, I'll sign the report."

"You can do it. You owe it to Petty Officer Dyer, his parents, and the United States Navy."

Woolsey picked up the file and headed to the copy machine. A Yeoman offered to do it, but he declined. He placed the copies in a plain envelope and wrote some numbers on the back. He handed the folder to Kevin and pointed out the phone numbers. "The first one's my direct line, the other's my home. Emergencies only."

"Fair enough." Kevin tucked the envelope under his arm and left.

The coastal fog was making its afternoon return as Kevin made his way to the car. The sun had disappeared behind the blanket of gray, the damp wind penetrated his jacket. He huddled in the pay phone next to the admin building. He took out Mike's card and dialed, eager to hear more about the divers. "Hey, Mike—Kevin. I hear they picked up Duncan and Ray. Are they headed your way?"

"How could you possibly know that? Aren't you off this case?"

"Come on, Mike—give me a break. Where are they?"

"On their way here, but they were only arrested an hour ago. Where are you?"

"The amphib base in San Diego. It's called being in the right place at the right time. I was with Woolsey when he got the call. There are some puzzling things about Dyers' autopsy."

"Not on the phone. Can you come to the office? We can talk before Duncan and Ray arrive."

"Sure. So, how'd they find them?"

Mike laughed. "It fits their pattern," he said. "They went on a drinking binge after they left *Atlantis* and shacked up with a couple of babes. They ended up getting arrested for drunk and disorderly conduct. When the officer called his report in, he finds out about their outstanding warrants. Imagine the girls' expressions when they heard their escorts are wanted for murder."

Kevin shook his head, disgusted. "Any chance I can speak to them in private? I don't care how long I have to wait, or what time of day it is—I just need a few minutes."

"So you're back in?"

"I'm in."

"Tell you what, Kev—plan on observing from a separate room, but I'll check with my supervisor and see what he says. I can't promise anything."

"Make sure security is expecting me."

"Rush hour" is a meaningless term in Southern California. In fact, the only quiet hour occurs between two and three at night. Kevin crept along the interstate averaging thirty to forty miles per hour. He got off the interstate two hours later.

He was at Mike's office by a quarter to four, surprised to see Mike waiting for him. He checked him through security and escorted him down the hall. "I don't know why, but my boss agreed to let you talk to them before we do. You'll be videotaped. It's for security purposes and to help us formulate questions, but whatever you guys say is officially off the record. Of course, Duncan and Ray still have to agree to talk to you."

"I understand. Are they here?"

"Not yet." Mike checked his watch. "They should be landing at LAX about now. They'll have to be booked, so we have plenty of time to talk about that autopsy report."

"How about if I show you?"

Mike's eyes lit up as Kevin handed him the envelope. "It's the drowning ruling that bothers me. You should talk to that pathologist. Something's not right—the currents were only five knots and Dyer's air tanks were nearly full."

Mike looked up. "Where'd you hear that?"

"That's what the oceanographer told Woolsey. Five knots was his best guess."

Mike stared at the report. "One way or another, we'll get to the bottom of this."

20

EOD divers Duncan and Ray looked pale as they entered the in-processing room. The Convair 580's vibrating props had pounded their already throbbing heads. Their bloodshot eyes made for outlandish mug shots. The booking officer issued them sweat clothes and locked them in a cell.

Agent Mike Pentaglia hung up the phone. "Good news, Kevin. They're being booked right now. I'll see if they'll meet with you. If they agree, I'll take you to the conference room."

"Great. Make sure they understand I have nothing to do with your investigation—that I'm on their side."

"I will."

Kevin thought about what he'd say—what he'd ask. How would he feel when he saw them? He jotted a few notes.

"You're in luck," Mike said, peering in the door. "Let's go."

Mike escorted Kevin into the holding facility. Kevin found himself looking for cameras; Duncan and Ray were too hung over to care. Duncan did not check Kevin out.

Mike said, "Mr. Hamilton's here because he wanted to speak with you in private. As I told you before, he's not here in any official capacity and represents no one. Nothing you say can or will be used in a court of law so it's in your best interest to level with him. He believes you're innocent. You still want to speak to him?"

Duncan nodded. "Why not? We didn't do nothin' wrong."

"Well, Kevin—I guess I'll leave you alone."

"Thanks, Mike. We'll be fine." Kevin waited until the door shut, then looked at Duncan and Ray. They reeked. The ventilation couldn't handle it. "Sorry we're meeting under such circumstances. I'm a retired Marine Corps pilot and have tremendous respect for what you do for our country. Thanks for meeting with me." Duncan stared at the floor. "Like Agent Pentaglia said, I don't believe you've committed a crime—at least outside Catalina."

"Whaddaya know 'bout us?" Duncan asked, his voice slurred. "An' why do ya care?"

Kevin leaned against the wall. "I suppose in a roundabout way I feel responsible for Dyer's death and putting you in this place."

"Say what?"

"You heard me. If we hadn't ditched, none of us would be here right now."

Duncan pulled himself up on the bench. "What's in it for Ray and me—to talk, I mean?"

"If you're honest, I'll share information about Petty Officer Dyer's JAG investigation. If you cooperate, I'll share it with your lawyer. By the way—I suggest you find a good one. Everyone around here thinks you're guilty of murder."

Mike winced watching the video monitor.

"That's a bunch of crap. We didn't kill anyone. Hell, we didn't even know Dyer. He was a kid, for Chrissake. Why would we kill 'im?"

"Beats me." Kevin looked at Ray, who seemed to go along with whatever Duncan said. He was Duncan's lackey. "Tell me the truth, Dan—were you diving when Dyer was killed?" Duncan didn't answer. "Is that why they couldn't find you aboard *Atlantis* when they paged you?"

Kevin's questions were taking their toll on Ray. Cooperating was his ticket out, and he wasn't about to blow the opportunity. "Sir, we did dive that night, but only 'cause we wanted to finish the job. Skipper Battock was out to get us the moment we showed up—just ask Lieutenant Commander Duncan. We couldn't do anything right. The only reason we got shut down was out of contempt. Believe me, we were as anxious to get off his ship as he was to get rid of us, and the only way to do that was to dive without his permission. Face it, Mr. Hamilton—underwater salvage isn't real exciting."

"That's Lieutenant Colonel Hamilton, USMC, retired." Duncan wasn't impressed. Kevin contemplated Ray's words. Maybe he wasn't Duncan's lackey after all. "Let's move on. You were both SEALs—why were you transferred to EOD?"

"It was bullshit, sir."

"Shaddup," Duncan said.

"Tim—is your resentment because you were kicked off the SEALs, or is it something else?"

Duncan cut Ray off before he could answer. "We weren't AWOL, ya know."

"That's not what the Navy says."

"Yeah? Well who gives a shit? We had some time off so we headed to Avalon. We found a couple of beach babes who were cruising for a good time so we helped 'em out. How're we supposed to know our all-night party would turn into an extra day? Everyone was drunk—no one cared. Next thing we know, cops are hauling us away. I couldn't believe it when they said we were wanted by the FBI." He released a rancid belch.

Kevin waited.

"Anyway, I figured our buds were playing a joke. Wudda been a good one, too."

"So you had some fun in Catalina. You still haven't answered my question about why you were kicked out of the SEALs."

"Colonel, you ever see any action?"

"Some," he said.

"Then ya know we don' fight to win anymore, right?"

Kevin saw where Duncan was heading. "Commander Duncan, whether we agree or disagree with US policy is irrelevant. We took an oath to defend our country. What's your point?"

Duncan's fists tightened. "You know they were broadcasting live fuckin' TV from the beaches we were assaulting? All the enemy had to do was turn on CNN. That stupidity cost me three men!" He took a few deep breaths and settled down, his hands relaxed. "So, Colonel—what kind of combat did you see?"

"I flew A-4's, then FA-18s. The Gulf, Bosnia, other places."

Duncan laughed. "And all police actions, right? I know all about 'em, but flyin's a whole different game. You drop your bombs and fly back to your nice neat bunk without knowing anything about the people you just killed. War becomes personal when you use a knife. Let me tell you, Colonel—we fought with everything we had on that fuckin' beach. And for what? So politicians could watch live fuckin' TV?"

Kevin sat down on the floor. "Can we get back to my question?"

Duncan's bloodshot eyes focused. "Look—we made some bad decisions and got kicked off the SEALs, but it was no big deal. We borrowed some air tanks, for Chrissake. We planned to fill 'em when we got back. No one would've known except a new guy, Freeman I think, was holier than thou and turned us in." Duncan laughed, tossing his head back. "He didn't last, though. Someone said he's an FBI agent now. Fits don't it?"

Mike reached for a notepad, still watching the video.

"SEALS don't rat on each other," he said, firing a gaze at Ray. "Anyway, after we checked into Mobile Three, we decided we'd enjoy life. After all, we'd already blown our careers, so we went to Avalon. Know what I mean?"

Kevin nodded. "You've been through a lot, Dan. As for the CNN coverage, you're right, it sucks, but it's in the past. Now give it to me straight—were either of you resentful enough about Skipper Battock to sabotage his salvage operation? Remember, you already admitted to making an unauthorized dive and had the know-how and opportunity to blow up the wreck."

"No fuckin' way!" Duncan said.

Kevin wanted a hardcopy of the transcript. Mike must be floored.

"Look, I already told you our mission was to secure the site so Battock could do his fuckin' salvage operation. If he'd let us do our job, we might've disarmed the bomb and they would've had something to bring up. Do you really think we'd try smuggling C4 aboard *Atlantis*? Besides, why blow up a wrecked cargo plane?"

Kevin looked at them. They weren't actors. They were pissed off soldiers. "Someone had a motive. Tell me about your unauthorized dive."

"Like I said, I figured if we checked everything out that night, we could make a brief dive in the morning, pronounce it safe, and be on our way with the rest of the day off. We were promised a helo, see, so we were pretty motivated." Kevin nodded.

"It only took a few minutes to inspect," Duncan continued. "The hole was like a shark's mouth, its teeth bent out. It was safer going in through the forward section where the cockpit used to be. Everything inside was trashed. Containers were smashed up against the cargo net. But there was a big enough hole where we could move around a bit. We were making our way aft when something hit the ceiling—a metallic *thump*. I signaled Tim to kill his floodlight. We waited, listening, wondering who else was out there. I looked out the over-wing window and saw a brief glimpse of light. Then everything was dark. I figured Battock must've sent someone down to look for us so we got outta there. We felt our way back with our lights off. When I found the anchor chain, I knew we had it made. My rope was still there. It was dark, and no one was expecting us. It wasn't hard to climb aboard undetected. We changed into our sweats, stashed our gear, and blended in. Battock saw me and was so pissed he sent me to my room like a kid. All was fine until he ordered General Quarters.

"I couldn't believe the chaos. I saw women crying and men puking but didn't have a clue why. I went aft and saw Dyer. XO McClintock and the corpsman were doing all they could to save him. They knew he wouldn't make it, but they weren't giving up. Battock told me to get lost so I did. I swear to God, we never saw anyone and I have no idea what happened to Dyer. I'm sorry it happened. I wish I could take it back."

"Anything else?" Kevin asked. Duncan had sobered up, perhaps from guilt.

"Not 'til the next morning. We performed our scheduled dive under much improved conditions. The water was clear and the light penetrated nicely. The hole looked bigger, but I'm sure that's because of the lighting. Anyway, I figured we'd try going through it this time. Somehow things didn't look the same. Then I noticed some explosives tucked inside a container. When I backed up, my flipper hit something and tugged at it. We were screwed. I expected an explosion, but it didn't come. *Atlantis* was right on top of us and there were other divers with us. We didn't have any option but to get outta there. *Atlantis* barely got moving before the goddam thing blew. We were lucky."

Something wasn't right. Kevin recalled Dyer's file. "Did you have any problems with an undertow?" Duncan looked at Ray, confused. Ray shrugged. "Let me rephrase that. Was the current sucking you into the hole?" Duncan and Ray looked at him like he was crazy. Kevin opened the envelope and showed them the autopsy report. "Dyer had severe trauma to his right side and puncture wounds to vital organs from behind. As you know, he was impaled on the fuselage with shrapnel poking clear through him, so if the currents weren't drawing you in... "

"Jesus Christ," Duncan said, gawking at the photos.

"Unfortunately, you two are still the only ones whose whereabouts weren't accounted for, so you're still the prime suspects. I wanted you to know that before you talked to anyone else."

"But we didn't do it," Ray said. "Like Dan said, we froze when that light went by. I never saw a thing, but I knew someone was out there. I felt a large fish swim against me. We were pressed against the ceiling, unable to move. It's like we were in a tornado shelter waiting for a twister to pass, except we couldn't ever be sure it did. We sure as hell didn't want anyone to find us so we got outta there when we could."

Duncan stared at Kevin. "Find out what hit the ceiling, what made the metallic thump."

Kevin stuffed the report back in the envelope. They were caged wolves, persecuted for being wolves. "For whatever it's worth, I believe you. You're a disgrace to the uniform, but you're not murderers. What can I do to help?"

"Testify at our hearing," Duncan said. "Look, Colonel—we'll do anything to get out of here. Even submit to a lie detector test. We've got nothing to hide. Yeah—we screwed up doing that second dive and I'll take the rap for that, but this other light, the metallic thud thing—that wasn't us."

Kevin handed Duncan his business card. "Here's my number. I'll do what I can. Good luck."

The guard escorted Kevin to the observation room where Mike was waiting. Mike continued to watch the video monitor. "Well?" Kevin asked.

"It was a convincing performance, but then they've had plenty of time to rehearse, put out red herrings. Since you left, they've been having quite a chat. They're truly mystified over the murder charge, though. Of course, I'm sure they know they're being watched so some of it's probably for our benefit. For now, I'm gonna hand them over to the Navy to face AWOL charges. They'll be easy to find the next time around."

"Sounds good. So, Mike—assuming someone else planted the explosives, how could they have done it without someone from *Atlantis* noticing?"

"I'm working on that."

"Must've traveled underwater, right? It's a fair distance from shore and there weren't any other surface ships nearby. Maybe that metallic thump isn't a red herring. Maybe we're looking at submarines."

"Some of those minisubs have pretty good range. Let's see what we can find out. See what you can find in the phone book while I check the computer."

Kevin began checking the various Yellow Pages for submarine charters, underwater exploration, and anything in between. Mike placed calls and worked the computer screen. After an hour, Mike was smiling. "Let's go for a ride."

Dense fog reflected off their headlights as they merged on the freeway. Traffic was heavy. "We're meeting a field agent in Long Beach. One of the dockworkers saw a ship with a piggybacked minisub depart the day after your accident. The sub's in a warehouse now." He noticed the concern in Kevin's face. "Relax, Kev—nothing's gonna happen."

Mike turned onto a deserted dimly lit street. Barking dogs challenged them. Seagulls flew away. "Where's your backup?" Kevin asked. "I mean, what if someone's guarding the warehouse?"

"Geez, Kevin, don't believe everything you see in the movies. All we're doing is checking out a warehouse. Besides, we are the backup."

Mike's car slowed to a crawl. He turned off the headlights and inched his way up to a Ford Taurus parked on the street. "Wait here," he said. Kevin slumped in his seat, watching Mike climb into the sedan. Two minutes later, he was back. "You sure you want in on this?"

"Yes."

"All right—here's the deal. The sub's definitely inside the warehouse, but we're waiting on a search warrant. The warehouse owner's on his way to open the building for us. With any luck, we'll be in and gone within the hour."

Kevin scanned the streets. "Does your friend in the Taurus have a camera?"

"Yup—infrared. You do realize there's no guarantee this is the right sub."

Kevin shrugged. "Still our best lead."

Boredom settled in. Kevin leaned back in his seat. "Bet you never imagined being on a stakeout, did you?" Mike asked.

"Nope."

"Most of our stakeouts are as interesting as filing paperwork." Mike kept scanning the streets and docks for movement. *Where's that warehouse owner?*

Kevin stiffened when a small sedan pulled up to the Taurus. This time Mike stayed put. "Another agent?" Mike nodded, intent on what was going on outside. The sedan driver passed something over and drove off. The entire event took less than a minute.

Mike quietly opened his door. "Be right back."

Kevin felt his adrenaline pumping. He wasn't tired anymore, especially since Mike was still in the Taurus. He watched a '72 Ford pickup stop in front of the warehouse. Then Mike was waving for him to join them. Kevin slid out of the car and ran to the Taurus.

"Kevin—this is Special Agent Rick Jordan." Kevin met his hand. "That should be the warehouse owner. Rick's gonna watch our backs while we're inside. If you prefer, you can stay here with him."

"No."

"Okay. Stay close and let me do the talking." Kevin nodded and followed Mike across the street. Mike approached the truck from the driver's side, shining his flashlight into the driver's face. "Special Agent Pentaglia—FBI. Are you the owner?"

The pot-bellied man in coveralls squinted in the light, his hands on the steering wheel. "Of course I am. And get that goddam light outta my face."

Mike lowered the beam and the man got out, his pajama pants hanging over his slippers. He reeked of beer, but that's not to say he was drunk, just crotchety.

"So why'd you drag me down here?"

Mike tucked his badge into his pocket. "We've been told you have a minisub in your warehouse. I have a search warrant—we'd like to see it." He showed the warrant.

The man was too tired to care. "Make it fast. I gotta be back at dawn."

The old man removed a huge set of keys from his pocket. "What's your name," Mike said.

"Farley."

"Okay, Farley, let's see what's inside."

Farley opened the door and flipped on the lights. "Sorry it's so dark. I had to take some bulbs out for energy conservation." Kevin and Mike stepped inside, surprised to find it so crowded.

Farley was closing the door when a car approached. "Might be one of my renters," he said, taking a look outside.

Jordan noticed the slow-moving car. Its rear window rolled down in slow motion. Someone was moving around inside. Something was wrong. He went for his gun. "Get down!" he yelled.

Shots rang out and Kevin knocked Pentaglia to the ground. Seconds later, a brilliant flash ignited a quick-spreading fire in the entry. Kevin was dazed but uninjured. He rolled over and saw the flames, his ears still ringing from the blast. He couldn't see; the flames were too bright. He shielded his eyes with his hand, expecting to find Mike at his side. He was startled neither he nor Farley were anywhere nearby. "Mike! Farley! Where are you?" The flames were deafening. A draft swirled about him as the fire intensified. "Mike! Farley! Talk to me!"

Mike was watching Farley when the bomb went off. He was blinded from the light and disoriented after Kevin knocked him down. He felt the heat, but couldn't tell which direction to go. He shined his flashlight in circles, hoping to get Kevin's attention. "Kevin! Over here," he said on his knees, gasping for air. "I can't see!"

Kevin heard Mike's voice and saw his light dancing in the smoke. He still hadn't found Farley. "I see you, Mike." He looked for Farley, then grabbed Mike's arm. "Give me the flashlight and hold onto my arm."

"All I see are spots. Where's Farley?"

"I don't know, but we can't stick around." He moved Mike to a corner and set him down. "Wait here—I've got to find an exit." He looked around the firetrap. Where were the exit signs? He took one last look for Farley. Flames consumed what used to be the entrance. He shielded himself as best he could, but the heat was too intense. Then he saw Farley's burning body. He made his way back to Mike. "Farley's dead," he shouted, helping him to his feet. Flames licked the ceiling, the roof creaked. The fire was igniting some of the boats and vehicles. "When the flames reach these oil drums, all hell's gonna break loose. Hang onto my shoulder, Mike. We have to find another spot."

Jordan reloaded his weapon as he watched the front of the building go up in flames. There was no way to get inside. He waited for the ambulance and fire trucks, fearing the worst.

Kevin huddled behind a steel girder, bouncing his flashlight beam off the walls. It was a combat zone; explosions sent molten shrapnel flying through the air. He hit the deck as another fifty-gallon drum blew, wondering how in the hell they'd get out. The windows were fifteen feet high and covered with steel security bars. There weren't any unlocked doors. Kevin's flashlight beam bounced off the answer to his prayers. He found Mike and pulled him to his feet. "Let's go. Hold onto my hand."

The tow truck didn't look like it had been used in years. He pushed Mike into the passenger's side and rolled up the window. "Stay low, Mike." Kevin ran to the driver's side and reached for the ignition, thankful the keys were there. He pumped the accelerator several times and held his breath as he turned the key. The starter engaged, but the engine failed to start. Flames swirled around him, burning debris flying past the windshield. More explosions. They were getting closer. He pumped more gas, cursing under his breath. The engine belched and came to life. *Thank you, God.*

The wheel was hot, the paint blistering on the hood. If they didn't move soon, either the fuel tank would ignite or the tires would blow. He forced the shifter into first gear and held the clutch. It was rough, but running. "Hold on," he said, revving the engine. He flipped on the headlights and popped the clutch. The tires screeched as the truck lunged forward. He steered it towards the wall where the fire seemed weakest.

They hit the wall at twenty miles per hour and everything went dark. For a second Kevin was back in the DC-10, then he had the truck stopped. He felt cool air on his face. He sat there, shaking. "Let's go, Mike," he managed.

Mike's vision slowly returned as they walked down the side street. They heard sirens. Lots of them, and barking dogs. Kevin sucked in the damp fog. "Farley's dead, more evidence destroyed. I swear to God, Mike, I'm the only common denominator."

"You're alive," Jordan shouted, running their way.

Kevin and Mike stopped and turned. Jordan had beads of sweat pouring off his brow. "I thought you were toast," he said. "Where's the old man?"

"Inside," Mike said. "I'm sure he was killed instantly."

"I screwed up, Mike. I aimed at the tires when I should've gone for the driver."

"Shit happens," Mike said, disappointed in his backup. Then again, maybe he was the one who misjudged his opponent.

Kevin watched the firefighters direct their stang guns, shooting streams of water from across the street while the explosions continued inside. Police cordoned off the area and kept the media vans at bay. Had it not been for the fog, a news helicopter would be circling overhead. He noticed Mike rubbing his eyes. "You need eye drops. I'm sure they'll have some in the ambulance."

"I'll be all right."

"Suit yourself, but they sure helped me," Kevin said. Mike nodded, flames dancing in his swollen eyes. "It's in there, you know."

Mike looked at Kevin. "What? The sub?"

"Yup. I saw it when I was looking for an exit. I can draw you a picture."

"Super. Rick, find something for him to write on—quickly." Jordan ran back to the car. As soon as he left, he noticed two ambulance attendants making their way towards them. The woman EMT asked if they were all right. Mike nodded, coughing while wiping the soot from his face. "We're fine, but the guy inside wasn't so lucky. You might want to stick around to take him away."

She nodded. "Was he a friend of yours?"

Mike hesitated. "Yeah, he was."

"I'm sorry. Guess I'd better find out what they want us to do. Let me know if you need anything. I expect we'll be here a while," she said.

"Thanks."

It took two hours to contain the three-alarm blaze, but finally the firemen were rolling up their hoses. One engine company remained on site to douse any hot spots. Kevin watched a lone fireman drag Farley's body outside. It was curled up like a roasted marshmallow. He recalled seeing an FA-18 burst into flames after it flipped over on landing. Its pilot looked the same.

Most of the firefighters had left by the time they loaded Farley's body into the ambulance. Mike noticed a police officer writing some notes and approached him. "This is an FBI investigation now."

The police officer looked at Mike's badge and went back to his notes. "Fine with me, but I still have to file my report. You okay? You don't look so good."

"It's been a long night. Would you secure the site 'til we inspect it tomorrow?"

"Consider it done." The officer went to retrieve a roll of plastic tape from his car to cordon off the building.

Jordan returned with a notepad as the officer was leaving. He pulled Pentaglia aside while Kevin scribbled. "I never saw 'em until it was too late," he said. "I don't know what street they came down—they just showed up. Couldn't see the plates either."

Mike Pentaglia nodded. "My guess is it was a phosphorous charge, someone with a military explosives background." Duncan and Ray came to mind, but this time they had a rock-solid alibi. "I can't imagine many people would have access to that type of explosive." He walked back to Kevin. "How's the drawing coming?"

"Okay," he said, eager to finish while it was fresh in his mind. When he closed his eyes he saw more details, but also saw flames. Too close, he mused. Damned lucky. He put finishing touches on and passed it to Pentaglia.

Mike was impressed with the detail, especially considering Kevin saw it under duress. There was no doubt it's what they were looking for, but how could it have survived the fire? Once again, the trail grew cold. "Someone's doing a fine job of covering their tracks," he said.

Kevin stared at the smoldering ruins. "Yeah, but there's a bright side."

Mike frowned. "How could anything good come from this?"

"It proves we're on the right track."

"Okay, so who tipped them off that we were looking for the sub?"

Jordan had been wondering the same thing. It takes time to set up a professional hit, and this was definitely professional. Was there a mole in the bureau, or had someone intercepted their phone calls? "Whoever's responsible must have unlimited resources."

Mike nodded. There were others with Duncan and Ray's qualifications who'd do the job. The investigation had turned lethal. They'd have to take extra precautions. "So Kevin, which one of your nine lives did you use tonight?"

Kevin smiled. "I think that was number eight. It was a lot safer in the Corps."

Jordan examined the sketch. "This sub looks like a torpedo with arms."

"Exactly," Kevin said. "It's about twenty feet long with two pincer-type robotic arms mounted in front of a glass nose. I imagine the pilot operates it from a prone position. It didn't look big enough to do it any other way."

"How many can it carry?" Pentaglia asked.

"Maybe two, but they'd practically be on top of each other."

"Rick, call the National Geographic Society first thing this morning. Fax them Kevin's drawing and see if they know of any minisubs out here that fit this description. We need to know more about its capabilities and crew, too. If the National Geographic doesn't know anything, see if they know someone who does. Also, get your film developed and leave the prints on my desk. That car may have been there all along just waiting for Farley to unlock the building."

"I'll get right on it. You guys heading back to the office?"

Mike stared at the docks. "Not yet. I want to check out that flat-decked ship over there. Maybe it carried the sub."

"Well, keep me posted," he said, disappearing into the darkness.

Mike walked over to the Battalion Chief, who was watching his firefighters turn over the hot spots. "How long before we can look around?" he asked.

The Chief stared at Pentaglia. "You're joking, right?" Pentaglia shook his head. "This was a hot fire. Who knows what was in there? I won't allow my investigator in until morning. If you come back around eight, it should be okay."

"Thanks. For whatever it's worth, there was a brilliant flash before the fire."

"I'll pass that on," he said. "Nothing surprises me anymore."

Mike walked over to the police officer. "Looks like the perimeter's secure. We'll be back in the morning."

"Have a good night."

Kevin watched a duck swim around a small dingy. A few boats had lights on, either for security or people were living aboard. It was low tide and the seaweed smelled. Seagulls slept in the parking lot, one atop a light fixture.

"What's so interesting? Mike asked, joining him on the dock.

"See that gray boat?" Kevin said. "Blends into the fog pretty well, doesn't it."

"Sure does."

"Camouflage makes sense for military vessels, but why a civilian ship?"

Mike aimed his flashlight. HEAVEN'S GATE was stenciled across the stern in large black letters. It was the ship's only markings. "Weird isn't it?"

"What, the color?"

"No, the fact that we come out of an inferno to find Heaven's gate in the fog."

"I guess," Kevin said, missing the irony, too tired to ask.

Mike stretched his back. "Let's go home. It'll be a short night."

"It's not too late for those eye drops. Lots of all-night pharmacies open."

21

Fog hovered over the warehouse site; it slunk out of the dark alleys and abandoned buildings. Seagulls still huddled in the parking lot. Dogs barked. A foghorn blared its lonely tune. Five hours of sleep hadn't helped. Kevin and Mike were tired.

It was a miracle the fire didn't spread. It was also understandable how Jordan missed the hit-car. Kevin spotted someone running on the dock, wondering if he was connected to the bombing. He went to investigate, but by the time Pentaglia joined him the man was gone.

"What's going on, Kev?"

"Nothing. Everything in place?"

"Yup. Lots of yellow police crime scene tape everywhere and there's an officer across the street to enforce it. If only the fire investigator were here."

"Maybe that's him," Kevin said, pointing to a man in coveralls and rubber boots walking towards an unmarked car.

Mike held up his badge as he approached. "Morning," he said. "Are you the fire investigator?"

"That's me. I take it you're the ones who were here last night."

"Yup. Your Chief said we could look around when it was safe."

"Have at it, but be careful. There's a lot of sharp metal and some warm spots."

"Thanks. By the way, can I get a copy of your report?" he asked, handing him his business card. "You can fax it to the number at the bottom."

The inspector stuck it in his pocket, continuing his work.

Kevin followed Mike into the charred wet muck. The damage was worse than he imagined. The walls and supports were warped, roof collapsed, contents either charred or destroyed. It seemed unlikely the sub survived, but he had to check it out. He paused at the spot where Farley died. He barely remembered what he looked like.

"Crap." Mike pulled his shoe out of the mess. Kevin turned. "Guess I picked a bad day to wear pressed slacks and loafers," he said.

Kevin smiled, no better off. "They don't match anyway."

"Not anymore."

Kevin retraced his route as best he could, pausing several times to imagine where he was last night. Everything looked so different. He edged his way through the twisted steel and rubble to a spot where the metal roof touched the ground. "I think this is it," he said, prying the roof up. "Give me a hand, Mike." Kevin jammed a piece of re-bar between a fifty-gallon drum filled with saturated chemical spill material and the roof and leaned into it, but the corrugated steel barely moved. Mike added his weight and the metal rose to a point where it balanced.

"Hold it there," Kevin said, sliding warped fifty-gallon drums underneath.

"Maybe we should wait for a crane."

Kevin grabbed the flashlight and ducked underneath. "I see it, Mike," he said, inching forward. "Get in here."

Mike squatted down, creeping towards the light in the muck. "Well, I'll be damned," he said. The paint was charred, but it was in better shape than either expected. "I'll bet this thing can tell a story or two. We'll get some heavy equipment in here."

"Give me a minute." He heard Mike's footsteps sloshing and planned to follow, but the stainless steel pincers were too intriguing to leave. Its claw reminded him of some marks on Dyer's body.

He peered inside the melted Plexiglas nosecone to see the control levers and pilot's cushion. As suspected, it was operated from a prone position. The cabin appeared large enough to accommodate an observer, but with only a single hatch, he didn't see how a diver could enter or exit while the sub was submerged. He'd just turned around when a brilliant flash blinded him. He ducked and covered his head, but there was no loud explosion or flames. Behind the spots in his eyes, Mike was preparing to take another picture. "You idiot. You scared the crap outta me!"

"Sorry," Mike said. "I needed you in the shot for a size comparison. I didn't expect you to turn around, but I should've warned you. Find anything interesting?"

"Yeah, as a matter of fact," he said, still angry. Blinking did nothing to clear the spots. "There's no flood chamber so no one could've gotten in or out. If this sub was used to plant the explosives, the bomb must've been carried externally and positioned with the pincers." Mike nodded. "Look at this, Mike." Kevin's beam reflected off the stainless steel appendages. He made a pass over their full length and stopped at the joints. "I bet these pincers can rotate three hundred sixty degrees and bend up and down like human arms. They may have limited range, but its claws look delicate enough to plant a bomb. You remember Dyer's autopsy report?" Mike nodded again, intrigued. "Don't you think these pincers match the marks on his body?"

"I'd say Dyer was rammed, grabbed by the pincers, and pinned to the plane like a butterfly," Mike said.

Mike took the flashlight and scanned the full length of the sub. Its curled pincers made it look like a praying mantis. He dug out his camera and took several close-ups of the pincers and a couple of the pilot's controls. When he finished, he returned the camera to its pouch. "Great theory, but why didn't they detonate the bomb after they killed Dyer? Why wait until morning when they could've made Dyer the fall guy that night? With the evidence blown to hell, the Navy might've ruled it a suicide and we would've had a helluva time proving otherwise."

"Maybe they didn't want to blow up *Atlantis*. Don't you remember the hoopla about it being the Navy's newest ship? Can you imagine the pressure if it sank?"

"Yeah, maybe."

On the way back to the car, Mike checked his voice mail from his cell phone. There was a message from Tony Perini of the lab saying both bombs used the same type of plastic explosives. There had to be a connection, but what?

Mike tucked the phone in his pocket. "You won't like this, Kev, but your company's safety reps are returning to Oklahoma City. They said since it was a bomb and not mechanical failure, their work is done."

"No surprise there. But I'm still in," Kevin said, grimly.

"Of course. Nothing's changed. You're still on loan to the FBI."

They both noticed the white pickup truck racing towards them. It was coming at such high speed that Mike drew his gun and took aim at the driver. If the driver so much as tossed a cigarette he'd be dead. The truck screeched to a halt in front of the warehouse and a man in a blue jumpsuit leaped out, his hands raised in disbelief. Mike holstered his gun as the man ran to the police officer. The officer said something and the man dropped to his knees, pounding his fists on the sidewalk. "We'd better see what's going on."

Mike assumed he was a relative of Farley's and wanted to offer his condolence. He was the last man to see him alive; it was the least he could do. "Excuse me. Sir?" The man finally looked up. "I'm Special Agent Pentaglia, FBI. What seems to be the problem?"

"My sub. First it's stolen and now it's burned up. I can't believe this!"

Mike looked at Kevin. "Your sub?"

"That's right. I run an underwater exploration business—or should I say, used to. I came out to work on her a few days ago and she was gone. Then I got this anonymous call saying she was in Santa Monica. I figured it was a joke, but sure enough, she was docked at the pier. Whoever stole her must've felt bad and called

211

me. Of course her batteries were drained, but at least nothing was missing. After that I decided to store her in Farley's warehouse so he could keep an eye on her. The harbormaster told me about the fire. I can't believe it."

"Was Farley a friend of yours?"

The man smiled. "Farley and I go back twenty years. I worked for him before starting my own business. He's gonna be real pissed when he sees this."

"What's your name, sir?" Mike asked.

"Wayne—Wayne Riley." He saw something in Mike's eyes. "What's wrong?"

"Wayne, I'm sorry, but—"

Riley's face went slack. "Ah, shit. He's dead? He was in there?"

Mike bowed his head. "Wayne, last night there was a drive-by bombing. I think it had something to do with your sub." Riley stared at the rubble. "I know it's bad timing, but I need your help." Wayne nodded. His chin quivered. "I'll give you a moment," Mike said, pulling Kevin aside. They moved far enough away so Riley couldn't hear. "You think he's legit?"

"Don't you?"

"I have to admit, if he's faking, he deserves an Oscar," Mike said. "Farley must've been a trusted friend. I wonder if he'd recognize the caller's voice."

"That's a thought," Kevin said.

Riley headed their way. "I can talk now."

Mike told him about the plane crash, the underwater explosion, and why they were looking for his sub. His eyes hurt. "I don't think Farley was a target," he said. "He just happened to be in the wrong place. Kevin and I were lucky to get out."

"You were in there?"

"Yeah," Mike said, putting a couple eye drops in. "The bomb blinded me. Kevin got me out."

Riley looked angrily at Kevin. "You both got out, but Farley didn't? You just left him there?"

"Wayne," Mike said, "there was a bomb. Farley was by the door when it went off. Kevin searched for him and saw him under the door, engulfed in flames and not moving. I was hoping to spare you the details. I'm sorry. He never had a chance."

Riley closed his eyes. "I can't believe someone would do this."

"I assure you, we'll get to the bottom of this. Someone saw your sub on *Heaven's Gate* three days ago. Did you have a charter lined up?"

"*Heaven's Gate*? That's impossible. My sub's never been aboard that ship." Mike made a mental a note to look into *Heaven's Gate*. "When was the last time you used your sub?"

Riley took a moment to blow his nose. "Three weeks ago when I was filming a documentary on kelp for PBS. It was no big deal. Just a few hours' work."

Mike removed the notepad from his pocket and began scribbling. "You think someone from that job might've had something to do with stealing your sub?"

"Nah. You ever seen the people that make those documentaries? Trust me, there was nothing weird about that job."

"What do you do when there's nothing scheduled?" Kevin asked.

"The yard, paperwork, whatever. I run the business from my house." His eyes were blank. What would he do now? Start over? He thought about *Heaven's Gate*. "Until she was stolen, I kept her aboard *Skimmer*. She's owned by Barney Fagan."

Mike looked around the crowded harbor. "Which one's *Skimmer*?"

Riley squinted his eyes at the docks. The sun breaking through the fog cast its rays over the area where *Skimmer* should have been. "She must be out on a charter," he said. Mike continued to take notes while he listened. "I can't say Barney's a friend, but we've been doing business for a few years. I don't know where he lives though."

"That's all right. By the way, you care to see your sub?" Riley's eyes lit up. "Wait here." Kevin and Riley watched Mike explain to the officer he was accepting responsibility. Mike was smiling when he returned. "It's a mess in there, so be careful."

While Mike waited on the sidewalk, Kevin guided Riley to the sub. Riley was shaken by what he saw. The sub looked repairable, but he had to face reality. "Thanks for showing me, but it still puts me out of business."

"How so? I mean, I thought you'd be elated. Don't you have insurance?"

"Sure, but my policy won't cover lost revenue. I was bidding a job that starts in two weeks. There's no way it'll be fixed by then. Let's get outta here."

They found Mike sharing a cup of coffee with the officer, steam rising from the Styrofoam cup. "Well?"

"Riley's concerned about his business," Kevin said. He told him about Riley's reaction and the job he was bidding. "He says it can't be repaired in time."

Mike didn't have the heart to tell them the sub would be detained as evidence for the foreseeable future. "Wayne, I know this is a long shot, but couldn't one of your competitors have stolen your sub? I'm just grasping at straws, but if they were bidding the same contract and now you're out of the picture, wouldn't they come out ahead?"

"Not likely," he said, looking over his shoulder at the charred remnants of sailboats and marine supplies. "It wasn't that big of a contract; just a small piece for the Discovery Channel. My bid was ten grand plus expenses. I can't imagine anyone sabotaging my business for that."

"Ten grand doesn't sound that small to me. How long was it going to take?"

"Two days plus another day of standby. I give the option for an extra day. My standard fee is five grand a day."

Mike expected the lab technicians and heavy equipment to show up at any time. Riley's story confirmed they were on the right track and he was eager to match the sub's pincers to the marks on Dyer's body. "Wayne, how many other businesses in the area operate minisubs like yours?"

"I only know of two, but if the money's good enough, people come from all over. I flew my sub to Australia for a rush job once.

It paid double plus expenses so it was worth it. That's the nice thing about being a small business. By leasing space on a mother ship, I have more flexibility and less overhead than those that own one."

"Interesting," Mike said. "How many operators have you worked with?"

"I dunno. Five, ten?"

"How many people would you say are qualified to pilot your sub?"

"Hell, I don't know," he said, pondering who had the know-how and opportunity to steal his sub.

"Try to think, Wayne. We have reason to believe your sub was used to plant a bomb that destroyed an NTSB investigation site. Can you think of anyone?"

"My God." The color drained from his face. He sat down. "Did anyone else die?"

"Yeah. A Navy diver," Kevin said. "He had marks on his body that seem to match your sub's pincers. We still don't know why he died, though."

Riley kept shaking his head from side to side. "This is all too much. Farley's dead—now a diver. I can't think of anyone off-hand, but there are probably a half-dozen people around here who could pilot my sub. If you want to stop by my house, I can get you whatever you need. It's only about fifteen minutes from here."

Mike checked his watch. Whatever Riley had to say was more important than waiting for the lab to show. "Give me a second and we'll go." He instructed the police officer on what the lab should look for and returned. "Okay. All set."

Riley's house was a modest stucco nestled among lemon trees. Lemons dangled precariously, their scent unmistakable. Robins pecked at the lawn while jays watched from the trees. There were no children. His neighbors were retired or the kids were in school. A French poodle barked from a window at the Japanese gardener blowing leaves.

They followed Riley inside. The house reflected his love of the sea. A large fish tank sat atop a bookshelf; a sailing ship's lantern was converted into the overhead light. There didn't appear to be a woman in his life. "Care for some lemonade?" Riley asked. "It's fresh from the tree."

"Sure," Mike said. "Wayne, I need some information on your sub's performance. You know, how fast it can go, how long it can remain underwater, what's the dexterity in the robotic arms? That sort of thing."

Wayne came back from the kitchen and handed him a glass, thinking about his sub's glory days. "She's no speed demon, but I've had her up to ten knots," he said. "With fully charged batteries she can stay underwater about twelve hours solo, half that with an observer. As for the robotics, you can write your name in the sand if you know what you're doing."

Kevin made some calculations. "Wayne, could it make a thirty mile round trip without surfacing?

"That would be pushing it."

Mike said, "But given the right contacts and enough money, your sub could've been underway within hours of the DC-10 going down and no one would've been the wiser."

"Yeah," Kevin said. "That would explain why *Atlantis* didn't see anything."

"Wayne, didn't you say you had a list of operators?"

"Oh, yeah. In my office. Be right back."

Kevin took in the rest of the surroundings, paying particular attention to a photo of a submerged sub collecting kelp samples with its pincers. It had an inscription from a PBS producer thanking Wayne for his work. Even the kitchen cabinets had a nautical theme, probably replicas from an old sailing ship.

Wayne came back and handed Mike a sheet of paper. Kevin looked over Mike's shoulder. Neither expected the list would include minisub operators from Washington State to the Texas

Gulf and Eastern seaboard. "This is exactly what we needed, Wayne. How many are local?"

"Three," Wayne said.

Kevin looked up from the list. "When did you discover your sub was missing?"

"Your friend has it in his notepad. I filed a report with the Long Beach and Santa Monica Police. If you want, I can give you the case number."

Mike looked up. "That might be helpful, thanks."

While Riley returned to his office, Mike studied the list again while sipping his lemonade. "Now that's what lemonade should taste like," he said. He pulled out his notepad to review his notes. Wayne returned with the case number. "Wayne, Kevin and I have been discussing how your sub might've been used. Mind if I run it past you so you can tell us if it would work?"

"Sure."

"We originally thought the sub would have to be deployed from a mother ship, but from what you've said, that may not have been the case. Could it make a submerged round trip from Santa Monica to Santa Cruz Island?"

Riley took out his nautical chart and measured the mileage. "That's over sixty miles one way. That would be an enormous task for the sub and crew. Of course, you could achieve the same objective by piggybacking her within twenty miles, then do the rest of the trip submerged. It doesn't take long to download the sub, and if the mother ship continued on her way, *Atlantis* wouldn't have noticed. Of course speed's still an issue, but if I were making the trip, that's how I'd do it."

"That would explain why she ended up in Santa Monica," Mike said. "Kevin, other than your crewmembers, who else knew your plane was going down?"

"Anyone monitoring the frequency, including any airline passengers that were tuned in through their headsets. If someone reported it to the media, there might've been a news flash. Basically, anyone could've known about it within seconds of our ditching."

Mike nodded. "Time is still the critical element, so it must've been a local job. Wayne, do you pilot your sub?"

"Of course. It's not only fun, I couldn't afford to hire someone else to do it. Does this look like a plush operation?" Kevin smiled. "Believe me, if I were in this for the money, I would've quit a long time ago. Don't get me wrong; I was making ends meet, but only 'cause I keep the overhead small."

Mike watched fish dart around the tank. "I'm still having a hard time understanding how your sub was stolen unless it was by someone familiar with your operation. What can you tell me about *Skimmer's* crew?"

"*Skimmer*? No way she's involved. Hell, Barney's had the same crew for as long as I can remember." He paused to look over the list, pointing at a name. "You know, these guys are just up the road and they're both qualified sub pilots. I've never had much contact with them, though. I only know 'em because they're competition."

Mike wrote the Barclay Brothers' address in his notepad. "Ever have any encounters with them? Undercut them?"

Wayne shook his head. "No. Nothing that I know of, anyway. In fact, other than asking about their rates once, I don't think we've ever spoken."

Mike closed his notepad and slipped it in his pocket. He took his and Kevin's glasses to the kitchen and reached for Wayne's hand. "Wayne, I'm sorry to meet under such difficult circumstances, but we sure appreciate your help. Again, sorry about Farley."

Riley escorted them to the door. As Kevin pulled the car door shut, he waved at Wayne. Wayne waved back. "I hope he'll be all right," he said. Mike nodded and put the car in gear. "Where to now?"

"Barclay Brothers. Kevin, I've got a problem and I need your help."

"Oh?"

"You see, these guys could be suspects and since I can't speak to them without disclosing I'm with the FBI, I need you to talk to them."

Kevin laughed. "You're kidding, right?"

"No, I'm serious. You have no idea how people clam up after I introduce myself. Even innocent people. Of course, you won't have that problem since you'll be posing as a potential client. Tell them you want to see some shipwrecks. Yeah. Tell 'em you're afraid of the water and a sub's the only way you'll ever get to see the ocean. Throw out whatever bullshit you want, but don't change your story. Trust me, you can pull it off."

Kevin stared at him.

"It's no big deal, Kev—really. I'm not asking you to be a secret agent. Just go in and take a look around, then tell me what they're like and what you saw."

Kevin sighed. "Fine. I'll go, but you'd better cover my ass."

The route to Barclay Brothers led to a series of dead-end streets. It took twenty minutes to get there. Kevin took in the view from the parking lot. He could see Farley's warehouse and dock a mile away. If they'd taken a boat, it would have been half that.

A faded Barclay Brothers sign squeaked in the breeze, giving no clue as to the type of operation it was. The building was run down and surrounded by rusty equipment. It looked abandoned. "You sure this is it?"

"That's what the sign says. Don't worry, I'll be right here. Remember, Kevin. Ask about their charters, but don't get carried away or they might get suspicious. Stay in character and you'll be fine."

Kevin nodded, hoping Mike was right. He stepped from the car heading straight for the door, not looking back. As he neared the entrance, he sensed he was being watched. Before he could knock, a large, unshaven man smelling of beer and sweat opened the door and stared at him. Whoever he was, he didn't represent the business any better than the sign. "Is this Barclay Brothers?"

"That's what the sign says, don't it?"

Kevin smiled. How could a place like this stay in business? Maybe it was a front for drug smuggling. Since the Coast Guard stepped up its patrols, maybe underwater smuggling was a new frontier. "I was interested in chartering a sub," he said. "I'm from out of town and wanted to see some shipwrecks before I went home."

"Who says we have a sub?"

Kevin shrugged. "Someone told me you ran a minisub operation. Guess I have the wrong place. Sorry to bother you." He turned to leave.

"Hold on." Kevin turned back. The man looked around and opened the door to let him in. "We don't usually cater to people off the street," he said. "Tell me again what you wanted?"

"I live in the Midwest and I've always dreamed of seeing shipwrecks. I've read about freighters and sailing ships running aground and sinking off Palos Verdes."

The man watched, scratching his beer belly. "I don't think we're right for you," he said. "But thanks for stopping by."

"Wait," Kevin said, trying to keep him from closing the door. "Can't you at least quote me a price? I really want to do this."

"Exactly what shipwrecks were you hoping to see?"

Kevin's heart raced. *Don't get carried away or they might get suspicious.* It seemed easy when Mike said it, but now he couldn't think. He concocted the best story he could, but even he had doubts about it. When he was finished, he smiled.

"You can wait inside if you want. I have to check with the boss."

Kevin watched the man disappear into the back room and close the door. Kevin moved as close as he dared. He heard voices, but couldn't make out their words.

Steve Barclay sat behind the beat-up metal desk with his hands behind his head, wanting to know who his brother had been talking to. "What's up, Larry?"

"There's a guy out there who wants to take a charter," he said, a finger finding his belly. "I dunno, but I got a bad feeling about him."

Steve peered out the window for the second time. Someone was still in the car. He saw Kevin's shoe under the door and smiled. "Come here," he said, quietly. "Now is that a government car or what?"

Larry began pounding his fists together. "I knew something was up. He said he wanted to see shipwrecks, then starts yackin' about Spanish galleons. Christ—he's only off by three hundred miles."

"If you were so sure he was conning you, why's he still here?"

"'Cause I didn't want him to think we were up to something. He doesn't know shit about subs, but he said he's from the Midwest so that made sense. Don't worry—I haven't told him anything."

Steve tapped his pencil, thinking. "Did this guy identify himself as a cop or anything?" Larry shook his head. "I'm guessing your friend is this guy's stooge. Just tell him we don't do sightseeing charters and get rid of him."

Kevin heard footsteps and quickly stepped back, pretending to admire the photos on display. He noted a shot of a bubble-nosed minisub, its pilot in a prone position smiling at the large fish in the foreground. It was taken to make the fish appear larger than the sub. He heard the doorknob turn and felt Larry's eyes on him. He turned around and smiled. "Well?"

"We don't do sightseeing charters. You might check with Wayne Riley."

Larry gave no phone number or directions. Their conversation was over and he wanted him out. "Okay. Thanks anyway," Kevin said. When he got back in the car, he fastened his seat belt and looked straight ahead. "Get me out of here."

Mike started the car and hit the gas. Once they were out of sight, he pulled off the road. "I take it you noticed someone was watching you."

"Yeah. Their eyes were burning a hole in my head." He looked at Mike. "I don't get it, Mike. I had him, then suddenly I didn't exist."

Mike smiled. "Don't blame yourself. They probably had us marked before you ever went inside. Someone kept peeking out the window. They didn't see me the first time because I was lying down, but after that—well, let's just say it's kind of hard being incognito in a stripped-down Chrysler with extra antennas."

"But our conversation didn't end until Bubba returned from the back room. I don't know how many were back there; I only heard voices. I tried listening in, but couldn't make out what they were saying. Oh, I did see a picture of their sub, though. It looks real similar to Wayne's. Even more interesting—Bubba referred me to Wayne like he didn't know anything about Farley's fire."

"Interesting, but if they're smart enough to make us, they're probably smart enough to sound ignorant."

Kevin leaned his head against the headrest. "So, what now?"

"I'll assign someone to keep an eye on the Barclays while we move on to other things. Trust me—this wasn't a wasted trip. They wouldn't have gotten rid of you so fast if they didn't have something to hide. Besides, you confirmed they had a sub like Wayne's and admitted they knew him. You saw how close Wayne's pier is. It would've been real easy to steal his sub. You did good, Kevin."

Kevin closed his eyes, thinking. Mike might have been more convincing if he didn't keep saying he should trust him. Especially after last night. He could be wrong about the Barclays just like he was about Duncan and Ray. "Nothing says they have to take my business, you know."

"Kevin, money's a powerful motivator and it sure looks like they could use some. As far as I'm concerned, the Barclays just became our prime suspects."

22

They reached the office a little before two. Mike went straight to the computer while Kevin divvied up their sandwiches and chips. While the computer booted up, Mike narrated his plan as though he were going through a checklist. Kevin watched from a distance. Mike entered the name Barclay and over thirty mug shots appeared of Barclays that had at least one encounter with the law. "Now for a regional sort," he said, entering another keystroke. The screen shrank to four suspects. "Well? Recognize anyone?"

Kevin studied the faces, surprised he recognized one. "Yeah. That's the guy who answered the door. What's he wanted for?"

"Nothing right now. You see, once you're booked, you've earned a place in the national database. Let's check his profile." With a few more keystrokes, Larry Barclay's bio appeared. "Interesting," he said, reading the screen. "Arrested but not convicted of drug trafficking, and arrested but not convicted of manslaughter. Looks like a real winner, doesn't he? He must have one helluva lawyer."

Kevin studied his record. "What about his brothers?"

Mike went back to the previous screen and compared the remaining photos. You sure you don't know how many people were back there?"

"No. I heard voices. Two for sure."

Mike nodded. It would have been useful knowing whether there were more than two Barclays at Barclay Brothers. He built a square around a bearded man having similar features and positioned him next to Larry. Some computer magic made the second man clean-shaven. He went back to the other suspects. "I don't think these other two are related. Look at their eyes, nose, jaw lines." Kevin nodded. Mike went back to the page with Larry and Steve Barclay. With the stroke of his finger, Steve Barclay's bio appeared. "Bingo." Mike leaned back in his chair, reading the screen. "Seems Stevie's been arrested for arson but no conviction. They certainly fit, don't they?" Without waiting for Kevin's response, Mike placed a call to the Long Beach harbormaster. "Hi. This is Special Agent Pentaglia, FBI. Do you maintain a log for ship movements?"

"How big?"

"Maybe a hundred fifty feet."

"That's too small for us to worry about. I doubt we'd notice anything that size unless it's an extravagant yacht or needs assistance, but if you come to the office I'll be glad to show you around."

"Thanks, but I really don't have the time. Would you keep your eye out for a minisub tender named *Skimmer*? It's got a flat deck and crane."

"I'll put the word out. If we see it, we'll let you know."

Mike gave his number and cradled the phone. "Another dead-end?" Kevin asked.

"He'll look for it. Meanwhile, I'll get some agents to snoop around. If the Barclays decide to run, we'll have reason to pursue them. If not, we'll question them whenever we need to. Either way, they won't get far without us knowing about it. We need to get a court order to tap their phone. If we match a call to someone that had a shipment on your flight, we might have something."

"Makes sense. Since you brought up shipping, did you find anything interesting about the DC-10 load manifest from Global?"

"Nothing so far," he said, searching his desk. "Crap. I know it's around here somewhere. I'll get someone to check on that while we're in the lab."

Mike took Kevin to the lab. They went inside expecting to see Tony Perini in his thick glasses. Mike didn't recognize the rail-thin technician with the slicked back hair. It wasn't like the bureau to swap techs. "Where's Tony?"

"He took the day off," the man said, wiping his hands. "He wasn't feeling well."

Mike checked out the man's ID. Everything appeared legitimate. Since Tony wasn't around, he had little choice but to put his confidence in the stranger. "Did Tony come up with anything new on the DC-10 case?"

"Hang on, I'll check." The tech returned moments later with a file labeled, "Global Cargo Express DC-10 Inflight Explosion." He turned to the summary page, scanning it for anything significant. "It says two separate charges were used, both were C4 plastic explosives most likely set off by timing devices. Microscopic fragments from a plastic wristwatch were found with the first bomb but there's nothing listed for the second. They found a slight amount of oily unexploded matter on some metal fragments. According to this, the second bomb was likely placed inside the aircraft after it ditched."

Kevin nodded. No new revelations there. He would've bet his next paycheck on those findings. "What did the fragments with unexploded material look like?"

The tech skipped to the appendix showing photos of a jagged piece of metal with arrows pointing to the explosive material. "It says it's a very strong alloy with an aluminum base, but there's no known material like it. It was definitely part of the cargo, not the aircraft. The bomb was hidden inside the casing so an x-ray scanner would've missed it. Oh, yeah. It says an oily film may have kept some of the C4 from igniting."

Kevin handed the file to Mike. If only he could visualize what the cargo looked like. "How thick was the casing?" he asked.

"Nearly three eighths of an inch. Pretty stout, whatever it was."

Mike passed the file back to the tech. "Thanks for the help. Let me know if you find anything different. I'll be in my office."

Mike went back to his computer and called up a document he'd been saving for Kevin. "Take a look at this, Kev. I kind of wanted to hear what Tony had to say before I showed it to you. These are the high-dollar claims against Global from your flight. Frankly, I was amazed at the variety of the stuff you haul. Blood, radioactive materials, explosives, money, gold; I had no idea. Anyway, I ran a sort for dollars-claimed versus what was shipped and came up with several potential suspects. Now I'll enter what we just found out from the lab." One name stood out. "Ever hear of Cougar Industries?"

"Nope."

"Neither have I, but they're right in your back yard."

"You're kidding."

"I'm serious. They're based in Oklahoma City, and according to their claim, they were shipping a heavily insured engine."

"That jibes with a heavy-duty casing."

"Yup." Mike checked out Cougar's web page. It featured a revealing description of their revolutionary engine, the Ultima E850. Things were falling into place. "Global reports that Cougar Industries has been persistent trying to get their ten million dollar claim paid off."

"Ten million dollars?" Kevin practically laughed in his face. "Who's ever heard of a truck engine costing ten million dollars? Is it gold plated?"

"Doesn't look like it. In any case, we'll need a warrant to collect metal samples from Cougar Industries. If their casings match these lab fragments, we can shut them down until we get some answers." Mike smiled, leaned back in his chair, and propped his feet on his desk. "You know, Kev, I think it's time you went home. I'll even buy the ticket."

"Pardon me? We're so close. I don't want to quit now."

"That's good because there's a catch. I need you for more undercover work. You'll still be working with me and getting paid for being home, but I'm counting on you to help out when I call."

Kevin's smile faded. "Why not get another agent or local detective? I'm a pilot, remember?"

Pentaglia smiled. "That's what makes you so perfect, Kevin. You couldn't pass for an undercover agent if you tried. Besides, I might need you to testify, and you're a very credible witness. We're a team, Kev. I figured you'd leap at the opportunity. I'll meet you there once I get the warrant. Until then, enjoy your time at home."

"A dream come true," he said under his breath.

"A piece of cake, Kev. Just wander around Cougar Industries and tell me what you see. You'll be wired and I'll be in the van recording everything. Maybe you can get a tour. All I want is feedback. You're not there to collect samples or poke around."

"And why would they possibly give me a tour?"

"I'll fill you in later, but you're wasting time. If I were you, I'd be booking that flight. Go on—get out of here. I'll catch up with you in a day or two."

23

Being home with his family was like a paid vacation. Kevin glossed over most of the details and tried to put the investigation out of his mind. All Nancy knew was that Mike would be calling.

He and the boys had been romping for over an hour. Brutus managed to claw Kevin's back in the process. He was a good dog, but like most two-year-olds had his own mind. The phone rang and Nancy said it was Mike. He struggled to his feet wearing two kids and ended up dragging one on each leg. When he reached the phone he was breathing hard.

"You sound tired," Mike said. "Everything okay?"

"Hi, Mike. Just doing my leg exercises. What's up?"

"We need you inside Cougar today. I'll pick you up in an hour. Apparently Cougar carries a lot of clout, because the judge turned down our request for a search warrant. Going undercover's the only way."

"Mike, we really need to talk about this. I'll see you when you get here." He hung up before Mike could say anything else. The boys sensed something was wrong and let go. "Sorry, guys—I need to talk to your mom." Randy turned on the TV.

Mike arrived forty-five minutes later, eager to get started. "You ready?"

"No, Mike. I said I wanted to talk about this. Nancy needs to know what's going on. She's in the shower; it won't take long."

"Kevin, we talked about this in LA. We need to get going. I've got people waiting in the van. We're on a time schedule."

"Gimme a minute," he said, darting up the stairs. While Mike waited, Brutus gave him a sniff. The boys never looked up from the TV. They knew Dad had to leave and didn't care to know why. Kevin emerged from the bedroom a few minutes later. "I know. I shouldn't be long. Love you," he said, pulling the door closed. He flew down the stairs and found his sons. "Come here, guys." He kissed them on the head and mussed their hair. "Take care of your mom, okay?" Jake and Randy nodded, hugging his legs. "I sure love you."

Kevin stepped into the unmarked panel van. The driver and technician inside smiled at him. "This is Stan and Vern," Mike said. "Stan's the man when it comes to electronics. Vern will watch our backs."

While Vern drove, Kevin's eyes wandered. Stan busied himself, sorting through bins of electronic equipment. Kevin couldn't help wondering what he'd gotten himself into. Everything happened so quickly it was like he was kidnapped.

"I need you to open your shirt, Kevin," Stan said, holding a tiny recorder. "This is a fully self-contained system with built-in microphone and is completely waterproof. It's quite powerful, so speak normally." He taped the device to Kevin's belly and checked the leads. "Okay, we're done. You can button your shirt now."

Mike saw the anxiety in Kevin's face. Maybe he should have waited to talk to Nancy himself. Time schedule. What a joke. No such thing for an operation like this, he just didn't want Kevin backing out. "Remember, Kevin. Just go in and check the place out. Find out what you can and we'll pick you up. With your engineering background, you'll be a perfect job candidate."

Kevin's eyes narrowed. "Wait a minute. How'd you know about my degree? I never said anything about that." Pentaglia shrugged. "Oh, I see. Big Brother's been checking me out, too."

"It came up," Mike said.

"Then you also know I haven't studied engineering in over twenty years. Tell me, Mike, do you really expect me to BS my way into a job interview without a resume?"

"Give it your best shot, Kevin. That's all I ask."

Cougar Industries was located in an industrial park surrounded by older suburbs. Vern knew he was getting close by the smell.

Kevin looked around. With the morning sun coming through the windshield, he knew they were heading east, but beyond that he didn't have a clue. Vern found every pothole, making the ride on the unpadded floor that much more unpleasant. "At the risk of sounding like my kids, are we there yet?"

"Take a look for yourself," Vern said.

Kevin moved forward to look out the windshield. Vern pointed out the nondescript two-story industrial building with a blue sign that read Cougar Industries. The reflective windows glowed from the sun. At least seventy cars were parked in a lot graced with large oak trees. A strip of grass out front completed their landscaping.

Kevin noticed that one of the surveillance cameras on the rooftop appeared to be tracking them. "This place is a damned fortress," he said. "What now?"

Mike patted him on the back. "Relax, will you? We'll drop you off behind those trees and move around the block. That camera won't pick you up until you leave the parking lot. Take your time, get a good look around, but don't fake your name. If anyone asks for ID, show them your driver's license. Oh, that reminds me—give me your military ID, pilot licenses, and union card."

"Say what? My entire flying career depends on those pieces of paper." His stomach cramped.

"It's for your own protection. If anyone saw that stuff—"

"Fine," he said, searching his wallet. "Make sure nothing happens to them."

Vern slowed to a crawl behind the trees so Kevin could jump out. Once Kevin was out, he drove off. Mike watched Kevin approach the entrance from a peephole. "Kevin, do you read?"

"Five by," Kevin said, barely moving his lips. He felt the sweat soak into his undershirt. As he opened the front door, a security officer in a light blue shirt greeted him. "Howdy," he said, smiling at the older man. "I'm Kevin Hamilton. I was wondering if I could talk to someone about an engineering position."

The guard's eyes looked twice their size through his thick lenses, curious why someone looking for a job didn't have a briefcase. "Do you have an appointment?"

"Unfortunately, no. I just moved to Oklahoma City and a friend told me about Cougar Industries. I hadn't planned on stopping by, but since I was in the area I thought I'd see if I could schedule an appointment."

"May I see your driver's license?" Kevin reached for his wallet, gaining confidence by the minute. The guard wrote down the information in his logbook and returned his license. "Have a seat. I'll see what I can do."

Kevin admired the polished floors and floral arrangements, a striking contrast to the drab exterior. He was inspecting pictures of engines and semi-trucks on the walls when the guard called him. "Mr. Kizka will be here shortly," he said. "We make photo IDs of all our visitors, so please step on the footprints." Kevin did as instructed and the guard centered a red dot on his nose. "Smile." Wearing a ridiculous grin, Kevin waited for a flash that never came from the digital camera. He was still grinning when the guard walked away. "You can step aside now." A minute later, the guard handed him a company badge with "VISITOR, ESCORT REQUIRED" in bold red lettering below his name. "You'll need to keep this on while you're here, and turn it in when you leave."

Mike smiled. "He's in," he said, pressing the headset to his ear.

Kevin didn't know who Mr. Kizka was and didn't dare ask. He heard footsteps. A moment later a middle-aged man appeared. He wore a white smock that offset his olive skin. He appeared of

Middle Eastern decent, though he could've been Italian. Kevin jumped to his feet. "You must be Mr. Hamilton," he said, reaching for Kevin's hand.

Kevin gripped it firmly. "I am, but I prefer to go by Kevin."

The man looked over Kevin's button-down shirt, slacks, and loafers. "Nice to meet you, Kevin. I'm Arvid Kizka, Chief Engineer for Cougar Industries. So you're interested in an engineering position?"

"That's right. I've always been fascinated with engines and heard about your radical designs when I worked for Rival Technology in California. Their place is nothing like this."

Kizka smiled. "What's your background, Kevin?"

"Before Rival, I was in the Marine Corps. I worked production management at Rival, but I was also an excellent organizer and quality control manager in the Corps."

"So you were an engineer in the Marines?"

"No, actually I was an aircraft maintenance officer. Being in charge of twelve planes and two hundred people gave me plenty of management experience, though. It was a great opportunity, but I missed engineering. I'm really hoping to find a job that utilizes my management skills as well as my engineering background."

"Interesting. In fact, there's a possibility something like that might open up in the not-too-distant future." Kevin's eyes widened. "You see, for the first time in Cougar's history, we're planning to mass-produce one of our own designs. Another manufacturer was supposed to but backed out. We believe in the E850 so we're going to give it a go."

"No kidding?" Kevin said, giving emphasis so Mike would hear.

"Talk in a normal voice," Mike whispered into Kevin's collar-receiver.

"What happened to the other manufacturer?"

Kizka mouth compressed in censure. "Let's just say our deal soured when the prototype wasn't delivered on time, through no fault of our own, I might add. It actually worked out for the better."

"How so?"

"Well, until now Cougar's only built prototypes and sold the rights. Such was the case with the Ultima E850, but then the cargo plane went down on its way to Japan. The deal sank with the prototype and we were suddenly out years of research and development money. Frankly, I didn't know if Cougar was going to survive."

"So what happened?"

"The insurance money came through so we're going to build another prototype. I was elated when the boss decided Cougar was going to manufacture the E850. If all goes as planned, it'll create hundreds of new jobs."

"Sounds great. But you only had the one prototype?"

"That's the way we've always done it. We never had a problem until this."

Kevin nodded. "So, what happened when the buyer heard the plane went down?"

"Oh, he went ballistic. Tigress figured they'd have the big-rig market cornered and went so far as to accuse Cougar Industries of industrial sabotage. Of course, I wanted Tigress to build it, but I would've preferred they wait another couple months for delivery." Kizka smiled. "Of course, the irony is Tigress was planning to export the E850 back to the States because their trucks are too small to handle it."

Kevin nodded. Everything in Japan was three-quarter scale compared to the US. "Who can blame them? It's all about competition, right? I hate to admit my ignorance, but I really don't know much about the E850. I don't suppose you have any engine specs I could look at? Nothing confidential, of course."

Kizka studied Kevin. "Well, I suppose I could show what was released at the sales presentation. The Ultima E850's my baby, you know. Let's go to my office."

Kizka handed him a printout dated July third. He hovered over him, waiting for a reaction. Kevin was grateful for his engineering degree. He could still interpret the values. "Very impressive," he said. "I've never seen anything like it. And what a great engine for the environment." He passed it back. "You mentioned you wanted a later delivery date. Were you making some improvements? Refinements?" He read Kizka's face. "Any bugs?"

Kizka looked away. "It was nothing really."

"You mentioned a sales presentation. Mind if I see the script?"

Kizka searched his desk, noting the clock. "I don't have a lot of time. How about if I show you the video? It's just a short clip, but at least it shows the engine in action."

"That would be great."

Kizka led Kevin into the posh showroom. It was nicer than the finest movie theater he'd ever seen. Thirty padded high-back chairs were mounted on a slight incline and angled towards the giant screen behind the stage. Lush curtains provided an elegant backdrop. "Mr. Goldstein does everything first-class. Have a seat," Kizka said, walking behind the curtain. The lights dimmed and the video started. Derek Goldstein appeared, introducing the E850. The ten-minute presentation was a good sales pitch on the engine and how it was to be marketed. Any potential buyer would be impressed.

When the lights came up, Kevin offered the desired enthusiastic response. "That's truly remarkable," he said. "Congratulations."

Kizka grinned. "Mark my words, Kevin. When the Ultima E850 goes into production, Cougar Industries will have raised the bar for energy-efficient truck engines."

Kevin relaxed in the seat, impressed by what he'd seen. Kizka turned everything off and sat next to him. "I'm curious," Kevin said. "The E850's engine block must be very strong and lightweight in order to provide that kind of performance. Is it a new alloy or a modification of something that exists?"

Arvid smiled. "I'm afraid that area's off limits."

"I understand." Kevin got up from the chair. "Mr. Kizka, thank you. I've taken enough of your time. I really appreciate your showing me around. This is exciting. Of course, I realize I'll be one of many applicants."

"Like I said, there's not much going on right now, but that could change within the year. I understand we're still waiting on some financing. Say, if you've got a minute, I'll see if Mr. Goldstein's available. He's the CEO. I'd like him to meet you."

"Sure. That would be great." He waited in the hall while Kizka went to see Goldstein. *Mike—I hope you're getting all this.* There was no response.

Kizka's eyes were full of vigor as he approached Goldstein's secretary. "I need to see the boss," he said. "I've got someone I'd like him to meet."

"One moment, Arvid." She rang Goldstein on the intercom. "Sir, Mr. Kizka would like a moment of your time. He says he has someone he'd like you to meet."

"Send him in, alone." Kizka tapped at the door and entered. Goldstein rolled his cigar to the other side of his mouth, tossing his issue of *Fortune* aside. "Have a seat, Arvid. So, you getting engaged or what?"

"Not exactly. There's an engineer I'd like you to meet. His name's Kevin Hamilton. Ex-Marine, good guy. I know we're not ready to hire anyone, but he seems eager and is an ideal candidate for production manager. I told him a little about the E850. He appreciates what we have."

Goldstein played with his reading glasses. "Is that so? Where's he from?"

"He just moved back here. He's waiting outside. Too bad he wasn't around when we were in development. Maybe we wouldn't have had so many problems."

"I thought that's why I hired you. Are you implying you should be replaced?"

"Of course not. All I'm saying is while we were focusing on research, it would've been nice if someone had been ensuring quality control. We had financial constraints, but that's in the past. So, would you like to meet him?"

"If it means that much to you, send him in, but I'll see him alone. I'm not paying you to baby-sit people off the street."

"Yes, sir."

Kevin walked in and sat where he was told. He couldn't believe Goldstein's office. It was bigger than his master bedroom.

Crown molding accented the two-tone wallpaper. The eggshell carpet perfectly set off the cherry-wood desk. Like Kizka said, Goldstein did everything first-class, and with impeccable taste. He studied the man in the three-piece suit who was doing the same to him. He figured Goldstein's custom-tailored suit cost more than he made on his last trip. "This is quite an office, Mr. Goldstein."

"I like it," he said, smiling. "Where'd you go to school, Kevin?"

"MIT, sir. Class of seventy-eight."

Goldstein flashed his MIT ring, declining to offer his graduation year. "Good school," he said. "Arvid's quite impressed with you. He seems to think you might be the right man for a job. What's your background in engine production?"

"Until two months ago, I was a quality control engineer at Rival Technology. Before that, I was a Marine Corps maintenance officer."

Goldstein nodded, doodling on a notepad. "So, what happened at Rival?"

"Nothing really. I just didn't want my kids growing up in Southern California. Nothing wrong with it, of course, but I'm originally from this area and wanted the kids to be closer to family."

"Rival, eh? You know Brittany Griffin? She left about a year ago."

Kevin's heart skipped a beat. Mike created a good cover, but he sure as hell didn't give any names. "Can't say that I do," he said, hoping Mike would give him a clue. Was Goldstein testing him? Nothing came through.

"Doesn't matter." Goldstein smiled and set his pencil down. He pressed his fingers together, occasionally tapping them to his lips. "So, what do you think of Cougar Industries? Arvid said he briefed you on the E850."

"Well, he showed me the video presentation and stats. From what I've seen, the Ultima E850's pretty amazing. I was interested in the alloy you used in the engine block, but of course Arvid said that was off limits. It must be quite a breakthrough."

236

"Yes." Goldstein stared at Kevin, his eyes full of contempt. "But surely you didn't expect him to reveal that to someone who worked for the competition." Kevin said nothing. He waited.

Goldstein smiled, chewing on his cigar. "I like your style, Kevin. You're not easily intimidated. A valuable asset when working through critical engineering decisions. Have my secretary give you an application, one that I've initialized. It'll bump your application to the front of the line. As Arvid probably told you, there's nothing going on right now, but I'll keep you in mind. Make sure you turn in your badge on the way out."

Vern made a sweep through the parking lot, stopping behind the trees just long enough to pick Kevin up. Kevin jumped in the back and lay on the floor, amazed he'd pulled it off. His heart settled once the van moved. Mike slapped him on the back, laughing. "You were fantastic," he said. "We have it all on tape. Pretty interesting stuff about the engine." Kevin nodded, trying to catch his breath. "I have something else in mind for when we get the warrant—if you're still in, that is."

24

Derek Goldstein sat at his desk, troubled over his interview with Kevin. He'd allowed himself to be overcome by Kizka's enthusiasm and Kevin's charm. Kevin's interest in the alloy still bothered him. Was he a corporate spy or something else? "Gwen, would you please get Brittany Griffin in here?"

"Yes, sir."

Ten minutes later, Brittany Griffin was standing uncomfortably in front of the CEO's desk. It was a well-known fact he didn't invite engineers into his office unless it was bad news. He didn't offer her a seat.

Goldstein looked into her eyes, which were fearful. "How long did you work at Rival Technologies, Brittany?"

"About five years, sir. Why?"

Goldstein leaned forward in his chair, chewing his cigar. "I'll ask the questions if you don't mind. How big is their operation?"

"Probably eighty employees. About the same as here."

Goldstein jotted a note, *Ask Arvid about Hamilton's resume?* Griffin shifted her weight from one foot to the other, her fingers curling and uncurling. What if she and Kevin were collaborating to steal his alloy? He made another entry, *Order new background check on Griffin.*

"Sir?"

"Sorry—I didn't sleep well last night. Did you know a QA engineer at Rival by the name of Kevin Hamilton? It's possible he got there about the same time you left."

Tension left her. *I'm not getting fired.* "That name doesn't sound familiar, and I knew everyone pretty well. Should I know him?"

Goldstein set his pen aside. "Thanks for coming in, Ms. Griffin."

"But—"

"I'm sure you have work to do. Good day." When she left, he stabbed his notepad with his pen.

Kevin waved to Vern as he drove off. "Hi everyone, I'm home," he said.

Brutus, Jake, and Randy ran to the door. "Hi, Dad. Can we go to the park?"

"I don't know, Jake. Where's your mom?"

Randy stood on his tiptoes and whispered. "She's real mad. Let's just go, okay?"

Nancy busied herself in the kitchen cleaning the counter tops. "No one's going anywhere until you help clean this house," she said.

Randy shook his head. "Guess I talk too loud, huh Dad?"

Kevin smiled. "It's okay. We'll do something in a while, but right now I'd better give your mom a hand." He went into the kitchen. Her eyes smoldered. His stomach wrenched. "It went well," he said.

"No fires this time, eh?"

"C'mon, Nance. This thing's coming to a head. Let's go upstairs and talk." She nodded, tossing the dishrag aside. "Be down in a bit, guys," he said. Jake shrugged and went back to the TV. Kevin closed the bedroom door and sat her down on the bed. "Okay—what's this all about?"

Nancy got off the bed and paced. "You have no idea what it's like being married to you. Every time I get comfortable having you around, you're gone for another week. If it's not a trip, it's the FBI. You're like a drop-in visitor, Kevin. At least I knew your schedule in the Marine Corps. I can't count on you anymore. I've been the mom and dad ever since the kids were born and I'm getting real tired of it."

"So, what do you want me to do? You're everything to me. We've already been through this, remember? You gave me your blessing, for Christ's sake. Do whatever it takes, you said. Well I did— and we're damned close to wrapping this up. I just met the CEO of Cougar Industries; got all kinds of things on tape. This thing can't go on forever. Stick with me, Nance. I need to know you're still behind me on this."

She stared at their photos. "Why don't you take the boys to the park? They need you."

"But, what about—"

"Just go."

It was a relief going to Mike's office. He and the boys had a good day, fishing, playing ball. They were asleep as soon as their heads hit the pillows. Nancy hadn't spoken a word all day and morning was no different. He massaged his neck as he sipped some strong coffee.

"You look like shit, Kev."

"Gee, thanks, Mike. Maybe you should try sleeping on the couch."

"Been there, done that. Sorry. I don't recommend divorce, though."

Kevin shrugged. "Either it'll work out or it won't. In any case, I want to nail these bastards. Goldstein's dirty, and he has reservations about me. Next time you pull something like this with an amateur, give a better background brief."

"I'll keep that in mind. You ready to hear the plan?"

"Shoot."

"I found a soft-spoken female agent who's perfect for this assignment. She's gonna make some calls for us. I didn't figure Goldstein will go for a face-to-face meeting."

"So you think Goldstein's dirty, too, eh?"

"Things are leaning that way."

"Okay, I'm in. My marriage is down the crapper. I have nothing to lose."

"Okay, here's the deal…"

Ginger Potmier sat across from Mike and Kevin, practicing her sweet talk to check out the tape recorders. She had to sound convincing or Goldstein would hang up. This was her game. After being hit on by every agent in the bureau, it was nice to give it back. Mike gave her the signal and she dialed Goldstein's number, pressing the phone to her wavy red hair. "Hi. This is Mary with Global Cargo Express' claims department. May I speak with Mr. Goldstein please?"

"One moment, please," Gwen said, putting her on hold.

Goldstein propped his feet on his desk, smiling as he took the call. "It's about time someone called back. Do you have my money?"

"I'm afraid not. Sir, we have a few more questions concerning your claim. This shouldn't take long and we'd really like to clear this up so we can forward your check."

"What did you say your name was?"

"Mary. Mary Kessler." Mike signaled her to keep it rolling; improvise. "Mr. Goldstein, if you prefer, you can swing by my office so we can discuss this in person. I can see you around four pm if that's all right. It should only take a few minutes."

Goldstein mulled over his options. Too many things fell through the cracks when he wasn't around. "I can't leave the office. What do you want to know?"

Mary looked over her script. "Sir, according to our records, you only shipped the one pallet. Is that correct?"

Goldstein sighed. "Isn't that what the bill of lading says?"

"Sir, I'm only trying to verify the facts."

Goldstein squeezed the phone. "Okay, Mary. I'll speak plainly and slowly so there's no confusion. I only shipped one pallet."

"And that was an engine, correct?"

Goldstein's face flushed. "That's right. An engine." His voice got tense. "A very valuable one-of-a-kind prototype. I'll send you a videotape if you want, but I want my money. Why do you insist on wasting my time?"

"I apologize for the inconvenience, Mr. Goldstein, but we have to verify that the contents claimed match the paperwork before any payment can be made. Do you have any idea how many pieces made up the hundred and twenty thousand pounds of cargo on that flight?"

"No."

Pentaglia smiled, passing her a thumbs-up. Ginger smiled back.

"Mr. Goldstein, as a businessman, surely you realize it takes time to sort these things out, especially when people aren't willing to answer the questions."

Mary's voice had an irresistible quality. As frustrated as he was, Goldstein found himself wondering what she looked like. Flowing red hair, green eyes, a hundred twenty pounds, late twenties; nothing like Gwen. "Okay, Mary, I get the point. Let's wrap this up. I've got work to do."

"Yes, sir. It's extremely rare to lose or damage airfreight, but we strive to handle claims as promptly and accurately as possible. While researching your claim, we found there had been two other claims for engines over the past twenty years, but neither came close to the amount that you declared. In fact, the prior highest value was a racing engine with a declared value of one hundred thousand dollars. Mr. Goldstein, how can your engine be worth so much more?"

Goldstein took a deep breath, trying to remain calm. "Mary, the Ultima E850's a revolutionary engine. A breakthrough in technology. There's nothing else like it in the world and it was being delivered to a foreign investor on a time-critical shipment. The amount claimed is what my investor agreed to pay me. You have certified copies of my agreement with Tigress Automotive of Tokyo. Since my engine never arrived, that contract became null and void. As a result of your plane crash, Cougar Industries lost all of its production costs and is now going broke. Is that clear enough for you?"

"Yes, sir. Thank you. Now, how much did you receive from your insurance company? Global can only pay the difference between what your insurance paid and the declared value."

Oh that's good, Mike thought. She was definitely the right person for the job.

"Mary, I don't have any private insurance. That's why I paid a premium for shipping it. I canceled my insurance policy two months ago to make payroll. I need my money now!"

"I understand, and I'm sorry I upset you, Mr. Goldstein. I believe we have everything we need. I'll do what I can to expedite your payment. Have a good day."

Goldstein slammed the phone down. For the second time he had the feeling something was wrong. Global must have a dozen copies of everything by now, so why were they still asking questions? He'd heard voices in the background, men's voices. He darted from his office and approached the security guard. "Max, get me a copy of yesterday's videotape. And bring me Kevin Hamilton's visitor's pass, too."

"Here's his pass, sir," he said. "I'll get you the video."

"Ginger, you were incredible," Mike said, hugging her. "Can you believe it? No private insurance? What do you think, Kev?"

Kevin smiled. "Definitely worth coming in for. What now?"

"We get our warrant. This time there shouldn't be any questions."

Goldstein mashed the intercom button on his desk. "Arvid, get in here—now!" Goldstein paced the room like a tiger. His cigar rolled in his mouth. He heard a tap at the door and watched Kizka come in. "Sit down, Arvid," he said, gritting his teeth. "I want to know what you told Kevin Hamilton about the E850. And don't spare any details."

Kizka's fingernails dug into the armrests. It wasn't like Goldstein to light his cigars. "Sir, everything we talked about was in your presentation. I showed him the spec sheet and the marketing video. That's it."

"So, you didn't say anything about our production plans for the Ultima E850?"

"Not really. I mean, I told him we were planning on producing it after we lost the Tigress deal, but I never mentioned Tigress. Besides, that's old news, boss. It was in all the papers. Anyone who reads the business section knows we lost that contract."

"Perhaps." Goldstein kept pacing. The lighted cigar didn't help. He snuffed it in the ashtray and put it back in his mouth. "Arvid, don't go into such detail with people you don't know. From now on, keep everything on a need-to-know basis."

Kizka nodded. "Sorry, boss. It won't happen again."

Goldstein escorted him to the door with his arm around Kizka's shoulder. "Thanks for coming in, Arvid." He waited at the door until Kizka was out of sight and caught Max's eye. "You got that tape?"

"It'll be ready in a few minutes, Mr. Goldstein."

Goldstein pulled his door shut and locked it. "Gwen, I have to run a quick errand. I'll be back in a few minutes. Max, that tape had better be ready when I get back."

"Yes, sir."

Larry Barclay sat listening to the faded Barclay Brothers sign squeaking in the breeze. When he answered the phone, he didn't hear anything. He was ready to hang up when a computer-generated voice said he had a collect call from Derek Goldstein. Having no time to consult his brother, he accepted the call.

"Took you long enough," Goldstein said, huddling against the phone booth.

"Hey, man, I probably shouldn't have taken the call. I never expected to hear from you again. What gives?"

"Cut the crap, Larry. Has anyone been snooping around your place?"

"A couple of jerks in a Chrysler were checking us out a few days ago, but nothing's happened since. I doubt the guy I talked to was a cop, though. Too bad of an actor. Why?"

"What'd they look like?"

"Hell, I don't know. You know how many people we get through here?"

"Yeah, I do. I've been to that outhouse you call an office and never saw another soul. Were they black, white, tall, thin? What?"

"One was about six feet tall, short blonde hair, bright teeth—looked like one of those Ralph Lauren Polo models. You know, Joe College, but older. The other guy never got out of the car. Can't say much about him except he was white."

Goldstein's eyes swept the passers-by. *Coincidence?* "Is your fax machine on?"

Larry checked. The electronic display confirmed it was ready. "Yup."

"Good. When I get back to the office I'll fax you a picture of a guy who was just here. Fax me a note if you think it's the same guy. Don't call."

"Sure. Anything else?"

"I'll let you know." Goldstein hung up. He looked around. No one at the gas station paid any attention. When he returned to his office, a large manila envelope marked "PERSONAL" sat in the middle of his desk. Max, the security guard, had written the date and time on the label, leaving no question as to its contents. He pushed the intercom button. "Gwen, I want to be alone," he said, then locked his door. He pressed a button under his desk and a cabinet panel dropped, revealing a VCR and monitor. He fast-forwarded through the security tape until a white panel van pulled into the parking lot. He stopped the tape and played it back in slow motion. The van disappeared behind the trees and suddenly Kevin appeared, walking towards the entrance. He reviewed it three more times, unable to determine how Kevin arrived. When Kevin left the building, the same van drove through the parking lot and he disappeared again. "You son of a bitch," he said. He picked up the phone. "Max, get in here!"

Goldstein heard a tap at the door. "It's locked. Use your key." Max came in and waited in front of the desk while Goldstein reviewed the tape. "I want a background check on Kevin Hamilton," he said, staring at the monitor. Max nodded, expecting more. "Well, what are you waiting for?" Max hurried out. Goldman studied Kevin's image, frozen on the screen. Then he called Mary Kessler, Global Cargo Express claim in hand.

"I'm sorry, sir, but I don't know anyone by that name," the Global Cargo Express customer service rep said. "Perhaps she works in a different department. Would you like to hold while I check?"

"No thanks," he said. Someone tapped at his door. "Yes?"

"Sir, it's Max. I have the information you requested on Mr. Hamilton."

"Bring it in." Max set the computer printout in front of him and stepped back. "Goddamit, Max, I don't have time to waste. What's it mean?"

"Sir, I plugged the information from his driver's license into the database. According to the computer, he's a retired Marine and works for Global Cargo Express."

Goldstein closed his eyes, never imagining the connection. Things were starting to make sense. Hamilton wasn't looking for a job; he was a fraud investigator for Global Cargo Express. "Thanks, Max. That's all." Once Max left, he enlarged the photo from Kevin's visitors pass and faxed it to Larry Barclay.

Larry was about to walk out the door when the fax machine started beeping. He was expecting Goldstein's transmission and went over, curious about what it might reveal. He read the handwritten note at the bottom of the page, *Does this guy look familiar?* Larry ran out the front door waving the fax in the air. "Hey, Steve. Look at this."

Steve looked it over and pulled out his lighter. He set it on fire, holding it from a corner until it was nearly incinerated, then dropped it to the ground, grinding the ash into the dirt. "Well, Larry, Goldstein just fucked us over by sending this fax. Whoever was in that Chrysler probably tapped our lines, so now there's a connection. What a fucking asshole." He looked around the docks, but didn't see anyone. "Remember how we talked about taking our business to Mexico?"

"Yeah."

"Well, I think it's time we went."

"But we need a crew, we're not packed, we're—"

Steve squinted. "Larry—we're toast unless we get out now. There's canned food and bottled water on board and she's gassed up. We're outta here."

"But what about Goldstein's fax? Aren't you gonna respond?"

"Fuck Goldstein. In fact, bring the fax machine. The last thing we need is to leave a fax behind."

Steve backed his car up to the office while Larry grabbed the machine and a few other things. "How long you figure we'll be gone?" Larry asked.

Steve looked around. "I don't plan on coming back. When it's safe, we'll transfer our bank accounts to Mexico. Get in the car, will you? For all we know, we're being watched."

Larry did as he was told, but Steve wasn't heading for the ship. "Where are you going? I thought we were in a hurry to leave."

"We are—to the sandwich shop." Larry looked at him. "What? I'm hungry and we don't need to draw attention to ourselves. You get the drinks and I'll get a couple of foot-longs to go." Larry nodded.

Steve backed the car up to the pier. Once they got their supplies on board, he returned the car to the parking lot. He ran aboard and started the twin diesels while Larry prepared to cast the lines. Larry stared at Farley's place, the gutted space where his warehouse once stood. He felt even worse about taking Barney

Fagan's boat, but desperate times required desperate actions. At least Barney would get his boat back—sooner or later. Their sub was already aboard; it was too perfect.

Skimmer normally carried a crew of ten, but she was docile enough to be handled by the two of them. They had crewed for Fagan several times. Her crane made off-loading the sub a two-man operation. Seeing Steve's thumbs-up, Larry let the last line go. As the fog began to filter in, *Skimmer* quietly slipped out to sea.

Goldstein was fixated. He watched the numbers change on his digital clock. Over an hour had passed since he'd sent his fax, but the Barclays had yet to respond. He was tempted to call them, but he didn't want the call traced to his office. *What in the hell's going on? Larry knew it was important. Why weren't they responding?* After another hour passed, Gwen's call caused him to jump.

"Sir, I'm sorry to bother you, but it's three o'clock and I have to leave to take my daughter to the dentist. Do you need anything before I go?"

"No," he said, slamming the phone. It was clear the Barclays weren't going to respond. He grabbed a cigar and locked his door. "I'm outta here," he said to Max, hurrying towards the front door.

"Yes, sir. Have a good evening, Mr. Goldstein."

"There's nothing good about it."

Goldstein pulled into the same gas station and huddled into the pay phone. This time he dialed direct using the pre-paid calling card he found in his desk. The answering machine came on after the sixth ring. *"You've reached the Barclay Brothers Charter Service. Leave a message…Beep."* Goldstein hung up slowly, anxiety gripping him. He recalled the sequence of events; the Chrysler, the panel van, Hamilton showing up, Mary Kessler's call, and now the Barclays were gone. Were the feds closing in? Exactly who was Kevin Hamilton, and what did he do at Global? Goldstein fought his way through traffic, cursing everyone he passed. He needed to leave the country, and the fastest way was by private jet.

Mike's search warrant was tucked inside his blazer as he sped towards Cougar Industries, two backups following. Kevin rode shotgun, unarmed, but determined to see this through. Nothing had improved at home; this is where he belonged. Mike screeched to a halt in front of Cougar's entrance. Kevin followed him and the others inside.

Max watched them on the monitor and crouched behind his desk with his weapon drawn. Three men burst through the door. "Freeze," Max said.

Mike held his hands in the air, badge in one palm, warrant in the other. "FBI," he said, looking at the frightened old man. The other agents held their badges. Kevin blended into the group. Max crawled out from his desk and put his gun away. "We have a search warrant," Mike said. "Go on, guys." They agents fanned out and began their inspection while Mike and Kevin remained behind. "We'd like to speak to Mr. Goldstein and Mr. Kizka." He could tell Max recognized Kevin.

"Mr. Kizka should be in his office. Mr. Goldstein's gone for the day."

Arvid Kizka came rushing down the hall, angry and confused. He saw Kevin and stopped, his jaw wide open. "Kevin? What's going on?"

"Sorry, Arvid, but the FBI needs answers." Several technicians were arguing in the halls, their voices echoing off the polished tile. They couldn't believe the FBI was taking their alloys.

"I'm Special Agent Pentaglia," Mike said to Kizka. "I understand the E850's your vision. Kevin was quite impressed. Is there someplace we can talk?"

"Let's go to my office," Kizka said, leading the way. Once inside, he didn't look at Kevin. "Have a seat."

"No thanks. Mr. Kizka, we have reason to believe Cougar Industries is involved in an insurance scam involving the prototype E850 engine." Mike spent the next few minutes briefing Kizka on all that had transpired, pointing out that two people had been murdered and critical evidence destroyed during the investigation. "The search warrant allows us to collect as many alloy samples as my lab techs deem necessary. Things will be a lot easier on all of us if you cooperate."

Kizka nodded and took them to the lab where agents were busy collecting samples. He unlocked a cabinet and removed two small blocks of metal, then handed them to Mike. "This is what we used to build the E850 casing." Mike handed them over to the lab technician, who compared them to one of the samples from the LA lab.

The tech placed one piece under a microscope and ran a simple chemical analysis. He repeated the process with the second sample. "They appear to match, but I can't say for sure until I run more tests in the lab."

Mike nodded. "Mr. Kizka, I want you to know that Kevin has spoken very highly of you. Unfortunately, I have to place you under arrest for conspiracy to commit murder and air piracy. You have the right to remain silent—"

"I know my rights," Kizka said, sounding dazed. "I didn't do anything. Mr. Goldstein may be a bit eccentric at times, but he's no murderer either. I'm sure he'll straighten this out when he gets back. You'd better pray he doesn't sue for false arrest. He holds a mean grudge."

"I'll keep that in mind," he said, cuffing Kizka. "But first we have to find him. Any idea where he might have gone? The security guard said he was in a foul mood and left for the day."

"How should I know? Have you tried calling him on his cell phone?"

"Do you have the number?"

"No, but I'm pretty sure he keeps it in his Rolodex for emergencies."

"Wait here." Mike instructed another agent to keep an eye on Kizka while he and Kevin went to Goldstein's office. After Max let them in, Mike closed the door. He spotted the Rolodex, surprised Goldstein still used one. "Here, Kevin. Help me out," he said, handing him a handful of cards.

"Found it," Kevin said. "It was under cell phone, if you can believe that."

"Good. Hang on to it. I want you to call Goldstein on my cell phone after I arrange a phone patch through Dispatch. If you can keep him on the line long enough, they should be able to get a fix on him."

Kevin waited to be handed the phone. He never wanted anyone so bad in his life. His life was a mess; revenge would be sweet. They went back to Kizka's office looking for more information. While Mike questioned Kizka, Kevin looked over the scale models of engines Kizka had designed. It felt strange. He'd earned a degree in engineering, yet never pursued it as a career. Had he done things differently, he would've been proud to work with Kizka.

Mike wrote in his notepad, *400 series Mercedes, gold, license plate, Ultima 1.* "Thanks, Arvid. Let's go. You're coming with Kevin and me." Mike double-checked Kizka's handcuffs and slid him in the back seat of his car. He closed the door and used his cell phone to call the FBI dispatcher with Kevin at his side. "This is Special Agent Pentaglia with an operational emergency. Put out an APB on a 400 series gold Mercedes registered to Derek Goldstein, license plate, Ultima One. Goldstein's wanted for murder and should be considered armed and dangerous. Also, I need a phone patch so we can record a conversation while running a trace."

Goldstein's cell phone wouldn't stop ringing. Thinking it was Larry Barclay, he finally answered. "Mr. Goldstein? It's Kevin Hamilton. Do you have a minute?"

"Hamilton? How'd you get my number?"

"Arvid gave it to me. I stopped by to drop off my application and was hoping to talk to you again. Sir, I really hate bothering you, but Arvid said you were the only one who could answer these questions. I'm really impressed with the E850, by the way."

Goldstein gripped the wheel. *Get rid of him. Don't let him know you're onto him.* "Look, Kevin—this isn't a good time. Would you call the office tomorrow?"

"Actually, I won't be around tomorrow. You know, the most amazing thing is how your alloy samples match the Ultima E850 pieces that were salvaged from the Global DC-10 wreck. Care to explain that?"

It was over. "Look, you devious fuck. I know you work for Global, but I'm curious. Is it their fraud division or are you working for someone else?"

"I work for Global. That's it."

"Don't bullshit me. You're obviously working for someone else. Who is it?"

"Take it easy, Derek. You sound really stressed." Mike passed him a note: *Get in the car and keep talking.* Kevin nodded.

"Why are you in this, Hamilton?"

"Why? Because you blew up my plane, you son of a bitch. My captain may never walk again and two men are dead!"

Kevin frowned at Mike. "Sorry, Mike. He hung up."

"Shit! They weren't finished with the trace. Call him back."

But Goldstein had turned his phone off.

The Oklahoma Highway Patrol desk sergeant plotted Goldstein's position based on the partial trace and passed the information to the dispatcher. "Attention, all units, be on the lookout for late model 400 series Mercedes, gold, license Ultima One. Suspect appears to be heading north on I-35, destination unknown. All units exercise extreme caution. Suspect should be considered armed and dangerous."

Goldstein, unaware of the broadcast, exited the freeway just as seven police cruisers converged on the area. None of the officers spotted him. The police dispatcher relayed the information to Mike.

Pentaglia pulled off the road and turned around to face Kizka. "All right, Arvid, here's the deal. We can't find Goldstein and your ass is on the line. He knows we want him, he's turned his cell phone off, and he's eluded the police, so I'm only gonna ask you once. Where might he have gone? Does he have a mistress, or is he going to the airport? What's your best guess?"

Kizka leaned forward to get the handcuffs out of his back. "How should I know?" He stopped abruptly. "Wait a minute. He's used Mach One Jet Charters before. They're at an airport on the north side of town, but I don't recall which one."

Mike reached for the radio. "Dispatch, have all units concentrate on airports on the north side of town and alert the Will Rogers airport police. Suspect may be fleeing by airline or private jet. Also, I need the location of Mach One Jet Charter." While awaiting a response, Mike sped towards the only small airport he knew of in the area. It was a long shot, but he was out of time. The dispatcher confirmed Mach One Jet Charter was at Wiley Post airport; minutes from their location. A report came in that Goldstein's Mercedes was found near Mach One Jet Charter; officers were searching the grounds.

As Mike turned into the parking lot, Kevin spotted a corporate jet taxiing towards the runway and leaped from the car. "Get Tower to cancel all takeoff clearances," he said, running towards the airplane ramp.

Mike threw the car in park and ran to the control tower, relaying Kevin's request through their hot line near the door. "That's right," he said to the controller. "Nothing moves. We may have a federal suspect trying to flee." Hearing a buzzer, he yanked on the door and ran up the stairs to monitor from the tower.

Kevin noticed a single-engine Cessna 172 that a pilot had just finished preflighting. He ran up to the man, shouting, "FBI," flashing his military ID. The startled man raised his hands. "It's an emergency. I need your plane."

"Sure—it's a rental. Keys are in it."

The Ground Controller focused his binoculars on the taxiing corporate jet. "Westwind One Zero Charlie Bravo, Ground, hold your position."

Mike noticed a blue and white single-engine Cessna taxiing at a quick pace. He nudged the controller. "What's that guy doing?"

Goldstein overheard Ground Control's transmission on the overhead speaker and felt the plane come to a stop. He unbuckled his seat belt and moved into the cockpit entry, leaning over the captain. "What's the hold-up? I've got an important meeting to attend."

"The controller told us to hold," the captain said.

"I can't wait. I'll triple your fee if you keep going."

The first officer looked at the captain. Tripling their fee meant he could eat for a month. "You know, Jeff, this plane's been having a lot of radio problems lately. I could swear that last transmission gave us takeoff clearance."

"Yeah. That's what I heard, too," he said, easing the throttles forward.

Goldstein breathed easier as they started moving again. He watched the first officer turn the speaker off. He smiled.

Mike watched the Westwind approach the runway.

"Westwind One Zero Charlie Bravo, Ground, hold your position. Unidentified Cessna, hold your position." He selected all tower frequencies. "Attention, all aircraft at Wiley Post, hold your positions!" Both aircraft ignored his orders. The controller took off his headset and threw his arms in the air. "I give up."

The Cessna and Westwind continued towards the runway, each increasing their speed. Mike speed-dialed Dispatch on his cell phone. "Have all units pursue the red and white corporate jet that's approaching the runway. Do not let that jet take off!"

Kevin kept his eye on the Westwind while he headed for the runway intersection. Goldstein had to be on board; otherwise its pilots would've heeded Tower's instructions. If he blocked the runway at midfield, the jet wouldn't have enough to take-off. He arrived just as the Westwind was pointing its nose down the runway. He looked over his shoulder at the jet, praying its pilots noticed him.

Goldstein came forward again. "What are you waiting for?"

"There's a plane on the runway," the captain said, pointing out the high-wing Cessna. "We'll have to hold until he clears. Sir, you'll need your seat belt on before we can take off."

Goldstein stared out the windshield. Clearly the Cessna wasn't there by accident. He saw police cars pulling onto to the ramp. He reached into his blazer and pulled out a 9mm pistol, holding it to the captain's head. "Sorry, guys, but I guess we'll have to do this the hard way. Now take off!"

"But there's not enough room."

"Die now or die trying. Captain, either get this thing moving or your buddy will." He heard sirens. The police were closing in. Before long, their cars would be on the runway. "Move it!"

The first officer turned on the exterior lights while the captain held the brakes and ran the power up. "Give me ten more flaps," he said. The FO lowered the flaps another ten degrees.

Kevin saw the landing lights come on and smoke billow from the engines. He had two options; move out of the way or block them. "Forgive me, Nance." He added power and kicked in full rudder to point his plane at the Westwind. He turned on his landing light and ran up the power. Now beak-to-beak, Kevin's heart pounded to the beat of the pulsating landing light, rational judgment overridden by rage. When the Westwind released brakes, so did he. The runway shrank as the planes accelerated. *Jesus! Why don't they abort?*

"This guy's nuts," the captain said, watching the Cessna fill his windscreen.

"Keep going!"

Death was a certainty. There was nothing to lose and Goldstein wasn't strapped in. The captain slammed the throttles to full reverse thrust and applied maximum brakes. When the rapid deceleration threw Goldstein forward, the first officer reached for the gun. Somewhere during the struggle, a shot was fired. Goldstein fell backwards.

The Cessna was approaching flying speed, but the Westwind was less than two hundred feet away and closing. Kevin slapped the flap lever full down and yanked back on the yoke, praying it would fly. "Come on, baby." The nose wheel lifted, followed by the mains. As he continued raising the nose to a near-stalling attitude, he recalled the old adage, pull back on the stick, the houses get smaller. Pull harder and the houses get bigger again. He knew the plane couldn't fly if the wing stalled, but he couldn't let up. He was ten feet off the ground, but the Westwind's vertical tail was about to split him in two. He eased in some left rudder and closed his eyes, expecting an impact. Two seconds later, he looked back and watched the jet come to a stop. "Jesus," he said. He thought of Nancy and the boys. "Jesus," he said again.

Police officers surrounded the jet with their weapons drawn. The captain held his hands in the air, pointing towards the door while the first officer restrained Goldstein. Someone opened the door and two officers charged aboard. Goldstein was bleeding from the shoulder, cursing, his pistol gleaming on the dash, out of reach. "Shot with his own gun," the captain said.

"We'll take it from here," the officer said, grabbing Goldstein. "You guys will need to stick around. The tower folks want a word with you."

Mike arrived as they were handcuffing Goldstein. He smiled at the Westwind pilots. "Hijacked, eh?" The captain nodded, saying nothing about radio problems. "You made a wise choice keeping her on the ground. For a minute there, I thought you were gonna get airborne."

"We might have if it weren't for that 172," he said, watching the Cessna circle the field.

Kevin smiled, waiting for the Westwind to clear the runway. Tower told him to hold overhead, but he wasn't in a hurry to land. He didn't realize how much he missed flying small planes until today. His body relaxed, his limbs as light as the air over his wings. Once the jet was towed off the runway, he landed and parked the plane where he gotten it, tossing the keys back to the astonished renter. "She flies great," he said, smiling. "I'll square things up inside."

"Kevin," Nancy said, running to him.

"Nancy? What are you doing here? How—"

"The boys and I were running errands when the news reported an FBI standoff at Wiley Post Airport. Someone intercepted Mike's cell phone calls and passed it to the radio stations. Since you never came home, I figured you had to be involved."

He wrapped his arms around her. "I love you, Nancy Hamilton—more than anything in the world."

Nancy smiled. "You sure you can't go back in the Marine Corps?"

Mike ran over, patting Kevin on the back before he could answer. "You're insane, you know that, Kevin?"

"What are you talking about?" Nancy asked.

As Mike filled her in, Kevin met her eyes. "It wasn't insanity, Nance. I was pissed off. I couldn't let him get away. Not after all he's done."

Nancy pulled him close. "Just don't do it again, okay?"

"I won't." He saw a police car pull alongside Mike's car, Goldstein locked in the back, his shoulder bloodstained. "That's Goldstein," he said. "I've got to see him, Nance. Be right back."

Goldstein was too busy cursing to notice Kizka slumped in the car next to him. When Mike opened the cruiser's front door, Goldstein's volume increased. "Hold it down, Goldstein. I wanted you to meet the Cessna pilot before they hauled you off."

Kevin stepped forward. "Hamilton! Still the devious fuck!"

"That's right. And I hope they lock you up for life." Kevin closed the door and walked away. He went to Nancy, embracing her. Her eyes told him they'd work things out. "Mike—I think it's time I got back to my real job."

25

When Mike learned Goldstein's fax machine sent a message to the Barclay Brothers, he instructed Agents Landis and Kidman to pick them up. They got there as quickly as possible, but found Barclay's office empty. Kidman peeked in the windows, hoping to find an easy entry. Landis found the Barclays' car, its engine cold. The place looked like it had been abandoned for months. Landis found Kidman checking out the yard. "You think they were tipped off?" he asked.

"Maybe. Or maybe they're on a charter. If you were trying to evade the law, where would you go?"

Kidman looked at the ocean. "South." Every second they wasted meant less distance to the border. "Let's see what we can find out."

They spread out, canvassing the docks. A boat owner told Landis two men cast off in *Skimmer* around one yesterday afternoon. He showed the man pictures of the Barclays and the man said the likeness was good. He quickly found Kidman. "They're running all right," he said. "They took their sub and a boat called *Skimmer*."

"At least we know what to look for. Hopefully the Coast Guard will find them before they get to international waters."

Landis retrieved the California map from his car and drew a perimeter radius. "Assuming their departure time was 1 pm and they headed down the coast, they'd be close to San Diego by now," he said to Kidman as he dialed his supervisor. He explained the situation and what assistance he needed. "…That's correct, sir. The fog's breaking up around here. Looks better to the south. Couldn't be too hard spotting a ship with a minisub on deck. Maybe the Navy would help. I bet those sub hunters from North Island would love a real mission."

"I'll see what I can do."

"Oh, sir, you might contact the Justice Department while you're at it. We'll need an extradition order if they make it to Mexican waters."

"Anything else?"

Landis noted the sarcasm in his boss's voice. "No, sir."

"Good. Check out all the local ports. They may have gone north to throw us off."

"Yes, sir. I'll keep you posted." Landis tucked his phone in his pocket and looked at Kidman. "Well, Fred, the boss wants us to check out the local piers. Before we go, let's search Barclay's office. Maybe we'll find a photo of *Skimmer* so we'll all know what they're looking for." Kidman nodded.

The doors and windows were locked. Landis was about to break a window when Kidman grabbed his arm. "You really gonna do that?" he asked, pointing to the metal security alarm box. Landis relaxed. "Probably better to call the alarm company than explain why we broke in, don't you think?"

Landis dialed the number on the alarm box and reached the Reliable Security dispatcher. Ten minutes later, a mini-truck with two ladders strapped to its camper shell approached. The driver strolled to the porch. "What's the problem?" he asked. "My boss said it was an emergency, but I don't hear any alarms going off. Did it quit on its own?"

Landis stared at the lanky young man, pierced ear and nose, tattoo on his neck, pondering his qualifications. "It never went off," he said, flashing his badge. The tech was intrigued with Landis's badge. "I'm Special Agent Landis, this is Special Agent Kidman. We need you to disconnect the alarm so we can get inside. We have a search warrant and we're running short on time."

"Just take a minute," he said. "Of course, once the alarm's off you might check the back door. I've worked on this place before. It doesn't lock."

Kidman smiled. "I'll go around back," he said. "Yell when the alarm's off." Once the technician said it was okay, he tried turning the knob but it wouldn't budge. He shouldered a few jolts to the rotted doorframe and the door pushed in. He ran inside to open the front door.

They found several photos of Barclay's sub on *Skimmer*, a few by itself, and a couple of the Barclays. A rectangular dust-free spot on the counter revealed where their fax machine used to be. "We don't have time to sort through all this stuff," Landis said. "Grab what you can and let's get back to the office. After we fax these photos to the authorities, we'll look for the boat."

They spent all afternoon and evening going over everything, but didn't find anything incriminating. They gave the lab several items to fingerprint, hoping for a match with Riley's sub, but so far there was nothing. They were about to call it a day when their supervisor called Kidman.

"Glad you're still here," he said. "I just received an urgent message from the Mexican Consulate that you might find interesting. Your bombing suspects were spotted on a beach south of Ensenada. The police are searching the area, but so far no one's been apprehended."

"Well, that's something, anyway. How can we get involved? We're not doing any good around here."

"I'm not sure yet. I was just forwarding information."

"Thanks. Keep us posted, okay? We'd sure love to meet these guys." Kidman cradled the phone. "Glad we stuck around. I should sleep better tonight. Let's hope the Barclays don't do anything to screw up their extradition. You headed home, Greg?"

"No. I'm gonna stick around awhile. Maybe there'll be some more news."

"Have at it; I'm outta here. Call me if something comes up."

"Will do." Two hours later, Landis answered the phone. He thanked his supervisor for the update and stared at the phone. He figured Mike would want to know.

"Whoever's calling, it better be good," Mike said, reading the clock.

"It is. It's Greg Landis."

"Jesus, Greg, it's two am. Did you forget Oklahoma's two hours ahead of you? I mean, couldn't it wait?"

"I thought you'd like to know the Barclays are in Mexican custody."

Mike sat up in bed, wide-awake. "Hey, that's great. Thanks for the update, but I think I'll wait 'til morning to pass it on to Kevin."

"Wait, Mike, it gets better. The Mexican government agreed to release them in our custody since the Barclays' only charge is illegal entry. No red tape. I'm flying to Ensenada in a few hours to bring 'em back. By the way, their fax machine was gone. Probably at the bottom of the ocean. Oh, one more thing. Barney Fagan's boat was recovered by the Mexican Navy after being abandoned at sea."

"I'm sure Fagan will be glad to get *Skimmer* back, but he'll probably have to pay a healthy fine first. What's the story on the fingerprints?"

"Unfortunately, whoever stole Riley's sub must've worn gloves. No prints yet."

Mike rubbed the sleep from his eyes. "Well, we have Goldstein on attempted hijacking, but Kizka can be out anytime. Neither are talking. Frankly, I'm amazed their lawyer hasn't sprung Kizka."

"But didn't the lab confirm the alloy samples matched the fragments? And what about the unexploded matter?"

"All circumstantial evidence," Mike said. "We have a match, but we can't prove who's responsible. Like Goldstein says, anyone could've planted the bomb after Kizka dropped it off at Global. Unfortunately, there was probably enough time for a Global employee to do it. Goldstein was also quick to point out that Global profited from their previous DC-10 loss. He swears he's a victim, but so far he hasn't provided any explanation as to why he held a gun to a pilot's head. Let's hope the Barclays talk. Call me when you get back from Mexico."

26

Agent Greg Landis was tired, but it was worth the trip to Mexico. He briefed the Barclays while the pilot completed his checklists. Steve and Larry were secured to their seats with seatbelts and plastic tie straps around their ankles and wrists. Landis had a captive audience. "Before we go, I have to remind you that anything you say can and will be used against you in a court of law and you have the right to an attorney. You're both under arrest for destroying evidence in a federal investigation, two counts of murder, and two counts of attempted murder. Do you understand your rights as I've explained them to you?" Both nodded. "Do you have any questions for me?" he asked, returning his Miranda rights card to his pocket.

Larry shook his head, but Steve wasn't as tranquil. "This is bogus and you know it. We were doing a photo shoot of the Baja coast when our sub started taking on water. The batteries began shorting out so we got her as close to shore as we could before we had to abandon her. We were trying to thumb a ride to town when the next thing we know a police helicopter's spotlighting us saying we're busted. Needless to say, I'm not real anxious to come back to Mexico."

"Sounds like quite an ordeal," Landis said. He poured himself a cup of coffee and bit into his sandwich. Larry watched. "Sorry, guys—nothing for you. It'll take a while to fly back to LA so you may as well relax. We'll talk more when we get downtown."

A van awaited them at Santa Monica airport. While they were asleep, Landis made a call requesting that food be available during their interview. Landis studied his suspects as the van headed for the office. Larry seemed to have a weakness for sweets, but Steve would be a challenge. "You guys look pretty uncomfortable in those clothes. I've got some fresh ones for you if you want to get cleaned up. All that salt must be miserable on your skin. I've only got one shower, so Larry, you'll have to wait." Landis turned around in his seat, not giving them the chance to respond.

As they approached downtown LA, Steve kicked Landis' seat. Landis turned around. "What about my phone call?"

"You'll have the chance just like everyone else."

They arrived at the FBI office ten minutes later. Landis escorted them into a holding room where they were booked. The guard picked out a pair of orange coveralls and escorted Steve to the shower while Landis took Larry into a small room. Larry ignored the mirrored window, focused on the feast in front of him. Cold cuts, baked bread, sliced fruit, sweet rolls, and orange juice were attractively arranged over a green tablecloth. "Help yourself, Larry," Landis said, cutting Larry's tie straps. Landis tore off a piece of roll and popped it in his mouth. Kidman watched from the other side of the mirror.

Larry fixed himself a sandwich, devouring half on the first bite. He polished off the sandwich and lunged for a sweet roll. He finished that and piled meat slices on a plate, adding some fruit on the side. He helped himself to a glass of orange juice, gulped it down, then poured another. "Take it easy, Larry. There's plenty to eat," Landis said, sitting at the table. "Have a seat. Relax." The only chair was across from him. Larry sat and took another bite, but his eyes stayed on Landis. Greg reached for a grape. "I bet you're glad to be back in LA."

"Damned right," Larry said, wiping his face on his sleeve. He spit out the salt. "They don't feed you in Mexico."

Landis nodded. "You know, Larry, one of the best things about this country is there are ways to go easy on those who cooperate in prosecuting criminal masterminds. Hell, everyone knows you didn't blow that DC-10 out of the sky, but we do know you and your brother planted that second bomb."

"I don't know what you're talking about."

"Come on, Larry. I'm talking about the underwater demolition that scattered the DC-10 wreckage all over Davy Jones' locker. Didn't you know the federal government protects civil aircraft even after a plane's crashed? Now, don't get me wrong. Destroying a commercial aircraft carries a stiff sentence, but whoever hired you to do the job's the real criminal.

"You remember how good your life was before you got involved in this mess? I bet you and your brother were doing fine with your submarine business, right?" Larry bit into a hunk of melon. Juice glistened as he chewed. "Don't play games, Larry. You talked to someone at Cougar Industries three times after the DC-10 ditched. Cougar had to destroy the wreck so we wouldn't find out the bomb was planted in their engine, but the lab proved otherwise. Of course, after you covered for them, Cougar left you and your brother to take the rap. Derek Goldstein probably forgot to mention that part when you took the job. Anyway, I hope you invested wisely because it'll be a long time before you can spend any of it. Oh, did I mention that air piracy is one of the least negotiable felonies? It's kind of like trying to talk a cop out of a speeding ticket in a school zone." Larry kept chewing, finding refuge in food. "Do you really want Goldstein to go free while you and your brother rot in jail?" Larry didn't respond. Landis rose from his chair. "Okay. Have it your way. Hope you enjoyed the buffet 'cause you won't be seeing it in prison."

Larry set his plate aside with angry eyes. "What's this air piracy crap? How does blowing up a wreck constitute air piracy?"

Landis tossed another grape in his mouth. "Like I said, Larry—right or wrong, that's the way it is. The government doesn't see any distinction between blowing up a wreck and flying a plane into the World Trade Center. If it involves a civilian airliner, it's still considered an act of piracy. Of course, some judges might consider it an act of terrorism, and you know how they feel about terrorists."

"Hey—we had nothin' to do with any air piracy."

"Fine. Let's hope the judge sees it that way." Landis cocked his head, staring into Larry's eyes. "You and your brother seem pretty smart, so how'd Goldstein get you to do his dirty work? I mean, thanks to him you're both sunk. Oh, sorry. Bad choice of words. Anyway, you and your brother were running a legitimate business and now it's gone. Even if you manage to get out of this, you've lost your sub and your business. Of course, if you found another sub, you'd still be hard pressed to find another sub tender who'd lease you space after you stole Fagan's boat. Yes, sir, about all you'd have is that dilapidated shack you call your office, assuming it's not torn down by then." Landis checked his watch. "Twelve-thirty in Oklahoma City. I bet Derek Goldstein's having a nice power-lunch right about now. You think he's having juicy prime rib or grilled salmon? Later, he'll be heading back to his office in his shiny gold Mercedes." Landis closed his eyes. "Mmmm. I can almost smell that prime rib. Those bay leaves sure give it a nice aroma, don't they?"

"I still don't know what you're talking about."

"No problem. But do you really think Goldstein or anyone else at Cougar Industries gives a damn about what happens to you? You guys are throw-aways. It's always like that, Larry. The big fish eat the little fish and you guys are minnows."

Larry stood up. His words when they came were surprisingly reserved. "I'm not going down alone. Goldstein set us up. Yeah, he paid us big bucks to blow up the wreck, but all we were doing was finishing it off. We even joked about it being an environmental cleanup."

"I suppose that's one way of looking at it. I can almost understand that part, but what about that Navy diver? Why'd you have to kill him?" Larry turned away. "Larry, he was just a kid. A good one at that. He enlisted in the Navy to earn money for college. He was an only child. His parents are devastated."

Larry sat down and buried his head in his hands.

"He's finished," Kidman said to the other agent. The videotape continued to run.

Landis patted Larry on the back. "He shouldn't have been there," Larry said.

"Go on."

"It was pitch black and we were running blind so no one would see us. We hadn't even seen the wreck yet, but all of a sudden we hit something. We turned on a headlight, and saw the diver struggling to the surface. We couldn't risk him telling anyone about us. Steve circled around, grabbed him with the free pincer, and dragged him down. He didn't last long. Steve saw the hole in the plane and slammed him into it. The guy just hung there, metal sticking through him. I keep dreaming about it. Steve slid the bomb that was in the other pincer in the hole and we were outta there. The timer was set to go off an hour later, but he rigged a tripwire with a short delay as a backup."

"For the record, who hired you?"

"Goldstein. Derek Goldstein. CEO of Cougar Industries."

"And you're willing to testify to that? It'll help your case if you do."

Larry nodded. A pastry crumb clung to his jaw, oddly innocent.

"You're doing the right thing, Larry. By the way, why'd you use Wayne's sub instead of your own? Wouldn't there have been less risk of being caught that way?"

Larry shook his head. "Goldstein had a strict time table and we were having problems with our robotics. It was easier borrowing Wayne's sub. I called him right after and told him where to find it. She was fine when we left her in Santa Monica, but when Steve heard about the Navy diver, he figured the pincer marks might come back to haunt us. We had no choice but to torch Farley's place."

Landis nodded. "Here's another thing that's been bothering me, Larry. While you and your brother were in the sub planting the bomb, who was running the sub tender?"

"No one. We dropped anchor about twenty miles from *Atlantis* and Steve picked her up on the way back. We worked with Barney all the time so he kept *Skimmer* at our dock. We had our own set of keys so we could load or unload the sub whenever we wanted. We pretty much had *Skimmer* at our disposal."

"Then why leave the sub in Santa Monica? Wouldn't it have been better to put it back on *Skimmer* and take it to the pier? I mean, if you would've done that, neither boat would've been missed."

Larry shrugged and began eating again. "Steve figured it'd take too much time to get the sub loaded again. He wanted *Skimmer* back before sunrise."

"You realize that Farley died in the fire, don't you? Farley's and the diver's deaths make it second-degree murder."

"I want to talk to my lawyer."

Landis sat back in the chair. "I encourage you to do so. Oh, you should know that an FBI agent and another civilian were in that warehouse fire with Farley. They survived, but that's where the attempted murder charges come from."

"That's bullshit."

Landis shook his head. "I promise you it's true, and if they hadn't escaped it would be four counts of murder. The law comes down real hard on people who kill federal agents. Another FBI agent was outside and saw the whole thing. Be glad he was aiming for your tires. Anyway, when can your lawyer get here? I'd like to wrap this up."

"Ask Steve. I'm sure he's been talking to him."

Landis nodded. "Like I said, I'll do what I can to get the judge to go easy. Be right back."

Landis walked into the opposing room. Kidman was all smiles. "I have to hand it to you, Greg. I figured one of 'em might break, but I didn't expect him to sing."

"Yeah," he said, dialing the phone. "Frankly, the whole thing sickens me." Greg waited. "Hey, Mike. Good news. Larry Barclay confessed to everything except the first bomb. As you suspected,

Goldstein hired them to destroy the wreckage. Larry has an electronic money transfer receipt to prove it."

Mike grinned as Landis filled him in. They still had unresolved issues, but it was a relief knowing the big fish would fry. "What did he say about Kizka?"

"Not a word."

Mike Pentaglia didn't call Kevin until later that evening. It was sad their partnership was breaking up. He'd been a good partner. He couldn't have done the job without him. If anyone deserved credit for breaking this case, it was that hardheaded pilot from Global Cargo Express.

Kevin frowned when he recognized Mike's voice. Nancy shook her head, praying he wasn't involved in something else. "What's going on, Mike?"

"I know how much you've been wanting closure, so I thought you'd like to know Larry Barclay gave it all up. Thanks to him, Goldstein's going down for conspiring to blow up the wreck."

"Hey, great. But what about my plane? Who brought it down?"

"We're still working on it. I was wondering if you felt like making one last trip downtown so you can spit in Goldstein's face when we break the news to him?"

Kevin smiled. "Hang on." He covered the phone and looked at Nancy. "Goldstein's stooges confessed. It's over, Nance. It's finally over."

"Thank God." She squeezed him tight.

"But there's more," Kevin said. "Mike wants to know if I want to give Goldstein a proper send-off. You want to go with me?"

"Hell, yes. After all this grief he's given our family—hell, yes. I'll see if Ann can watch the kids."

"Hey, Mike? Can you pick us up? Nancy wants to come, too. She deserves it."

"No sweat. I'm on my way."

They arrived at the federal building shortly before three. On the way, they passed the memorial for the old federal building. Kevin couldn't help thinking about Farley's burning body and the Navy diver. Would Goldstein hire someone to take him out, too?

Their footsteps echoed through the parking lot. He sensed Nancy's apprehension. He felt the same. If anything happened to them, their boys would become orphans. He should have left her behind.

Mike helped them with their check-in and escorted them to the debriefing room. He expected Goldstein, but not Kizka. Both men were dressed in orange jumpsuits, sitting with their arms folded across their chests. Arvid's face was cold, his pleasant features lost. Kevin and Nancy stood with their backs to the wall near the door.

At the opposite end of the room two men in three-piece suits stood in front of their attaché cases, looking like the lawyers they were.

"Thank you all for coming," Mike said as though it were a business meeting. "Kevin, Nancy; Mr. Liebert and Mr. Frierson are lawyers for the defense." He looked their way. "Gentlemen, I invited Mr. and Mrs. Hamilton to sit in. Any objections?"

Liebert and Frierson shook their heads.

Kevin looked around the room. He suspected they were being taped, but he wasn't sure if he and Nancy were in a blind spot. There was nothing special about the setting. One long table, a few chairs, tile floor, camera holes, no two-way mirror. Mike was the only FBI agent in the room. Kizka's face remained cold, thinner than he remembered. Kizka refused to look his way.

"Since we have a quorum, perhaps you'll tell me why I'm here," Kizka said.

Mike took a seat across from Kizka, leaning over the table until he smelled his breath. He wanted to make sure he had Kizka's attention. "Mr. Kizka, does the name Larry Barclay mean anything to you?"

"You don't have to answer that," Liebert said.

Kizka's spirit was broken. He didn't care about legal advice. Sitting next to the man who ruined his life was punishment enough. Goldstein was a sociopath, a workaholic who trod on anyone in his way. Kizka should have left years ago. The autonomy is what kept him there. He barely looked up. "Larry Barclay? Can't say I know the name. Why?"

"Well, your boss hired Larry and his brother Steve to blow up a DC-10 wreck. The one with your engine aboard."

"You don't have to say anything," Liebert said.

"That's true," Mike said. "Of course, we do have his signed confession."

Liebert stepped forward. "You failed to mention that. I need a recess so I can talk to my client." Goldstein sneered, waving his hand.

"We also have a money transfer receipt from Mr. Goldstein's Swiss bank account. Apparently Mr. Goldstein was able to get it erased, but Steve Barclay made a copy of the transaction. Guess they're not as dumb as they look." Kizka was pale with shock. He stared at Goldstein. "There's more, Arvid," Mike said. "You see, Larry also confessed to murdering that Navy diver. Actually, he pointed the finger at his brother on that one, but he adamantly denied having anything to do with the inflight explosion. That's where you come in."

Kizka found new life. "If you're suggesting I had anything to do with planting a bomb, you're wrong."

"Arvid, you don't have to say anything."

"Will you shut up?" Kizka said to Liebert.

Kevin squeezed Nancy's hand as he watched Kizka and Goldstein.

"Mr. Kizka," Mike said, "the lab fragments of the Ultima E850 had traces of C4 plastic explosives inside of the casing. In other words, the E850—your baby—was the source of the explosion." Kizka said nothing. "Now here's the clincher. You're the one who insisted on handling the shipment. You nailed the crate shut and delivered it to Global Cargo Express. You were also the last one to see the E850."

Kizka nodded. "That's true. But I only handled the shipping because the E850 was everything to me. It took a lifetime to create. How could I possibly destroy it?"

"I don't know, but the evidence singles you out."

"Arvid—" Liebert began.

"I thought I told you to shut up," he said. Kizka glared at Goldstein. He recalled the day he shipped the E850. "Well, Derek, I guess it's down to you and me now, isn't it?" Kizka looked at Mike. "I may have been the last one to see the E-850, but Derek was the last to inspect it before it was crated." He looked at Goldstein. "So, what did you do, Derek? Slip some C4 in the valves or was it something more sophisticated?"

Goldstein's voice went quiet. "Arvid, you don't know fuck-all about the business. We were losing our asses. I did what I had to."

Liebert slammed his attaché case shut. "That's it. I give up. Mr. Goldstein, you'll get my bill, but there's no way I'll represent you in court."

"Don't get too upset with him," Mike said. "We already located the C4 provider and they confirmed Mr. Goldstein signed for the shipment. It's a pretty airtight case, Arvid. You see, Derek, plea bargaining's a win-win proposition, except in your case."

"I don't get it," Kizka said. "If you knew Derek was responsible, why in the hell did you put me through all this?"

"Believe it or not, it was for your own good," Kevin said, approaching him. "Arvid, you're a brilliant engineer, but you're very short-sighted in other things. You never would've believed it if you hadn't heard it first-hand."

Nancy looked at Kevin, wondering what other surprises Mike held in store.

"He's right," Mike said. "Besides, you were still in custody when everything came together. Telling you earlier would've only gotten you out a few hours earlier. I thought it would be best if it played out in front of you. You're a free man, Arvid."

Kizka declined to shake Mike's hand. "A free man." It tasted like ashes.

"Mr. Frierson, would you please tell Mr. Kizka about the company?"

Frierson came forward. "Mr. Goldstein, fifteen years ago you hired me to represent Cougar Industries. During that time I did everything possible to look after the company's interests. When you lost your engine in that crash, I was appalled to discover you'd recently canceled your insurance policy. I started looking into your personal affairs and found your financial situation equally disturbing. Of course, I didn't know about your Swiss Bank account until Agent Pentaglia told me. After I learned of your arrest and was briefed on the charges and evidence against you, I met with the Board of Directors in a special closed-door session prior to this meeting."

Goldstein lunged at Frierson. Mike tackled and cuffed him. "You sleazy son of a bitch! I'll kill you!"

Frierson caught his breath. "As I was saying, after speaking to Special Agent Pentaglia, I asked Mr. Liebert to meet us here. After briefing him on the charges against you, he agreed to serve as your defense counsel. Of course, that seems to have changed. Not that my opinion matters, but it appears the government has an ironclad case against you, thanks in part to your stunt at the airport and what's happened in here."

"Hey, Pentaglia. What about my rights?" Goldstein asked. "I'm entitled to a lawyer. Not someone who just sold me out."

Mike stood in front of Goldstein. "Everything's on tape, Derek. Mr. Liebert advised you and Arvid several times to keep quiet, but you both ignored him. You were read your rights when you were arrested and before this meeting. Everything you've said will be used against you in a court of law. You have the right to choose a new lawyer, or if you prefer, one will be appointed for you. Mr. Frierson, we've kept Mr. Kizka here long enough. Would you please tell him what's happening at Cougar Industries?"

Frierson opened his attaché case. "Arvid, the members of the Board still believe in the Ultima E850, so they agreed to buy out Mr. Goldstein's shares and have assumed control of Cougar Industries."

"That's bullshit and you know it," Goldstein said. "I'll never sell my shares! I built this company from scratch!"

"You may have built the company, but you're flat broke," Mike said.

"That's an understatement," Frierson said. "You drained your Swiss Bank account to buy the Barclay's services, and mortgaged everything to make your last payroll. Even your stock won't cover your expenses. While some might consider your dedication admirable, you knew that DC-10 would crash, and the insurance scam was your ace in the hole. Mr. Goldstein, business transactions are easily traced. The Tigress deal was a good one, but the money never came in time to get the E850 into production. Cougar Industries was in a downward spiral and without that insurance money, you either had to sell out or leave nothing to your stockholders. I suppose that's why you forged the Tigress agreement increasing the E850's value tenfold. It was my duty and in the best interest of Cougar Industries to use your Power of Attorney to sell your shares. Simply put, you no longer own stock in Cougar Industries."

"No!" Goldstein yanked at his cuffs. "You'll never get away with this! I have my rights! I'll take this to the Supreme Court if I have to!"

"Quiet down or I'll gag you," Mike said.

Kizka watched him. "You're right, Derek. I don't know much about business and had no idea we were going under. I suppose that's why you went through with the Tigress deal even though we didn't have all the bugs worked out. We were so close. Good God, man—we only needed a few more weeks!"

Goldstein stared at the table.

Kevin reached for Kizka's arm. "Come on, Arvid. We'll take you home."

Once outside the conference room, Arvid looked at Kevin, his eyes thoughtful. "You know, Kevin, we'll be needing an engineer with qualifications in quality control and logistics management. We're going to build this engine. I could use you."

Kevin was about to respond when Nancy spoke up. "It's a fine offer, Mr. Kizka. But my husband's a pilot; flying's his life."

Kizka smiled. "Of course. And I suspect flying's a demanding mistress."

"Yes. But what we have—Kevin and I and the children—is beyond price."

Arvid shrugged. "Well, I had to try. Kevin, do you realize I never even saw your resume?"

Kevin laughed. "I appreciate the vote of confidence, Arvid, and I'm sure you'll select a fine candidate for the job. I wish you well with the E850. I expect I'll be reading about it; changing transportation for the better in this country."

Arvid's eyes lit with passion, color back in his cheeks. "The world, Kevin. The world."

Later, in the quiet of their car, Kevin watched Nancy. She sat quite still, staring ahead. "Thanks for what you said back there," he said.

"You know it's the truth and I've come to terms with it. Not easily, but I've worked through it. I always want you in my life, Kevin."

Kevin smiled. "But one thing you should know. Flying's a passion, but it's not my mistress. It's important you know that."

Nancy reached over and squeezed his arm. "I know."

"I was thinking of taking a simulator instructor job."

Nancy laughed. "Stay in the sky, Kevin. Stay in the sky."

Coming in 2003

The Innocent Never Knew

When Senator Sam Tinsdale's plane crashes one stormy night short of the runway, NTSB investigator Bob Stambler is sent to Albuquerque to investigate—and runs into quick trouble. The crash site has been tampered with; critical evidence is being removed without his authority. Then his boss, Ralph Dietz, issues a statement that the Cockpit Voice Recorder and Flight Data Recorder don't work. Stambler is stymied in doing his job and becomes convinced there is a government cover-up. When the FBI confiscates the flight recorders, Stambler finds himself alone, working against time as he seeks out the truth of the Senator's crash.

The key is in the tail section of the Boeing 737 that broke off on impact. It didn't burn like the rest of the aircraft, and if he was to find any lead, it had to be there. He finds it when he examines the flight attendant's seat. Somewhere out there, in hiding and on the run, is Polaris Airways Flight Attendant Erica Hayes. Now the problem was finding her, and finding out why she had disappeared…

In the tradition of DANGER WITHIN, author Mark Danielson brings his aviation expertise to another yarn of murder and double-dealing set against today's pressures of flying the commercial skies.

Check out these other fine titles by
Durban House at your local book store.

Exceptional Books
by
Exceptional Writers

Current Titles

BASHA   John Hamilton Lewis

DANGER WITHIN   Mark Danielson

DEADLY ILLUMINATION   Serena Stier

DEATH OF A HEALER   Paul Henry Young

HOUR OF THE WOLVES   Stephane Daimlen-Völs

A HOUSTON WEEKEND   Orville Palmer

JOHNNIE RAY & MISS KILGALLEN   Bonnie Hearn Hill & Larry Hill

THE LATERAL LINE   Robert Middlemiss

THE MEDUSA STRAIN   Chris Holmes

MR. IRRELEVANT   Jerry Marshall

OPAL EYE DEVIL   John Hamilton Lewis

PRIVATE JUSTICE   Richard Sand

ROADHOUSE BLUES   Baron Birtcher

RUBY TUESDAY   Baron Birtcher

SECRET OF THE SCROLL   Chester D. Campbell

SECRETS ARE ANONYMOUS   Frederick L. Cullen

THE SERIAL KILLER'S DIET BOOK   Kevin Mark Postupack

THE STREET OF FOUR WINDS   Andrew Lazarus

TUNNEL RUNNER   Richard Sand

WHAT GOES AROUND   Don Goldman

Nonfiction

FISH HEADS, RICE, RICE WINE & WAR: A VIETNAM PARADOX
   Lt. Col. Thomas G. Smith, Ret.

MIDDLE ESSENCE—WOMEN OF WONDER YEARS   Landy Reed

PROTOCOL   Mary Jane McCaffree, Pauline Innis & Katherine Daley Sand
   For 25 years, the bible for public relations firms, corporations, embassies, governments and individuals seeking to do business with the Federal government.

Basha John Hamilton Lewis
Set in the world of elite professional tennis and rooted in ancient Middle East hatreds of identity and blood loyalties, Basha is charged with the fiercely competitive nature of professional sports and the dangers of terrorism. An already simmering Middle East begins to boil and CIA Station Chief Grant Corbet must track down the highly successful terrorist, Basha. In a deadly race against time, Grant hunts the illusive killer only to see his worst nightmare realized.

Danger Within Mark Danielson
Over 100 feet down in cold ocean waters lies the wreck of pilot Kevin Hamilton's DC-10. In it are secrets which someone is desperate to keep. When the Navy sends a team of divers from the Explosives Ordinance Division, a mysterious explosion from the wreck almost destroys the salvage ship. The FBI steps in with Special Agent Mike Pentaglia. Track the life and death of Global Express Flight 3217 inside the gritty world of aviation and discover the shocking cargo that was hidden on its last flight.

Deadly Illumination Serena Stier
It's summer 1890 in New York City. Florence Tod, an ebullient young woman, must challenge financier, John Pierpont Morgan, to solve a possible murder. J.P.'s librarian has ingested poison embedded in an illumination of a unique Hildegard van Bingen manuscript. Florence and her cousin, Isabella Stewart Gardner, discover the corpse. When Isabella secretly removes a gold tablet from the scene of the crime, she sets off a chain of events that will involve Florence and her in a dangerous conspiracy.

Death of a Healer Paul Henry Young
Diehard romanticist and surgeon extraordinaire, Jake Gibson, struggles to preserve his professional oath against the avarice and abuse of power so prevalent in present-day America. Jake's personal quest is at direct odds with a group of sinister medical and legal practitioners who plot to eliminate patient groups in order to improve the bottom line. With the lives of his family on the line, Jake must expose the darker side of the medical world.

Hour of the Wolves Stephane Daimlen-Völs
After more than three centuries, the *Poisons Affair* remains one of history's great, unsolved mysteries. The worst impulses of human nature—sordid sexual perversion, murderous intrigues, witchcraft, Satanic cults—thrive within the shadows of the Sun King's absolutism and will culminate in the darkest secret of his reign: the infamous *Poisons Affair*, a remarkably complex web of horror, masked by Baroque splendor, luxury and refinement.

A Houston Weekend Orville Palmer
Professor Edward Randa11, not-yet-forty, divorced and separated from his daughters, is leading a solitary, cheerless existence in a university town. At a conference in Houston he runs into his childhood sweetheart. Then she was poverty-stricken, neglected and American Indian. Now she's elegantly attired, driving an expensive Italian car and lives in a millionaires enclave. Will their fortuitous encounter grow into anything meaningful?

Johnnie Ray & Miss Kilgallen   Bonnie Hearn Hill & Larry Hill

Johnnie Ray was a sexually conflicted wild man out of control; Dorothy Kilgallen, fifteen years his senior, was the picture of decorum as a Broadway columnist and TV personality. The last thing they needed was to fall in love—with each other. Sex, betrayal, money, drugs, drink and more drink. Together they descended into a nightmare of assassination conspiracies, bizarre suicides and government enemy lists until Dorothy dies…mysteriously. Was it suicide…or murder?

The Lateral Line   Robert Middlemiss

Kelly Travett is ready with an Israeli assassination pistol and garlic-coated bullets to kill the woman who tortured and murdered her father. Then the CIA calls with a double warning: she ought to know about Operation Lateral Line and her enemies are expecting her. Revenge is not so simple in the ancient killing alleys of Budapest. There's a Hungarian Chief of Police and his knife and a smiling Russian Mafia boss who has a keen interest in her Israeli pistol....

The Medusa Strain   Chris Holmes

A gripping tale of bio-terrorism that stunningly portrays the dangers of chemical warfare in ways nonfiction never could. When an Iraqi scientist full of hatred for America breeds a deadly form of anthrax and a diabolical means to initiate an epidemic, not even the First Family is immune. Will America's premier anthrax researcher devise a bio-weapon in time to save the U.S. from extinction?

Mr. Irrelevant   Jerry Marshall

Sports writer Paul Tenkiller and pro-football player Chesty Hake have been roommates for eight seasons. Paul's Choctaw background and his sports gambling, and Chesty's memories of his mother's killing are the dark forces that will ensnare Tenkiller in Hake's slide into a murderous paranoia—but Paul is behind the curve that is spinning Chesty out of his control.

Opal Eye Devil   John Hamilton Lewis

From the teeming wharves of Shanghai to the stately offices of New York and London, Robber Barons lie, steal, cheat, and kill in their quest for power. Eric Gradek will rise from the *Northern Star's* dark cargo hold to the pinnacle of high stakes gambling for unrivaled riches. Aided by his beautiful wife, Katheryn, and the devoted Tong-Po, Eric fights for his dream and for revenge against the man who left him for dead aboard *Northern Star*.

Private Justice   Richard Sand

After taking brutal revenge for the murder of his twin brother, Lucas Rook leaves the NYPD to work for others who crave justice outside the law when the system fails them. Rook's dark journey takes him on a race to find a killer whose appetite is growing. A little girl turns up dead. And then another and another. The nightmare is on him fast. The piano player has monstrous hands; the Medical Examiner is a goulish dwarf; an investigator kills himself. Betrayal and intrigue is added to the deadly mix as the story careens toward its startling end.

Roadhouse Blues Baron Birtcher
Newly retired Homicide detective Mike Travis is torn from the comfort of his chartered yacht business into the dark, bizarre underbelly of LA's music scene by a grisly string of murders. A handsome, drug-addled psychopath has reemerged from an ancient Dionysian cult, leaving a bloody trail of seemingly unrelated victims in his wake.

Ruby Tuesday Baron Birtcher
Mike Travis sails his yacht to Kona, Hawaii expecting to put LA Homicide behind him: to let the warm emerald sea wash years of blood from his hands. Instead, he finds his family's home ravaged by shotgun blasts, littered with bodies and trashed with drugs. Then things get worse. A rock star involved in a Wall Street deal masterminded by Travis's brother is one of the victims. Another victim is Ruby, Travis's childhood sweetheart. How was she involved?

Secret of the Scoll Chester D. Campbell
Colonel Greg McKenzie has unknowingly smuggled a first century Hebrew scroll out of Israel into the U.S. Someone wants it back. McKenzie's wife Jill is taken hostage: her life for the scroll. A Nashville wants to know why McKenzie hasn't filed a missing persons report on his "missing" wife. And the secret of the scroll has the potntial to turn the Arab-Israeli disput into a raging holocaust.

Secrets Are Anonymous Frederick L. Cullen
Bexley, Ohio is a quiet, unremarkable town in the heartland of American. But its citizens have secrets and amitions which they reveal in interesting ways: chat rooms, instant messaging, e-mails, hypnosis, newspaper articles, letters to the editor, answering machines, video tapes, eavesdropping, vanity plates and coctail napkins. All-American "unremarkable" Bexley is suddenly beseiged by The National Security Agency, the FBI, the Securities and Exchange Commission and a drug cartel—and the guy who runs the ice cream parlor lets them all use the restroom—at a price. What's going on?

The Serial Killer's Diet Book Kevin Mark Postupack
Fred Orbis is fat—very fat—but will soon discover the ultimate diet. Devon DeGroot is on the trail of a homicidal maniac who prowls Manhattan with meatballs, bologna and egg salad—taunting him about the body count in *Finnegans Wakean*. Darby Montana, one of the world's richest women, wants a new set of genes to alter a face and body so homely not even plastic surgery could help. Mr. Monde is the Devil in the market for a soul or two. It's a Faustian satire on God and the Devil, Heaven and Hell, beauty and the best-seller list.

The Street of Four Winds Andrew Lazarus
Paris—just after World War II. On the Left Bank, Americans seek a way to express their dreams, delights and disappointments in a way very different from pre-war ex-patriots. Tom Cortell is a tough, intellectual journalist disarmed by three women-French, British and American. Along with him is a gallery of international characters who lead a merry and sometimes desperate chase between Pairs, Switzerland and Spain to a final, liberating and often tragic end of their European wanderings in search of themselves.

Tunnel Runner   Richard Sand

Ashman is a denizen of a dark world where murder is committed and no one is brought to account; where loyalties exist side-by-side with lies and extreme violence. One morning he awakens to find himself paralyzed in a mental hospital. He escapes and seeks vengeance, confronting old friends, the Pentagon, the Mafia, and a mysterious general who is covering up the attack on TWA Flight 800.

What Goes Around   Don Goldman

Ten years ago, Ray Banno was vice president of a California bank when his boss, Andre Rhodes, framed him for bank fraud. Now, he has his new identity, a new face and a new life in medical research. He's on the verge of finding a cure for a deadly disease when he's chosen as a juror in the bank fraud trial of Andre Rhodes. Should he take revenge? Meanwhile, Rhodes is about to gain financial control of Banno's laboratory in order to destroy Banno's work

Nonfiction

Fish Heads, Rice, Rice Wine & War: A Vietnam Paradox
Lt. Col. Thomas G. Smith, Ret.

This memoir set in the Central Highlands of Vietnam, 1966–1969, draws on the intensely human and humourous sides of the strangest and most misunderstood war in which American soldiers were ever committed. Lt. Col. Smith offers a powerful and poignant insider's view of American soldiers at their most heroic who in the midst of the blood and guts of war always find the means to laugh.

Middle Essence—Women of Wonder Years   Landy Reed

Here is a roadmap and a companion to what can be the most profoundly significant and richest years of a woman's life. For every woman approaching, at, or beyond midlife, this guide is rich with stories of real women in real circumstances who find they have a second chance-a time when women blossom rather than fade. Gain a new understanding of how to move beyond myths of aging; address midlife transitions head on; discover new power and potential; and emerge with a stronger sense of self

Protocol   Mary Jane McCaffree, Pauline Innis & Katherine Daley Sand

For 25 years, the bible for public relations firms, corporations, embassies, governments and individuals seeking to do business with the Federal government.

This book contains a wealth of detail on every conceivable question, from titles and forms of address to ceremonies and flg etiquette. The authors are to be complimented for bringing us partially up to date in a final chapter on Women in Official and Public Life.
—Department of State Newsletter